THE BLACK BOOK OF BADON

BY

KEVIN BAYTON-WOOD

The characters and events portrayed in this book are fictitious. Any similarity to real persons, living or dead, is coincidental and not intended by the author.

ISBN: 9798703379431

This book is dedicated to Mum and George, Mark, Karine, and Rhian.

PLACE NAMES

ALT CLUD---THE KINGDOM OF STRATHCLYDE.

ANDREDES CAESTER---PEVENSEY, SUSSEX.

ANDREDSWEALD---WEALD OF SOUTH ENGLAND.

ANNWN---THE CELTIC OTHERWORLD (HEAVEN).

ARMORICA---BRITTANY, FRANCE.

AQUA SULIS---BATH, SOMERSET.

BADON---BATHEASTON, SOMERSET.

CAER EDYN---EDINBURGH, SCOTLAND.

CANTWARA---KENT.

DUMNONIA---DEVON AND CORNWALL.

DURNOVARIA---DORCHESTER, DORSET.

ÉRIU---IRELAND.

GAUL---FRANCE.

GLEVUM---GLOUCESTER, GLOUCESTERSHIRE.

GWYNEDD---KINGDOM IN NORTHWEST WALES.

ISLANDS OF THE MIGHTY---BRITISH ISLES.

INIS BASSA---BASCHURCH, SHROPSHIRE.

LONDINIUM---LONDON.

MONA---ANGLESEY, NORTH WALES.

NEORXNAWANG---SAXON HEAVEN OR AFTERLIFE.

POWYS---WELSH KINGDOM.

RHOS---A PRINCIPALITY IN GWYNEDD.

RHUTHUN---RHUTHIN, DENBIGHSHIRE.

SULIS HILL---SOLSBURY HILL, SOMERSET.

SUMMER ISLE---GLASTONBURY TOR, SOMERSET.

TAMESIS RIVER---RIVER THAMES.

VIROCONIUM---WROXETER, SHROPSHIRE.

AUTHOR'S INTRODUCTION

When I was a small boy, I attended Wellhouse School in Mirfield, West Yorkshire, and it was there that I read my first King Arthur story. I immediately became hooked on the idea that a great king called Arthur Pendragon, along with Merlin the wizard and the Knights of the Round Table rode throughout the land righting wrongs and winning battles. The idea that King Arthur might be a real person, intrigued me but, being more than interested in history I knew that he did not appear in the list of Kings of England. Armed with a desire to know the truth, I began a quest that took me over thirty years into the future, and the final resting place of the man who became known as King Arthur.

Historians who specialise in the so-called 'Dark Age' period of British history, do agree that a major three-day battle and siege took place at a place called Badon, sometime around the beginning of the sixth century. This, you could argue, is history. Unfortunately, no one can claim to know for certain who the victorious leader was; some say it was King Arthur, others claim it must have been Ambrosius Aurelianus, nor does anyone know for certain where Badon was.

During my decades of research into those times, I inevitably drew my own conclusions as to who the warrior of Badon might be, and the likelihood of him being the legendary King Arthur. There are those who won't agree with my assumptions, but from what I've discovered over my many years of searching through the ancient writings and genealogies, listening to the little-known songs and tales passed down orally from generation to generation, visiting the many Arthurian related sites and sifting through their archaeology, only one man, in my opinion, can possibly be the warrior who became known as King Arthur.

While reading the extensive Welsh and Teutonic genealogies, I noted the men and women who were related to the man I believe to be Arthur, and the various other kings and princes of that time, including the Germanic invaders we now collectively refer to as 'Anglo Saxons'. Researching these characters was difficult and time consuming, but over a period of many years, doors opened and light flooded in, illuminating these people and presenting me with a series of stories I believe are well worth telling.

I must, however, add a disclaimer because although I believe that I know who the real King Arthur was, what he did and who joined him in his battles with the Teutonic invaders, I can prove none of it; King Arthur will always remain a figure of myth and legend. This book, therefore, and the four that will follow it are fiction, a bit of swash and buckle mixed with a pinch of Otherworldly magic and philosophy, a good smattering of romance, humour, fun, battles, heroes and villains set within a series of events that could have happened. I must also add that although most of the characters in my stories are based on real people, some are my own creations, and I hope you'll enjoy getting to know them as new additions to the Arthurian Pantheon. KBW.

BRITON

CIRCA 500 AD.

EARLY SPRING

1.

The bright face of the waxing Moon shone brilliant over the unusually quiet forest. No fox barks pierced the wary night, no night birds screeched or cawed warnings to snuffling boar or sleeping deer, because the distinctive scent of humans had worried the creatures into remaining hidden within their sanctuaries.

Walking his nut-brown warhorse through the woodlands, Owain ap Einion, the Prince of Rhos and the second born son of the High King Einion ap Cunedda, turned slightly in the saddle to look up at the huge face of the dominant, cold Moon. He'd never seen the like of it, and in awe of its presence and fearing its influence he wondered why tonight of all nights, it must swell so silver-bright. Halting his mount, he patted the animal's neck and ran his hand through its mane, considering whether he should leave his prey to their sleep or, cede to his need to kill?

Sliding down from the saddle so that he could empty his bladder, he punched his spear into the soft forest mulch, rested his black, oval shield against a tree and while relieving himself into the spreading root-web of a massive oak, he again looked up through the budding branches, concerned that the clear and bright night might betray him.

He'd never seen so many shining stars, and drawing in a deep breath of cold air, the earthy scent of the damp forest thrilled his reason to be here, tingling his belly with adrenalin, prickling his skin with anticipation and fear. A few fingers of mist slid over the forest mulch, soon the new dawn would replace the silver Moon, so if he was going to make the charge, he must do it now, before the first touch of sunlight ruined his plan. Picking up his shield, he remounted, pulled his spear from the earth and clicked his horse forward, letting the animal pick its own route through the woodlands.

Having reached the scrublands at the edge of the forest, the young Prince looked across the vale. Tendrils of creeping mist drifted heavy across the crescent shaped meadow, the surrounding woodlands secretive and spectral, the borderlands quiet and still. Within a blanket of mist at the far end of the meadow, the dying embers of dozens of campfires glowed weak, their comfort forgotten while the sleeping warriors lived inside their dreams.

Walking the margins of the night-camp, a handful of spearmen patrolled their watch without concern, their minds relaxed because when the new Sun climbed above the mists, King Aelle's South Saxon warriors would begin the long march back to their homeland, after weeks of raiding outlying Celtic villages.

Before setting out on his first border patrol, Owain's father had insisted that if he came across a Saxon warband, under no circumstances was he to pick a fight, he must defer all major decisions to his experienced warriors. But he wanted to blood himself, he needed to know if he had the coldblooded instincts required to fight and kill a man. If he chose to attack, he must rely on surprise and the speed of the charge: would he make it across the meadow before the Saxons awoke and grabbed their weapons; could he slaughter them before they formed their famously formidable shield-wall? He doubted they'd be caught so cold, but the chance must be taken, he had to know if he had the courage to back his warrior-skills.

From what he could see only five Saxons patrolled the camp's perimeter, but that was five too many, surely one of them would see his approach and raise the alarm? Risk was everything in war, so his father claimed, yet the odds were heavily stacked against him, and why take unnecessary risks when a fight can be avoided? Rash as his decision might be, the Prince of Rhos tied the chin-straps of his helmet, raised his spear, lowered it and fifty mounted warriors of his newly formed horse-legion, all wearing identical conical helmets and brightly polished chainmail byrnies, emerged from the woodlands to form a battle-line either side of him, their spears pointing to the stars. Cai, the blonde-haired son of the Dragon of Caer Edyn, took his place on Owain's shield-side and, not wanting the other horsemen to overhear him, he quietly said to the Prince, "Is this wise?"

"No, but if we can slaughter a large warband, my father might take the Legion seriously. What do you think, Bedwyr?" Owain asked the warrior on his spear-side.

"You know what your father's orders were; but I'd rather fight than run." Bedwyr never shied away from a fight, he lived for battle and was considered to be the most ruthless killer in Celtic Briton.

Now that the time had come to charge, Owain felt less sure of himself. He believed in the courage and skill of his warriors, but he knew that practicing the battle-charge in the fields surrounding Viroconium City, wasn't the same as attacking a Saxon shield-wall. His moment of doubt shivered his skin when he imagined a Saxon war-axe slicing through his neck. Turn aside now and he'd never blood his sword, and if he was to meet his death tonight, so be it.

Looking along the line of warriors to his left and right, he pointed his spear at the sleeping Saxons and, walked his mount slowly into the meadow's swirling mists. His warriors followed; the scattered clinking of chainmail, weapons and tack swallowed by the creeping fog; the plod of heavy hooves dampened by the soft earth. Owain hoped that if they could advance twenty or thirty paces without being seen, they'd have a chance of reaching the campfires before a wall of shields and spears was raised against them. But the first spring Moon was way too bright, so the Prince had hoped in vain.

At the edge of the Saxon camp a sentry glanced over his shoulder to see what he initially thought was a cloud of twinkling lights, moving slowly through the grey mist. Realisation hit him and his bellowing voice rang clear into the dying night, "Celts! shield-wall! Celts!"

"Britannia!" Owain yelled, a call repeated to his left and right and, his warriors charged, galloping in one tight line towards the dozens of campfires colouring the mists. Hooves pounded the earth and men yelled their battle-cries, sweaty hands tightened around spear-shafts, gripped shield straps and bridle reins, and the fifty-one horse-warriors closed on the Saxon camp.

Panicking Saxon sentries dragged cloaks off sleeping warriors, or kicked them awake as the Celtic horsemen closed. Bleary-eyed spearmen reached for weapons and shields, then ran for the camp's perimeter, hoping to form a cohesive shield-wall before the Celts smashed into them.

Loving the feel of the charging horse beneath him, Owain knew that if his reckless attack reached the Saxon spearmen before their shield-wall came together, numbers would count for nothing because one horse-warrior was worth a dozen infantrymen in an open fight. Spurring his warhorse on, leading his men towards the disorganised panic of weapon grabbing warriors, his first battle-charge had his blood boiling as battle-lust smothered his conscience.

Galloping across the misted vale, the Prince saw the few fully awake Saxons rushing like bees around a smoking hive, trying desperately to organise a defensive line of shields and spears, but their efforts were panicked and chaotic. He knew that he had them, so tightening his grip on his still raised spear, he yelled, "Britannia!" again, focused on the throat of the spearman standing directly in his path and, he slowly lowered his spear.

"Britannia!" his warriors replied to his call. Lowering their spears, they closed on the confusion of Saxons.

Owain could see the terrified eyes of his chosen victim reflecting the silver Moon as the man raised his shield and gritted his teeth. Galloping the final few strides, the Pendragon's son aimed his spearpoint and leaned forward in the saddle, veered slightly to the left and punched his weapon through the man's throat. Thrown backwards by the force of the thrust, the Saxon's gurgled scream died as he fell into the mist. The horse-warriors smashed into the loose wall of shields and spears, and the feeble defence splintered into small, fighting groups.

Drawing his sword, Owain wheeled his mount and charged into a loose collection of spearmen. His conscience gone, his sword swung and with no thought for the pain he was inflicting his blade cut across a man's face, flicked back and hacked off a man's hand before it sliced through the throat of another. Wildly swinging his sword, he slashed into another group of Saxons gathered protectively around a tall axeman. Parrying a spear-thrust with his shield, he saw the axeman yell and aim a chop at him, so he pulled hard on his reins to turn his snorting horse and, the axe narrowly missed his thigh. Wheeling his mount, he saw the axe swing back so he clanged it away with his shield, and without needing to think he plunged his blade into the Saxon's chest. Turning his horse in circles, his sword cut wide arcs at the growing number of warriors surrounding him. "Come on!" he roared at their snarling faces, hacking desperately at limbs and blades as the spearmen closed in for the kill.

Realising he must get out of the death-circle or this would be his first and last battle, his sword flashed right and left as he cut into the ring of attackers, slashing his blade at moonlit faces and fire-reflecting byrnies, slicing his sword across necks, faces, backs and arms. His horse reared and brought its hooves crashing down, smashing to bloody pulp the face of a man too slow to get out of the way. An axe-swing barely missed Owain's exposed back, a spearpoint flashed towards his face so he raised his shield and swung his sword back in a low, curving arc that sliced through the Saxon's forearm. Someone grabbed his black cloak and tugged at it, so he turned and hacked down, howling with pleasure when his blade cut into gripping muscle. Yanking his sword free, he urged his horse forward while slicing his blade into and across a man's teeth, the pleasure of the grind thrilling Owain's need to kill. Kicking his iron-capped boot into the face of another warrior, he punched his shield-rim into a spearman's neck, and at last he was free of the death-circle.

Sucking in cold air, he turned his mount and charged back into his wreath of Saxons, slaughtering the ones prepared to fight the blood-soaked warrior with the lightning-fast sword arm. His sword killed and maimed without mercy, and although his head ached from the pressure of subduing the horrors of battle, he didn't want the killing to stop. Something hit the back of his helmet, and before he could think he'd hit the ground in a crash of metal. Instinct told him to get up or die, but there was a heavy weight pressing down on his chest; a Saxon had him pinned to the damp, bloody earth.

Desperately swinging his sword at the dark blur above him, his blade clanged against metal and broke in two. Without releasing the stub, he smashed both of his fists into the Saxon's chest, knocking the man off-balance, so he pushed with all his strength and was relieved to feel the weight lift when the Saxon tumbled backwards. He leapt on the man and thrust what remained of his sword into the Saxon's throat, pushing and twisting the stub until he felt warm blood shoot up his arms. For a few heartbeats the Saxon twisted beneath him, clawing in futile desperation at Owain's bloodied hands. The man's life-blood pumped away, leaving his dead-eyes staring blank at the face of the killer. Exhausted, the young Prince flopped off his victim, his battle-lust fading, the cold night chilling his lust to kill.

Sitting cross-legged beside the dead Saxon, he grinned through blood-spattered teeth as he took in the carnage he had caused; the campsite scattered with limbs, heads, pools of blood and the dead and the dying. Pinching his nose to mask the revolting stench of battle-gore, he watched the final throws of the massacre while listening to the pain-filled cries of the wounded. He'd never imagined battle would be like this, exhilarating yet gut-churningly disgusting. It was such a mess, a savage, bloody mess but he'd felt something new, something desperately primal that consumed, elated and repulsed him in the same breath.

Removing his helmet, Bedwyr flopped down beside the Prince. "They are all dead or dying," he said, and after dryly coughing, he added, "I need a drink."

"We killed them all?" Owain asked, surprised the fight had been so easy.

"A handful of them escaped into the forest, so I sent some of our warriors after them." Grabbing a Saxon ale-skin, Bedwyr swallowed a huge swig then offered it to Owain. "You were right," he said, watching the Prince greedily gulp down ale, "the Saxons don't know how to fight against cavalry. Your first battle, Owain, and you've won a great victory." Noticing his exhausted friend didn't seem to be listening, he asked, "Are you alright, are you wounded?"

Owain touched some of the dark smears of congealed blood clogging his iron-ringed byrnie, revolted by its tacky warmth. With his battle-lust gone and his conscience returned, he looked at the Saxon with the sword-stub stuck in his throat and, something hit him hot in the gut, a boiling punch that surged in burning waves, outwards from his stomach. His left hand began to shake, his body felt so hot with panic that he wanted to cut a hole in his belly wide and deep enough to release the growing furnace of heat.

Seeing Cai bringing his nut-brown horse to him, he heard a sudden explosion of drumbeats pounding through the woodlands, and a ripple of fear slithered cold over his skin. Instinct took over. He threw aside the ale-skin, got unsteadily to his feet, ran to the horse and leapt onto its back. Before Cai and Bedwyr could react, Owain had galloped into the forest. Cai called after him but the Prince wasn't listening, all he wanted was to free himself of the stench and gore of this night of slaughter, and the guilty madness the battle had fostered in him.

Flinging back the worn leather door-flap of her roundhouse by the Forest Lake, Gwenwyfar filled her lungs with cold forest air and stepped out into the hazy morning sunshine. Spring was her favourite season, the time of rebirth, growth and a hope as clean and fresh as the cool mornings. It was also the time for lovers to meet, but her man hadn't visited her for the passing of at least three Moons, which both worried and frustrated her.

Sitting on a log on the pebbled shore of the lake, she closed her eyes to better feel the Sun warm on her face, imagining her part of the forest as it would soon look, thick with green leaves and the purples, blues, yellows and whites of spring flowers. "How can anyone live in cities and towns?" she asked the high, white clouds. "Why do people hide from the beauty of nature's nurturing cycle?"

Before her shimmered the wide lake, her gateway to the Otherworld. Here she could drift, let nature move her to its rhythm, a rhythm that had turned the wheel of life long before men stuck their hunting spears into the earth to claim the land as their own. "The land is eternal," she said to the gentle wind flitting through the trees, "mankind is not."

The wide sheen of glimmering blue was crowned in the centre by a tree covered island, large enough to house the village of an almost forgotten people. Like her they kept themselves to themselves, leaving the outside world to those who needed it. The island was far enough away for her to forget it whenever she chose, though all its inhabitants were her friends, and had been so since her mother had birthed her.

Tucking the hem of her brown, tanned-hide skirt into her waist-belt, she stood and pulled off her blue woollen tunic, exposing her goose-pimpled skin to the almost white sun. It only took a few barefooted steps for her toes to feel the shock of the lapping cold as she threw her tunic under the hanging, leafless spines of a nearby willow tree. Wading into the water up to her thighs, she rubbed her goose-pimpled arms, leaned forward and her long, raven hair spread like tree roots on the breeze-rippled lake surface. "Come on, Gwen," she urged herself. "The water isn't cold, it's alive." Crouching slightly, she immersed her head.

Hearing a muffled rumble permeating the water, she flung back her water-spraying hair and listened. Her tranquil world was being invaded by the same drumbeats she'd heard the previous night, thundering across the lake from the oak and hawthorn covered island. "The Mother Goddess is awake," she whispered. She often wondered about the rituals of the Island People, knowing very little about the mysteries they denied her, even though she'd been conceived during their Spring-Moon couplings, and had lived with them throughout the early years of her life. What did it matter? We are born, we are free, we live we love we die and whatever else happens just fills in the gaps.

The pounding drumbeats made her sigh because they'd probably boom for at least a day and a night, or longer because the rising of the Mother Goddess from her winter slumber was an important time for those ruled by the old gods. Turning, she looked at her smallholding, which was just big enough for one, sometimes two. She grew vegetables, kept a few chickens for their meat and eggs, a goat for its milk and she had a pig which she fed and allowed to roam free until the falling leaves of autumn reminded her to sharpen her butchering knives. Her home sat idle beside the lake, a wattle and daub roundhouse, thatched with straw to let out the smoke and shelter her from the rain. Did she need more than this? Apart from satisfying her occasional lusts with her lover, what more was there? This was her world and she'd never let anyone take it from her, but then who would want to?

Feeling like a swim, she waded back to the shore, removed her skirt and undergarments and stepped back into the lake. Slipping smoothly into the clear water, she turned onto her back and kicked to glide herself through the light-shimmering surface. Her cold shivers didn't last long, soon the refreshing waters were passing comfortingly over her body, so she gracefully twisted and turned with the pleasure, joy and freedom of it.

With her eyes wide open she dived beneath the surface, watching entranced as her fingers parted the water plants blanketing the bottom of the lake. Turning, she saw sunlight dance like thousands of sparkling crystals on the surface. Reaching up, her feet kicked her towards the tiny water-stars and she tried to grab one, then laughed at her own foolishness when her face burst through the surface and, she flipped onto her back. Rolling onto her front, she dived again to enjoy the beauty of the swaying greens, wishing she could remain in the water until the Mother Goddess took away her soul. But the cold was beginning to chill her bones, it was time for her to return to her warm hearth and see what the day would bring.

Back on land, she picked up her discarded clothes and headed for her roundhouse, to warm herself beside the hearth-fire. As soon as she entered the dimly hearth-lit, circular, one roomed home a feeling of cold and clammy dread squeezed the freedom of her soul, so much so that she hadn't the courage to look into the shadows. A glowing hearth-ember sparked and spat a small piece of ash onto the circle of hearthstones. Taking a tentative step towards the eating knife she'd left on one of the stones, she came to a cold stop when a dark figure moved out from the smoky shadows. "Hello, Gwen, seeing so much of you is a pleasure!" The smirking face of a man she despised, smiled lustfully at her.

Pulling her bundle of clothes to her chest, she covered some of her nakedness and spat his name at him, "Huail ap Caw! Get out of my roundhouse!"

"I'd rather stay," he mockingly told her, greedily staring at her body. "And you are in no position to make demands."

"Will you do me the curtesy of turning away while I get dressed?" She wasn't afraid of the son of King Caw of the Picts, but his unashamedly lust-filled looks were making her feel very uncomfortable.

"You don't need to be modest, Gwen." Stepping around the fire, he drew attention to the beating drums. "The pagans are at it again; it must be the mating season. I wouldn't mind a little ritual-coupling myself, and you do look lovely."

She looked disbelieving at the tall man; whose sneering face told her she was in great danger. "You could be handsome," she said, her stomach churning at the thought of his grubby fingers touching her skin. "If it wasn't for that sneer and the dark, almost vacant look in your callous brown eyes, I might find you attractive."

"That wasn't very nice, be careful what you say. I've come for a little sport, but if you insult me again, I might have to hurt you." Running his hand through his greasily lank, long black hair he was about to step towards her when the sounds of clucking and squawking chickens made him look at the door-flap. "Don't mind that," he laughed, "it's two of my warriors. I guess they've found their lunch! My appetite requires a different kind of nourishment."

"You'll get nothing from me!"

"You know, Gwen, I may be the son of a king, but I'm also a man." Taking his knife from his belt, he used it to clean some of the dirt from beneath his fingernails. "You are beautiful, I can't believe you are still unclaimed. Why aren't you married, do you prefer the company of women?"

"I'd prefer a woman to you!" she hissed.

"You might enjoy the pleasure of having a man."

"Not much of a man." Her reply was curt, she'd had enough of this game. "I know you for who and what you are, a well-known rapist and coward who runs from battle. I'm not afraid of you, and………"

"Brave words for one so vulnerable." He took a step forward, close enough to touch her if he chose.

She made a hurried attempt to sort out her clothes and cover herself, but he grabbed them away. Instinctively, she wrapped an arm across her breasts, her free hand hiding what he wanted between her legs. Slipping his knife back into his belt, he spoke softly to her, "Having to undress you would be so tiresome." He threw her clothes on the fire and they burst into flames, brightening the home. "You can waste our time and pretend you are not interested, but I know you are, what woman wouldn't want to mate with a prince? And you can protest your womanly innocence as much as you like, I enjoy pleasuring a reluctant woman. But there are limits to my patience, so come to me now or I'll be forced to use you then pass you on to my men."

"You wouldn't dare! You know who my parents are and what they'd do to you if you hurt me!"

"The Merlin and his whore, I'm not afraid of their imaginary pagan powers!"

She knew she was in trouble; this oily, odious beast of a man wasn't going to take no for an answer. She was about to try reasoning with him when his warriors came in, both carrying dead chickens. She leapt over the fire to get out of their way.

Pointing at his men, Huail joked, "I think they'd like a little sport; do you mind being shared, Gwen?"

There was no way she was going to let these pieces of filthy, Pictish shit take that which she only gave to the man she had chosen. Realising her only weapon was her naked body and, believing she could outwit the Prince, she lowered her arm to reveal her breasts, forced a smile and took a daring step towards King Caw's son. "Is this what you want?" she asked. "Touch me, Huail, you can if you want to, but only if you dismiss your lapdogs first." This was the hardest thing she'd ever had to do, but for the first time since the Pict had stepped out from the shadows, she felt in control.

He spread his arms to welcome her naked body. "My warriors won't touch you; you have my word."

As the two of them came together in the smoky, dim light of the hearth, he wrapped his arms around her and felt her skin with his cold, clammy hands. He could hear his men laughing, they knew well enough that his word meant nothing, they'd have her when he'd finished. Looking him cold in the eyes, Gwen said, seductively, "Would you like us to lay down?"

"Oh yes," he grunted like a feeding pig.

Before he knew what had happened, she'd pulled the knife

from his belt, jabbed it into his thigh and yanked it out again. Yelping, he stepped back to inspect the slender, blood-oozing wound. Before he could think, she threw herself at him and punched the knife through his raised, protective hand. Firmly gripping the wooden handle, she jerked the blade up and pulled so that it turned the screaming man around, forcing his hand over his shoulder and behind his head. "Bitch!" he shrieked. "Let me go!"

His men dropped their chickens, drew their swords and moved towards her. Grabbing a handful of Huail's hair, she pulled his head back, slid the knife free and held the point to his throat. "Call them off or you are a dead man!" Pressing the knife against his skin, she cut a thin trickle of blood. "Stay where you are!" she screamed at the men when they edged closer.

"Get out!" Huail yelled at them.

The two men backed out of the roundhouse. Hearing a rider galloping towards the homestead, they ran along the forest path to where they'd tethered their horses. A heartbeat later the Merlin rode out from the forest and into the clearing, his raven-feather cloak hanging loose from his broad shoulders as he drew his sword. Without a thought for their Prince, Huail's men leapt onto their horses and galloped away into the woodlands.

In full control now, and enjoying the shift in power, Gwen pushed her attacker through the door-flap, the knife still pricking his throat. "Do you need my help?" the Merlin asked.

"I can handle this piece of rat-shit." Using the knife-blade to force Huail towards the lake, she raised her foot and used it to shove him into the cold water.

Landing with a huge splash, the Pict coughed out water and turned to see Gwen running back into the roundhouse. Understanding the look on the Merlin's face, he swam the lake's edge as far as he could, climbed out and hobbled into the forest.

Dismounting as his daughter returned after throwing on a blue, woollen dress, the Merlin asked, "Did he hurt you, Gwen?" Throwing herself into his arms, she reassured him that she was fine, if a little shaken, and told him how she'd tricked Huail. Smiling proudly at her, he asked, "Who taught you how to fight, I suppose it was your lover?"

"I don't know what you mean." She blushed.

"Have it your own way, Daughter."

"Did the Pict drown?" she asked, looking hopefully at the lake.

"No, but he'll be dealt with at the appointed time. Until then you'd better keep your wits about you. I'm sure he'll return when his wounds have healed."

If a person was to visit the former Roman Civitas of Viroconium, it wouldn't be the sights and sounds of the market place that took their breath away. Those who chose to wander through the forum would see white walls and marbled columns supporting red tiled roofs, which sheltered painted walls and multi-coloured mosaic floors. Maintained by the grandsons of Roman artisans, the city was kept in such good repair that anyone walking its streets would believe Rome's authority hadn't abandoned the people of Briton. Strolling amongst the vendors stalls in the daily markets, you wouldn't just see the products of local harvests and trades, you'd be

"What use would thirty men be in such a vast forest?" Einion shot back at him.

"We could send the entire Legion into the woodlands?" Cai suggested.

Shaking his head, Einion walked around the table and retook his seat. "You could summon the ghosts of every Celtic warrior who has ever wielded a sword in battle, and they still wouldn't find my son. The forest is massive, Owain could wander its expanse for years without meeting a soul!"

"But you said you'd ordered a search!" Bedwyr unwisely reminded him.

"I sent one man!"

"The Merlin." Cai realised.

"Yes, he'll bring Owain back. No one knows my son or the forest better than him." Restraining his anger, he poured himself a cup of wine and calmly asked, "Did my son really fight with savage courage?"

Bedwyr felt the tension break. "He did, he is born to the saddle and the sword."

Imagining the sight of his second son leading the Legion into battle, he said as if nothing had happened, "You may go." Relieved, the two young men were about to turn and leave when the High King spoke again, "If my son returns in one piece, you might live, if he doesn't, you won't enjoy your deaths."

Sitting cross-legged on the floor beside Gwen's hearth, the Merlin understood why his daughter needed so little; her life was simple and she liked it that way. Apart from practical essentials such as clay pots, dishes, knives and spoons, a wooden bucket and a barbed fishing spear, her small harp was her only luxury, which he'd given to her when she was a child. Her bed was a pile of furs, beside which lay a makeshift wooden shelf holding tanned leather leggings, a couple of green woollen tunics and a blue dress. Her leather boots stood near the door-flap, beside her hunting bow and a bunch of arrows.

Her home was a smoky pulse, where a person could sit alone, eat and listen to the weather without having to consider anything unnecessary. It was a simple place in which to sleep, make love or gently stroke the ringing strings of the harp. If the Island People weren't still banging at their drums, the Merlin would envy her, but the intrusion was impossible to ignore and, he knew what the Island People were doing and why it was so essential. Gwen didn't care for chairs or stools, preferring instead to sit on the hard-packed dry earth, which didn't bother him because it had its charm. Looking at her through the hearth-smoke, he watched her plucking chicken feathers into a clay bowl as he sipped apple cider from a clay beaker, wondering how she'd cope with what he knew would soon happen.

Having used his renowned sight to search into her future, he knew all the joys and pains she'd live through. He wanted to tell her about the visions, to guide, encourage and protect her but he could say nothing because it wasn't his place to interfere with the fates, to do so might bring the cruellest punishments from the gods. Sometimes he wished he was an ordinary man, not gifted with the knowledge and workings of the sight. If it was a burden, it could also

Merlin continued grumpily, "he opened his eyes to see that he was hunting, riding through a forest where the leaves shone so bright, he thought millions of hand-sized emeralds had fallen onto the forest. He saw riders, led by the hounds of Cuchulain, chasing a great white stag, a beast he'd believed was entirely mythical. Through the valleys and forests the old ones chased the white stag for what seemed like an eternity, with Gwydion leading; but how could time have moved because there'd been no night? He asked the father of Bran the Blessed where the night had gone to? The father of Bran shook his head and asked him what he meant by 'night'? Onward they chased through the jewelled valleys, though Gwydion never closed on the animal, nor was he meant to because the chase was a question, not an action. As the stag leapt a trickle of sapphire blue, the ancients who'd built the stone circles and tombs called his name and he reined in his horse, looked to where he thought the summons had come from, and he marvelled at the feast prepared in a valley filled with the most beautiful of white souls. The valley stretched through the shining forest, the feasting tables and honoured guests trailing beyond the limits of his sight, narrowing into what he thought could be the heart of the palest of suns, but there was no sun in Annwn. Walking amongst the miracle, he saw every kind of delicacy he could imagine, but no meat because this was the land of eternal youth, where neither man nor animal grew old or died. There was an empty seat at the table, so he sat and ate a fruit that tasted of every food he could imagine in one thought. While eating his fill, he heard the most delicate of sounds, like the kiss of the wind rustling the emerald leaves of the forest. The sound brushed against his ethereal skin and, he thought he recognised it. It was as familiar as a recent dream yet, just as distant, hanging beyond his thoughts while giving him an inner warmth and feeling of wellbeing. Maybe it was a breath, or even thousands of breaths though it could just as easily be the sound of knowledge, wisdom, love or the future. He soon realised it could only be the breath of the Goddess Enaid, sent in advance to warm Annwn as she made her way to the feast. She was coming, he believed, to answer the silent prayers of those who'd danced on the Isle of Mona. A rainbow of light flashed into the valley, dazzling Gwydion who turned away to mourn his weakness, his heart begging him to turn and look. Listening to the tears of his soul, he risked a glance, and before he could wonder why he wasn't blind, the light exploded, dispersing into a million stars that evaporated into the soft, blue-yellow sky. When he saw her, he could do nothing but kneel and cry, because her beauty was beyond anything his heart could cope with, and the loving goodness radiating from her soul, pure as it was, was more than he could accept or offer in return. The Goddess Enaid was tall and lithe, with translucent, almost pearl white skin. Her knee length hair had no colour, except for the reflections of a rainbow that caught the light around her, crowning her with a shimmering myriad of colours that sublimely faded into the trails of her hair. He tried looking into her eyes but how does one catch and hold a moment of bliss? Smiling at Gwydion, the mother of the gods offered him her breast so that he might feed upon the goodness that is the combined soul of everything that has ever existed. Spreading his lips around her nipple, he closed his eyes as she cradled him in her love, the warmth

2.

In the sleeper's dream a snarling warrior swung an axe; blood coloured the forest trees and the sounds of battle-dreams raged into pounding and scattering drumbeats. The dreamer, wanting no escape from the pleasure of killing, strolled amongst the already slain carpeting the forest floor and, he jabbed his sword repeatedly into the dead, enjoying the feel of the blade puncturing flesh. The dream shifted and a woman he didn't know took hold of his sword arm, placed her hand on his bloodied but now broken blade, and smiling she said, "Leave it, the Goddess has made you a stronger blade."

On the edge of awakening, Owain's head throbbed to the sound of beating drums, his confused dream fading to leave a metallic taste in his dry mouth. Opening his red-rimmed eyes, he looked at his hands, rubbed away some of the encrusted blood, sat up and turned to see his horse chomping grass beside a trickling brook. He'd no idea how many days the horse had carried him through the forest, how long he'd slept for or where he was, but he did know that he never wanted to kill again.

Irritated by the drumbeats slamming flat against the trees, he walked over to the stream, knelt beside it and washed Saxon blood from his arms and face. From what he could see, through the leafless treetops, the Sun was fading into an orange haze, so he decided he'd follow its progress because Viroconium was in the west. Changing his mind when the greasy aroma of roasting meat caught his sense and tempted his hunger, he mounted his horse, splashed into the brook and chased the delicious smell deeper into the forest.

He hadn't ridden far upstream when he realised the darkening forest was closing in on him, and the drumbeats were getting louder. There was little to see except for trees, which made him nervous, so he halted and listened, trying to work out if the beating throbs were coming from the same direction as the greasy aroma. Unable to tell because of the many echoes, he felt for the sword he knew no longer hung by his side but, he did find his knife tucked into his belt. With that small piece of comfort to hand, he continued his ride upstream, towards the cooking meat.

Noticing the pebbly-brook was thinning, almost to a trickle, he guessed he couldn't be far from its source, which had to be a spring. Riding on, he whistled a tune to the beating drums until he came to a glade dominated by looming, moss covered rocks the height of two or three men standing on each other's shoulders. To the side of the rocks emerged the spring, which bubbled into a thick patch of bracken before sliding west and north.

To his left the wall of rock climbed to a tree-lined ridge that sheltered a small cave in the base of the granite. Riding closer, he saw it was more of an overhang than a cave, and a spitted hare was roasting above stone-circled flames, so someone obviously lived here. Having found his meal, he dismounted and left his horse to graze.

Before walking to the meat, he noticed a short hunting spear leaning against the rock below the overhang and, tilted beside the fire lay a clay water jug dripping its contents, so someone had left in a hurry. He couldn't see anyone, but whoever had set the hare to none of which were Saxon. Searching amongst the dead, I came across my grandfather first, he'd been hacked to pieces."

"What about your father?"

"The Saxons hanged him upside down from a branch at the edge of the forest, and lit a small fire beneath him. One side of his face was scorched, blistered and blackened, and they'd cut his belly open so that his guts spilled onto the fire. I found my little sister's body in a patch of brambles; she'd been thrown there. They'd pulled a knife across her throat, but I didn't see that until I removed her dress from her little face. She only had four summers behind her, and I remember thinking how unfair it was that she'd died so young. She looked so tiny and vulnerable, her face twisted into helpless sorrow, all the love and joy shocked out of her." He paused to wipe his eyes. "I never found my mother, Carys, all that was left of her was her long golden hair, they'd cut it off! I buried my family in one grave, which I dug deep to prevent wolves and dogs from feasting on them. I then burned the rest of the dead villagers and waited a few days by the charred circle where our roundhouse had stood, in case my mother returned, but she didn't. Perhaps the Saxons had chased her into the woods and killed her there, and left her body for animals to devour. I came to the sanctuary of the forest because I didn't want to be near humans for a while." For a few moments the only sound was the incessantly beating drums, neither of them wanting to speak. Slapping a stick into the embers, the boy wiped away a tear and said to the warrior, "Now I'll hunt in the forest, grow and become strong. When I'm ready I'll walk to Viroconium, find Owain the Prince of

Rhos and join his horse-warriors, if he'll have me. Then I'll kill Saxons, I will have my revenge."

Wrapped in his cloak beside the campfire, Owain stirred from sleep, awoken by the pounding drums as sunlight poured into the rocky glade. Standing over him, silhouetted by sunbeams, a dark figure looked down. "Is that you, Gal?" the Prince asked, squinting to try and make out the features of the shape he felt sure he knew.

"No, the boy has gone hunting for your breakfast," the feather-cloaked man replied.

"Gwion!" Owain exclaimed with surprise, rubbing sleep from his eyes as the wise man stepped out from the sun's rays.

"Call me the Merlin, or Merlin. If you ever become king, then you may use my birth name."

"I'm sorry, Merlin. How did you find me?"

"I followed your thoughts."

"Can you do that when someone is sleeping?" Owain sat up and looked through the woodlands for Gal.

"Following someone's thoughts is easier when they are asleep because their dreams are more powerful than their woken thoughts."

"But we don't always dream?"

"From the moment you fall asleep, to the time you become conscious, a continuous flow of dreams passes through your mind. You don't always remember them, but if you don't dream you eventually go mad."

"That's all very interesting, but why are you here?"

carrying on in and around the collection of wooden huts and storehouses surrounding his feasting hall.

Whilst casting a fatherly eye over the people going about their business, the doors to his hall opened and he saw his daughter, Gorpe, walk out, carrying an empty basket. Being an unmarried virgin, her long, golden hair hung loose down the back of her leaf green dress, swaying with her hips when she delicately stepped along the muddy winter duckboards that led to the fleece barn.

Seeing how his younger warriors greeted her, not all of them showing her due respect, he grunted with amused pride. She wasn't popular because she was a princess, his warriors loved her because she was a rare beauty and a fine prize for any man who could win her heart. He could guess what his warriors in the courtyard were thinking, but none of them were high-born enough to win her hand, so none of them would bed her.

Although she had fifteen summers behind her, she hadn't been promised to a king yet, and, as his wife Queen Aelice kept reminding him, it was about time Gorpe was given to someone worthy of her status. Her monthly moon-bloods had begun over three years ago, her body had developed some very impressive curves so if he didn't act soon, she might begin to look at his warriors in the same way they looked at her, and who'd have her if her womb was fat with child?

The wind gusted, whisking up his beard as he walked along the battlements. Looking north to the forest his people called Andredsweald, he remembered that somewhere within the vast spread of woodlands his two surviving sons, Wlencing and Cissa, were returning from the borderland raids. Their return, with the two hundred spearmen who'd accompanied them, was well overdue but that didn't worry him because they'd probably captured a large selection of slaves, and the plunder from the raids would slow their march home. Wlencing would inherit his throne and lands, and being wise, brave, a ruthless killer and popular with the ladies, he'd make a fine king.

The further downstream Owain's plodding horse took him, the quieter the beating drums became. As the shallow brook cut through a spread of blooming snowdrops colouring white a forest glade, the young Prince raised his head to savour the warmth of the climbing sun. The winter had been long and hard, the last of the snows having only recently melted, so the spring warmth was welcome.

The warmth made him think of his lover, guessing that perhaps a day's ride from here she'd have set about her daily chores. His duties as a Dragon had kept him from her for some time, and he longed to see her again. But after the months of separation would she welcome him with a loving smile and a warm bed, or with a cold heart and harsh words? If she turned him away, he'd deserve the rejection, but first he must find the Merlin, who'd no doubt tell him his travels were over and he must ride to Viroconium.

He didn't want to return to the city, much preferring the idea of visiting his lover for a few days before turning his mind to the never-ending Saxon wars. But it was his duty to lead the Legion he'd created; they were his warriors and he was proud of them. Over the winter their fighting strength had increased to two hundred, and with help from Bedwyr and Cai they'd been drilled into an effective unit of cavalry. He didn't want to let his comrades down, but right now the thought of the battle-charge didn't stir his blood, he much preferred the idea of idling away his days in his lover's bed.

Further downstream his horse plodded, the brook deepening as he knew it would. It wasn't long before the Druid came into view, sitting on a low branch that overhung the stream. Dipping a fishing line, tied to his finger, into the clear water, the Merlin either didn't hear the splashing of the approaching horse or, chose to ignore the Prince's arrival. Owain laughed at the serene scene, amused because the Merlin was obviously feeling as lazy as he was. Without greeting the Druid, Owain dismounted, tested the strength of the branch, and shuffled along it to join his friend. The Merlin jerked the line to give the impression he was fishing seriously, before asking, "Do you enjoy fishing, Killer of Saxons?"

"Yes, but what do you expect to hook here? It's too shallow, you are too close to the source so you won't catch anything."

"Won't I?" Chuckling, the Merlin wiggled the line. "Before making assumptions, a wise man would ask what I am fishing for?"

"Riddles."

"There are no riddles if your eyes are open. I'm not here to debate or teach, so rest your soul and be lazy, Owain, while you can."

"How can I with the endlessly pounding drumbeats splitting my head? Do you know who the drummers are, and why they've been beating away for at least three days?" Owain looked closer at the fishing line, then back to the Merlin. "There's no bait on your hook!"

"Why would there be when there aren't any fish here?"

"Are you going to tell me what you want, or must I wait until you've caught an invisible fish?" To his surprise, he found himself watching the bait-less hook, just in case a fish did leap onto it!

"My intension was to take you home immediately, but something happened during my journey, something you should know about. Huail ap Caw has been making a nuisance of himself."

"Must you tell me now?" Owain's sigh was long and deep, he'd only just begun his journey back and already the troubles of the kingdom were being heaped on his shoulders.

"I think you'll want to know," the Merlin warned him, winding up his line.

"I don't want to know what's going on with a boorish Pict who'd rather kill and rape the weak than fight the strong enemies of the Celts."

"You aren't listening to me, Owain, I said you'd 'want' to know."

"What do you mean? No riddles, tell me straight, what's so important that it couldn't wait? Has my father died, has my brother Cadwallon been taken ill?"

"Calm yourself, the emergency was dealt with and none of your loved ones were hurt. If you promise not to overreact, I'll tell you what's been happening while you've been skulking in the forest."

"I wasn't skulking, I was trying to make sense of my feelings."

"Did you succeed?"

"You are the one who sees and understands everything," Owain said a little too aggressively.

"You are a petulant young fool sometimes. Do you want to know what Huail has been up to?"

3.

The latch of the birthing chamber door lifted with a click, the door opened and a serving girl, carrying a bowl of bloodied cloths, slipped out without making eye contact with the anxious man sitting on the chair by the door, who watched her quickly close the door and run along the stone-flagged, torch-lit corridor in Viroconium's royal villa. Seeing the bloodied rags, Prince Cadwallon, the dark haired, first born son of the Pendragon, felt sick to the core but what could he do? Being a man, he wouldn't be allowed into the room until the midwife summoned him, and she wouldn't do that unless his child had been born or, his wife was near death.

Princess Meddyf, his beautiful, sweet-hearted young wife had been at the birthing post for most of the previous day, night and well into the new morning. Her painfilled screams regularly ripped through the villa like iced-spears, though her gentle sobs were only heard within the room. Cadwallon desperately needed to hear the cries of his new-born, not just because he wanted to welcome the child into the world, but because he couldn't bear the thought of Meddyf's suffering continuing.

Since the Sun had risen her cries had become weaker, more subdued, tired and strained. Cadwallon knew something was wrong, and if they'd let him in maybe he could help. But that wasn't the main reason he wanted to be with his wife, if she wasn't going to survive the birthing, he needed to hold her one last time before the light of her soul flickered and fled.

The serving girl scurried back, carrying three more clay bowls, a bundle of white cloths and a sharpened knife. Lowering her eyes while edging past him, she opened the door just enough for her to slip through without him seeing in. Frustrated at being denied a part in his child's birth, Cadwallon stood and faced the closed door as another fragile scream chilled his bones.

Although their marriage had been a political union between two royal families, he deeply loved Meddyf. From the first moment he'd seen the heart-warming smile on the prettily freckled face of the petite, auburn-haired woman, he'd known his marriage would be a happy one, and he'd been right. From her first days in Viroconium her infectious joy had spread throughout his household. Everyone loved her, and he often wondered how such perfect goodness and strength could come from such a fragile young woman. There wasn't one spark of darkness in her, she was the light of the city and if she died, the people of Viroconium would openly mourn.

Another laboured, withering scream thickened his blood and a cold, heavy silence strangled his heart. He heard nothing, no encouraging words from the midwives, no sighs of surrender or gentle sobs, then a gut-stabbing, high pitched shriek ricocheted along the corridor walls. Staring at the door, he held his breath, hoping for a whisper or a sigh, anything to reassure him that his wife still lived. The serving woman slipped out from the room again, carrying another bowl of bloodied rags.

Unable to withstand the torment, he decided to open the door, rush in and take his wife in his arms. He couldn't leave her to die without telling her he loved her, and he was about to lift the latch when he heard the first shrill wail of a new-born child. Tear-filled emotions surged over him, relief first, then fear, followed by a host of questions.

Tensing, clenching and unclenching his fists, he waited for the midwife's call to beckon him in. The door opened, and Ina the midwife stood before him, cradling a bundle of new-born life. "You have a strong, healthy son," the buxom woman said, trying to smile as she pulled back the cloth to reveal the boy's wailing, screwed up face.

Gently placing his little finger into the baby's tiny, open hand, Cadwallon thinly whispered, "I have a son." The boy's tiny fingers squeezed tight around his father's, and for a few moments the Prince couldn't speak. Taking the child from the midwife, he held him warm and close, instinctively protective.

The child looked perfect, with the thick bush of the black hair of the Cunedda line sprouting from the top of his head. His eyes were the emerald green of Meddyf's family, which reminded him that as well as having a son to consider, he had a wife. Looking at the midwife, he saw concerned sadness clouding her eyes. Certain that something was seriously wrong, he tried stepping around her but she matched his sidestep. "There were complications," she told him. "For the time being the birthing chamber isn't the place for you."

"But I must see my wife."

"Please," Ina pleaded, "let us do what we can for her, then you can see her." The midwife's voice wavered and cracked when she said, "The child, the child wouldn't be born, we'd no choice but to cut, to cut him from his mother's womb. Meddyf lost a lot of blood, she may not survive the night." Seeing his pain, it almost broke her heart to continue, but he needed to know the truth. "I can't lie to you, it's unlikely the Princess will live, prepare yourself to mourn her passing."

"Does she know she has birthed a Votidini prince, has she seen him?"

"Yes, your wife held the child and offered him a name. I have stitched her wound, now she must sleep. I've given her a drink to dull the pain, that's all I can do. For the time being she needs healing, not love, that must come if she survives the night."

"What name did she choose?" the words almost choked him.

"Maelgwn."

"That means 'Princely Hound'. She chose well, it's a strong name for a future king."

Taking the boy from him, Ina spoke with genuine caring, "I must take him to the wet-nurse, your wife was too weak to offer him her nipple. I'll return to the Princess when I've given the child to the nurse, and be assured, Cadwallon, we'll do everything we can to save your wife. You are a Christian, aren't you?"

"Yes."

"Go to your private rooms and pray for your wife. I'll send for you if and when you are needed."

Saxons like to feast, drink and enjoy women at every opportunity, so they don't need an excuse to join their king in his feasting hall when food, ale and women are in plentiful supply. On this day a chilly, easterly wind was blowing across Andredes

Caester's battlements, so almost every warrior no out on patrol, had gathered in the hall.

Sitting on a bench beside one of the three hearths in his feasting hall, King Aelle drunkenly pointed at the smoky, sooted rafters, chuckling to himself because from the inside the hall really did look like the upturned keel of a boat. After pouring himself another horn of ale, he took a long swig, swayed to his right and fell backwards onto the straw covered floor. Getting up, he rubbed his elbow and laughed when a drunken warrior slipped off his stool and landed on a startled hound, that yelped and bit the man. Retaking his seat, Aelle remembered that a King's true wealth is measured by the strength of his sons, not the size of his hall or the number of warriors who'll follow him into battle. He glanced at the closed doors, hoping they'd open so that he could welcome home his sons.

Princes Wlencing and Cissa would need lands of their own soon, so a choice had to be made. He could march east to invade the valleys of the Jutish King Aesc or, lead his army north and west into the lands of the Britons. "Celts are soft," he said to the ale-sodden warrior sitting opposite him. "They fight like plucked chickens and run from battle squealing like pigs!" A woman, just as drunk as himself, fell onto his lap while trying to escape the attentions of a warrior. "Get off me," he growled after squeezing her breast, then he slapped her arse and rolled her off. "Go and fetch me another jug of ale."

He liked women, all of them, whatever their shape and size. Some of his favourite kingly possessions were the strong, well-built women who knew how to keep him warm in bed. They weren't all freeborn, some were slaves, Celtic women he'd captured during raids. Having a fondness for Celtic women, because they did exactly what he told them to do, once he'd threatened them with the edge of his battle-axe, his private chambers were regularly frequented by them.

Unlike his women, his warriors were given all they could desire, and more, some had even been granted land taken from the Celts during his many wars, which was a good policy because this strengthened his borders. He often thought the Celts had no fight in them, except for their so-called Pendragon. When the spring buds finally burst into leaf, he'd lead his warriors to the Western Sea, which would force the Pendragon to march south against him. And what a fight that would be, the two most powerful kings in Briton, battling for the right to claim the entire island as their own.

Seeing through drunken vision, Aelle just about recognised the woman he'd spent the previous night with, hanging herbs to dry from nails hammered into the tall posts supporting the roof. She was a pretty, golden haired Celtic slave whose name he couldn't remember, but that didn't matter because he did remember how she'd let him rut her like a bull.

Although many warriors were enjoying his generosity, most of his spearmen were out on patrols or raiding parties. The spring thaw always heralded the murder and rape of Celts, which was one of the many pleasures of being a Saxon. But he was getting too old and fat for such adventures, his joints ached in the mornings and he didn't have the energy to chase Celtic women as their husbands died on Saxon spearpoints. It was fun being a Saxon, he decided, farting beef and cabbage stew in the direction of last nights bed-mate. Saxons were a civilised people, unlike the savage Celts, some of whom shaved their faces, trimmed their hair and ate with two-pronged forks as well as with knives and spoons. When he conquered them, he'd make a point of civilising them, that was his duty.

Becoming curious about a 'game of insults' developing around the hearth closest to the doors, which was getting rowdier as each insult was offered, he staggered over to listen. It was his favourite game for breaking the tedium of the colder days, and the rules were simple: the warriors insulted each other, the best insult winning a prize. He wasn't sure what the prize was today, sometimes it was a purse of silver, but it could just as easily be a cask of ale or a good hunting spear. The game was usually played in good spirits, rarely becoming violent though he had seen men killed while playing the game. But that wouldn't be a problem here, he didn't allow weapons in the hall, except for his own.

A roar of laughter thundered as the game neared its conclusion and, from what he could see through his ale-misted eyes, Algar and Cenric were enjoying the duel. Cenric stood, and in an ale-sodden drawl he shouted for all to hear, "Algar, I see the lice from your beard have fled to find a cleaner pig!"

The hearth-warriors roared with laughter. Aelle slapped the insulted warrior on the back, sat down next to him and pushed him to his feet. Algar, as drunk as everyone else, swayed a little before turning to face the previous insult. "Your lice feed from the slops gathered on your beard," he slurred back at Cenric, "was it grown in a cesspit?"

Amused, Cenric roared at one of the warriors who'd fallen from his stool in drunken laughter, "You might laugh, Paega, but the lice from your beard have found a warmer bed on the arse of your woman, I've heard her beard is long!" Everyone, including King Aelle, erupted into raucous laughter, except for Paega's wife, who broke a clay jug of ale over Cenric's head.

"My woman may have a full beard between her legs," Paega offered in reply to the sore-headed man, "but your woman, who looks remarkably like one of the cows on your farm, you know, the one you hump every night before finding your bed, she has a beard that......."

The game was cut short when the hall doors swung open, letting in streams of bright sunlight. King Aelle saw four silhouetted figures walk through the hazy beams, carrying what looked like a body on a wooden pallet. "Who enters the hall of King Aelle!" he bellowed as he got up and strode towards the newcomers.

"Prince Cissa," the tallest of the silhouettes replied, "with the flesh and bones of Prince Wlencing, once heir to the South Saxon throne."

The King stopped in his tracks, groaned and fell to his knees. Not wanting to show any weakness, he took a deep breath, got to his feet and walked over to the body. "How did he die?" Lifting the cloak from Wlencing's corpse, he saw a dark, blood-encrusted wound in his son's chest.

"He died with an axe in his hand, in battle. His axe drank Celtic blood!" Prince Cissa shouted, holding aloft the blade so that the truth could be seen.

King Aelle took the weapon and ran his thumbnail along the iron edge, scraping away Celtic blood. "My son died killing his enemies!" he shouted across the tables. "Soon, he'll feast with Hengist and Horsa in Woden's hall, which is as it should be. My third-born son, Prince Cissa, will follow me as king of the South Saxons. Does anyone challenge his right to lead our warriors after my death?" No one spoke. "So be it." Turning to some of the wives of his warriors, he ordered them to prepare Wlencing's body for cremation.

Knee deep in the lake, with her skirt hitched up, Gwen held her barbed bone fishing spear at an angle to the water, ready to strike. Below the spearpoint nothing moved, except for an insect skimming over the lake's surface. She'd been on her guard since Huail's intrusion, but from the moment her eyes focused on the greens foresting the lake's underworld, the idea of another violent intrusion was forgotten.

Hidden within the forest, which here and there almost crept into the lake, a mounted warrior watched her, fascinated as her upper body turned with the swim of her prey. He blinked when she plunged the spear through the film and lifted it in an arcing spray of water, a carp wriggling on the barbed, bone point. Unaware of the watching man, Gwen waded to the pebbly shore, pulled the fish free, cracked its head with a stone and, she stepped back into the lake to spear another fish.

The warrior couldn't help but admire her skill, and her beauty. Never had he seen a woman quite like her, and with the sun's rays shining on her long, raven hair, giving it a sheen of glowing red, he felt that a part of her must have been created in the Otherworld. A light breeze wafted her hair as she stood perfectly still, her concentration focused as another fish swam into range.

Tempted by her Otherworldly beauty, the warrior could watch no longer, so he clicked his horse through the budding twigs and branches. Hearing the rustle of twigs and the crunching of pebbles, Gwen raised her spear and turned, determined not to let Huail ap Caw get close to her a second time. Her wary blue eyes saw the warrior ride out from the trees; his arms held wide to show that he meant no harm. Using his legs to guide his mount, he rode into the lake.

Neither spoke as the horse splashed closer, their sight fixed upon each other, watching for the slightest movement that might signal an attack. He circled his mount around her, excited by the vision of determined beauty, cautious of the spear pointing at his throat. Turning to match his circle, she softened her heartbeats just as her lover had taught her, relaxing while remaining alert to danger, ready to strike if need be.

Irritated by the way he was circling her, she thrust her spear. The horse whinnied as the barbed bone flashed close enough for the warrior to pull hard on the reins, jerking the horse's head to one side. The beast stumbled and splashed away, so he patted its neck to calm it, rode back and continued circling her. Again, she lifted her spear, so he raised his arms, offering her his surrender. Deciding he should make a peaceful offering, he halted his horse and said, "You look like a goddess."

"You look and smell like a butchered pig!" she instantly threw back.

"Please, lower your spear, Gwen."

"Stay where you are!" she warned, prodding the barbed bone at him, "unless you want me to scar your pretty face!"

"I haven't come here to hurt you."

"Did I say you had?" Within the blinking of an eye, she'd turned the spear and swung it. Cracking him on the side of his head with the spear-butt, she laughed when he tumbled head first into the lake. "Owain the Prince of Rhos, the great Dragon of the Legion, unhorsed by a woman with a fishing spear!"

Coughing out a mouthful of water, he rolled over and sat up, chest deep in the cold lake. "Was that necessary?" He tried to stand, so she jabbed the spear-butt into his chest, knocking him splashing backwards.

"You are not coming anywhere near me until you've had a wash," she warned, standing over him like a warrior who'd just made her first kill. "Get yourself and your clothes clean of all that dried blood. I'll be in the roundhouse when you've done, I've chicken stew cooking if you are hungry?" With her head held triumphantly high, she splashed back to the shore, picked up the fish and disappeared into the roundhouse, leaving him sitting in the water, defeated but amused.

After washing, he hung his clothes and chainmail on branches, and stepped naked and cold into the smoky warmth of her roundhouse. "I've washed my clothes and hung them to dry."

“Good.” Kneeling beside the hearth, stirring the contents of her cooking pot, she admired his muscle-toned, naked beauty then threw him a fur. “Don’t ever come to my home stinking of other men’s blood again.” She glared at him, not wanting to let him off the hook.

He sat beside the fire to warm himself. “You usually have a warmer welcome for me, have I done something wrong?”

“You don’t usually come to me with your clothes covered in blood,” she snapped. Softening, she asked, “Where have you been, Owain?”

Wisely, he thought before answering, unsure of her trap. “There’s been a battle and.........”

“I know about the battle, and you know that’s not what I meant. Why haven’t you visited me?” Her voice softened a little more. “I’ve missed you.”

He shuffled closer. “I know I should have come to you sooner, and I’m sorry but the Legion kept me busy throughout the winter, I’d hardly time to breathe. Battle season will soon be upon us, so we’ve had to increase our training and double the border patrols. I wanted to be with you.” Tentatively putting his arm around her waist, he pulled her close and smiled into her beautiful blue eyes. “Out on cold night-patrols it was only the thought of you that kept me going, kept me warm. I love you, Gwen, I hate every moment we are apart. If I had the choice, I’d stay here with you, but how much choice do princes get?” He tenderly kissed her.

She responded by folding her arms around his neck, her lips melting into his warm kiss. Before he could become aroused, she pushed him away and said, “I’ve something to tell you.”

"The Merlin told me about Huail's visit."

"It's much more serious than a visit from a piece of Pictish-weasel-shit."

"Tell me, Gwen," he said softly, feeling her anxiety. "Whatever it is, we'll face it together."

Closing her eyes, she blurted her secret, "I'm pregnant, you'll be a father within the passing of six moons."

West of Andredes Caester, the final touch of daylight faded into a smudgy, purple haze, it was time for the funeral rites to begin. It wasn't easy for King Aelle to accept the loss of two sons, but at least they'd died in battle so, they would share Woden's feast in the God's great hall. In the wastelands to the west of Andredes Caester, King Aelle, dressed in his finest chainmail and wearing his ceremonial, gold-crowned helmet, waited beside the pyre with Queen Aelice, Prince Cissa and Princess Gorpe as hundreds of firebrand-holding mourners looked on in respectful silence.

Now that it was time to send his second son to Woden, King Aelle couldn't help but wonder what might have been. If his two eldest sons had lived, what kind of an empire would they have carved out, how far would the lands of the South Saxons have stretched? Only Prince Cissa remained to stand beside him in battle, so he'd place his hopes for conquest on the young man's shoulders. Seeing the north star shining bright above the rings of mourners, he felt Queen Aelice touch his hand as she offered him a burning torch.

Taking the firebrand, the King raised the smoking flame to the stars and a low, guttural groan hummed from the mourners. Placing a jewelled pendant on the mouth of the corpse, he lowered the torch and called to Neorxnawang, "Woden, prepare your feast. A warrior comes to your hearth who owns many battle-scars and trophies of war. You'll hear his tales of love, lust and battles until all your ale-horns have been emptied, and those stories will be true. Watch him when he runs with your hounds in the great hunt, there'll be none to match his strength, grace and speed. When he fights, he will defeat all the strong champions you set against him, and remember his reputation as a warrior is great amongst mortal men. He is Wlencing, winner of battles, gold and women. God of our ancestors, his bloodied sword and axe are now yours!"

Several of Wlencing's closest friends and sword-brothers stepped from the circle to place offerings on the pyre, including a shield, a spear, drinking horns, bowls of food, a full cask of ale and the head of a horse, everything the soul would need on its journey to the next life. When the last of the gifts had been placed, King Aelle lit the pyre. Stepping back to stand beside Prince Cissa, he felt for his sword, gripped its handle and silently swore to have his revenge, when he'd discovered who the killer of his son was.

Hundreds of firebrands stormed in arcs and fell onto the smoking logs. The mourners began a high pitched, one note keen. The wind whipped through the pyre, feeding the flames and pulling them high into smoking spirals as the spitting, fiery tongues enveloped the body in a furnace of sorrow-filled flames. Queen Aelice stepped forward with rivers of tears flooding her cheeks. Drawing from the depths of her motherly soul a profoundly loss-fuelled sadness only a mourning mother could feel, she began the funeral dirge, her sorrow etched on her grieving face while the watching hundreds added their respect to strengthen her song.

Grief hit Aelle and, beating his chest he fell to his knees, his weeping, upturned eyes begging Woden to accept his dead son's soul into his hall. Regrets waisted themselves and his tears flowed, his sorrow scouring a hole in his heart that would never be filled. Queen Aelice helped him up and held him close, her broken heart howling her sorrow into the acrid black smoke.

The dirge wailed long into the night, the circling mourners releasing their grief as the glowing logs collapsed in a shower of sparks and greasy smoke. With Wlencing's soul released to find its way to Woden's feasting hall, the citizens and spearmen walked away, leaving the royals to mourn alone.

While the black shades of his people walked back to the fort, King Aelle said to Cissa, "We must talk, alone. Wlencing's soul has left us, respect has been paid so you must tell me everything that happened when he was killed. I want to know what tactics the Britons used, and which filthy, pox-ridden Celt must pay the blood-price for my son's death."

4.

The stone walls of Meddyf's bedchamber flickered with light and shadows, the dying candle on the table beside her bed glowing its last, so Prince Cadwallon, sitting on a stool, used the flickering flame to light another. Meddyf still clung to life, her faint breaths less than a whisper so he closed his eyes and prayed that her body would find the strength it would need to heal itself. What he wouldn't give for her to open her eyes and smile her forgiveness, which he badly needed because if she died, he'd never forgive himself for getting her with child.

In the thin, glimmering candlelight he gently touched her cheek with the tips of his fingers, and was surprised by how warm her skin felt. He wanted to kiss her cheek, but should he risk waking her? Let her sleep, that's what the midwife had ordered and she was a sensible woman. Ignoring Ina's wisdom, he bent down until his lips almost touched her skin, then he hesitated, his uncertainty overriding his need. Turning on his stool he looked out of the small window that wasn't shuttered against the night. He'd been as proud of his impending fatherhood as any man could have been, but with Meddyf close to death he felt robbed, useless and ashamed for feeling sorry for himself while his wife's gentle breaths grew weaker.

The window shutter rattled and a light breeze pushed dark storm clouds across the night. Walking to the window, he investigated the death-black sky and its thickening clouds, whispering a prayer to the Christ as raindrops blew into his face. Closing the shutter, he walked back to the stool to continue his vigil and, he took a risk and lightly smoothed Meddyf's sweat-dampened hair away from her eyes. Kissing the tip of her nose, he thought he heard her sigh through the faintest of breaths. Intently watching her mouth, he waited. Both her eyelids flickered so he whispered her name, and her lips parted just enough for her to release a soft sigh. His mind panicked, what should he do, would it be wise to leave her alone while he went to find Ina? Her dry tongue touched the front of her top lip, she tried to swallow as her eyelids opened and her tired but beautiful green eyes looked up at him. "Water, please," her dry whisper croaked from her parched throat.

Suppressing his joy at hearing the first words she'd spoken since naming her son, he picked up the jug from the table and poured a little herb-water into a small bowl. Sitting himself on the edge of her bed, he gently lifted her head and held the bowl to her lips. Taking a few small sips, she smiled and thanked him. After drinking a little more, she closed her eyes so he lowered her head onto the pillow, expecting her to sleep again. Instead, she asked how her son was?

"He thrives, his nurse must already be deaf from his wailing, and he feeds like a pig, the boy is never satisfied."

"He's a Votidini prince," she said through faint breaths. "He'll be a strong king."

He had to agree, but for now he wanted her to sleep so that the Christ could heal that which mortals could not. "Close your eyes, Meddyf, the more you sleep the sooner you'll be well again."

“I won’t heal, I’ve accepted that and so should you. Pray for my soul, Husband, and don’t ever forget that I love you.” Her eyes closed, her breathing softened into a peaceful sigh and she slept. Accepting the inevitable truth, Cadwallon wept.

Sitting cross-legged beside the hearth in her roundhouse, Gwen studied Owain through the hearth-smoke. He’d been gazing into the fire for some time, and she was fascinated by his constantly changing facial expressions. It was funny watching his face shift from frowns to grimaces as he nodded or shook his head, but she was concerned.

When she’d told him she was pregnant, he’d kissed her, and to her surprise he’d thanked her for giving him such a gift. Since then, he’d hardly spoken a word, which convinced her there was more going on than she knew. Feeling bored and ignored, her eyes trailed the hearth-smoke up and into the roof thatching. Rainfall was gently tapping on the thatch, a sound she’d loved as a child because it was so comforting, reminding her that the finest gifts of life are given by nature.

She guessed that Owain might be thinking about the battle and his time in the forest, although she knew he had decisions to make because he’d briefly spoken about them. He’d told her that the life of a prince didn’t sit happily on his shoulders, though he did want to lead his people in the fight to take back the ‘Lost Lands’ from the Saxons. But he was confused, while wanting to help his people, he also wanted to be free of them so that he could live the way he chose, instead of having his life dictated to him by duty. Out of the corner of her eye, she saw her small harp standing next to her bow and hunting spear, which gave her an idea.

Seeing her pick up the harp and return to sit by the fire, he was both curious and surprised that she was about to play the instrument, because she'd never played to him. After plucking a few strings, she began to tune it. He then remembered he'd never heard her sing, though that wasn't true because she'd been singing when they'd first met in the forest, two summers gone. With the harp tuned she plucked a few notes and chords and, she said to her lover, "I'm going to sing about the 'Lost Lands'. My father taught me the song when I was a child, and sometimes, usually when it's raining, I sit by the fire and sing it to myself."

Watching her fingers pluck a regular pattern, he felt the gentle tones soothing him, which had him believing there was magic within the sound. Closing his eyes as she hummed the slow melody, he felt himself melt into her smooth tones. Some songs create magic, the Merlin had once told him, so he let the song have its way and Gwen's voice swirled with the smoke, the words suggesting the images she wanted him to feel and see, "The winds of the valleys, they whisper a name, the name of the lost lands, and freedom again. The lands of our fathers, lost in the storm, wait for a calling, again to be born. The tears and the shadows, the ghosts of the day, sing of our fathers, and where they lay. The dust and the ashes, beneath the stones, will be awoken, to guide us home. There is a wakening, to comfort the day, the people returning, homeward again. There is a dream that, so many can see, returning to lost lands, where we were free."

With the final note falling thoughtfully into the hearth, he said in a childishly sullen voice, “I don’t want to go back, Gwen, I want to stay here, with you.”

“You can’t, you are a Votidini prince.” She’d never have guessed there was such deep sadness within him. Sitting with his head bowed, he looked like a scolded child, defenceless and small. He may be a warrior and a prince, but he was still a motherless, vulnerable boy. “Can anyone hide from who they are?” she asked.

“I don’t know. Perhaps I’m not who I’m supposed to be?”

“You must be honest with yourself, Owain, or you’ll blind yourself to yourself.” Putting down the harp, she moved around the fire, sat beside him and took him in her arms.

Sinking his head onto her comforting chest, he began to tremble so she smoothed her hand through his long, black hair. For a while, he wept. Humming sweetly, she gently rocked him while his silent tears fell. He didn’t mind her rocking him, because he needed her to be his mother, and as his tears wet his cheeks the weight of his lust driven savagery, and the shock that had oppressed him since the battle, drifted away and his mind cleared.

His tears ceased and, lifting his head from her breast he confessed to her, “I ran from the killing-field to hide from myself, because I enjoyed the killing. When I first plunged my spear into a man it gave me a feeling of overwhelming power, lust and joy and I wanted more killing. I needed to feel warm blood on my hands, I had to slice through flesh and send heads and limbs tumbling. Kill, kill, kill that’s all I wanted, not you, not my father or brother, not even my mother. Can you feel that, Gwen, do you understand? When all the Saxons were dead, my mind settled and I was forced to look upon the bloody mess I'd created. Hating myself, I ran, hoping to leave the worse part of myself behind on the battlefield. When I awoke in the forest, I realised that savagery is part of battle survival. It's in our nature, as it is with every animal, we kill to survive. It's primal so will happen whenever I fight and kill, and I don't think I can face that again. I'm afraid that if I enter battle's madness a second time, I won't see the other side of that insanity."

Gwen understood, so she asked him a simple question, "What else can you do?"

He didn't have to think before replying, "I can walk away from my responsibilities. Live a simple life within the turning wheel of nature's cycle, with you. I want to remain here and watch my child grow."

So that's why he'd thanked her, she thought. The growing child in her womb had given him a reason to turn his back on his duty, which angered her because she wasn't sure she wanted the child to be his reason for abandoning his people. "We all have our given paths to follow," she reminded him. "You have responsibilities, a place in the world given to you by the Goddess."

"Did she ask me if I wanted to carry that burden?"

"No, but that's not the point."

"Then what is the point? The people who work in the fields have a choice, as do the tradesmen in the cities, so why can't I choose?"

"You already know the answer, and you are asking the wrong question."

"How do I walk away, Gwen? How do I face my father and tell him I am no longer the Prince of Rhos and the Dragon of the Legion?"

She kissed him. "The only answer I can give is that you must find your own answers. We all know the truth to any question we ask ourselves about our lives, so be completely honest with yourself and you'll realise all you need to know. Whatever you decide, my love is always yours."

A clay ale jug flew across the feasting hall and smashed at King Aelle's feet, who, sitting beside Prince Cissa in the drunken wake, laughed when the thrower was floored by a woman's punch. Although the Sun had long since risen, Wlencing's funeral feast was still going strong, his warriors' lust for food, women, ale and a good fight increasing as they became more drunk. The speeches had been said and battle-songs sung, and while Aelle was content to let the wake degenerate into a drunken brawl and orgy, he was more interested in taking revenge for Wlencing's death. "We can't talk here," he said to his son. "Come with me."

"It won't look good if we leave."

"I don't care, there are things I must know and I'm not waiting until this lot sober up before setting a plan in motion."

Stepping over copulating couples, kicking, pushing and punching people out of their way, they forced a route out of the hall.

Having just enough space to house three stools and a table, Aelle's private, wood-built room was small but well-lit, and warmed by a glowing brazier. He'd had it built against the rear of the hall so that he could find peace when needed, and it had proved its worth. They both sat beside the brazier, initially ignoring the Celtic slave-woman who'd followed them out of the hall carrying a jug of ale and two clay cups. "Put them on the table, then go," the King ordered the slave. "The Celts usually run like chickens when they know our warbands are raiding," he said to his son, "so what happened, why is Wlencing feasting with Woden?"

Cissa felt uneasy, his father could be quick to anger but, what could he say other than the truth? "They came at us while we were sleeping."

"Did you post guards?"

"Yes, and they raised the alarm. But the Celts didn't attack on foot, as they usually do, they charged from horseback so there wasn't time for us to organise a strong defence. We did attempt to form a shield-wall but they smashed right through it, and we were cut to pieces. I was standing beside Wlencing when he was killed, he was run through by a black-cloaked Celt. I don't know who the man was, but I've never seen anyone fight like him. He killed without thinking, even when surrounded by a group of our spearmen he easily cut his way out."

"We'll probably never know his name," Aelle said, thinking. "Are you sure no infantrymen supported their cavalry?"

"I'm certain. The Celtic horsemen charged right as us, lowering their spears just before impact. We must work out a defence because if they come against us with a full legion of horse-warriors, all our gains could be lost."

"I don't need you to tell me that."

"Is there a way of defeating a full cavalry charge?"

"I don't know." Aelle understood there'd been a shift in tactics. He'd fought many battles against the Celts, but they'd always fought on foot. Why the change, who was the black-cloaked warrior? "Roman legions were often supported by cavalry," he thought aloud, "though they were used to protect the flanks of their infantrymen and, mop up the post-battle rout." Pausing to think, he poured himself some ale, and asked, "We outnumbered them, yes?"

"By at least four to one."

"I must know which Celtic Dragon led the attack, spies must be sent to Celtic towns and cities; do we have any who speak their language?"

"Most of them do."

"Make sure at least two go to Viroconium, only King Einion the Pendragon has the money to equip a cavalry legion. By the bones and flesh of Woden, the blood-price for Wlencing's death will be paid!"

Having made love, Gwen and Owain were drowsily spent. Warmly caught in the afterglow of their passion, they lay in each other's arms beneath her furs. Gently stroking her raven hair, he remembered the first time they'd met, two summers ago when the Sun had been high and bright.

Along with Bedwyr and Cai, he'd been given permission by King Einion to go hunting in the forest, to practice their tracking and archery skills. Having tracked a good-sized deer for most of the morning, they'd cornered it sometime around the height of the midday sun. Hunting deer was a precarious business, not only should hunters move through the forest in silence but, they must remain downwind of their prey because if it was approached from the wrong direction, the animal would pick up their scent, bellow its alarm and take flight through the trees.

Their prey had led them into the darker regions of the woodlands, where very little light penetrated the green mesh. Keeping low and downwind, the three hunters had used tree trunks for cover as they stalked the deer into a rock-walled corral, where the forest screen opened and sunlight flooded in, illuminating a scene Owain couldn't quite believe.

Bordered on three sides by mossy rocks almost as high as the surrounding oaks, the corral opened around a bracken covered sward. Beneath the brilliant sunlight a trickling spring flowed into a small pool in front of the rocks, where the magnificent hart lowered its head to drink, unaware of the watching danger. With the deer at bay, the archers moved in for the kill.

For the first time while hunting, an unknown feeling touched Owain's soul and he thought twice about killing the deer because it was such a magnificent beast. Catching the sun, its summer coat shimmered in various shades of red and brown, its flexing muscles as well-developed as the antlers crowing its proud head. Cautiously, the animal lifted its head and looked in his direction, sniffing the air for predatory scent.

Hidden behind a grey-barked sycamore, Owain remained still, slowing his heartbeat to narrow his concentration and steady his aim. Seeing the deer lower its head to drink again, he so much wanted to let the animal live, his conscience telling him to walk away. He'd been sent to do a job, people must eat so the animal had to die, but he'd regret the killing.

Looking over his shoulder to the left and right, he saw no signs of Bedwyr and Cai, but he knew they were ready, their arrows nocked, waiting behind trees for his signal to shoot. The signal would be the whipping sound of his bowstring, and the fizz as the barbed dart sped towards its target. With his back to the tree, he slowly drew an arrow from its quiver, nocked it and pulled the chord partway back. Lowering his body until he was almost kneeling, he turned slowly while raising his bow, and delicately, he stepped a little to the side of the tree whilst rising to his full height. Taking a slow, deep breath he pulled the bowstring back to his ear and looked along the arrow shaft, aiming the point at the deer's heart.

His fingers were about to release the bowstring when he heard a sweetly singing voice, coming from behind the rocks. Lowering his bow slightly, he saw the singer walk into the shafts of sunlight, her arm outstretched towards the deer. Standing waist deep in the bracken, her unbound, raven hair tumbling down the back of her green dress, a girl smiled and sang to the animal, offering it something sweet from her hand. Owain relaxed the bowstring, watching as the deer welcomed the young beauty. Realising this must be a regular scene, though he'd never heard of a deer being tamed, he slipped back behind the tree and peered around it. To his surprise and shame, without turning her head to his hiding place, the girl called across the bracken sward, "Come closer, he won't run!"

The three friends reluctantly emerged from behind trees. Shrugging his shoulders, Owain waved them forward. The girl turned and smiled, and although she was about twenty paces from him, the moment Owain saw her face his movements shifted into slow motion. He felt like he was walking in deep mud, slow and heavy as his burning stomach churned. His heart beat with such force he thought it would burst from his chest, and he couldn't look away from the girls red lips and bright blue eyes so perfectly framed by her tumbling, ebony locks.

Forcing his legs to move, he made his way slowly through the bracken, certain his feet would catch a root, trip him and make him look a fool. Her first smile almost made his legs buckle, the second had him wanting her as he'd never desired anyone. Closing, he could see she wasn't so much a girl as a young woman, her curves stirring something wonderful in his loins. His feet eventually moved him close enough for her to take his hand and gently place it on the curve of the deer's neck. She then parted her lovely lips and said, "Stroke him, he enjoys it."

Without taking his gaze from her lovely blue eyes, he did as she'd suggested. "Does he have a name?" he asked.

"No, of course not," she replied. "He is free, if I gave him a name, he'd become my captive, and no animal should be caged or limited in any way by humans."

"Then please, tell me your name." He stroked the deer as Bedwyr and Cai arrived, not that he would have cared where they were.

"I am Gwenwyfar, and you were going to kill my friend, but I won't hold that against you."

"I am Owain, these are my friends, Bedwyr and Cai. I'm sorry we were hunting your friend, we'd no idea he was tame."

"How could you have?" She took his hand in hers, which made him blush. "I don't suppose any hunter considers the feelings of their prey, or the sadness the kill might cause."

"People must eat," he replied. "If you are not hunting, why are you in the forest?"

"I live here." Raising her arm, she swept it in a wide arc. "This forest is my home; its creatures are my friends."

He was brought back to the smoky half-light in the roundhouse by Gwen gently kissing his cheek. Turning onto his side to face her, his fingers brushed aside some of the silky soft raven hair that had fallen across her face. "What were you thinking about?" she asked as his fingers touched her cheek.

"The day we first met, in the forest."

Taking his hand in hers, she kissed a fingertip, slid his middle finger smoothly between her lips and onto her tongue, and she began sucking it, sliding the finger provocatively while her eyes looked lustfully into his.

He knew what she wanted, and usually he'd oblige but they'd just made love and he was spent. Anyway, there was something he was curious about, and now was as good a time as any to find out. Sitting up, he pulled back the furs to reveal her naked body. Placing his hand where he thought his child was growing, he said softly to her, "Is it a boy or a girl?"

She placed her hand on top of his to create a union of three souls, and asked, “Does it matter?”

“No.” He kissed the soft skin where their hands had been. “It’s such a miracle, yet every creature must be born. Is life a miracle, is it sacred?”

“Yes,” she replied, smiling at his innocence. “Can bees making honey be anything other than sacred?”

Covering her with the furs, he searched for the right words to ask her a question, but his heartbeat quickened and his mind went blank. He’d planned and rehearsed this moment, but now that he was certain of what he wanted, his anxiety robbed him of his courage. Composing himself, he nervously said, “I’d like you to be my wife. I’ll never love another woman the way I’ve loved you since the first day we met. Will you please become my wife, Gwen?” As reality registered its full burden, she felt sadness swamp her, and her tears came. “What’s wrong?” Panic swept away his joy. “Shouldn’t I have asked?”

“You know we can’t marry,” she whispered through her tears, “your father would never allow it. You are the son of a king so must take a high-born woman as your wife; it is your duty. I love you, Owain, but I’m not high-born, not in a way your father would understand.”

“The Forest People see you as their queen,” he pleaded, knowing his words carried no weight.

“I am not royal, I’m the daughter of a priestess and a druid. Whilst it’s true that many people in the forest show me a certain respect, that doesn’t make me royal, just loved, and I’ll forever honour them for that. We must enjoy what we have and be thankful for it."

He didn't want to believe she was turning his proposal down, but everything she'd said made sense. He wasn't going to give in so easily though. "My father might have ideas as to whom I should marry, he may feel it's his right to choose a bride for me but I will have my say. My choice will be made through love, not politics." He felt anger growing towards his father, though he realised it wasn't entirely his father's fault. Tradition dictated a marriage to nobility, King Einion hadn't created that policy, though he firmly believed in it. "I choose you Gwen," he said a little too angrily. "I'll only ever take one wife, and whatever my father says, I will only marry you."

She believed his sincerity, but couldn't believe such a marriage would be allowed, nor did she think it could work, so she spoke honestly, "What kind of wife would I make? I'm not a woman of the royal courts. I couldn't live in Viroconium with all its rules and etiquettes, it would choke me. It takes a certain kind of woman to maintain a royal household, and since when have I been a woman who falsely paints her face and styles her hair in the hope of becoming something she is not? Can you really see me gossiping the nonsense of fashion, jewellery, décor and who's taken who as a lover? I'd rather die than live like that. Viroconium's ladies are sheep, following whatever shepherding trend is popular at the time; I think for myself. In the forest I am free, I can look and think the way I choose. I follow no one and no one follows me, I wouldn't give that up for anyone. Nature is my kingdom and the seasons are my fashions, the animals and birds, the leaves, the grasses and the summer flowers are my court and my values. You've known me long enough to know this is my place, I'd suffocate in city-culture, I'd hate it."

Although it hurt, he had to agree with her, but he was determined to be with the woman he loved, whatever the cost. "I'll renounce my title and leave Viroconium, marry you and live here, in quiet peace," he said as if it was nothing.

Taking him in her arms, she held him close. "Do you understand what you are saying, what you are asking yourself to do? Would you leave your whole life behind, knowing your father and your people might never forgive you?"

His reply was immediate and strong, "I know my own mind. Not being with you would be a far greater sacrifice. I want you to be my wife, nothing else matters. Will you marry me, please, if I live here, with you in the forest?"

He was so determined that it scared her. If she had a free choice, he'd be her husband but the consequences of him walking away from his duty were beyond her thinking. On the other-hand, if he could face the inevitable repercussions, so could she. "If you are freely making your offer, then I freely accept, though I've a feeling the marriage won't last long because your father might hunt you down and kill you."

"I doubt it, and anyway......"

The door-flap swept back, a rush of cold night air flickered the hearth-flames and, the Merlin walked in.

5.

Walking Viroconium's battlements, King Einion stopped above the south-wall gateway and looked across the river to the vast spread of the Middleland Forest. Somewhere within the dark, sprawling woodlands his missing son was still avoiding his responsibilities, which worried him. He knew about his son's lover, Gwen, and so long as she kept her place, he didn't mind her limited influence over him. Believing Owain must be with her, and therefore safe, he turned his mind back to the more pressing problem of the Saxons, because one of his spies had informed him that the Sea-wolves were preparing for war.

For the best part of his life, he'd fought to protect his people from the invaders, and when the Saxons had first attacked, they'd swept like a firestorm across the southern kingdoms, killing, burning and raping, mercilessly sacking towns and cities as the Britons ran for their lives. Some of the southern Celtic battle-lords had fought the gale of iron and fire but, being overly proud they'd refused to unite and fight together, so they'd been quickly defeated.

Realising that only a united Celtic Briton could repel the invaders, Einion had attempted to convince his fellow kings that putting aside their pride to fight as one great army, would benefit them all. Some had refused, forcing him to conquer them and bring them together to fight beneath one banner, his. When the spring leaves escaped their buds, he'd use the threat of his sword to summon to Viroconium every Celtic king, prince and warrior, then he'd march a vast army south, supported by Owain's Legion, and put to the sword every Saxon living in Briton.

Thinking again about his son, he leaned thoughtfully on the battlements and cursed the raven-haired forest woman. The Forest People might call her their queen, but to him she was a low-born bed-mate for his son, a rutting whore to be used and discarded. If the woman tried to claim his son's soul, he'd hunt her down, use her then cut out her heart with his eating knife; no low-born woman was going to make her bed in Viroconium's royal villas!

Whether his son had deliberately run from the battle or not, he was proud of him. He was the boy who could ride almost before he could walk, who could swing a sword with devilish speed and had learned to read just so that he could study the tactics of the great Roman and Greek generals. There was no doubting that Owain was born to be a warrior and, his place was at the head of the Legion, not in the bed of an open-legged, forest-whore.

His eldest son, Prince Cadwallon, was the opposite of his brother. He was more like his dead mother; thoughtful and considerate; openminded and gentle; someone who saw every side of an argument so he sought the common ground. As a warrior he was no more than useful, and though his courage could never be questioned, he wasn't an inspirational battle-lord like his brother was. Cadwallon was a politician and a diplomat, who'd make a good and fair king, if he didn't die in battle first.

Distracted by the sound of snorting horses and jangling metal, Einion walked to the battlements above the east gate-arch, to watch his son's warriors ride their warhorses into the north meadow.

Wearing waist length chainmail, conical helmets and carrying Roman style oval cavalry shields, he noticed they were wielding spears longer than the usual body-length weapons favoured by the infantrymen. Unusually for horse-warriors, they had unstrung hunting bows tied to the sides of their saddles, with quivers of arrows strapped to their legs. Owain had explained how they'd be used, and he fully approved, though the new idea had yet to be tested in battle.

Forming a single line, the Legion, under Bedwyr's command, charged across the hoof-churned field at full gallop, wheeled and charged back as if they were the sweeping arm of one body. They wheeled again, and at the sound of two horn notes they galloped easily into four lines and lowered their spears, their mounts racing towards dozens of posts at the far end of the meadow. Yelling their battle-cry, "Britannia!" the four ranks skewered the posts while at the charge, leaving the stakes bristling with spears.

Einion was impressed and, seeing them charge then split into two sections as they wheeled at the gallop, one section circling around to charge in behind an imagined enemy's rear, he envied what his son had achieved. But although the Legion had been Owain's idea, equipping it had cost the crown a small fortune in silver, so they'd better prove their worth in battle or he'd disband them without a second thought.

Many of the British kings, princes and chieftains had been reluctant to send their sons to join the Legion, but as its reputation grew more young nobles had arrived to begin their training. Einion laughed to himself, remembering how Owain had once begged him for the money to pay for a thousand horse-warriors, swearing that if he had them, he could put to the sword every Saxon in Briton. The lad could be right, but he wasn't prepared to hand over the silver necessary to arm, feed and house a full army of horse-warriors.

Hearing approaching footsteps, he turned to see Prince Cadwallon walking his way. His son and heir looked tired, and well he might with his pretty wife close to death. "How is Meddyf today?" he asked while watching the Legion string their bows. "Is Maelgwn still waking the dead with his wailing?"

"She's sleeping peacefully. As for the boy, I'm sure he's driving his wet-nurses to distraction with his demands."

"Who could criticize him for demanding his wet-nurses nipples, I'd do the same in his position!"

"They are pretty girls!" the Prince agreed, laughing.

"Impressive, aren't they, the Legion I mean?" Einion asked as the ground thundered beneath charging hooves.

"I wouldn't like to fight them. If war comes, they'll need Owain, he is their Dragon, their heart, pride and power."

"Tell him that." The Pendragon looked back to the dense mass of forest, willing his son to come to his senses and return before the Saxons marched. "The Merlin will bring him back." Putting his arm around Cadwallon's shoulder, he led him along the battlements. "Walk with me, I've something to tell you."

"You don't want me to talk to Owain about Gwen again, do you?"

"No, I'll deal with her. When I die, you'll become king of the Votidini. It's your birth right and I believe you'll rule well because you think before speaking. Although you are courageous in battle, you are not the warrior your brother is. The Legion worship him, they follow his commands without question, he's a true leader of warriors. For that reason, I've decided that he, not you will become Pendragon after me. With you wearing the crown and, Owain being your sword arm, the future of our people should be secure. What do you think?"

"Talking about the succession is a little premature."

"It's a king's duty to plan ahead."

"I understand that, but I see no reason why you won't still be ruling and fighting ten summers from now."

"Would you challenge your brother's right to become Pendragon?"

"No, but isn't the Pendragon elected by the council of kings?"

"Not if I say otherwise."

Sitting beside the lake on the trunk of a fallen tree, Owain, Gwen and the Merlin were well advanced into a tense, sometimes angry discussion about the young Prince's future. Having told the Merlin that he wanted to resign his positions of Prince of Rhos and Dragon of the Legion, Owain nevertheless still relished the idea of leading a full cavalry charge into battle.

The Merlin had argued that such a resignation would prove to be a recklessly foolish choice, it wouldn't only threaten the future of the Celtic nation, but also the life of the child growing inside Gwen's womb, because the Prince's horse-warriors might prove decisive in the battles with the Saxons. Briton's warriors needed him more than

Gwen did; the Prince should put his people before his love for Gwen.

The high Sun had long since burned away the last of the morning rain clouds and, was shimmering gold on the lake's surface. Not far from where they sat, there was a silver splash, just before a flapping duck ran across the water in wild panic, to escape the needle-toothed jaws of a hunting pike. "Some people, Owain, are born to hunt," the Merlin said, "while others nest and nurture."

"That depends what you believe," the Prince countered.

"No one knows what you believe," Gwen said, nudging into the conversation. Something hot pricked her womb and she put her hand to her mouth. The shot of pain eased and she relaxed again.

"I believe that all people have the right to choose their own destinies," Owain said, thinking Gwen was looking a little pale.

"Do you?" the Merlin asked. "Are we greater than the gods, can we alter the rhythm and flow of nature?"

"Again, that depends what you believe." The Prince was determined to remain with Gwen and their unborn child.

"Tell me!" the Merlin snapped, "do you believe in any of the gods?"

"No. I love Gwen and I believe in our future together. I want my child to be free from politics, war and the unnecessary responsibilities men place upon each other. I believe in freedom and the right to choose."

"And how many men do you think are free to choose their fates?" the Merlin asked calmly, looking across the shimmering lake to the island at its centre. "Peace for all mankind is a beautiful dream, and will remain so until men find a considered way of resolving their differences. In the greater scheme of things, all peoples are one, though I don't expect you to believe that because in these less than subtle times hate and prejudice are the masters. In time, war will be forgotten and all peoples will take up the plough and the loom, but not if warriors like yourself hide from their responsibilities."

"The fate of the nation doesn't rest in the palm of my hand. Find another beast to carry the weight."

"If another man could carry it, I wouldn't be here."

"I respect you, Merlin. If you tell me you have seen my future and Briton will collapse without me, I'll return to Viroconium."

"You know I can't disclose the futures of individuals; I may advise and guide, that is all. So why don't you........." He was about to suggest a compromise when Gwen let out a gut-wrenching scream. Lurching forward onto the pebbled shoreline, her arms wrapped tightly around her waist and she curled into a screaming ball. "What is it?" the Merlin asked, kneeling beside her. "Tell me, Gwen, I can't help unless you do."

"It's my womb," she squeezed the words through gritted teeth. "A stabbing, burning pain in my womb." A warm liquid trickled down the inside of her thigh, and another bolt of searing pain made her scream again.

Lifting her into his arms, the Merlin said to Owain, "You see the fallen willow tree, the one half-hanging into the lake?" Owain looked and nodded. "On the other side there's a rowing boat, it's Gwen's, use it to row to the island. There you'll find 'Graine the healer' tell her what has happened and bring her back as fast as you can, Gwen's life may depend on how quickly you return."

The Prince ran and leapt the fallen willow, pushed the small boat away from the bank, jumped in and began rowing as if this was the last thing he'd ever do. It was about a hundred paces to the island, and he wasn't used to pulling oars so his arms soon began to ache. But he couldn't relax his pace, even if his lungs burned so hot that he thought they'd explode. The picture in his mind of the panic on Gwen's pained face kept him pulling hard at the oars, skimming the boat through the water in the hope of saving her life. His muscles were about to burst when the underneath of the boat scraped the pebbled shore of the wooded island. He leapt out, tied the boat to a bush and ran along the only path he could see in the scrublands.

The island was an almost flat mass of trees, and large enough for him to waste most of the day searching for Graine. Without knowing which way to go, he'd no choice but to trust his instincts and run. Still breathless from rowing across the lake, he ignored the burning pain in his chest and forced his legs to sprint. Had he come the wrong way, he wondered as the thin track narrowed beneath his feet? Dashing around trees, his heart pounding like a fiery thunderstorm, he leapt fallen branches and ran through bushes and bracken, uncertain of where he was going or what he hoped to find. Every bush and tree looked the same to him, so he could be running in circles, and every passing moment could mean death for Gwen and their unborn child.

Like the Sun bursting through dark storm clouds, the trees parted and he saw a small village in a clearing. Halting his run, he looked for signs of life, taking a moment to catch his breath and restore his exhausted wits. The village, which seemed deserted, was a collection of small roundhouses made entirely from mud and thatch. At the entrance to the village stood two tall posts, carved with animal faces. The Merlin had once described to him these most ancient of symbols, but it was the first time he'd seen totem poles, and the sight of them made him shiver.

In the centre of the village stood a much larger roundhouse, at least four times the size of the others. On either side of the path that led to its entrance, stood more lines of poles, painted in many colours, each one about the height of a man. These posts were hung with grotesquely rotting animal heads, except for the two framing the entrance to the large roundhouse. These posts were taller, painted black and had what appeared to be the skulls of children hanging from the black beam that formed a crude arch.

From within the big roundhouse a melancholy hum filtered through the thatching, which sounded like thousands of bees on the wing. The sound faded slightly, and he heard rhythmic clapping. The clapping grew louder and softer along with the hum, like the ear-splitting sound of a mythical beast the Merlin might sing about in one of his ancient songs. But he was wasting time. Remembering why he was here; he walked the totem-edged path towards the strange sounds. A red-haired, naked child emerge from the half-open door of the big roundhouse. She ran to him, took his hand and pulled him towards the doorway. Stopping outside the low entrance, the girl pointed him in, then she slid through the gap.

Entering the dark and smoky, firelit glow of the circular building, his heartbeat skipped when the clapping and humming stopped, and the many villagers, all seated on the dusty earth, turned to look at him. Naked except for black feathers platted into their hair, their faces painted blue to make their bright eyes seem much larger, they looked like the ancient tribe they were. Adjusting to the half-light, his eyes were caught by the flash of a turning sword hanging above the smoking hearth. For a moment he wondered at the vision, unable to believe that a silver sword could hang in the air. Focusing on the weapon, he saw a thin thread, probably horsehair, suspending the sword from a rafter.

A throat drying, smoky aroma of roast apples and acorns fogged his senses, making him feel a little queasy. Realising he'd stepped into a ritual, which might be considered an unforgiveable intrusion, he waited, hoping one of the searching faces might welcome him.

Drawing on his courage, he was about to speak when a beautiful, golden-haired naked woman stood and smiled at him. He felt sure he'd seen her somewhere, but he couldn't have, as far as he knew these people never left the island. Confused by her familiar beauty, he found he couldn't speak, or had the heavily scented fire-smoke muted his voice? "You don't need to speak," the beautiful woman said, walking gracefully towards him. Raising her hand in welcome, she spoke in a creamily soft, calming voice, "I am Graine the healer, Priestess of the Mother Goddess Enaid. I am ready to come with you, second son of the High King Einion known as Uther the Pendragon." Someone handed her an animal-hide dress and a small sack. Taking Owain's hand, she led him outside.

Walking out of the village, she let go of his hand and without speaking she ran, barefoot and naked into the woods and, he followed. How she knew where he'd left the boat he couldn't guess at, yet she led him straight to it. After pushing it into the water, he helped Graine in then joined her. Again, her creamy voice warmed his heart as she slipped herself into the dress, "Row, Owain ap Einion ap Cunedda, a life needs saving."

Having made Gwen as comfortable on the furs in her roundhouse as he could make her, the Merlin was kneeling beside her when Graine burst in. "Thank the Goddess you are here," he said. "All I could do was give her some herbs in warm wine for the pain; saving her life is your work."

"Husband," she said to the Druid, "take the Pendragon's son outside and tell him what you think he should know."

Owain looked with surprise at the two servants of the Goddess, before the Merlin lead him outside. Sitting beside the lake, a little confused after what he'd just heard, he threw a pebble into the water and watched the surface ripple. "You have a wife," he said, then remembered how he thought he'd seen Graine before, now he knew why, she looked just like her daughter.

"I lay with Graine during the Beltane fires, when I'd only fifteen summers behind me," the Merlin began, enjoying remembering. "I'd been sent to the Forest Island to oversee an initiation, one of their young boys was to begin his journey into the druidic arts. Graine chose me to lay with her on the night of the fire-leaping, being a daughter of the Goddess that was her right. You've seen her, Owain, what man could refuse such a beauty? After the Beltane festival I left for Mona, taking the boy initiate with me. During the journey I couldn't get Graine out of my mind, I was in love, which saddened me because I knew my future didn't run alongside hers. The first sending I received from her, informing me I was to become a father, quite knocked the life out of me. My first thought was to run, but you can't hide from fate, so when the time for the birth grew close, I left Mona to be with Graine. We were both filled with joy when Gwen was born, and I spent a full cycle of the Moon on the island with them." Thinking he heard the name 'Rohanna' passing on the breeze, he looked up at the thin clouds. Dismissing the whisper as an imagining, he continued his story, "For the first years of her life, Gwen lived with the other children on the island, but Graine's sight told her the child's destiny lay elsewhere. When Gwen had seven summers behind her, and I'd taken my place beside your father in Viroconium, Graine and I built the roundhouse by the lake for our child, believing she'd be close enough for one of us to visit her every day, and the Island People could watch over her. Gwen loved her freedom, she ran as wild as a child could in the forest and, watching her grow into the nature surrounding her was an honour and a pleasure. On one of my visits, she emerged from her roundhouse carrying a small deer, claiming hunters had killed its mother, so she'd look after it."

"I think I saw it once." Owain smiled at the memory.

“Few have shared that honour; she guarded the animal with a ferocity akin to a she-wolf. Not long after you met Gwen, she told me she feared the deer had been hunted, because it no longer visited her. It was the first time I saw my daughter cry. Gwen is a child of the forest and should remain so, remember that when you insist on taking her as your wife. It may or may not be your destiny to be with her, but there’s a great storm coming, a war so destructive that thousands will die. If the war goes against our people, Briton will be thrown into a dark pit, from which it may never again see the light of hope. Consider well your decision to remain here, Owain, weigh it alongside how you might feel if the Islands of the Mighty were to die and be reborn as the land of the Angles, ‘Angleland’. Do you understand?”

Feeling the weight of the moment, Owain looked across the lake, trying to think of a thousand reasons why the Merlin might be wrong. Was he so important that to walk away would bring disaster to Briton? “I want to remain here,” he said, though he knew he couldn’t.

“I’m sorry for you, and for Gwen. But think, Owain, see reason and return to Viroconium until King Aelle has been defeated.”

For a while, the two of them talked as the Sun climbed. Time seemed to slow to almost nothing while the Druid told the young Dragon more about Gwen’s childhood, and how they’d chosen her name. He also told him about his own younger days on Mona, and some of the less secret trials he’d endured to win the robes of a druid.

“Son of the Pendragon,” Graine said as she emerged from the roundhouse carrying a small but bloody bundle of rags. “Your daughter is dead, but my daughter will live to birth more children.” She turned to the Merlin. “This child,” she held out the small bundle, “was a daughter of the Goddess so will be treated accordingly. Although her soul existed for three Moon cycles only, Gwenwyfar gave the unborn a name and, asked us to bury Rohanna on the island, where life returns to life.”

“The Forest Island?” Owain asked.

“No,” the Merlin replied. “Rohanna will be buried on the island of her ancestors, the Summer Isle.”

Owain saw a knowing look pass between the two servants of the Goddess, which had him wondering why the name Rohanna was so significant? He was about to ask when Graine answered his unspoken question, “You are not ready to know the significance. Be patient, all will be revealed at the chosen time.”

On night-blackened cliffs overlooking a pebble and sand beach, a lone rider halted his horse, his attention caught by a flickering light on the horizon of Briton’s Stygian Southern Sea. With no stars shining through thick clouds, the tiny flicker had to be the prow-light of a boat. His suspicions were confirmed when the dark outline of a Saxon keel took shape and, as the mast-less boat closed he saw oars plunge and rise, leaving him certain that a Saxon longboat was racing towards the shore. Within a heartbeat he saw four more lights pricking the night. Calculating that if each long-keeled vessel carried about ninety men, near five hundred warriors were heading for the land of the Celtic Durotriges. King Nathanleod needed to know and levies must be mustered, so he turned his horse and galloped away.

Standing at the prow of the lead boat, a tall, fair-haired warrior saw the black image of the rider galloping away. "Good," he said to the calm sea, pleased that soon Nathanleod the usurper would know that he'd returned. He'd been away a long time, helping his cousin fight the Franks in Armorica. Returning to Briton to take back his kingdom, his revenge would be swift and brutal.

King Ceredig of the Durotriges looked over his shoulder at his warriors, who were pulling hard on their oars as the boat sliced through the dark breakwaters, the pebbled beach nearing with every oar-stroke. Holding the prow, he yelled to his warriors, "Raise oars!" and braced himself for the keel-scraping shudder. Drawing his sword as the boat crunched over pebbles, he looked inland for signs of watching warriors, saw no one, so he jumped down. Taking a handful of the pebbles, he turned to the first warrior to join him. "This is my land; I won't leave it again."

"Your kinsman will die before the new Sun sets," the fully armed warrior encouraged the King.

"I'll cut his fetid heart out." Turning to face the sea, Ceredig filled his lungs with cool, salty air and called to the hundreds of Celtic and Saxon warriors leaping ashore from the boats. "Where is their king, where is their army? Only cowards hide behind city walls when true warriors come to conquer! Worry not my brothers, you'll have your battle, the blood of my kinsman Nathanleod, and his cowering spearmen will be yours before another night darkens my land!”

6.

Weep silent soul, mourn throughout the quiet night, sooth your pain with a smothering smoke-dream; hold your tears within your soul and stir your pain into drying your eyes while holding you solemn, yet bereft, within a parallel channel of grief. Weep silent soul, and when the Sun rises numb your pain so that you might hold love fast within your being.

Warm beneath soft furs, Gwen slept peacefully beside Owain, who for some time had been humming a mellow tune. She hadn't stirred much since the ordeal of her miscarriage, Graine's brew of sleeping herbs having done its work. Owain had joined her beneath the furs after the Merlin had left, but his sleep had been fitful, and the further the night progressed the less tired he felt. With dawn fast approaching he began gently stroking Gwen's hair, for comfort. Birdsong told him the Sun was about to rise, soon he must face the day, which set him thinking.

After weighing the pros and cons of returning to Viroconium, he decided he couldn't leave Gwen when she was so fragile. The threat of Huail ap Caw's return remained and, Gwen couldn't fight him in her present condition. Thinking he had a solution to the problem, that's if she approved, he put it to the back of his mind, they could discuss it later.

It wouldn't be long before the Merlin returned, so he'd a decision to make. All the Druid's arguments had made good political sense: King Einion was getting old and Prince Cadwallon was no general; Bedwyr was a fine Dragon but, being ruthless his battle-tactics were questionable; Cai was respected by the Legion and the Viroconium infantry, but he was too pragmatic and during battle risks must be taken if the victory was to be won.

Believing his place was with Gwen, it was with a heavy heart that he accepted he must return to Viroconium. Graine had told him they were two young people just beginning their journey through life; there was a time to fight and a time for settling down, whilst not forgetting there was a time for seeing and believing the truth. Feeling Gwen move, he expected her to wake and shed more tears, instead, she looked at him with clear, dry eyes and asked, "Have you slept?"

"I've had enough sleep," he lied, not wanting to burden her.

"Will you return to Viroconium today?"

"No, there's something I must do first, I'll discuss it with you after we've eaten."

"What is it you want to discuss?"

"It can wait. Let's hold each other for a while, I don't know when we'll have the chance again."

Two armies faced each other across a fording place, where an iced-brook divided the shallow valley. It was a bitterly cold spring morning, with grey clouds pitching angled sheets of freezing sleet into chilled faces. Men blew on their hands while stomping their numb feet, both sets of warriors wishing they were somewhere else.

King Ceredig's union of Celtic and Saxon mercenaries waited on the west side of the valley, a small army of professional, efficient killers. Facing them across the iced-brook, King Nathanleod's larger force of Celtic levies hoped the two kings would find a peaceful solution.

King Ceredig wasn't impressed by Nathanleod's army, from the look of their rustic weapons and lack of body-armour they'd been dragged from the plough-fields to fight. He'd expected the usurper to bring a battle-hardened legion of warriors, not a rag-tag army who'd probably been forced at spearpoint to join the ranks. His kinsman had about thirty well-armed warriors who looked like they knew how to kill, most likely his personal guard. Obviously, Nathanleod hadn't prospered since taking the throne, or maybe he didn't like spending his gold on spearmen.

Ceredig's mercenaries had been forged into hardened units of fighting men on the vicious battlefields of Armorica, so they'd make short work of the desperate host of pitchforks and scythes across the ford. Having arranged his men in two lines, a short distance from the brook, his Celtic brothers in the centre, the Saxons taking the flanks, he saw Nathanleod, along with a dozen of his chosen warriors, step out from their muster and walk down the sleet-soaked slope, to parley. "Ceredig!" the usurper shouted across the brook. "We should talk before good men die!"

"Women talk, men fight!" Ceredig called back, determined his cousin would die today.

"I have an offer for you!"

"You are going to give me back my kingdom?" Ceredig mocked. Pushing through his ranks, he taunted the King, "You are a thief and a coward!"

“Do you want to parley or throw insults?” Nathanleod looked closer at Ceredig’s mercenaries and his heart sank. He must think fast, or he was a dead man. “I want to offer you a fair deal, one that will satisfy us both.”

“No deals, you stole my crown and my land so I’m going to kill you!”

“Surely we can settle this without bloodshed?”

“What are you offering?”

“I keep Durnovaria City!” the usurper shouted, believing his offer was fair, “and the lands east of the city. You get all the lands to the north and west, surely that’s worth considering?”

“You want my city?” Ceredig laughed. “Here’s another idea, throw yourself onto your sword and only you will die today. If our people’s lives are so precious to you, you won’t hesitate!”

“You must be mad, Ceredig. I’m a Christian, suicide is a great sin.”

“You raised your levies to fight me, isn’t that suicide?”

“I’m sorry you aren’t prepared to bargain; we could have saved lives.” Realising Ceredig wouldn’t compromise, the usurper led his guards back to his ranks. Taking his place in the centre of his regulars, he tied the cheek pieces of his helmet and drew his sword.

Ceredig’s battleplan was simple; with Saxon shield-walls on the flanks, he knew his centre would be the weaker part of the line so it would slowly fall back when the two armies met, leaving the two Saxon flanks to swing around and encircle the levies. Having seen Nathanleod’s ramshackle army, he wasn’t sure his plan was necessary, but he’d stick with it and get the battle over with quickly.

Realising what he was up against, Nathanleod considered holding a defensive line on the slope of the hill. If he'd been outnumbered, that would have been his choice but Ceredig's army was small, so a frontal charge and attack was preferable. He guessed his cousin would expect him to fight a defensive battle, so he'd use the element of surprise, see if the shock of the charge could be decisive.

As the cold north wind strengthened and sleet lashed through the valley, Nathanleod called to his warriors, "Men of Durnovaria, we are here to protect our women and children from ruthless, foreign invaders! Yes, their battle-lord was once your king, but don't be fooled by his birth, he returned to his homeland in a Saxon keel! If we lose this battle, those Saxons will rape and murder your loved ones. You must fight hard my brothers; kill to protect the ones you love because there'll be no mercy for them if we are slaughtered. Fight for your families!" He nodded to one of his warriors, who raised his cold copper horn to his lips. A horn-blast touched the ice-clouds as the King pointed his sword at the frozen brook and shouted, "Forward!" His army roared defiance and poured down the icy slope in a disorganised mess.

Cracking and splashing through the thinly iced brook, the momentum of their attack was lost as they reluctantly waded through the freezing water, their courage faltering with each dragging step. The first levies to step out of the water formed a hesitant line, each man wanting to run before battle was joined. The last to cross was Nathanleod and, after pushing his way to the front, he called to his terrified warriors. "Charge!"

The battle was violently short. Nathanleod's reluctant warriors were brushed into Ceredig's centre like a breeze caressing hard granite cliffs. Prodding and poking their tradesmen's weapons, they wildly slashed at the shields of their enemies, foolishly hoping their press of numbers would force Ceredig's army to run.

The centre of Ceredig's line fell back with practiced precision, drawing Nathanleod's army into a triangle of death. Sensing the time was right, Ceredig raised and rotated his sword, signalling the Saxon flanks to encircle their enemy and close the trap. The rear ranks of the two flanks ran in behind Nathanleod's army and enclosed them in a wall of shields and spears. With shields locked and spears bristling, the Saxons pushed their shields against the trapped, panicking levies while stabbing, slashing and chopping in a synchronised rhythm of death strokes.

With Nathanleod's army surrounded, Ceredig's Celts pushed forward, joining their Saxon brothers in the slaughter. Pressing inwards, stepping over the dead and wounded as they progressed, the front ranks thrust their spears as the following ranks stabbed down at the fallen wounded. It was a savage massacre, the ineffective levies cut down to the very last farm-boy, leaving only a field of torsos, heads and limbs in pools of blood where an army had disintegrated.

A great cheer erupted when Nathanleod's head was raised on a spear, he was the last to die. Walking amongst the stinking mess of the dead, Ceredig felt saddened by the loss of so many, these were his people and seeing them hacked to pieces gave him no pleasure. But he'd killed a king and taken back his lands, so the slaughter had been worth it. When the slim pickings of the looting had been completed, he ordered his men to march to Durnovaria, where he expected the gates to be open.

Sleety rain had been falling for the entire day, soaking Owain and Gal, who were working through the weather to complete the small roundhouse that would be the boy's home for the foreseeable future. Gwen had agreed that when Owain left, leaving Gal behind as her protector, was an idea, but was it a good idea? The boy might be sly and fleet of foot but, how would he defend her if Huail returned, when the lad wasn't even a grown warrior?

With darkness descending, the last of the straw thatching was almost in place, much to Owain's relief. He was cold, wet, tired and felt miserable enough knowing he'd soon be leaving Gwen, without him having to build a roundhouse in this weather. Lying flat on the ladder, which was resting on the thatching, Gal lifted the straw cone into place, and smiled with relief when Gwen called from her roundhouse, "There's fish stew if anyone is hungry?"

Gal adjusted the straw cone as Owain deliberately wobbled the ladder. "Are you trying to kill me?" he shouted down, but the laughing Prince was running for the shelter of Gwen's roundhouse. The dark sky rumbled so the boy slid down the ladder and ran. Thunder burst over the lake and a heavier downpour of icy sleet soaked the forest.

Kneeling beside the fire, Gwen was spooning thick stew into bowls when Owain dashed in, followed by Gal, both soaking wet but laughing as they playfully jostled to reach the heat of the hearth.

"Get out of here!" she yelled as they warmed their hands by the fire. "You are soaking the place, go on, get out!"

"You're feeling better. It's sleeting out there," Owain objected.

"I don't care, go outside and take off your clothes, or you'll catch your deaths."

Owain shrugged his shoulders and made his way outside. Gal remained as close as he could to the hearth.

"What are you waiting for?" she asked. "The sooner you get out of those wet clothes, the sooner you can warm up."

"These are my only clothes and," he blushed and looked down at his feet, "I'm growing out of boyhood."

She put a comforting hand on his shoulder. "I'll leave you a fur by the door-flap."

Owain came back in completely naked. Rubbing his hands together, he unashamedly sat cross-legged beside the hearthstones, and looked up at the boy. "Go on, Gal, get your clothes off."

The boy attempted a smile before heading outside.

"Don't think you are going to sit there naked all night." Gwen handed him a bowl of the stew.

"Why not, I usually do?" he replied, the first spoonful of the meal warming him.

"Only when we are alone. How do you think Gal will feel having to look at you with nothing more to cover your modesty than that inconsiderate smile of yours? Here," she threw a fur at him, "wrap yourself in this."

Sheepishly lifting part of the door-flap, Gal looked for the promised fur. Finding it, he pulled it around himself and pushed his way in.

"Doesn't that feel better?" Gwen asked, handing him a bowl of stew.

"Yes, and thank you." Taking his place beside the glowing warmth, Gal swallowed a spoonful of stew and closed his eyes to let the delicious flavours sooth him. It had been so long since someone had cooked him such flavoursome food. "It tastes beautiful, Gwen, I haven't eaten anything so good since my mother," he cut himself short, not wanting to explain why he had no mother.

After they'd eaten, Gwen picked up her harp and plucked a slow, melancholy melody. Watching her closely, Owain felt her thoughts were elsewhere, because she'd hardly spoken during the meal and, she was staring blankly into the fire. Wondering where her thoughts were, he decided not to ask until they were alone.

It had been a long day, Owain was exhausted and the beautifully soothing harp music soon had him feeling drowsy. Seeing the boy curled up in a ball beside the fire, deep in sleep, he felt a little sorry for him. The lad wanted to accompany him to Viroconium so much that he'd seen pain in his eyes when explaining that he must remain with Gwen, just until the threat from Huail had passed. The boy had accepted his mission with good grace, so Owain decided he'd reward his services with something special, when his stay was over.

"We should let him sleep in here tonight," Gwen said without looking away from the hearth.

"But I thought........."

"I know what you thought; think how he must be feeling." As she put down the harp, she felt a rush of cold air sweep in. Looking at the door-flap, she was surprised to see the Merlin. Wrapped in his raven-feathered cloak and dripping rain onto her floor, he walked over to the fire to warm himself and, he looked down at the sleeping boy. "This lad will save your life," he told her.

Startled by the revelation, she said nothing. She knew the power of her father's sight, but wished he wouldn't use it with her, she'd rather discover the pains and pleasures of life when they arrived. Handing him a beaker of warm cider, which he quickly guzzled down, she offered the Druid a place by the fire for the night, but he shook his head. "I'm not staying." Handing her the empty beaker, he turned solemnly to Owain and said, "I have something for you." With a dramatic flourish he swept open his cloak and produced a shining sword.

Owain recognized it immediately, it was the blade he'd seen hanging above the hearth in the roundhouse on the island. The Merlin looked along the length of its silvery beauty, then pressed the point into the compressed earth floor. Leaning on the hilt, he closed his eyes for a moment. Opening them, he spoke to Owain with a voice that seemed to drift up from the deepest caverns of the earth, "No other mortal must touch this sword, it can only be used by yourself. During your first battle, Graine felt the vibrations when your sword broke, so she instructed her smiths to make you this. It is no ordinary weapon; it is the first of its kind in Briton. The secrets of its forging were brought from the east by a Roman trader, whose name I forget. The metal is known as steel and, it isn't brittle like iron or bronze. The blade will cut through iron swords and armour, nothing can withstand its edge. You'll remember that when lost in the forest you heard beating drums in the distance, that noise came from the Forest Island. The people were dancing in ritual to the beat of the drums and the blacksmith's pounding hammer, while calling upon the Goddess Enaid to temper the steel to its perfect strength and finish. Now, heed my warning, always remember to keep the weapon close, others will desire its invincible strength and killing edge." Without further comment, the Merlin held out the sword for Owain to take.

Wrapping his fingers around the hilt, the warrior felt its weight. Lovingly smoothing his fingers over the shining blade, his eyes widened with longing to hear its battle-song. The steel, reflecting the flickering hearth-flames as he turned it, felt as cold as ice and never had he seen anything so beautiful. The sword was thin at the hilt but broadened towards the end of the blade, before tapering into a razor-sharp point. Longer than the Roman Gladius he was used to using, he thought it looked like the old swords of the tribes who'd mustered to battle the first Caesar to invade Briton. Holding it in both hands, he felt its power. "It is magnificent. Will the Island People permit me to cross the lake to thank them?"

"No," the Merlin replied. "Protect them, that's all they require from you."

"Look, Gwen, it's a king's sword." Offering her the handle, he was surprised when she refused to take it.

“Only you can feel its power, Owain. Remember what my father said, let no other human touch the weapon.”

“Does it have a name?” he asked, turning to thank the Merlin, but he’d gone so he looked back at Gwen with his lust for battle flaming bright in his eyes.

“Perhaps you should name it,” she said sadly, knowing she’d lost him again.

“What name could possibly match its beauty and strength?” Stepping around the fire, he put his arm around her waist. “I’ll return as soon as I can, that’s a promise.”

Stirring a frothy mug of ale with his fat finger, drunken King Aelle sat alone in his private room, grumbling into the smouldering brazier, his morose thoughts pulling him from memories of his dead sons, to his living daughter. Choosing her a husband wasn’t proving to be straightforward. Sucking ale from his finger, he again went through the list of unsatisfactory suitors. He knew most of them personally, others by reputation, but they were either married or hadn’t yet grown enough of a beard to father children. Not wanting to wait because her virginity was a great prize, he must find someone before one of his warriors tempted and ruined her.

Perhaps he didn’t want her to marry, he thought as he farted and took in the aroma with satisfied pleasure. She’d always been the light of his life; his hall wouldn’t be the same without her joy. Unfortunately, not long after he’d broken his fast Gorpe had taken him aside and told him she wanted a husband, and as she’d inherited her mother’s fiery temper and wicked tongue, he knew he wouldn’t get any peace until she was satisfied. As his ale-fogged head slumped forward, there was a knock at the door. "Go away!" he shouted. But the door opened, letting in chilly air and windblown rain. Prince Cissa, shaking the weather from his hooded cloak, walked in and sat down beside the brazier. "I told you to go away," the King grumbled.

"My news can't wait," his son replied, pouring himself a drink of ale.

"Tell me, then leave me alone."

"One of the spies I sent to Viroconium has returned."

"Just the one?"

"Yes, the other was caught, he'll be dead by now."

"We'll have a small feast in his honour," Aelle slurred, and as an afterthought, added, "If he had a wife, give her a cow, a goat or whatever you think is appropriate. What did the spy say?"

"The Pendragon has created a cavalry legion, two hundred strong. It is led by his second son, Owain the Prince of Rhos, who is responsible for killing Wlencing."

"Owain ap Einion!" Aelle growled into his ale. "I'll kill the runt. Is that all the spy told you?"

"No. After the battle, the son of the Pendragon fled into the forest and hasn't been seen since."

"What?" Aelle supressed a laugh, took a huge swig of ale and looked questioningly at his son. "Is he a coward?"

"If he was the savage warrior I saw, the one with the black cloak, he is no coward."

"All Celts are cowards, if they weren't, we wouldn't have a kingdom." The King rose unsteadily to his feet, farted again as he opened the door and shouted through the rain to a slave girl carrying a basket of wood to the feasting hall. "Woman, bring me some ale, and you'll be warming my bed tonight!" Closing the door, he sneered menacingly at his son. "So, now we know that King Einion must die."

"Not the Prince?"

"No, he's no threat, he's a coward who runs from battle. I'll kill the Pendragon, burn his city to the ground and if Owain is there, I'll slice the skin from his back myself!"

7.

Frustrated by the prospect of being left behind, Gal sat alone beneath a willow tree, throwing pebbles into the lake. Bored of watching the spreading ripples, he plucked a blade of grass, clasped it between his thumbs and blew through it, releasing a shrill squawk, and he laughed when a nearby duck answered his call. He felt more disappointed than he'd ever let on, and if Owain hadn't explained to him the importance of his mission, he'd return to his forest cave.

Looking over his shoulder to the roundhouse, where Owain was saying goodbye to Gwen, a pang of sadness touched him. He liked his new mistress, she was pretty, cooked the most delicious food and every time she smiled his heart fluttered warm. Protecting her was an honour, he supposed, and should Huail return he'd do his best for her. But what could he do against an armed man, surely there were others better suited to the job?

Inside the roundhouse, Owain kissed Gwen. He'd no idea when he'd return, the wars might keep him away until the first frosts covered newly fallen leaves, longer if the Saxons forced a breakthrough. But he was determined to return and marry her, and had told her so, promising that when the Saxons had been defeated, he'd lay down his sword and live with her in the forest.

In uncertain times like these, Gwen knew she might never see him again. There'd be battles and could he honestly say he'd survive them? Yes, he had the sword of steel, but if Owain returned unharmed luck and skill would play the greatest part in his survival. She buried her head in her hands and wept.

Placing his finger gently under her chin, he lifted her head and, looking lovingly into her watery, crystal blue eyes he attempted to reassure her, "I promise you, Gwen, no Saxon blade will take me from you. My father can protest against our marriage as much as he likes, my mind is made up." He softly kissed her forehead. "The day I return, that's the day we will marry."

She pulled herself away. "How shall we marry?" she asked. "I'm not of the Christian faith and neither are you, nor do we worship the Goddess?"

He hadn't considered what form the marriage ceremony would take. If he wasn't King Einion's son, he could claim her like a fieldworker would, and that would be it, a promise and a kiss. But he was a prince and because the Christ was the chosen deity of most of the nobility these days, he'd be expected to speak his vows in church, to a god he neither felt nor believed in.

"In the old days," she said, trying not to smile, "before the Caesars came to Briton, the tribes had a very special marriage ceremony. I know of it because the Island People still marry this way."

"Tell me about it before I agree to anything." He was easy with whatever she suggested, but there was an ominously playful look in her eyes, and that worried him.

"It's quite different from the Christian marriage ritual," she began, "and it lasts for seven days and nights. Although it isn't easy,

I promise you'll never forget our union. Have you ever stood naked in public?"

"You are joking?"

"No, do you want to know more?"

Gal was still in a dark mood when Owain walked out from the roundhouse. Sitting down beside the boy, the Prince said, "Gwen's just told me about the Island People's marriage ceremony. There are three parts to it, and I'll be naked in front of everyone!"

A very pleasant image shot into Gal's head. "Will Gwen also be naked?"

Owain laughed and, ruffled the boy's hair. "Yes, she will."

"Will I be invited?"

"I take it you've never seen a naked woman?"

"Only my mother," Gal replied regretfully, "and she doesn't count."

"We must be serious for a moment." Owain broke the mood. "You know why I'm leaving you here, what Huail might do and I suppose you've realised you won't be able stop him. I don't expect you to fight him, you are here because you can run faster than the wind. When Huail arrives you must hide, watch and listen then run to Viroconium and find me, and don't play the hero because he'll slit your throat. If you do as I ask, there'll be a place for you in the Legion when you've completed your warrior training."

Accepting he wouldn't be here forever, the boy's glum mood lifted. "Will you teach me how to use a sword?" he asked enthusiastically.

"I'd like to, but it depends on my duties. Don't think about that yet, Gwen is your only concern until I've killed Huail. Look after her for me."

"You can rely on me."

Calling the Prince's name, Gwen emerged from her roundhouse holding a blood red, woollen cloak. With a heavy heart, Owain stood and took her in arms. "I will come back."

"I know." She pulled herself away and held the cloak to her chest.

"Promise me you'll be on your guard, Gwen, never stray too far from the lake."

"Don't worry, I can handle Huail. You are the one riding to war, it's you who needs to take care. Here, take this with you." She handed him the cloak. "I made it for you during the dark months, there's no magic woven into it, just my love."

Taking the cloak, he held it up to admire it. "It is beautiful, thank you, and what greater magic is there than love?"

"Come back to me, Owain."

After fastening the cloak over his shoulders, with its silver brooch and pin, he took Gwen in his arms, kissed her and said, "Keep an eye on the lad." Before he'd time to change his mind, he took the reins of his horse and leapt into the saddle. He blew Gwen a kiss, waved at Gal, turned his horse and galloped away to meet the Merlin.

Gal slipped his arm comfortingly around Gwen's waist. "He'll be fine."

"What makes you think that?"

"He promised me a place in the Legion, so he can't die."

She wondered which of them he was trying to comfort. "Come, if you've nothing to do there's a pile of logs that need chopping."

Imagining how riding to war with the Legion might feel, Gal remained where he was, staring along the path Owain had taken.

Fat King Wihstan of the East Angles, rode across Andredes Caester's north meadow for the meeting King Aelle had requested, with his son Prince Wuffa and twenty of his warriors. He'd expected a frosty reception, but not the total silence the watching Saxons offered his arrival as his horse trotted through the gateway. He felt very nervous as he rode between two lines of heavily armed Saxon warriors, an honour guard he supposed, their antagonistic looks warning him the meeting might turn bloody if he didn't show King Aelle full respect.

He understood the frosty welcome because his warriors had often crossed Saxon borders on cattle-raids, and vice versa, though never had the two peoples waged war against each other. The East Anglian and South Saxon kingdoms had never formed an alliance, but he was happy to meet the South Saxon King, so long as there was a profit in it. King Aelle needed his help so he'd honour the peaceful parley, at least until he'd heard him out.

The further into the fort he rode, the more impressed he became. The place was packed with warriors, and the preparations for war looked well advanced: blacksmiths hammered at lengths of iron; spearmen trimmed and worked straight ash-tree branches into spear-shafts; women scraped fur from hides and cut tanned leather into strips of varying lengths and widths. Aelle was obviously expecting to arm many warriors, so he'd make a better friend than an enemy.

As the riders reached the centre of the fort, King Aelle walked out from his feasting hall. Carrying no weapons, the King, followed by Prince Cissa and a dozen hearth-warriors, held out his arms to show his intentions were peaceful, then he bellowed across the courtyard, "Welcome King Wihstan!"

Wihstan dismounted and spread his arms to show he'd come in peace. Aelle took his hand, shook it firmly and presented the Anglian King with a small but ornate, jewelled silver knife. "I am King Aelle of the South Saxons, and this is my son, Prince Cissa, a strong warrior who has killed many Celts and shall become king when I am dead."

"Whilst you are living amongst us, I am your servant," Cissa said, bowing slightly to the East Anglian.

"Well met and well spoken," Wihstan replied. "This is my son, Prince Wuffa, he is also a killer of Celts." Delving into his saddlebag, he pulled out a gift and handed it to the Saxon.

King Aelle admired the finely decorated, gold drinking horn, passed it to Cissa then he roared across the fort for all to hear, "Before this time our peoples had never united to fight our common enemy! It is time the Germanic peoples settled their minor differences and marched together, to chase the Celts from their dung-heaps!" The crowd roared and cheered until he raised his arm to silence them. "Furthermore, I hope this first gathering will be remembered as the first among the many, and we become brothers in war, peace and within the drunken revelry of the feasting hall! All hail King Wihstan and Prince Wuffa, friends of the South Saxons!"

Again, the crowd cheered, and with the formalities over, King Aelle led his guests into the feasting hall. The rest of the day and night would be an indulgence of drunken feasting and rowdy, bawdy songs and speeches. Women would be provided for their guest's comforts, which was customary at such gatherings, so everything was set to forge an alliance that might make Aelle king of the whole of Briton, not that he'd let Wihstan in on that little secret. The real business would begin the following day, when the meeting would mark the beginning of the end of Celtic Briton.

Approaching Viroconium, Owain's mount ambled lazily along the rutted cart track. The Merlin, who'd ridden part of the way with him, before disappearing into the woods, had been excellent company, telling him stories passed down from druid to druid. With Viroconium's grey walls looming large before him, he felt a strong urge to turn back, the royal city being the last place he wanted to be. The closer he got to the city walls, the more they seemed to be looking down in judgement, warning him that King Einion's anger awaited his return. How would he explain his absence, and how would his father react when he told him he'd decided to marry Gwen?

Catching sight of the practice fields, he felt a rush of excited blood when a horn blasted four short notes, telling him the Legion had formed battle-lines and was about to charge. Kicking his horse into the gallop, he turned his mount away from the city's east gate-arch and raced towards the practice fields. Trotting the animal into a copse of hawthorns in the corner of the meadow, he watched the Legion's battle-charge, remembering the thrill of the attack against the Saxons.

Having completed their charge, the Legion wheeled and galloped to the centre of the field, so Owain nudged his horse into the open and urged it into an excited race towards the ranks of horsemen. Closing on them, he drew his new sword and charged directly at Bedwyr, his red cloak billowing as he yelled the battle-cry of the Legion, "Britannia! Britannia! Britannia!"

Bedwyr instinctively drew his sword as the unknown, helmeted and red-cloaked rider galloped across the meadow. But the battle-cry fed a seed of recognition that brought a smile to his face. Sheathing his blade, he called to his sword-brothers, "Our Dragon has returned!" A great cheer spread throughout the ranks and, completely losing their discipline, they raced to welcome their battle-lord.

On the city walls, King Einion and Prince Cadwallon watched the reunion unfold. Seeing Prince Cadwallon smile, the King asked him if he found this amusing?

"I'm sorry, I didn't think," the Prince replied, and he laughed when Owain knocked Bedwyr off his horse.

"As soon as this little display is over, bring your brother to my private rooms." With a wry smile Einion changed the order, "No, march him to the guardroom."

“He takes after you.” Cadwallon risked a sideways glance at his father and, he caught him smiling.

“If I wanted your opinion, I’d ask for it. Fetch him and be damn quick about it!”

8.

Only moments ago, Owain was being hailed by the Legion as a conqueror returned, now he was marching in step with Cadwallon across the cobbled courtyard. “How angry is he?” Owain asked as his iron-studded leather boots scraped to a halt in front of the guardroom door.

“Angry enough for us not to keep him waiting.”

“All I did was disappear for a few days, so why bring me here of all places?”

“I’m just following orders.”

“Are you coming in?” Rarely did Owain feel fear.

“No, this is your mess.” Cadwallon knocked on the door, patted his brother on the shoulder and walked away.

The guardroom door opened and Owain was greeted by the Merlin, which was both a surprise and a comfort. “It’s good to have you back, come in,” said the Druid, and he stood aside to let the Prince pass. “I’ll go and have a chat with the Saxon prisoner,” he said to the stony-faced King.

“Don’t kill him, I want that pleasure,” Einion growled. “I’ll join you after I’ve dealt with this.”

Owain had always feared this room, it was so cold, dark and full of painful childhood memories. In the past King Einion had often punished his growing sons here, and if any place in Briton disturbed Owain’s soul, this room was it. The routine was always the same, his father would make his victims stand in silence until he was ready to speak, enjoying their discomfort while the presence of the place fed their failing courage.

Sheepishly eyeing the King, who was staring blankly at him, he waited for his father's anger to explode. He'd learnt to his cost never to speak first when summoned to the guardroom, it was part of the ritual and today would be no different. Einion would ignore him for as long as his temper allowed, then a fowl-mouthed, violent tirade would burst across the room, followed by another period of menacing silence. "Close the door and sit down," Einion ordered in a surprisingly calm tone.

Doing as ordered, Owain closed the door, wondering why his father hadn't vented his wrath, then he sat at the opposite end of the table. Having had plenty of experience of how the Pendragon would set his traps, silence, rage, silence then often a gently spoken question, the young Prince rested his sweaty palms flat on the table, took a deep breath and waited.

"That was quite a display in the meadow."

"It was well earned." Immediately regretting his arrogant and hasty response, Owain shuffled uneasily and reminded himself to think before speaking.

"Do you think so?" His father tapped the table once with his index finger. "I understand you've been away; did you enjoy your time in the forest, with your lover?"

How was he supposed to respond to that? "Yes, I've been away."

"Maybe I should take a break, what do you think?" the King asked, for the first time unable to hide the menace in his voice.

Confusion set alarm bells ringing, usually by this time Owain would have felt the full force of his father's anger. It could prove to be foolish, but he decided to change the subject to one he knew would send the King over the edge. Better to make him explode and get this over with, he thought, though it was a dangerous gamble. Looking the King straight in the eyes, he confidently said, "The first chance I get I'll return to the forest and marry Gwen. I'd be delighted if you'd attend our wedding, though it's only fair to warn you that we've decided to follow the ceremony of the old tribes, not the Christian marriage rites."

Closing his eyes, Einion sat back and took a few moments to gather his composure. His son had obviously decided not to play the game his way, which was new though not unexpected, a son always eventually challenges the father, just as he'd done with Cunedda. Was Owain about to lock horns with him? He doubted it, though the thought of teaching his son who the bull of the herd was, amused him.

Einion's silence had the Prince wishing he'd kept his mouth shut, theory was one thing, reality another. Leaning forward with his hands on the table, the King shook his head, muttered something under his breath, sighed and sat back to let the atmosphere hang a little longer. If the boy wants to be the bull, he decided, he needs to learn how to do battle. Whether with swords or words, both forms of warfare require the same thought and judgement.

Deciding he'd kept his son stewing long enough, Einion calmly spoke across the table, "You've created a force of horse-warriors that might turn the tide of the Saxon wars in our favour, and, you've proved yourself in battle. As a swordsman you have no equal, with the Legion you've shown yourself to be a forward-thinking leader of men. Unfortunately, after the battle you ran, and spent days sharing the bed of a lowborn woman. I've given this much thought, and my decision will be final." Seeing fear in his son's eyes, he realised the young Dragon wasn't yet ready to challenge the bull.

The Prince braced himself for the full force of his father's rage. Pushing back his chair, Einion rose from his seat like a huge forest bear, calmly walked around the table and stood behind Owain. Placing his hands on his son's shoulders, he gripped them tightly. The Prince stiffened. "I'm no longer a young man," Einion said, relaxing his grip. "So, I've decided that from this day forward, you are the Pendragon of the Britons, my warriors are now yours to lead."

"Father?"

"You heard me, now listen and keep your mouth shut. I won't be announcing this to the kings and princes until the next gathering, so don't breathe a word to anyone."

Shock hit Owain. He'd come here expecting to be taught a severe lesson, instead, he'd been given what he'd wanted since he'd first wielded a wooden sword as a small boy. "That's it, you summoned me here to make me the Pendragon?"

"Yes, are you pleased?" Walking back to his chair, Einion sat and grinned at his son.

"I don't know what to say, except thank you. I won't let you down, I'll make you proud of me, although I think you've a few years of fighting left in you."

King Einion laughed at the last part. "No, I've had enough of war. You'll become Pendragon and your brother will be crowned king. As for myself, I'll live out my final years in a positive orgy of wine, food and women, in fact as many women as I can get my hands on. Your mother has been dead many years, and I've kept her memory long enough. Although I've missed her more than you can imagine, and I'll love her until my last breath is blown away by the wind, it's time for me to live my life as I choose, not how I think I should live it. I'm going to have some fun while my old bones are strong enough to support me when I chase as many women around the mulberry bush as I can find."

"So that's it, you'll cast aside your crown and sword as if they are trimmings from your beard?"

"That's a good way of putting it, I'm shaving off my whiskers to make room for kissing!" He roared with laughter, then looked seriously at his son. "If you live to be my age, and I hope you do, have the wisdom and courage to step aside so that you can enjoy your final years. Crowns and swords are passing vanities, don't let them rule your life." Owain was about to speak when his father raised his hand. "One more thing before you go: if you marry the lowborn forest woman, I'll kill you!"

The naked, tortured Saxon spy had been tied to a post in the dark and damp cellar longer than he cared to remember: one of his eyes was blackened and encrusted with blood; a patchwork of scabbed or leaking knife-cuts lacerated his body; scorched blisters, raised by the touch of hot irons, stank from suppuration; his testicles were bruised and his lips were swollen and cut. In the rancid, cold darkness where his life would end, he wished he'd died with his sword in his hand while trying to escape.

He'd been tied to the post for so long that his back ached constantly, but he couldn't adjust his position because the holding chains were too tight, all he could do was loll his head to one side or the other, which brought him little comfort. Licking his punch fattened lips, he prayed to Woden for just one small sip of water, not that his torturer would allow it, the man called Einion was far too cruel to grant such a mercy.

Alone in the dark, he thought about the woman he loved and the dreams they'd shared. They were hopeless dreams now, all he could hope for was a quick death, but he doubted the brute who'd cut, punched and burned him would put him out of his misery with just one knife cut. It was hard for him not to think about the next series of tortures, though why King Einion would bother was beyond him, he'd told his torturer everything he knew, which wasn't much.

He'd known the risks when choosing to become one of King Aelle's spies, having agreed to the uncertain existence because of the promised rewards and the future they'd buy. Never had he imagined the cruelty he'd suffered, having assumed that if he was caught, he'd be quickly put to death. Having discovered the identity of the battle-lord responsible for the death of Prince Wlencing, he and the other spy had attempted to escape together, and if the night-guard hadn't been so alert, he'd be a free man now, enjoying the fruits of his secret labours.

Though his torturer may have control over his physical pain and final breath, his mind was still his own, and until his skin was cut again, he'd use his mind. From his memory he pulled an image of his fair-haired, blue-eyed Annis. Her name meant 'Pure' though that's the last thing she was. Smiling at the thought, he recalled the sunbathed meadow the previous summer, where they'd first made love and discussed their future life together. At least he'd had those moments, though he regretted not having had more of them in his young life.

Hearing the rattle of keys and the cellar door creaking open, he turned his head towards the cellar steps as a firebrand illuminated the face of his visitor. Stepping carefully down the slimy steps, the newcomer made his way towards the tortured spy. The man, whose long dark hair ran smoothly over a feathered cloak, had a kind face, which gave the prisoner hope. Following the eyes of the torch holding man, his split lips attempted a painful smile as the man sat on a stool in front of him.

"I am the Merlin; I want to talk with you before your torturer returns." Moving the torch to get a better look at the Saxon's many wounds, he felt sickened by Einion's cruelty. "I'm told you understand the Celtic language?" The Saxon nodded. "I've asked the King to spare your life, but he won't, do you want to live?" The Merlin was surprised to see the man look away. "I think I can save your life, but only if you cooperate." Picking up a jug of water placed on the floor some days ago, he sniffed it then said to the victim, “Open your mouth.” Tilting the jug, he poured some of the sour water into the dry cavern. “Do you want to live?”

“Yes,” the spy almost choked on the word, so the Merlin gave him another drink. The prisoner coughed then asked, “Why torture me with false hope?”

“Because I want to save you.”

“Why, we are enemies, if our positions were reversed, I’d slit your throat.”

“Being a druid, I’ve sworn an oath to protect life, not abuse or destroy it. All life is sacred, and I hope that one day all humans will agree with my sentiment.”

“You are a philosopher?”

“Sometimes, yes, as all people are. I’d like you to help me save your life.”

“How?”

“By telling me everything you can about King Aelle’s plans and your mission here, including the number of Saxon spies there are in the city.”

Hope fled the Saxon’s exhausted mind. These were the same questions he’d answered time after time. “I honestly don’t have anything else to tell you.” His head flopped forward, and he sobbed liked a child.

The Merlin placed his hand gently beneath the man’s chin and lifted his head. Searching the desperately forlorn blue eyes, he saw no deceit in then. The cellar doorlatch lifted again, he glanced at the door, stepped back and sat down. “I fear your pain is about to increase.”

Einion walked in, looking very pleased with himself after his chat with his son. "Has he told you anything?" the King asked, walking down the steps.

"No, he's already told us everything he knows."

"That's a pity, I'd like to know King Aelle's campaign plans."

"Why would a Saxon king share his strategies with a spy?" the Merlin asked.

Einion shrugged his shoulders, took his knife from his belt and walked around the prisoner, admiring his bloody handiwork. "Have you anything to say, Saxon, before I increase your pain?"

"I've told you everything." The spy's desperate words fell pointlessly to the floor. "Just kill me, end my suffering."

"Not until I'm satisfied."

"For pity's sake," the Merlin pleaded, "either kill him or let him go."

"Not yet." Einion pressed the point of his knife against the man's cheek. "How many pieces of your fat king's shit slither over Celtic land?"

"I don't know." The man raised his eyes to meet the King's. "We work in pairs; I only know the man who accompanied me here."

"I don't believe you. Imagine your pain as my blade slowly carves a slice from your scabby cheek."

"Einion, stop this!" The Merlin placed his hand on the King's arm. "It is barbaric!"

"Sit down, Druid." With his knife hand, King Einion pushed his friend away, then returned the blade to his victim's cheek.

“There’s nothing more I can tell you,” the man whimpered, and he turned his head as Einion’s blade pricked his cheek.

Applying just enough pressure to puncture the skin, the King twisted the blade slightly and the man yelped. Enjoying his task, he pushed a little harder. The man’s shriek bounced from stone wall to wall and floor to ceiling, until the blade met cheek bone. “Kill me!” the Saxon screamed at his smiling torturer, “please!”

Einion forced the knife hard into the bone, turning the grinding blade and, warm blood oozed down the spy’s neck. Unable to carry the pain, the man tried to scream but no sound flickered the Merlin’s firebrand. His head sagged forward and, he passed out.

“Is that enough blood for you?” the Merlin asked, grabbing Einion’s knife holding arm. “Let him go or I swear I’ll leave this city!”

“Don’t threaten me, Merlin! You may be my oldest friend and the Archdruid of Mona, but that won’t save your life if you touch me again!”

“I’m sorry, Einion, but this isn’t the work of a good man, animals don’t stoop to such levels of cruelty. Slit my throat if you need more blood, but leave this man alone, he’s told you everything he knows.”

The King looked at the limp, naked body, wiped clean his knife on the spy’s chest then he handed his friend the blade. “You do it, slit his throat and have the body thrown over the city walls.”

“I will not, druids don’t kill unless it is absolutely necessary, nor must you have this man killed. Give him to me.”

“I can’t do that, if I let him live, he’ll return to spying.”

"He won't, just look at him, Einion." The Merlin lifted the spy's head. "Can you see that lost, jaded look in his good eye? He's a broken man, he could no more return to spying than you could offer King Aelle your crown. For the rest of his life, he'll live in permanent fear of Celts, his mind has shattered, only the gods know how his tortured dreams will torment his sleep. Let him go and I'll send a man with him to guide him back to Saxon lands."

"Why are you doing this, Merlin?"

"I want you to feel."

"Why?"

"Because you are human."

"That piece of Saxon vomit isn't."

"He is; he feels, sees, understands, loves and mourns just like you do. All humans are one, whatever their race or beliefs."

"All Saxons must die!"

"Violence breeds more violence. Give his life to me, please."

The King shrugged his shoulders and walked to the steps. "Have him if you want him, get him out of here."

Standing to attention by the door inside King Ceredig's private chamber, Gareth anxiously watched the King read again both of the parchment messages. Pacing the straw covered, dark-planked floor, Ceredig muttered a few well-chosen words and kicked over a chair. Furious at the High King's snub, he turned to Gareth and shouted, "Damn the fat Pendragon!"

Ripping the parchments to shreds, he threw the pieces into a brazier and said to the spearman, "I'm not invited to the gathering of kings, should I ignore the insult?" One of the messages was from the governor of Glevum, asking him if he'd received a summons to attend the annual council of Celtic kings; the other parchment, from King Aelle the Saxon, contained a cryptic message about an alliance. "Well, Gareth, should I accept the snub or march my army to Viroconium?"

"It could be an oversight, My Lord; the Pendragon might not know you've returned from Armorica."

"He knows, Einion has spies everywhere."

"Perhaps it's because you keep Saxon mercenaries?"

"Do you know, Gareth, that might be the truth of it. Einion could have jumped to the wrong conclusion. But the snub could be provocative; being a wily old fox, he might want me to march against him. Do you know how many warriors King Einion can put into the field, without the support of the other kings?"

"No, My Lord."

"He has at least five hundred experienced infantrymen, so if he marched against us, we'd have trouble defeating him."

"There's also his son's cavalry."

"From what I've heard the Legion's future is precarious, it can be disbanded at King Einion's whim. If I'd another two hundred warriors, I'd be tempted to march on Viroconium before the High King invades my lands."

"But he's a Celt, why would he attack you, surely he needs you to protect the south coast from raiding Saxons?"

"He could do that himself if he held Durnovaria. Politics is an uncertain game, given power and wealth the most stable of us can become unpredictable. Have my horse saddled, I've a visit to make. And saddle one for yourself, you are coming with me."

Gareth saluted and left the room. Considering the consequences of making a wrong decision, Ceredig walked to the window and looked out at the gentle meadows and woods spreading eastwards beyond the city walls. Kingdoms rise and fall on the back of alliances, and having fought to regain his lands he'd be damned before losing them again. If King Einion wasn't prepared to consider an alliance with him, others would.

Meddyf, supported by Ina the midwife, walked slowly into the walled royal-gardens, delicately tiptoeing towards the soft cushioned chair. "Now sit yourself down, My Lady," Ina said, plumping up the cushion. "Make yourself comfortable and I'll go find something for you to eat and drink."

"Thank you, you are an angel."

"I'm just doing the work the good Lord gave me," the midwife replied, then she went to order some refreshments.

This was the first time Meddyf had been outside her room since nearly dying in child-birth. Feeling she wasn't yet strong enough, she'd initially resisted the idea but Cadwallon's point had been well made, time in the garden might lift her spirits.

No one had expected her to survive, how she'd hung on through the worst of it, especially the nights of burning fevers and searing pain, was nothing short of a miracle, confirming to her the presence of the Christ God, because all her prayers had been answered. Lowering her hands to the sore and swollen bulge where

Ina had cut her child free, she untied the front of her nightdress and tenderly felt the stitches. Thankfully, there was no visible sign of infection, just a slightly red, folded line held together by crude stitches. Though her pain was now slight, she still felt exhausted so guessed her battle to survive wasn't yet over.

It was late afternoon and the soft Sun was high, so she raised her head and let the Sun linger on her face because it felt good to be outdoors, and with the colours and aromas of her garden stimulating her relaxing senses, she felt glad to be alive. Hearing footsteps on the stone path behind her, she turned just enough to see Cadwallon. She gave him a welcoming smile, while wishing she could have this time to herself. Sitting on the grass beside her chair, he took her hand and tenderly kissed it. "Where's Ina?" he asked.

"She's gone to fetch me some food. Where's our son?"

"He's at his wet-nurse's nipple. I'll bring him to you before he sleeps."

Accepting her husband's answer, she was glad someone else had the responsibility of suckling the child for a few more days, even though the thought of someone else feeding little Maelgwn pricked at her heart.

"It's good to see you out of bed," Cadwallon said kindly. "Ina said you shouldn't be up yet, she also let me know what she thought about you taking some air. That woman does have a sharp tongue."

"I know, she made me promise I wouldn't stay out long."

Ina returned carrying a bronze tray of food and drink. "A bowl of warm broth will do you good, My Lady." Placing the tray on the grass, she poured warmed wine into a cup. "Drink this, I've added some healing herbs but it doesn't taste too bad. I'll come and clear up when you're ready to go back inside, and don't stay out too long, I don't want the cold getting into your stitches." Handing Meddyf the cup, she walked away.

"She does go on." Cadwallon looked over his shoulder to make sure the midwife hadn't heard.

"I thought I would die," Meddyf whispered, looking at the herbs floating on the surface of the wine.

"But you didn't."

"I was blessed by the Christ. I've never known that kind of fear, I don't think I'll ever forget how slowly slipping away felt. You'd imagine that when dying you'd fight for every breath, but it wasn't like that. It was more like slowly sliding into a warm, scented tub of water, though that could have been because of the healing herbs. I couldn't go through that again, I wouldn't cope, I was terrified throughout the entire birthing." Taking a small sip of the drink, she looked seriously at her husband. "I don't know what Ina has told you about the damage done to my womb, and what I can and cannot do, but she thinks it would be unwise, dangerous even for me to get pregnant again." Having no reason to hide her tears, she cried.

Cadwallon sat in silence while her tears fell, remembering again the sound of his wife's screams during the birthing. When she'd cried away her tears, he said softly, "Ina told me everything, and made me promise never to make love to you again."

"What kind of marriage would that be?" She sniffed then wiped her nose on her sleeve.

"There are other forms of lovemaking," he reassured her. "There's much we can do for each other without me entering you. You are my wife and I love you. I won't put you aside for the sake of fathering more children. I'm just glad you're alive, and we do have a beautiful, healthy son."

"But I can't be a real wife to you," she blurted as her tears fell again, "and can you imagine how it feels knowing you can never carry a child in your womb? I'm a woman, Cadwallon, who no longer feels like a woman." She gently squeezed his hand in the hope it would soften what she was about to say. "I won't stop you if you want to seek your pleasures elsewhere. You have a right to express your seed and I can't and won't ask you to refrain from the full joys of the flesh. But if you do climb into another woman's bed, please be discreet, I don't want gossips spreading their malice. And don't ever tell me who you take as a lover."

9.

Sweat, ale and gluttony, sexual excess and fights; songs of war and boasting drunkards, raucous depravity of every kind; vomiting and urinating, hedonistic and pointless and unmarshalled, grotesque humans unleashed and enjoyed. There'd been many feasts held in King Aelle's hall, but none as indulgent as the one to celebrate the union between the South Saxons and the East Angles, which had stretched into a three-day orgy and although few of the Angles and Saxons had slept much, the celebrations showed no signs of flagging. Having had their fill of ale and women, the two kings had left the orgy to talk over the details of Aelle's plans and, they were now facing each other across the table in the King's private room.

Their two peoples shared a ready lust for adventure and war, and Wihstan was happy for his warriors to join a venture, if it meant killing Celts, thieving and raping. He'd never fully trust King Aelle though, even if an alliance was agreed and sealed with blood. Nor did he want to be considered the junior partner, so he decided to come straight to the point. "What exactly do you want from me?" he asked.

"Our peoples are cousins," the Saxon began, "we speak the same language and we kill Celts. Your prowess as a warrior is well known, the strength of your sword-arm is……"

"Yes, yes, yes, we've done all that," Wihstan butted in rudely. "Let's get on with this."

Aelle patiently acquiesced while refilling his ale-cup. "I want you to divert the Celts so that I can attack Viroconium and kill the High King. If my plan succeeds, we'll divide Briton between us."

"And if your plan fails?"

"It won't, and your warriors might not even have to fight."

Wihstan didn't like that at all. "War, you wrote in your message! Are you telling me that my army won't now be needed?"

"No, your diversion will draw warriors out of Viroconium, but when the Celts close on your position, you'll have the option of retiring to your own lands or, fighting."

"So, I'm the bait to weaken Viroconium's defences?"

"Yes, as are my warriors. While your men progress west along the valley of the Ouse River, my larger force, led by Prince Cissa, will follow the Roman road west and north to Glevum. If both armies' cross Celtic borders simultaneously, the Celts will have to leave Viroconium and divide their forces."

"You are hoping that by dividing the Celts we'll have a better chance of defeating them?"

"No. Once the Celts have left Viroconium largely unguarded, the best of my men will attack the unprotected city."

"There's a flaw in your plan. King Einion's getting old, he'll probably remain behind with a strong garrison, while his two sons lead his armies."

"I'm hoping he'll remain behind because I want to kill him myself. If my plan for getting into the city works, King Einion will be dead before he's drawn his sword. All you have to do is cross their border with at least two hundred warriors."

King Wihstan took a gulp of ale and considered the plan. He was about to give his opinion when there was a knock at the door. "Enter!" King Aelle shouted angrily, unhappy at the interruption.

A drunken guard stepped into the room, took a deep breath and slurred, "My Lord, King Cere, Cere, Ceredig of the Celtic Duro, Duro, Celts is here."

Aelle stood to welcome the King of the Durotriges.

"Why is he here? If I'd known a Celt would join us, I'd never have left my hearth!" Wihstan spat across the room at Ceredig, and looked around for a weapon. There wasn't anything to hand, so clenching his fists he moved menacingly towards the Celt.

Aelle stepped between them. "I invited him because he can be useful to us. King Ceredig has been using Saxons in his shield-wall for more than two years, and those mercenaries were hired from me, so he isn't our enemy, he is our friend." Reluctantly, Wihstan backed away and sat down. King Aelle then said to the Celt, "Please, sit and warm yourself by the brazier, you are welcome here."

Warily, Ceredig took his seat while Aelle poured him a horn of ale. The two bulky kings looked like men it was best not to pick a fight with, so he kept his mouth shut, took a sip of ale and considered the wisdom of coming into the wolf's cave. Having lived amongst Saxons in Armorica, he knew their language and customs well, but this situation was different, here he wasn't in control.

"We've run out of ale," King Wihstan said grumpily, upturning the jug to make his point.

"Woman!" Aelle shouted at the door. A beautiful, golden-haired young woman entered, carrying a large jug of warmed ale which she first offered to Ceredig. Aelle then made the formal introductions, "King Ceredig of the Durotriges, allow me to introduce King Wihstan of the East Angles, my good friend and ally." They both grudgingly nodded to each other.

Ceredig held out his drinking horn for the woman to fill. "Beautiful," he said without thinking, and he smiled at her.

Aelle saw the lusty look in the Celt's eyes and, was surprised to see the girl return the smile. "Ceredig, my friend, this is my daughter, Princess Gorpe, and yes, she is beautiful."

"Aelle, I'm sorry, I didn't know who she was."

"Be at peace, I'd have been insulted if you hadn't noticed her." Seeing an opportunity, the Saxon took it. "She only has fifteen summers behind her, or is it fourteen?" He slapped her backside as she stepped around him to fill his cup. "Don't you think she'd make a handsome wife?"

"Slap me again and I'll break this jug over your head," she snapped.

"She has enough fire in her belly to warm any man's bed!" Aelle laughed and raised his hand to slap her arse again, then thought better of it. "As it happens, I've been trying to find her a husband, do you have a wife, Ceredig?"

The Celt shuffled uncomfortably on his stool. "No, she died in Armorica, two years ago."

"Have you considered taking another wife?" Having seen a way of increasing his power, his less than subtle question was deliberate.

"There are many women prepared to share my bed," Ceredig replied, "why complicate that with marriage?"

"You could have both!" the Saxon suggested.

"Are we here to discuss war, or women?" King Wihstan asked impatiently.

"Good point, and I apologise." Aelle pulled a parchment from within his bearskin cloak, and unrolled it onto the table. "Let's get down to it."

Ceredig's eyes followed the sway of Gorpe's hips as she left the room, then he looked at the rough map of Celtic Briton.

"Aelle, can we trust a Celt with our plans?" Wihstan growled.

"This one, yes, he has no love for King Einion."

"Are you prepared to seal the alliance with blood?" Wihstan asked, looking accusingly at Ceredig.

"If I like what I hear."

"No!" Wihstan yelled, slamming his fist on the table. "First, pull the knife across your palm and mix your blood with ours."

King Aelle, seeing the wisdom of the idea, handed the Celt his eating knife. "Prove to us you won't betray the alliance."

Ceredig took the knife, sliced a red line along his palm, clenched his fist and passed the knife to Wihstan, who did the same then handed the knife to Aelle. After drawing the blade across his hand, the Saxon held it out to Ceredig, who grasped the hand, released it then did the same with Wihstan. Watching the Angles and Saxons mix their blood, Ceredig wondered what this alliance might mean for the future of Briton.

"Brothers in battle, brothers in peace," Aelle said.

"Brothers in battle, brothers in peace," the two wary kings replied.

The three of them closed around the map to plot the downfall of King Einion.

Having been escorted into the feasting hall by two of King Aelle's warriors, Gareth had been half hidden in the darkest corner for quite some time, sitting on his own, unable to believe the extent of the drunken orgy. The Saxons and Angles were indulging in every form of sexual act he could imagine, and many he couldn't! It wasn't just couples writhing about on tables, benches and the ale-soaked floor, groups of people were wrapped around each other, groaning and groping like balls of slithering worms.

Those not immersed in sexual lust were filling their bellies with roasted pigs, cows and various birds, or pouring endless jugs of ale down their throats. Fights had inevitably broken out, and one bloodied man, who'd found himself caught in a scrum of at least a dozen wrestling bodies, had been carried from the hall on a bench. Not wanting to join in, Gareth was thankful for the sanctuary of his wooden bench in the dark corner.

Sooner or later, someone was bound to challenge him, because he was a Celt, and if they did, he'd be defenceless because no weapons were allowed in the hall. Perhaps their hospitality would spare him from their brutality, assuming their customs extended to Celts? Deciding he shouldn't attraction attention, he looked at the floor as around the room the various grunts, groans and screams of drunken, sexual excess had him wishing he was in Durnovaria.

He was getting comfortable with the idea of spending the night looking at the floor, when a dark shadow slid into his limited vision. Slowly raising his head, he saw the bulkiest, blonde-bearded Saxon giant he'd ever had the misfortune to meet. The man beat his barrel-chest with his clenched fist and said, "Osgar." Believing that to be his name, Gareth replied in kind.

A fair-haired serving girl walked over, carrying an ale jug, which she offered to the giant Saxon. Osgar snatched the jug, took a huge swig then hurled it across the hall. Grabbing the girl by the throat with his huge right hand, he pushed her forward. "Celt?" he grunted.

"Celt," Gareth replied nodding, not wanting the Saxon to know he spoke his language.

The Saxon whispered something to the girl, and pointed at Gareth. The girl smiled warmly at the Celt and, smoothed her hands provocatively over her curves. Deciding it might be wise to play the innocent, Gareth raised his hands, shook his head and shrugged his shoulders, hoping the Saxon would think he didn't understand. Pointing at the girl, Osgar said, "Eva." Pushing her onto the bench beside Gareth, he walked away.

Not knowing what to say, Gareth nervously returned her smile and wondered if Saxons always gave women as gifts to their guests. Eva smiled, placed a warm hand on the inside of his thigh and stroked his leather leggings. His blood warmed when she extended her little finger and touched very close to where he hoped her hand would go next. Enjoying the look in her teasing green eyes, he shuffled closer and she slipped her hand beneath the flap at the front of his leggings. Lost in his lust, he succumbed to her touch and the releasing spirit of the feast.

In King Aelle's room, the business of the three kings was being concluded. "That's settled then," Aelle said. "With Ceredig's two hundred Saxons added to Cissa's diversion, I'll be able to lead more men into the forest when I leave for Viroconium."

"We should offer a sacrifice to Woden," Wihstan suggested, eyeing the Celt mischievously. "What better offering than the head of a Celtic king?"

"He's my guest, Wihstan!"

"I was joking!"

"With our future territory satisfactorily divided, I should find Gareth and set off back to Durnovaria." Ceredig stood and bowed to his new allies. "It's been a pleasure meeting you, Wihstan, and if you are ever in my part of Briton, don't visit my city!"

"What?"

"That was a joke also!" Laughing, Ceredig held out his hand in friendship.

"I've never taken the hand of a Celt," Wihstan growled as his chair scraped back and he got to his feet.

"Well, now's your chance." Aelle held out his own hand to Ceredig. "We are brothers in war, there must be no enmity between us."

"I'll shake his hand only when he's kept his part of the bargain," Wihstan replied. He bowed to Aelle but not the Celt, then made his way to the door. "Remember this, Celt, if you betray us my entire army will come looking for you." Kicking open the door, he left to re-join the feast.

Ceredig waited long enough for Wihstan to be well out of the way, then he went to find Gareth. Walking into the feasting hall, he was amused to see that his spearman had found a girl to hump, and a good-looking one at that. There was one very tempting girl he'd like to take into a dark corner, so picking his way through the mass of writhing, grunting and groaning bodies he looked to see if Gorpe was in the hall. She wasn't, so he veered towards Gareth's corner.

Kneeling in front of Eva, who was still sitting on the bench, Gareth's pumping crescendo came to a rude halt when he felt someone tap his shoulder. Pausing in mid-stroke, he turned to see Ceredig standing over him. "She's a pretty girl, Gareth. When you've finished, I'll meet you outside, we've a hard 'ride' in front of us!" Supressing a laugh, he knelt beside his warrior and joked, "Do you think you can manage two 'rides' in one day?"

"Very funny."

"I'll meet you in the stables." Laughing, Ceredig made his way back through the hall, leaving Gareth to conclude his own Saxon-Celtic alliance.

During the centuries of Roman occupation, the stone-built building where Owain and Cadwallon were sitting, had been the legionary temple dedicated to the war god Mithras, and because of its size and importance, the building had been kept in excellent repair. White marble columns supported the terracotta tiled roof, which protected painted walls depicting colourful scenes of bull-leapers, dancing maidens and battles. On the back wall, opposite the age-darkened double oak doors, an image of Mithras the bull-god, a heavily armoured man with the head of a bull, overlooked the geometric patterned blue, white and red mosaic floor.

Hanging and standing oil-lamps and candles illuminated the room, highlighting the martial scenes painted on the plaster walls. In front of the fresco of Mithras was a purple cloth covered, waist high dais that supported four chairs. In front of the dais, rows of backless benches stretched most of the way back to the oak doors. Everything was ready for the gathering of the kings, when royals from all parts of Celtic Briton would take their places at the annual council.

Seated on a bench near the dais, Einion's sons had been talking for some time, discussing the responsibilities soon to be heaped on their young shoulders. "It's right that our father is giving you the title of Pendragon," Cadwallon said without any hint of jealousy. "I can use a sword and spear as well as most men, but I can't command the hearts and minds of warriors in the way that comes so naturally to you."

Owain had always admired his brother's giving nature, even as a boy Cadwallon had happily stood aside in favour of his younger brother, if he believed the sacrifice would be beneficial. Cadwallon did have ambitions, though they were directed towards the welfare of the people. As for absolute power, he'd gladly sacrifice it to benefit the greater good. "There's something I must tell you," Cadwallon said. "I've spoken to our father and asked him not to step down as high king, not yet anyway."

"Why, you'll make a fine king?"

"I think something big is coming," the elder brother replied. "The Saxons have been quiet for more than a year, and my instincts tell me we are about to face a vicious war-tide, so we'll need a strong and experienced king at the helm."

"But what you've just said proves you are ready to become king."

"Seeing a storm is one thing," Cadwallon said, walking to the dais, "having the power to stop it is another." Looking thoughtfully at the four purple cushioned chairs on the dais, he said to his brother, "Having created your Legion and proved yourself in battle, you are ready to become the Pendragon. I have very little experience of dealing with ambitious men, I'm unfamiliar with their manipulations, conniving's, ambitious politicising and plotting; I'm not yet ready to become high king of the Britons."

Owain walked over to Cadwallon and put his hand on his shoulder. "I know who you are and how you'll rule, so when you eventually take the crown, my sword and the Legion will be yours."

"The kings and princes will arrive soon," Cadwallon reminded him. "We'd better find our father so he can refuse to tell us, as usual, what he'll say at the gathering!" They both laughed as they walked to the small door behind the dais, the door to King Einion's private chamber.

Foetid, muddy and loud, a cesspit of stinking savagery, a shantytown haven for cutthroats built by the newly arrived spearmen, had swallowed the meadows surrounding Andredes Caester; the time for war had come. Since the wolf-banner had been raised above the fort's gates, a steady stream of warriors eager to kill Celts, had arrived from outlying farms, villages and towns. Standing beside Prince Cissa on the fort's battlements, King Aelle looked down at the ramshackle collection of wooden huts, pleased that so many spearmen had answered his summons.

The chosen day to march had arrived, and the King could barely control his excitement as dozens of firebrand-wielding warriors stood ready to torch the shantytown. In the east, a ghostly slither of misty orange shone through thin clouds, promising a good day for a march. Waving his sword to the torch holding men, Aelle signalled the burning to begin. Mustered beyond the shantytown, his hundreds of warriors roared when the first huts burst into flames. Soon, thick black smoke drifted up into the brightening day, swirling in clouds as flames leapt from hut to hut. "Are you ready for war?" Aelle asked his son.

"I want to kill the Pendragon as much as you do."

"Good." The King lifted his eyes to the clouds and thrust his sword high. "Woden, god of war, victory and death!" he hollered, "lead us to our enemies so that we may strengthen and glorify your name by shedding Celtic blood! Prince Wlencing, warrior of Woden and murdered son, look down upon your armies of revenge, join us in battle when we claim the blood-price for your death!" Clasping Cissa's forearm, he said, "Let's go and kill Celts."

In the meadow, the entire shantytown now blazed bright as battle-horns blasted through the acrid smoke. The warriors roared, they lived for war, measuring their worth not in coin or wheat but in the celebratory songs of their prowess in battle. To them, dying with their swords in their hands was the greatest of all triumphs, and pitied was the man who died at the plough, because he wouldn't enter Woden's feasting hall.

With the last huts tumbling into smoking piles, the hundreds of gathered warriors split into two battle-groups. Prince Cissa would lead the first, two hundred strong. They'd follow the Roman road west until they met King Ceredig's Saxon mercenaries, and together they would march north to Glevum. The second group would be led by King Aelle, and they were four hundred of the best, battle-hardened warriors he had. They'd head north through the vast Middleland Forest, picking their secret way to its farthest edge, just short of Viroconium. These men would deliver the blow that would send Celtic Briton into a chaotic, final collapse.

"Woden be with you, Father. May the hunt be swift and your victims many."

"Thank you, Cissa. Remember, burn every village and town you come to; kill anyone who can't outrun your advance, and the moment your scouts inform you that a Celtic army is marching your way, you must retreat so that the preparations for the next phase of my plan can begin. This war won't end with the death of King Einion ap Cunedda."

10.

From the battlements on Durnovaria's north wall, King Ceredig watched his two hundred Saxons leave the city to begin the march to meet Prince Cissa's warriors. A part of him wanted to recall his small army but, he couldn't risk provoking a war with the South Saxons, at least not until he'd hired more mercenaries. He'd made his choice so would stand by it, and this wasn't the time for regrets, survival was the name of this game. Cynric, Ceredig's son born nine summers ago, watched his father closely, noticing the tightness of his jaw and his white-knuckled, clenched fists. "You could call them back," the boy suggested, having read the situation.

"I can't." Ceredig swore and turned away from the marching warriors. "I wasn't invited to the Pendragon's gathering, so I rashly formed a foolish alliance."

"But we are Celts, so you are making war against your own people."

"I haven't sent my Celtic spearmen." He looked down at his precocious but increasingly irritating son. "And I'm not leading them."

"What if the attack fails?" the boy asked. "What if the Pendragon discovers you've sent your Saxons to join Prince Cissa?"

"The Britons will only see Saxons; they'll assume they are King Aelle's warriors; why would they think otherwise?"

"Because High King Einion has spies everywhere, and he......"

"Look, Cynric!" Wanting to strike the boy, he took a deep breath and reminded his son that he should be practising his swordplay with Gareth.

"Can't I stay with you and learn how to rule a kingdom?"

"Don't you want to become a warrior?"

"Yes, but when I'm old enough to fight I won't march against my own people."

"That's enough, Cynric! Go and find Gareth, he's waiting for you in the main hall."

"But I want to……..."

"I said go!" Ceredig impatiently pushed his son away. Since the Sun had risen, he couldn't stop thinking about how the coming days might mark the end of Celtic Briton. If King Aelle's plan succeeded, the fall of King Einion's kingdom was a definite possibility, and that prospect frightened him because with Saxons burning, killing and raping across Briton, an emboldened King Aelle might turn his warriors against Durnovaria. But time cannot be turned back, and regrets are a waste of emotions.

Filing into Viroconium's Temple of Mithras, speculation was rife amongst the kings and princes. Taking their places on the benches, they openly discussed the possible reasons for the early summons. The annual council usually took place during the summer solstice, so there must be a specific reason for the change. Many believed they were here because a Saxon attack was imminent, while others thought the birth of Prince Cadwallon's son was the reason.

Only one of their number suggested that King Einion was about to hand over power, and he was mocked for his perceived stupidity.

As was customary on such occasions, those entering the hall did not bring their weapons with them, and with the last of the expected guests seated, the huge oak doors were banged shut, hushing the chatting royals into silence. To the surprise of everyone, a horn blasted a long, shrill note from beyond the oak doors. The doors swung open again and all heads turned towards the sound of marching warriors. Before anyone could protest, forty red-cloaked warriors of the Legion had marched up the temple steps and into the room, their studded boots crunching on the mosaic floor as they marched in two columns down the central aisle. At the end of the aisle, they split to form protective lines in front of the dais.

The room burst into uproar, never had the High King insulted the royals in such a manner. The horn blew another note, and with the nobles on their feet protesting, forty more red-cloaked warriors marched in and formed ranks along the rear-wall of the temple. The doors banged shut and Briton's royals turned to the dais, the implications of the change sitting uncomfortably on their shoulders. The show of power told them they were here to listen, so one by one, they wisely sat down.

The small door behind the dais opened and the Merlin walked into the room, holding a tall, ebony rod. All eyes watched him as he walked to the front of the dais, where he took his place in the centre of the red-cloaked guards and, rapped the butt of his rod three times on the floor, signalling the beginning of the meeting. Seeing the many angry faces of the seated kings, he took a moment to compose himself before addressing the gathering. "You will 'all' stand for High King Einion ap Cunedda, Prince Cadwallon and his wife Meddyf, Owain the Prince of Rhos and Maelgwn, the King's first grandson!"

"Einion wasn't introduced as the Pendragon," King Erbin ap Constantine of the Dumnonians whispered to his neighbour, King Loth.

"What of it?"

"Don't you think it's significant? The Merlin doesn't make mistakes when introducing the King," Erbin pointed out as King Einion led his family onto the dais. They took their seats in almost complete silence, which surprised Prince Owain because usually men would cheer and clap as the royals entered the gathering. He looked at his father, who seemed unmoved by the cold reception.

When his family were seated, the High King took a small step to the front of the dais and bellowed in his bear-like manner across the room, "Welcome, kings of the Britons. I've an announcement to make before the business of the council begins!" Turning to Meddyf, he beckoned her forward, softened his tone and said, "My fellow kings, there has been an addition to our family, one that has brought us great joy." Taking the sleeping baby, he held it up for all to see. "With great pride I introduce to you my first grandson, Prince Maelgwn. He has strong lungs and from what his wet-nurses say he has a healthy appetite for the female breast, just like his grandfather!" A low ripple of forced laughter trickled throughout the room. Carefully passing the boy back to Meddyf, Einion told her she must leave the meeting because she was a woman. "I've called this meeting early because there is to be a change in the defence of our nation, the time has come for younger blood to carry the Pendragon's burden."

Surprised murmurs questioned the announcement, then King Loth stood and asked, "Are you telling us you are stepping down as the Pendragon?"

"I am."

"No!" Some of the kings shouted, though with little conviction. If there was to be a change, many believed they had the experience and respect necessary to lead the armies of Briton.

Einion raised his hand to silence the murmuring hum. "Thank you for your muted response," he said sarcastically. "I'll have a role to play in the wars against the Saxons, I am still the high king, and before your minds race too far ahead, I'd advise you to keep that in mind. Times change, and so should our methods of making war, which until recently have had limited success. We need new tactics and a respected man to lead our armies, one who understands how to wage a new kind of warfare. It is time we put the Saxons to the sword!" He paused, expecting the room to erupt with cheering. Accepting the wary silence, he spoke again, "There are some here who believe themselves capable of leading our combined armies, but only one amongst us has the necessary foresight, tactical knowledge and ability to command, to defeat our common enemy."

"Tell us, Einion!" King Ban of the West Brigantians shouted from the back of the room. "Who is this great battle-lord you consider to be so worthy?"

The kings cheered, stamped their feet and roared their approval. Einion waited for the room to calm, and spoke directly to Ban, “I’m sure you are aware of the mounted legion my son, Owain, had the foresight to create. It cost me a fortune but it’s value has already been proved on the battlefield.”

“We’ve all heard about the battle-charge,” Ban replied. “Why is it significant?”

Convinced the conversation was pre-planned, Owain listened to the exchange, believing the nobles wouldn’t fall for this.

“The significance of the charge is simple,” King Einion called to his northern ally. “The Saxons don’t know how to fight against horse-warriors.”

“Cavalry has been used before,” Ban delivered the pre-planned point.

“They have, but not in the way my son has devised. Owain led just fifty horse-warriors against a Saxon warband of at least two hundred spearmen, and the Saxons were cut to pieces. In the past, cavalry units were used to protect flanks, attack enemy flanks and kill fleeing warriors during the rout. My son has devised a method of frontal attack which no shield-wall can withstand. We have a new weapon, and like my son we must embrace the new tactics because they’ll bring us total victory. So, from this day forward I am handing the Pendragon banner to the one whose brilliant young mind saw the potential of organised, heavy cavalry and had the courage to prove that his idea would work.” Einion turned to Owain and waved him up. “My son, the Prince of Rhos is now the Pendragon of the Britons!”

The room exploded into outraged uproar and the gathering rose as one to protest against the insult; fists were shaken at the King, fingers pointed at the young Prince and if the warriors of the Legion hadn't been there, some of the royals might have physically challenged the High King. The room quietened and someone shouted, "You can't do this!"

"The Pendragon must be elected by us all!" another man yelled.

"The right to raise a Pendragon is ours, not yours!" one of the kings challenged the High King.

"As the campaign season is almost upon us!" Einion bellowed at his disobedient royals, "I've decided to change the law and make the choice of the Pendragon exclusively my own. If anyone wants to challenge my authority, let them do so with swords drawn, then we'll find out who has the power to elect Pendragons!"

Uproar met the King's words, and this time the royals wouldn't be silenced by the King's raised hand. Stomping their feet in rhythm, they yelled insults at the High King. They were proud men and wouldn't follow an almost untried youth into battle. The Prince had barely begun to shave let alone fight, surely one of them was better qualified to lead the Celts in times of war?

King Erbin of the Dumnonians, nephew of the High King, walked down the aisle as far as the lines of red-cloaked guards, and turned to face the shouting kings. Raising his arms, he hoped their curiosity to hear him might silence them, it did. Lowering his arms, he turned to King Einion. "My Lord, do you honestly expect us to follow an untried boy who hasn't been elected? He may have won a battle, and it is possible he has the loyalty of his small Legion but the army of the Britons will only follow a warrior who has proved himself many times in battle. Our Pendragon must be a warrior whose courage cannot be questioned, who has shown that his tactics and ability to lead can be trusted when a battle hangs in the balance. Yes, your son has shown great courage, but his battle was over before it had started, he caught the Saxons sleeping so no special tactics were needed. I say he's too young and inexperienced to lead us. If we are to have a new Pendragon, let's choose another, a leader who has proved himself and can be trusted by all the Dragons and kings who'll fight under his command."

The kings cheered Erbin's speech full voiced and heartily, some of them calling out alternative names, usually their own. Owain, distracted by the sight of his warriors wearing red cloaks, like the one Gwen had made for him, smiled at the honour. Chuckling to himself, he wondered what Gwen might say when he told her she'd instigated a trend amongst warriors. He liked the look though, so considered the idea of making the red cloak a reward for newly trained warriors when they graduated to the Legion. His attention was brought back to the issue by the Merlin rapping his rod and shouting, "You will be silent!" He was ignored, so he rapped the rod again and raised his voice. "You will be silent in the presence of the High King!"

The disturbance continued, so Einion nodded to the centurion of the guards, who drew his sword and barked an order. The red-cloaked warriors drew their short swords and stomped their feet to attention, awaiting their next order. The threat worked; the room fell as silent as cold-death. King Einion then spoke with gentle, practised, calculated menace, "This is not a debate; I will be obeyed. If any of you want to leave the alliance, you know what you must do. I have no wish to go to war against any of you, but I've done it before and I'll do it again if you force my hand."

"Father, please, let me speak." Owain got to his feet and walked to the front of the dais.

Nervously taking a deep breath as his father stepped back, the Prince licked his dry lips when the seed of an idea germinated. "I agree with you all," he said almost apologetically. "I know I am young but I've seen how the times are changing, we must understand and embrace the change if we are to survive. The Saxons won't give us back our lands, every day more of their boats arrive laden with warriors, farmers and their families. If we are to survive, we must not be one step ahead of the Germanic peoples, but three, or four. Across the sea the kingdoms of the old Roman Empire are falling as entire nations from the east sweep westward, displacing tribes and peoples who must find new lands to settle in. There is burning, killing, raping and slaughter on a scale that's never been known before: Rome has fallen to the Barbarians; Gaul is close to collapse and it isn't difficult to see that we are next in the line. With this change comes the need to find a new way of making war, a tactic the Saxons cannot combat. They have no cavalry and only use bows for hunting, they'll ride to the battlefield but won't go into battle on horseback because they worship horse-gods so won't dishonour them in war. With a well-trained army of infantrymen, we might hold the Saxons back for a while, perhaps for our lifetimes. But more warriors from the continent will come to cut down our forests, burn our villages and towns and slaughter our people, and eventually we will be pushed into the margins of our own island. We are one nation fighting the displaced warriors of four nations, so wouldn't you agree that the odds are stacked against our survival? You all know that if we break up the alliance, they can take us one kingdom at a time, and that would be a slow death for all of us. But my mounted Legion can beat them. I know some of you will be thinking we've tried mounted warriors before, and they were only useful for protecting the flanks of our shield-wall. Look beyond what's already been done, see the possibilities of new battle-tactics and the victories they can bring. A charge by heavy cavalry is neither easy to control nor does it guarantee victory, but if the horse-warriors are also archers, we move into the realms of the unknown. Out in the meadows my Legion has practised being this kind of cavalry unit, and it has proved to be devastating against a shield-wall. An infantryman cannot defend himself against death from the front and death from above, unless he carries two shields, which would make it impossible for him to wield his weapons. Using the new method, we can defeat our enemies and send them back across the sea, taking with them the knowledge that Briton is no longer there for the taking. If you give me your trust and support for one campaign season, you'll see how effective the Legion can be. My father as good as ordered you to accept me as the next Pendragon, which he did because he knows what is coming. In the harbours across the Southern and Eastern Seas, keels are being packed with warriors; King Aelle is planning an onslaught so devastating that our nation may not survive it. His main challenge might not come until the high summer, but it will come so we must prepare to fight a vicious and prolonged war. One campaign season is all I ask, give me that and I'll show you how we can gain victory and freedom!"

Silence. Not a whisper was spoken while Owain's words were absorbed: Einion looked at his son with pride; the Merlin understood the Prince's wisdom; Cadwallon wondered if his brother was becoming a politician.

"The Pendragon has always been elected by the gathering," Owain broke the silence, "and that's how it should be. My father has put my name forward to lead you. Does anyone else want to carry the Pendragon banner into battle, if so, I'll happily accept the result of an open vote?" No one spoke, so Owain sat down again, accepted, for the time being at least, as the Pendragon of the Britons.

Hidden in the forest, a good walk south of Viroconium, King Aelle's warriors waited out the days before the planned attack on the city; the waiting was uncomfortable, but hopefully it would be worth it. Having posted a ring of guards, a spear's throw from the camp's perimeter, Aelle felt secure enough to relax until his scouts returned to inform him that the Celtic warriors had left the city.

They'd only been there a day when Aelle's spies had informed him that almost all the Celtic kings were inside Viroconium, attending their annual council. His first instinct had been to order the attack, the chance of removing every obstacle to his conquest of Briton in one glorious battle was tempting, but he knew he couldn't move until the Celts had ridden out to meet Wihstan and Cissa's armies. If he attacked when Celtic spearmen manned the walls in their hundreds, his men would be cut to pieces before they reached the city gates.

Sitting on a mossy rock in a sunlit sward, where a stream trickled through thick patches of bracken, Aelle ran a whetstone along the cutting-edge of his sword, remembering some of the many women who'd shared his bed. He would have drifted further into his memories if he hadn't noticed two of his spearmen on the other side of the stream, dragging what looked like a bound and gagged, scruffy Celtic boy. "This had better be good, Alric," he called across the stream.

Alric, the taller of the two warriors, picked up the kicking, red-haired prisoner and leapt over the stream with his victim slung over his shoulder, followed by the other spearman. Dropping the Celt at the King's feet, he saluted Aelle and kicked the curled creature in the ribs.

"You need me to deal with this?" Aelle snarled. "Take the boy away and slit his throat."

"If it was a boy, I'd already have done that," Alric replied. He then sucked the bloody semi-circle of teeth marks on the palm of his hand. "She's a ferocious bitch."

"Looks more like a boy to me," Aelle said. He growled in Celtic to the prisoner, "What's your name?" He then asked Alric if he was sure the filthy creature was a girl?

The girl ignored him, her tear-filled eyes flashing violence at the Saxon. The other warrior grabbed the girl's hair and pulled her head back, Alric then tore open the front of her tunic to reveal small, budding breasts. "Look, teats."

"Where did you find her?" the King asked.

"There's a hovel about four spear-throws from here," Alric replied, prodding the girl's breast to prove she wasn't a boy, "and from the look of the place it could be inhabited by more than one person."

"Why didn't you kill her there?"

"We thought some of the men might like a little entertainment," the other warrior spoke up. "After you've had her, of course."

"You are fools, both of you." Aelle drew his knife, grabbed the girl by the hair and pulled his blade across her throat. A single tear slid down the girl's cheek as her head flopped forward. "That's what you should have done, now go back to the hovel and kill whoever turns up."

11.

Murder, death, desolation and degradation, slaughter and abuse, the intention of every invader who had crossed Briton from east to west. Marching along the Roman Road to Glevum, Prince Cissa and King Ceredig's four hundred Saxons closed on the Celtic city. Behind them lay a spread of death and destruction marked by dozens of grey smoke plumes; signs of the many Celtic villages they'd burned. Their orders were to make themselves as visible as possible, so they'd torched even the poorest of hovels, no Celtic home had survived the Saxon progression.

Hundreds of Celts fled before the advancing army, heading for the open gates of Glevum. The peasants had run with whatever they could carry, while farmers drove their livestock in the direction of the City's high walls. Those caught by the Saxons were mercilessly killed, except for the women, who were raped before having their throats cut. The trail of destruction and slaughter would live in the memories of the displaced and orphaned for generations to come, as would their hatred of the Saxon people.

Prince Cissa had been ordered to march to the city, build a small fort with a deep ditch and rampart, and wait until his scouts returned with news of the advancing Celtic army. His father had told him not to engage the Celts unless he was attacked and cornered, his spearmen were only the bait in a very wide net. When the advancing Celts closed, his warriors were to abandon their defences and return south, their job done. Cissa thought it was a good plan, by the time the foolish Celts realised their mistake it would be too late, they'd never return to Viroconium in time to save it from King Aelle's slaughter.

Hearing Celtic horns blaring in the distance, Cissa realised he was closer to Glevum than he'd thought, so he sent runners ahead to scout the City's approaches. So far, the plan was working: Glevum was filling with cattle and frightened village folk; villages were burning for as far as could be seen, and news would soon reach King Einion of the invasion led by King Aelle's wolf banner.

As no one had come forward to challenge him, Prince Owain would become the Pendragon before the Sun began its slide. Sitting alone in the guardroom, King Einion reflected upon the gathering that was now officially over. He'd ordered the kings to stay and witness the raising of the Pendragon, and he'd demanded they publicly swore loyalty to his son. It was possible that after returning to their own lands, some of them might renounce their allegiance, perhaps even leave the alliance but he hoped they weren't foolish enough to take such drastic steps. He'd done all he could to help his son, from now on Owain must win over the nobles on his own. Deciding he should have a talk with the Prince before the ceremony, he went to find him.

Sitting on a bench in the Roman Temple, Owain wasn't worried about addressing the crowds, but he did fear the possible reactions of the kings and their sons, who might use the occasion to bring the house of Cunedda down a notch or two. If they did scorn him, he'd be powerless before he'd taken command of the armies, so he needed a solution to the possible threat. Hearing the door behind the dais open, he looked over to see his father, dressed in his richest purple robe, smiling proudly at him. "Is it time?" Owain asked, nervously.

"It is, but before we go, I've something to say." Einion crossed the room and sat next to his son. "I want you to know that I believe in you, unreservedly, and, because I have faith in your ideas, I'm going to give you enough silver coin to double the number of warriors in the Legion."

"Thank you, Father, I......."

"No, don't say anything. Some of the kings may turn their backs on you when you are raised on the Votidini shield. If they do, you'll need the extra warriors when invading their kingdoms."

"Would they risk civil war?"

"Oh yes, they are a fickle lot and given the opportunity to humiliate us, some might take it. When you step onto the shield you must face the kings and demand their allegiance, not with words but with the authority of your presence. Show them your strength, you must neither bow to them nor hesitate, be their master."

"Will such an arrogant display win me their respect?"

"Just do as I say," King Einion replied, shaking his head because his son had much to learn about politics. "When you walk into the meadow for the shield raising, the people will cheer every step you take, which will make you feel like a god. Don't be fooled by this, keep a level head and remember you are just a man. Never forget that the people can turn against you; you might be their salvation when the Sun is high, and the reason for their woes when the Sun falls, that is politics. Now go to the meadow and become a true Pendragon, which I know you are."

The ceremony to raise the Pendragon would take place in Viroconium's north meadow, so that's where the common people had gathered in their hundreds, dressed in their finest clothes, giving the occasion a multi-coloured splash. At the west end of the meadow, the ground sloped gently to a mound where the nobles waited, some wearing gold circlets to mark their rank.

With the day officially declared a celebration, a host of jugglers, fire eaters, singers and musicians were entertaining the crowds in the hope of relieving the people of their few coins: bull-necked wrestlers challenged those stupid enough to try a few falls with them, offering a tempting purse to the man who could put them on their backs; minstrels sang about old war-heroes and gods, some adding Owain's name to their songs and stories, lifting him prematurely to heroic status. Pigs, cows and sheep were roasting on spits, ale tents had been erected and stocked to satisfy thirsts, and tables were piled high with loaves of bread and baked pies.

At the appointed time, horns blasted a fanfare from Viroconium's north wall. The people turned and cheered, swarming like bees to the procession as it passed through the east gateway. First came half of the red-cloaked Legion, carrying shields and spears, marching in two columns to the sound of a beating drum. Behind them walked the Merlin, dressed as always in his raven-feather cloak. Owain, carrying before him his upheld sword, followed the Druid, wearing a blue tunic with matching leggings, simple but royal. High King Einion marched two steps behind his son, with Prince Cadwallon and Meddyf by his side. Cai and Bedwyr led the rest of the armed red-cloaked warriors. Loud the masses cheered, shouting Owain's name as their colourful swarm parted to allow the procession through.

The Red Cloaks led Owain to the centre of the meadow, where a large stone protruded from the earth. It had always been known as the 'King's Stone' a tradition that many believed trailed back to when the Pretani had first colonised Briton, after the age of ice. Many kings and pendragons had stepped onto the smooth rock, and Owain understood that once a man climbed onto it, no man had the right to challenge his authority, except in battle, because those whose feet felt the sun-warmed stone, had been chosen by the Goddess.

To the sound of the beating drum and the cheering masses, the first columns of the Legion formed a wide circle around the stone, locking their spears horizontally to form a protective barrier as King Caw of the Picts looked on from the mound, scowling as the royal party entered the circle. Halting in front of the stone, Owain closed his eyes to imagine and feel the moment. Following in the footsteps of generations of pendragons and kings, he wanted their souls to combine with his so that he'd be one with them. Realising the solemnity of the moment, the people fell reverentially silent as the following Red Cloaks formed an outer ring of spears. The drum stopped beating and silence hung over the crowds. Hearing the caw of a hunting bird, Owain searched the hazy blue sky. Seeing an oily, jet-black bird fly over the heads of the crowd, he felt an icy shiver chill his bones when the raven's screech pierced the quiet.

"Rohanna," the Merlin whispered to no one, while watching the bird soar away.

Owain stepped onto the stone and turned to face the Druid, who raised his arms and called to the Mother Goddess Enaid in a language only the druids spoke. As one the crowd gasped as the rhythmic words touched their souls, they then collectively sighed when instinctual understanding settled upon them. The Merlin pointed a commanding finger at Owain, who raised his sword and swung it in a wide arc, the singing blade catching the light as he thrust the point towards the high sun. A shiver of power slid down the blade and into his outstretched arm, cooling in shifting surges throughout his entire body. Now he knew why he'd been born. Sunlight touched the shining steel and split into angled arrows, the blade glinting as reflected light shot into the awestruck crowd, spreading a power of confident strength, a power everyone believed they felt. Spontaneously, the crowds roared the Prince's name, their shouts increasing when a wide smile spread across the young man's face. Looking down at his father, he remembered his wise words, accepting he was neither a god nor a king, he was a servant of the people.

The Merlin raised his arms, and the crowd fell silent. "Britons!" he called to the milling masses, "you've gathered to witness the raising of a new Pendragon, which is how it should be because it is for you the title is bestowed upon the one considered most worthy!" The crowd listened intently, caught in the ritual moment as the Merlin turned to face the Prince and asked, "By what right do you claim to be the leader of battles and defender of the people?"

"By my proven strength in battle, through the blood of the royal line of the Votadini people from which I was sired, and with the acknowledgement of the kings, princes and the common people of Briton."

"Declare yourself to the people," the Merlin commanded.

"I am Owain ap Einion ap Cunedda ap Edeyrn ap Padarn Beisrudd ap Tegid. I stand before you all as your servant, not just the people of Viroconium and the Votadini clans, but all who claim the blood of the Celts as their own. To all the Celtic nation I give my soul, my body and my sword; this is my unbreakable oath."

The voices of the swarm thundered their reply across the meadow, shaking the veil between worlds that only fractured when the opaque, rainbow shades of Samhain walked between worlds and times. Owain felt the shifting veil without knowing what it was, and turning in a full circle, his sword still pointing to the sky, a window in his mind opened and he saw the ripples of Annwn's gateway-pool, shimmering over the heads of the people. The ripples stilled into a black mirror, a cavernous hollow that cleared to free the faces of ancient souls he'd never met, but in that moment, he believed he knew them.

On the city wall a horn sounded and, Owain's vision faded so he lowered his sword. Turning to face the city, he saw the parting crowds reveal two beautiful, dark-haired women dressed in animal skins, carrying the polished bronze shield of the Votidini people. King Einion, Prince Cadwallon, Bedwyr and Cai walked to the women, who bowed to the King and held the shield high, turning its polished brilliance in a circle so that all may look upon the seal of kings and Pendragons. Lowering the bronze, the women held it for the Merlin to bless. Placing one hand upon it, he called to the Goddess in the language of the druids, his invocation felt by everyone in the meadow. The Merlin then took the shield from the women and offered it to King Einion, who placed his hands beneath the rim. Prince Cadwallon, Bedwyr and Cai did the same and, together they carried the shield to the stone. With their heads bowed, the four men humbly held the shield at Owain's feet.

With the crowds cheering, the Prince stepped onto the warm bronze nobly, reminding himself he wasn't a god, just a man with a sword. The Merlin waited for the noise to subside, before calling to the crowds, "Behold, Owain ap Einion, Prince of Rhos and Pendragon, son of a king, defender of all the Britons!"

The shield was raised to shoulder height as Owain thrust his silver sword up to the sun, and the crowd burst into a thanksgiving song, the song of 'Bran the Blessed'. The people sang as Owain was carried around the meadow so that everyone could see him, his sword catching the sunlight above the singing, cheering and smiling faces.

The four nobles carried the new Pendragon to the west mound, where the kings and princes waited, many of them watching in arrogant, envious silence. On top of the mound, King Caw of the Picts turned to his many sons with a defiant sneer darkening his face. "I'll never bow to this so-called Pendragon; I'll break my sword before I kneel to the whelp of King Uther."

Huail ap Caw was the first to reply, "I doubt the other kings will stand with you. They are weak, they fear King Einion so will bow to him and his sons for as long as they must. But I've conjured a plan that will culminate in the death of Owain."

Caw looked mischievously at his son. "Tell me about it later; if I can help you, I will."

"If he was a Christian, I'd bow to him," Gildas ap Caw, dressed in his priest's robes, joined the conversation. "Our people need a strong war-leader, but he doesn't follow Jesus so I can't support him, instead, I must condemn him to eternal damnation."

The shield carrying the Prince came to a halt before the kings. He looked up at them then turned to face the common people, snubbing their royal dignities. "You, the many peoples of our ancient tribes have made me Pendragon," he began his address, "and I promise I'll use my sword for the good of you all, protecting those who cannot fight for themselves. My sword is a sword of freedom, fired and tempered to bring unity and peace to our nation. This sword doesn't belong to me, this blade is yours!"

Understanding something different was happening, the crowd remained silent but expectant. Owain turned back to face the nobles. "You are the kings and princes of the Britons, born to privilege, riches and power. Whatever you might think, your people weren't born to serve you, you were given your authority to serve, protect and nurture them. They are the power behind your thrones, and if you forget that, I shall not. I was given this sword to unite, not divide, and I tell you nobles that our people shall be one, a single Celtic nation sharing a common cause, and if I must make this so with my sword, that's what I will do. You are either with the people or against them, make your choice now and live by that choice. Come, you who call yourselves royal, give your allegiance to myself and our people, or leave this place and prepare for war!"

As his words faded, a gentle murmur of anticipation spread amongst the commoners. The Prince hadn't simply challenged the kings, he'd removed their power, giving it instead to the people. All eyes turned to the mound, eager to see how the nobles would react. King Erbin of the Dumnonians was the first to move. He walked slowly down the slope, stopped in front of the shield and lowered his head, exposing the back of his neck. Held high on the shield, Owain gently pressed the soul of his foot onto the back of Erbin's neck, accepting the Dumnonian's submission. The crowd cheered as one by one the nobles reluctantly followed King Erbin's example, only King Caw and his sons turned their backs on the new Pendragon, and walked away.

A rider splashed through the stream that cut through a valley not far to the east of Viroconium. Urging his mount up the valley-side, he heeled the horse to push it harder because the news he carried must reach the High King before it was too late for Einion to react to the invasions. Having crested the hill known as the Wrekin, the steaming horse galloped down the slope and raced for Viroconium's meadow. Bedwyr, putting half-a-dozen infantry recruits through their first day of training in the meadow, saw the galloper charging his way, so he raised his arm to halt the rider.

Owain wasn't given the time to enjoy his new status, news arrived of the Saxon incursions the day after the kings and princes had left Viroconium. He was with Cadwallon and Einion in the High King's private room, discussing how to deal with the possible threat from King Caw and his Picts, when Bedwyr rushed in, and between gasped breaths he said, "King Aelle's Saxons are invading from the south, and King Wihstan's warriors have crossed our eastern border!"

"Where in the south?" Einion asked.

"Glevum. Could I have a cup of wine, I ran all the way from the practice meadow?"

"And the Angles are marching west?" Cadwallon asked as he poured a cup.

Bedwyr took the wine and swallowed it in three gulps. "Yes, two hundred of their warriors are rowing and marching towards the Middleland Forest."

"If they are invading from two directions," Einion began, "we must send the Legion east and the infantry south. There isn't time to fight off one then attack the other."

"It's our only option," Cadwallon agreed. "I'll lead the infantry south."

Einion felt for the hilt of his sword, excited by the prospect of going to war again. "King Aelle must take Glevum before moving north."

"I'll order the Viroconium infantry to march immediately," Cadwallon said, wondering why Owain hadn't joined the discussion.

"Yes," Einion agreed, "get going."

"Isn't there something you are both forgetting?" Owain asked, looking from one to the other.

"What would that be?" Exerting his authority, the King puffed out his chest.

"I am the Pendragon, and whilst I am happy to be guided by you, all decisions concerning wars are mine to take." He then asked Bedwyr if the messenger had said anything else?

"Yes. King Wihstan has positioned two groups of twenty spearmen along either bank of the river, to deter flanking attacks. By the time we are ready to leave, they may be less than two days' ride from here!"

"What about archers, do they have any?" Owain asked, already planning how to defeat the boatmen.

"No, and they burn their campfires high at night," Bedwyr said. "As for the Saxons at Glevum, they burned villages and small towns as they marched north."

Pacing the room while he thought, Owain stopped, looked at Bedwyr and said, "This doesn't feel right to me. Saxons don't lay siege to cities; they fight their battles in the open. Why are they............"

"They want us to know they are coming," Bedwyr cut in.

"There's only one reason they'd do that," Owain said to the Dragon. "Prepare the Legion to ride immediately, and make sure every man takes his hunting bow. Then tell Cai to ready four of the five centuries of the Viroconium infantry, they'll be marching to Glevum."

Bedwyr saluted and left the room.

Einion was quick to raise his doubts. “Why send only four centuries? If we send all five, we’ll have a better chance of forcing the Saxons back into their own lands.”

“Why would Wihstan want us to know he’s coming?” the Pendragon asked, pouring himself a cup of wine.

“You suspect diversions, with a third attack directed at Viroconium?” Einion asked.

“I do. If I ride east while Cadwallon marches south, the city will be open to attack, that much is obvious, so you, Father, must remain here. Can you hold the city walls with one hundred infantrymen?”

“Yes, if the city gates are closed before the Saxons reach them. When you’ve dealt with Wihstan, you must ride back fast, one hundred warriors won’t hold the walls for more than three or four days.”

“A twilight curfew must be instigated until the Legion returns,” Owain suggested. “There’s enough open space between the edge of the forest and the city wall for a Saxon charge to be seen during the day, so expect a dusk or night attack.”

“I would have done that anyway,” the King replied, puffing out his chest again. “I have done this before; I am not a fool.”

“I’m sorry, but I had to make sure. If there is another Saxon force, they’d come through the forest to maintain secrecy, in fact they could already be in place. Scouts should be sent into the forest, because if I am right, Viroconium is the main target.”

12.

Having tortured and executed a Celtic scout caught near his camp, King Aelle, wrapped in his fur cloak, sat uncomfortably with his back against a tree. The falling Sun was close to breathing it's last for the day, fading into deep reds and purples it sank into the treetops; soon the cold night would ache his bones and he felt old, wishing he hadn't made the journey north. He could have remained by his hearth, enjoying his choice of buxom maids but, suffering the privations of a spring campaign was vital, his dead son must be avenged. Seeing Algar running through the camp towards him, he got to his feet and asked eagerly, "Have they left the city, is it time to march?"

"Yes, the entire Legion has galloped east. About four hundred infantrymen marched south to attack your son, leaving no more than a single century inside Viroconium."

"Excellent! Do you know who led their warriors south and east?"

"No, My Lord, but King Einion's banner still hangs above the east gate-arch."

"They've taken the bait," Aelle said with boyish excitement. "How close are we to the edge of the forest?"

"About a thousand paces, we can be in position to attack before dark."

"Good, get the men ready to move. We'll be inside the city before they know what's hit them. It will be days before their horse-warriors return, by then their king will be dead, their city in ruins. Choose the warriors who'll hold the gate, and tell them to ride."

"Our scouts found a handful of horses only."

"That's all we'll need." Drawing his sword, Aelle licked his thumb and flicked the cold iron to test its cutting edge. "I'm going to enjoy this."

Crossing a ploughed field on their journey east, Owain's horsemen galloped towards a sparsely wooded hill. They'd ridden hard, and with the light fading the Pendragon decided his warriors and their horses needed to rest. Torn between pushing on to engage King Wihstan's warriors sometime after dawn, or making camp, he wrestled with his options. The second was a risk, if his plan was to work, he must attack the invaders before they reached the forest, because horse-warriors cannot charge through dense woodlands. Nearing the edge of the field, he saw a rider at the top of the hill so he raised his hand to halt the column, and watched the horseman charge down the slope and into the ploughed field-ruts in a flurry of flying dirt. "The edge of the forest is beyond the hill!" Bedwyr shouted as his horse slid to a halt beside the Pendragon's.

"Should we keep going or make camp?" Owain asked while the rider caught his breath.

"We are close to where the River Ouse enters the woodlands, we should ride on until we reach the river valley."

Owain turned in his saddle, his men looked exhausted and he was tempted to halt their journey. "How long will it take us to reach the river?" he asked, wanting to attack Wihstan's warriors before nightfall.

Checking the position of the sun, Bedwyr said, "We could be there before sunrise. There isn't much daylight left, but if we ride hard, we'll reach the river in time to get some sleep."

"Don't you ever tire?" Owain joked. "You might have limitless energy but our warriors are exhausted. We'll camp here tonight, then ride before dawn."

"Are you sure?" Bedwyr asked. "If the Angles reach the forest, we'll never get them out."

"I'd rather keep our warriors fresh for battle than engage the Angles with two hundred tired men and horses. Set the night guards, we'll have some food and discuss how we'll attack without getting our feet wet."

In Viroconium's guardroom, Einion looked over the parchment plan of the city, discussing with Cai how to deploy their century of spearmen. "You know what, Cai, I'm not sure that one hundred warriors will be enough."

"I've ordered the militia to act as sentries," Cai replied.

"How many militiamen?"

"Fifty-four answered the duty call, but they are not trained warriors. They can throw spears and use bows, but if it came to hand to hand fighting their lives would be cheaply spent, not one of them can use a sword."

"Desperate times," Einion mused. "When the Sun sets, militiamen walking the ramparts will look like warriors, which might be enough to deter the Saxons from attacking."

"I'll order them to man the walls before ringing the night bell and closing the gates." Cai wasn't convinced the Saxons would be so easily fooled, even in the dark an armour-less man holding a spear looks nothing like a helmeted warrior wearing chainmail.

"Half of them should be enough, split the militia into two shifts. Order our infantrymen to remain in their barracks, I want them fresh for battle. Open the armoury and see if there are any useable shields, mail-byrnies and helmets. The militia might not be warriors, but they'll feel like warriors if they are better armed."

"I'll see that it's done."

"With the militia on the walls, our infantrymen will be free to sally out, should they need to." Tapping his finger on the map, Einion said, "Half our warriors will protect the east gateway, it's the most vulnerable part of our defences. The city walls are too high to scale, so we'll leave them to the militia."

Cai wasn't sure that was wise. "Some of our infantrymen should at least man the wall above the east gate, while the rest wait in the courtyard, just in case the Saxons fire the gate, it's a tactic they've used before."

"I agree, the Saxons will want to get men into the city quickly, if they fail, we could hold out for days. Order a centurion to organise women into bucket-chains, just in case the gates are torched. Have all the scouts you sent into the forest returned?"

"No, one is unaccounted for."

"So, King Aelle is definitely out there somewhere." The High King trailed his finger along the line of trees drawn on the edge of the map. "We don't know how many spearmen King Aelle has, but they'll be his finest warriors. Saxons never attack at night; my guess is they'll come at us when the Sun rises. Let's make sure we are ready to meet them in the morning."

"The Sun hasn't fully set," Cai pointed out.

"Saxons don't attack fortified cities during the height of the midday sun, let alone when it's going down, so I'd guess we've one more night to make sure we are well prepared."

Militiamen wearing rusty chainmail and helmets taken from the armoury, climbed the steps to Viroconium's battlements as the falling Sun faded beyond the western hills. It was time for the curfew-bell to be rung and the gates closed. With militiamen taking their sparse positions along Viroconium's four walls, and the infantrymen ready to sally out from their barracks when the alarm bell rang, the city seemed secure. Still looking at the map in the guardroom, Einion felt certain the Saxons wouldn't attack tonight because scaling the city walls in the dark would be suicide. "You won't be needing that," he said to Cai, who was strapping on his sword-belt just in case King Aelle chose to defy logic.

"The Sun hasn't set," the Dragon reminded the King. "I'll order the curfew-bell rung and the gates closed."

"You may as well, I doubt any more travellers will arrive tonight."

Walking across the cobbled courtyard, Cai glanced along the battlements of the south wall, where most of the Militiamen had been posted. Approaching the bell tower overlooking the east gateway, he looked up when a militiaman shouted down from the battlements, "Riders, three horsemen closing from the east!"

Cai assumed they could only be messengers from the Legion. "Are they wearing red cloaks?" he called up, then he signalled the two gatemen to come to arms.

"I think so!" the militiaman shouted down, "and there's a small group of Saxon horsemen chasing them!"

Panicked shouts of "Saxons!" from the three riders, caught everyone's attention.

"Close the gates the moment the three riders are inside," Cai ordered.

"Saxons!" the riders yelled again as they charged for the gateway.

Cai watched with horror as the three horsemen rode beneath the arch, lowering their spears. Having caught the Celts unawares, the first two riders speared both gatekeepers before they could defend themselves or close the gates. The third rider tried to skewer Cai, but he rolled away. Leaping from their horses, the three red-cloaked Saxons formed a short shield-wall just inside the gate-arch. A heartbeat later, the following group of horsemen were dismounting to join their sword-brothers.

Scrambling to his feet while drawing his sword, Cai yelled, "Saxons in the city! Ring the bell!"

"Come on!" King Aelle shouted to his hidden warriors, and with the alarm bell clanging hopefully-wild, the edge of the woodlands sprang to life and hundreds of Saxons ran for Viroconium's east gates. Charging through the gloomy twilight with swords, spears and battle-axes ready to kill, they poured across the meadow, their battle-cries echoing off the walls as they overtook their fat King, who knew he'd caught the Celts cold.

Within moments of King Aelle's call to attack, hordes of warriors were streaming through the open gateway. More Saxons joined the shield-wall in the courtyard, while others ran for the stone steps that led to the ramparts. King Aelle was the last to enter the city and, seeing a dozen or so Celts organising themselves into a shield-wall, he laughed with relief and pleasure, taking the city would be easier than he'd thought.

Bellowing a command, he joined his warriors and the wall of shields and spears moved slowly forward, thrashing their weapons against their shields as they surged towards the few organised Celts. The rhythmic pounding of weapons was a sound he loved and, following a pace behind his warriors, he clenched his teeth as the thunderous din bounced from building to wall to building. Not wanting to miss out on the killing, he pushed into the centre of the front line, roaring his challenge to the Celts, knowing that Wlencing's killers were as good as dead.

Hearing clashing weapons and the tolling bell, infantrymen ran out from their barracks, shocked to see so many Saxons bringing death to their city. Cai had managed to form a short battle-line with the first few warriors to respond to the alarm, but it was nowhere near enough to stop the flood. Some of the infantrymen ran to bolster Cai's line, while others, seeing the militiamen on the walls being slaughtered, went to help.

Pointing his sword at the approaching Saxons, the City Dragon urged his shield-wall forward but they wouldn't move, fear had them rooted. Cai bravely, and perhaps foolishly began slowly walking towards the Saxon shield-wall. Heavily outnumbered, his spearmen realised the gravity of the situation so one by one they swallowed their fear and strode forward, knowing they were walking to their deaths. They might buy some time and that was all, but it could be enough time for the arriving infantrymen to form a stronger wall of shields behind them.

With the two lines closing, Cai prepared himself for the first clash of swords and shields. Stepping reluctantly towards the snarling face of the Saxon directly in front of him, he heard shouts and fighting coming from the ramparts, as well as screams from women and children. Also, he was sure that flickering flame-shadows were moving on the darkening east wall. Looking to his left and right, he guessed about fifty warriors were with him. Not enough to force the advancing Saxons back through the gate, but enough to make a fight of it. "Phelan," he said to the man next to him. "Round up as many women and children as you can, and get them into the temple, we'll hold the Saxons here until you are safe inside, with the doors barricaded."

"What about the rest of you?"

"Go! Before it's too late!" The advancing Saxons were only a few paces away, so Cai raised his sword and shouted his order,

"Halt!" Celtic shields locked together as sweat-slicked hands held tight to weapons.

"Kill them!" King Aelle bellowed.

With fires licking the falling dusk, the roaring Saxons threw themselves forward, meeting the Celtic wall in an ear-splitting, metallic crash and swords, axes, spears and shields came together in ringing blows. Swinging swords and axes chopped and slashed, ripping and hacking at shields to expose bodies; blades sliced into faces, necks and shoulders; sword pommels jabbed into squelching eyes, cheeks and lips; thrusting swords and spears skewered groins, thighs and bellies as the fire-shadows ghosted Viroconium's walls.

King Aelle's more solid wall of warriors rained down blow after blow, shattering bit by bloody bit the Celtic line. Hack and push, hack and push, an endless Saxon killing rhythm, each forward step forcing the shrinking Celtic line back across the courtyard towards the temple steps.

Fighting to keep his balance as Saxon shields pushed him back, Cai ducked and a vicious blow swished over his head, then he thrust his sword into the armpit of the axeman. The axeman yelled to Woden and choked on his own blood as a sword punched through his throat. "Give ground!" Cai shouted, hoping to be heard above the battle-din. "Give ground fighting!"

A long-handled axe swung down, hooked the rim of Cai's shield and ripped it from his sweaty grip. Unprotected, he backed out of the line, which automatically closed in front of him. Taking a few exhausted breaths, he took stock of the many one-sided battles within the city. On the walls the militiamen had been cut to pieces, to his left he saw warriors being hacked down as they emerged from their burning barracks. He saw Saxons running from street to street and house to house, killing without mercy, murdering a city. Anyone could see that fighting on was a futile gesture, so he'd a decision to make. Phelan, herding into the temple the few old men, women and children he'd found alive, called to the Dragon but his words were swallowed by the battle-din.

Cai saw a child-carrying woman run out of a burning building. "No!" he yelled as she was slashed in the back by a Saxon axe. She fell to her knees still clutching the child as her home collapsed in an eruption of black smoke and spiralling embers. He ran to help but before he was close enough to strike, the Saxon tore the screaming child from its mother and casually tossed it into the red glow of the collapsed building. Cai stopped in his tracks, appalled by the unnecessary brutality, then threw himself at the Saxon, who doubled over as the Celt's sword cut into his guts.

With flames leaping into the night and, Celts falling everywhere he looked, Cai knew what must be done so he ran back to the temple steps and called to his men, "Fall back! fall back to me!" His warriors disengaged and ran to form a defensive line behind him, bracing themselves for another attack as the last of their surviving women and children fled up the temple steps.

Seeing the Celts forming a pathetically short battle-line on the steps, King Aelle wiped sweat from his blood-spattered brow and, ordered his spearmen forward. Slamming the flat of his bloodied blade against his shield, whilst stomping out a rhythm his warriors could kill by, he yelled to his warriors, "Kill them all!"

With somewhere near two hundred blood-hungry Saxons striding towards him, Cai made an instinctive decision. "Into the temple, run for your lives!" he shouted, and ran for the open oak doors, followed by the last of his spearmen.

Slamming and barring the doors behind them, the Celts built a flimsy barricade with whatever furniture they could find, and in the total darkness they collapsed, exhausted, their tired minds deaf to the screams of those outside, caught in the death throes of Viroconium. Hoping his few dozen people would be safe here, Cai thanked the Romans for building the temple's high stone walls and tiled roof. Then a sickening thought hit him, where was King Einion?

King Einion grabbed his doublehanded broadsword and ran out of the guardroom as soon as he heard the clanging bell. Before he could cross the courtyard to join Cai's faltering shield-wall, he and the few warriors fighting with him found themselves cut off by a thick press of Saxon spearmen. Powerless to prevent the killing and burning, he stood his ground and swung his heavy sword in wild cutting arcs, fighting to escape the corner he'd been backed into. The few fighting alongside him died quickly, falling beneath a blizzard of killing strokes.

Not sure of what to make of Cai's retreat into the temple, which from what he could see was the only building not burning, Einion gripped the hilt of his broadsword with both hands and growled a challenge to the hesitant Saxons. With flickering flames reflecting from his chainmail-byrnie, he looked like a giant war-god only a fool would challenge. Urged on by one of their battle-lords, the snarling wolves closed, their flame-filled eyes peering over their shields as the semi-circle of death moved in for the kill. Standing alone in the dark corner, his pointing sword challenging the wary pack of wolves, King Einion prepared himself to kill and be killed.

Determined not to die a coward's death, he took a giant step forward and began swinging his heavy blade in a figure of eight, stepping closer to his enemies with each rotation of the broadsword. "Come and die!" he bellowed, splitting a Saxon's head clean in two. Seeing the skull-splitting power of the powerful swordsman, the Saxons backed away. "Come on you cowards!" he screamed at them. "Die like men!"

The Saxons edged together, linking themselves into a strong shield-wall, keeping their heads low as the mighty sword clanged against and bounced off their shields. Behind them, a second line formed to support the front rank. The Celt's broadsword crashed down, crunching through a Saxon helmet. The dead man flopped forward, his brains spilling onto the cobbled yard. Another man reluctantly took his place, ducking just in time to avoid the swinging blade that severed the head of the man standing next to him. A warrior thrust his spear, catching the forearm of the bear-like Celt, who roared with pain when the spearpoint sliced along his lower arm.

With the tendons of his left wrist cut, Einion retreated, holding his sword one-handed. Edging towards the defensive comfort of the wall, he felt his ankle touch the soot-smeared stone as a spear flew and slashed the inside of his thigh. Dropping to one knee, he snarled at the warriors moving in for the kill. Gritting his teeth against the pain, he forced himself to his feet and raised his heavy sword as the arc of Saxons edged closer.

Trapped like a wounded, cornered bear he braced himself for battle as a dozen spearmen ran at him. Taking a great gulp of air, the bull-of-a-man summoned every bit of his failing strength, let out a mighty roar and began circling his sword above his head. Moving forward in huge, limping strides, swinging the heavy blade in as wide a cutting-arc as he could manage, he hammered into the shields and spears, the weight of his sword hacking through flesh and chainmail like they were soggy bread. High King Einion, once known as Uther the Pendragon, came on, hacking, slashing, maiming and killing, screaming his wounded fury for what he knew would be the last time. Scything through flesh and bone, flooding the courtyard with Saxon blood as men dropped like stalks of harvested wheat, he twisted and turned, killing with every swing of his broadsword.

With adrenalin feeding his battle-lust he felt young again, so he forced his great bulk forward, driven by the strength and courage that had won him his name. Slicing his sword through faces, flesh and bones he killed without mercy, unaware of the cuts and stabs wounding red his unprotected limbs. He saw the flashing Saxon blades but he was numb to the pain they caused, while his rotating sword hacked, chopped and sliced into warriors scrambling to get away.

Smelling blood and bile and stinking guts and, stepping over the butchered remains of the men he'd killed, the fighting King swung his sword and splintered an upturned shield, severed an arm and his blade slashed across the back of a running man's neck. Was he floating, he wondered as he killed, his battle-roar more like a song than the screams of pain emanating from his gaping mouth? Feeling cold pain stab into his back, he twisted his body and swung his sword, the vicious slice sending a head spiralling into the flame-lit dusk.

Once again something crunched into his back and, wracked with pain he dropped to his knees, surrounded and exhausted. Glancing over his shoulder, he wondered why his killers were backing away. "Cowards!" he spat at them. Ignoring the many wounds leaking his life-blood, breathing heavily and turning on his knee to face the largest group of watching spearmen, he waited for them to kill him. "Cowards!" he heard his own shout bounce from the walls of collapsed, burning buildings. "Who wants to kill a king?" he bellowed. "What are you waiting for?" he roared to the reluctant wolves. Clenching his blood-smeared teeth, he snarled a challenge to the fat man who was pushing through the circle of shields and spears. "You!" he raged, pointing his blade. "Fat man, you fight me!" The tip of his sword dropped with a clang to the cobblestones. Looking at the bloody point, he realised his many wounds were releasing the last of his strength. Not wanting to die on his knees, he tried forcing himself to his feet, but his strength had gone. Lowering his head, he felt a tear slide down his blood-freckled cheek.

"Are you King Einion of the defeated Celts?" the fat man asked in well-spoken Celtic.

"I am," he replied weakly, his sideways glance warning the man not to come any closer. "Who are you?"

"King Aelle of the South Saxons; your executioner."

Leaning heavily on his sword, the dying Celt looked down at the blood-soaked cobblestones, his weak laugh sinking into his defeated reflection. Looking back at the Saxon, he clenched his teeth against the pain, and again vainly tried to force himself to his feet. Shaking his head, he whispered over the bodies of the dead he'd slaughtered, "Make it quick, Saxon, if you don't, I'll kill you."

"You haven't the strength," Aelle said as he walked forward, kicked the defenceless King's sword away and laughed when the Celt fell flat on his face. "What does Saxon blood taste like? Lap it up, enjoy your last meal in this life."

Gasping for air, the dying King glared with hate as Aelle pressed the point of his blade against the blood-slicked skin of Einion's throat. "Before I kill you, Celt, I want you to know that I am here because your second whelp drove his sword into my second son's chest."

"I couldn't give a shit about your stinking runt! And know this, Aelle the fart, my sons will avenge this slaughter, you won't live long enough to enjoy your small victory!" Einion winced as the Saxon's sword pricked the skin next to his windpipe.

"That's if they are still alive, King Einion the dead. This is for Wlencing!" Aelle pressed down on his sword, turning the blade as the body jerked. King Einion sighed and his shrieking soul fled its mortal flesh.

13.

Viroconium, the city the Romans had built, burned throughout the night. Raging fires collapsed buildings into piles of smoking rubble, charred timbers and white-hot ashes. Hundreds of corpses littered the streets and courtyards, some fully clothed, others not. The city had died with its king, but who would weep for the dead, who remained to mourn and rebuild?

King Aelle, walking with Algar amongst the dead and the groaning dying, came to where King Einion's body lay, surrounded by a flesh-strewn butcher's yard of slaughtered Saxons. "Is this what you brought me to see?" Algar asked, stepping over bits of dead warriors to get a closer look at the man. Turning the body over, he said to Aelle, "He is covered in wounds, how many men did it take to kill him?"

"I killed him," Aelle said proudly. "I considered hacking his body to pieces but, I couldn't bring myself to do it."

"Why not?"

"He was a brave man and a true warrior. I hope his god welcomes and feasts him well, he deserves every horn of ale his ancestors raise to him." Picking up the dead King's sword, Aelle felt its weight, surprised by how much strength would be needed to wield it. "If the rest of his warriors had fought like him, we might be feasting with Woden tonight." Dropping the sword into a pool of King Einion's congealed blood, Aelle turned as a warrior approached him. The spearman saluted the King. "My Lord, a small group of Celts have barricaded themselves inside one of the buildings."

"Which building?"

"The only one that isn't burning." The man pointed to the temple across the courtyard.

Had it all been worth it, Aelle thought as he led Algar and the messenger across the courtyard? His revenge had been total, he'd killed a king and raised Viroconium to the ground. Sneering at dead Celts littering the blood-pooled cobbles, he picked his way towards the temple. Climbing the temple steps, he stopped when he saw a small group of Celtic women and children being led at spearpoint towards him.

"These are all the Celts we found alive, My Lord," a warrior informed him.

"Well, deal with them."

"Yes, My Lord, but we thought you might like some new slaves to warm your bed."

"I'm not interested, do what you want with them."

The prisoners were led away, and Aelle turned his attention back to the Celts inside the temple. Laying the palm of his hand flat against the solid, oakwood doors he considered the time it would take to smash his way in, and how many of his warriors might die beyond the doors. "Have we plundered everything we can carry?" he asked Algar, kicking away a severed head that in death seemed to be smiling up at him.

"We have, though there wasn't much worth taking, what with the fires and the buildings collapsing."

“Then forget these Celts, someone needs to live to spread the word of how I deal with those who kill my sons. We’ve done what we came here to do, their king is dead and his city isn’t worth a silver coin. Kill every prisoner, then order the muster, we leave as soon as we’ve gathered our dead and wounded.”

Walking back across the courtyard towards the east gate-arch, he saw the first rays of the new Sun pricking through the last of the night. A villa wall crashed into smoky dust, dirtying his face with windblown soot while to his right his men were slitting the throats of the wailing and screaming Celtic women and children. Picking his way back to where King Einion lay, Aelle lifted the dead man’s sword, looked along its bloody length and turned to face the rising sun. “Woden!” he called to his god, and every Saxon in the courtyard stopped what they were doing to listen and watch. “By the blood on this sword I swear I’ll have Owain ap Einion’s head before the autumn leaves fall! I’ll not rest until the Celtic whelp’s body has been hacked apart and fed to my hounds!” Turning back to the body, he spoke to the corpse, “King Einion of the Celts, if I meet you in the afterlife, you’ll be needing this.” He rammed the blade into Einion’s chest and left it there. “Nobody touches that sword,” he said to Algar. “Post a guard until we leave, the sword is a message for the killer of my son.”

Shame and guilt are heavy burdens to carry, more so if such exhausting emotions are worn by the leader of warriors. Tired eyes might search the dark for excuses and reasons, but truth is what is required, acceptance and an understanding that the guilty must answer for their actions, and pay the required price.

Within the gloom of the unlit temple, the wounded groaned while the children wept into the dark. Cai hung his head in shame as he walked amongst the unmoving, forlorn grey figures sleeping on benches or slumped against walls. Not many warriors had escaped the slaughter, nor had more than a few dozen women and children. One of his warriors, a centurion, was slowly bleeding to death from an axe-gash in his belly, and Cai wished he was that man because he deeply regretted running from the battle when his people needed him to stand and fight.

He could understand why few of the survivors wanted to talk, the horrors they'd witnessed would haunt their dreams for as long as they lived. As for the heart-breaking, blood-boiling screams they'd heard outside, they'd been enough to drive a spear into the heart of the coldest soul. How the survivors hadn't been driven to madness by what they'd seen and heard was beyond him, he'd certainly felt a touch of anxious madness when hearing the screams and cries for help beyond the thick, oak doors. Darkness doesn't mask suffering, it enhances it.

As the clashing metal and screams of battle had subsided, the sound of aftermath told its own grim story. Punctuated by the barks and snarls of fighting dogs, collapsing buildings were all the survivors could here: no moans from the wounded filtered in; pleas for mercy had long since been silenced; violated women no longer screamed for release. The vulgar sounds of the Saxon language had also fled into the fading night, so it was probably safe to go outside.

Stroking the hair of a weeping girl curled up on a bench, Cai shamefully remembered how some of his warriors, the ones with families outside, had begged him to tear down the barricade so they could return to the fighting. But he'd stood with his sword drawn in front of the piled-up benches and chairs, warning them not to come too close because he'd use the weapon if he had to.

Walking to the front of the temple, he saw the first rays of sunlight creep under the doors, the time had come for him to lead the survivors out. His warriors also noticed the thin light seeping beneath the piled barricade, so they looked at him, waiting for orders. Not wanting to see the truth of what must be faced, he hesitated, giving himself the excuse that he must be sure the Saxons were far enough away, before he removed the barricade. In the dark he couldn't quite see his warriors angry, unforgiving looks but he could feel their hate. "We should open the doors, Cai," Phelan deliberately accentuated the Dragon's name, adding a touch of derision.

"We can't be sure yet," the Dragon pleaded.

"Sure, of what?" a man called from a dark corner.

"That it's safe to walk out."

"It might never be safe for one of us to walk the streets," another voice remarked.

"The Saxons have left," Phelan said, stepping closer to confront his Dragon. "Put up your sword, Cai, let us search for our dead loved ones."

"But I can't, not……,"

"Oh, but you can," Phelan insisted. Leaning forward, he seethed into the Dragon's ear, "Out there in the streets and courtyards our people are being picked apart by hungry cats, dogs and carrion birds. You know people who've died, what are you waiting for?"

"We don't know that it's safe yet."

"My wife is out there!" Phelan placed the flat of his sword on Cai's belly as a warning. "I want to protect what's left of her from hungry animals! Will you get out of my way, or must I kill you?"

More angry warriors stepped forward to join Phelan. Having little choice, Cai sheathed his sword and turned to face the barricade. Grabbing a bench, he pulled it free and the defensive pile collapsed. His warriors sprang forward to help clear the way as Phelan lifted the heavy door-bar, threw it to one side and opened the oak doors. Stepping aside as dawn light flooded in, he let the other warriors run past him before leaving to begin his gruesome search. The burning city helped the brightening dawn illuminate the savagery they didn't want to see, and as they ran down the steps most of them stopped, appalled by the aftermath of slaughter. A warrior vomited, there were hundreds of butchered, burned and mutilated corpses littering the courtyard and streets.

Seeing the hundreds of mutilated corpses, made Cai want to vomit, and walking amongst the dead he couldn't believe the pain twisted into the soot-smeared, tear-stained faces of the many victims. This wasn't war, he'd witnessed the aftermath of battle enough to know it wasn't like this. What kind of animals could rape and butcher a child, what drives humans to such savagery? Forcing himself to pick his way through the butchery, pathetic shame strangled his tired emotions: why hadn't he died protecting these people?

Walking into a corpse littered street with his head bowed, dragging his fingers along the soot-smeared remnant of a collapsed wall, he heard a crying child. Stepping over body parts and toeing his way around pools of blood, he followed the sound to a smouldering, tumbled-down and smoke-blackened house. Stepping inside what remained, he crunched over blackened roof-tiles, pushing aside charred and smoking timbers to where he could see a dark-haired, soot-covered girl curled up in the corner. He guessed she could have no more than ten summers behind her, not that he could tell because she was curled up so tight, and almost completely blackened with soot.

As soon as he'd entered the smoking ruin, she'd covered her face with her dirty hands and, she tried curling tighter into the corner. Understanding her fear, he knelt a few paces in front of her, holding out the palms of his hands to show he meant no harm. Squinting warily through her fingers, her red-rimmed eyes begged him to stay back.

Shuffling his feet to get a little closer, his right foot trod on something soft. Shifting a rooftile, he saw what looked like a finger, but it was so badly burned he couldn't be sure. Swallowing back bile, he shifted more tiles and his heart broke. The burnt and blistered body of what was probably the child's mother, turned his stomach and he vomited. Wiping his mouth, he wondered how the girl had survived the flames and the collapse of her home? Seeing a chance to redeem himself a little, he spoke to the child as softly as his parched throat would allow, “Don’t be afraid. I am Cai, the city Dragon, I’m here to help you.” The girl looked at the remains of her mother, then back at the kneeling warrior. Reluctant to move any closer, Cai held out his hand and said, “I can’t fix what has happened, but I can help you feel safe again, if you’ll let me.” She looked at him through soot-smeared eyes, the tracks of her tears clear on her dirty face. He saw no trust in her, which didn’t surprise him, only the future would shed light on what she’d been through. Lowering his hand, he spoke to her again, “Can you tell me your name?”

“Kareen,” she whispered. “Do you know my father?”

“What’s his name?”

The girl, searching for a memory that had been driven to another place by the shock of the night, didn’t immediately answer. Again, she looked at her mother’s remains, then back at the kneeling man. “He is Calin, the keeper of the east gate.”

Tears trickled from Cai’s eyes. He only knew one man named Calin, and he’d been one of the guards at the gate when the Saxon riders attacked. How could he tell her that both her parents were dead? Drying his tears, he said, “It isn’t safe here, Kareen, what’s left of the roof might collapse. Will you come with me?”

He held out his hand again, the girl looked at it and shook her head. Realising she wouldn’t be able to step over her dead mother, he stood and placed one leg on the other side of the body, then he leaned forward. She didn’t resist, melting easily into his arms as he picked her up. Stepping towards the almost complete, outer front wall, he remembered the slaughter awaiting them in the streets. "You must close your eyes," he told her, "and keep them closed until I tell you to open them. Can you do that for me?" She nodded and closed her eyes.

Moving as quickly as he could through the streets, he hoped she'd keep her eyes closed long enough for him to reach the temple. After climbing the temple steps, he stopped in the entrance, surprised to see that Kareen wasn't the only survivor. Others, mostly women and children, had made their way here because it was the only building untouched by fire and murder. Carrying the child towards the dais, he recognised Branwen, an inn keeper's daughter and a good friend. After telling Kareen she could open her eyes, he raised a hand to Branwen and beckoned her over. Her smile turned to concern when the child looked at her. "This is Kareen," he said to the woman. "Will you look after her while I help with the clear up?"

The woman held out her arms. Kareen moved easily into the softness of her ample bosom, the soft feel of a woman giving her familiar comfort. "I am Branwen," she said, smiling at the girl. "I'll look after you until Cai returns."

Having gathered his warriors, Cai ordered them to pile the bodies in the small courtyard on the other side of the temple and, post guards to keep hungry animals away from the dead. Leaving them to get on with their gruesome task, he made his way to the guardroom.

Glancing at the faces of the corpses littering the cobbles near the east gate, he began a search that filled him with dread. He had to find the bodies of King Einion, Princess Meddyf and the infant Prince Maelgwn. Taking deep breaths as he checked each body, he felt like running but told himself this was something he must do, for the sake of Cadwallon and Owain. It wasn't easy to see and walk amongst the slaughter, there were so many mutilated corpses to check and not all could be recognised as some were headless.

Nearing the guardroom, he saw a great circle of blood and what looked like a bloodied bundle of clothes and chainmail, with a sword standing at an angle in the pile. Walking closer, he saw it was a man with a sword rammed into his chest. The body was so hacked and slashed with wounds that he wasn't sure at first, but he quickly realised he had found King Einion.

The circle of blood, what did that mean he wondered, pulling the sword from the King's chest? There was so much it couldn't be Einion's, it must be the blood of many men but, where were they? The obvious occurred to him; all the dead in the city were Britons, the Saxons had taken their dead with them. Realising Einion must have caused great slaughter before being killed, he removed his cloak and lay it over the body. Kneeling, he closed the King's eyelids and whispered, "I'm sorry I ran."

Hearing a woman scream, he turned to face the courtyard where the dead were being piled, and he saw a grey figure holding a child, standing in the doorway that led down to the royal cellars. He was too far away to see who it was, but others, adults and children were following the woman out. Walking towards her, his heart leapt with relief and joy so he ran, calling out her name as he closed. Meddyf had survived, as had little Maelgwn.

Through the woodlands the unseen, grotesque souls of the ancients follow the horse-warriors, the salivating children of the Goddess Enaid eager for the killing to begin. The Sun might be bright and the night forgotten, but shades still move through the day, they don't need the dark-time to hide them because only those gifted with the sight can see their movements. At the forest's edge the horsemen halt their advance, the shades skimming through the undergrowth to the mass at the flanks.

Men will be lazy when the Sun shines, so on either bank of the Ouse River, warriors strolled towards the Middleland Forest, spears resting on shoulders, their shields thrown over their backs, enjoying the Sun and the pleasant walk through the green sprouting wheat fields. Between the two sets of flanking spearmen, the high prows of King Wihstan's war-boats could just be seen above the tall grass and reeds lining the riverbanks.

King Wihstan, sitting lazily with his back against the prow of the leading boat, enjoying the sun's warmth while chewing on a hunk of bread, threw a few pieces of crust to the ducks that had been following the boats all morning. Picking up a goat-skin of ale, he poured some of the brown liquid down his throat, wiped his hand across his mouth and called to the nearest boat, "Wuffa, if we haven't met any Celts before we reach the forest, we should row to the banks and wait for them in the meadow!"

"Suits me!" the Prince called back as his boat veered towards his father's. "Raise oars!" he suddenly yelled.

"Raise oars!" the King echoed to prevent their blades from clashing. Two banks of oars quickly lifted and Wuffa's boat slid alongside his father's, with a clunk and a grind. "That was close!" Wihstan laughed as the two keels scraped to a halt.

"Why don't you think we should enter the forest?" Wuffa called across.

"Because the Celts are bound to know we are coming, there could be a warrior hidden behind every tree, waiting for us to row into their trap."

"I could throw a spear into the forest from here, so why don't we head for the riverbank now? It won't take our warriors long to dig a defensive rampart."

"I hoped we'd have come across them by now," his father replied before pouring more ale down his throat. Standing, he rested his hands on the flat top of the prow and, he looked ahead. "I can't see that far upstream, the river curves to the right, just after entering the forest. Order the boats to row for the south bank."

Prince Wuffa shouted to the other boats, "Make for the south meadow, disembark and form a shield-wall!" He then asked his father, "What about the warriors on the other bank, shouldn't we ferry them across first?"

"No, send a boat across after we've secured our position."

The boats pulled towards the south riverbank. This far upstream the river wasn't at its widest, but was still about thirty paces across, which wasn't far to row so King Wihstan braced himself and waited for his boat to bump into the riverbank.

"Celts!" one of the warriors walking the south bank shouted. "Mounted warriors!"

"Row back to the middle!" Wihstan's panicked voice bellowed across the river. "Row for your lives!" Standing tall in the boat, he saw two hundred red-cloaked warriors casually ride out from the edge of the dark forest, and form four battle-lines in the scrubland.

"Second, third and fourth ranks, string your bows and draw your arrows!" Owain called to his warriors. "Front rank, ready your spears!" They'd practised this battle-charge many times, but with only twenty of King Wihstan's warriors forming a wall of shields and spears against them, the new tactic would hardly be tested. "Britannia!" the new Pendragon shouted.

"Britannia!" the Legion called back.

"Charge!"

Two hundred sets of pounding hooves thundered through the green sprouting wheat field, an uncountable number of the invisible dead following the charge, the howls of the snarling shades heard only by the Goddess. As Owain began lowering his spear, a shower of arrows flew over his head. Seeing the arrow-storm, Wihstan's twenty warriors instinctively raised their shields as the death-rain plummeted, just before fifty spears plunged into their exposed torsos.

"They have archers, row for the opposite bank!" Wihstan yelled, having watched the Celtic charge ride right over his flanking guards. "Row, hard you bastards!" Looking over his shoulder as he clung to the prow, he saw the cavalry wheel and ride to the riverbank. “Row, pull those oars or we are dead men!”

“Archers!” Owain’s voice was quickly answered by warriors drawing arrows from their quivers. “Rear rank, fire them high, front rank shoot them low!......... Loose!”

One hundred arrows flew high as the boatmen let go of their oars to reach for their shields. The arrowheads dipped and dropped towards the waiting shields, just as the low-aimed arrows stung into bodies.

“Loose high!” Owain ordered again. “Loose low!”

Shields fell and men rolled and screamed in pain, more arrows dropped, doubling their pain. Again, Owain’s order was repeated, and pointed iron shredded the panicking, scrambling spearmen. Wihstan didn’t know what to order his men to do, if they raised their shields, they were dead men, lower their shields and they were dead men. Some of his warriors leapt into the water to escape the stinging death, and the idea had crossed his mind but, he’d realised the weight of his mail-vest would pull him under.

Needing double protection with arrows falling from the sky or skimming across the river, some boatmen grabbed for other men’s shields. Individual fights broke out, causing enough chaos for helmsmen to be knocked aside. Boats turned and crunched into each other, jamming escape. More flights of arrows hit their targets and more Angles screamed in pain.

Prince Wuffa, crouching in one of the colliding boats, realised he’d no chance of surviving if he stayed where he was. His father’s boat, clear of the boat-jam, still had enough rowing warriors so it was pulling towards the opposite bank. Without thinking he forced himself to his feet and leapt onto the adjacent boat, then used his momentum to throw himself towards his father's keel. More Arrows dropped from the sky, and, leaping he felt a sharp pain pierce his shoulder. Screaming, he flew like a four-pointed star and landed with a crunching thud in his father's boat. A crack appeared in the planks beneath his chest, he rolled over, grimacing from his wound as water trickled through the breach.

"Lower your bows!" the Pendragon ordered.

"One of the boats has made it to the opposite bank, shouldn't we finish them off?" Bedwyr asked.

"We've done what we came to do, the survivors won't be back in a hurry." Owain watched the surviving warriors climb out of their boat and claw their way up the bank. "We ride hard and fast!" he called to his men while turning his horse. "Let's go home!"

Gulping in mouthfuls of air, King Wihstan lay exhausted on the riverbank. It had been a long time since he'd had to row a boat, he wasn't used to that kind of menial work. Wuffa, his shoulder bleeding, yanked out the arrow and slumped down beside his father. "Most of our men are dead," he said, catching his breath.

The King surveyed the chaotic scene floating downstream. Boatloads of dead or dying warriors, slumped over their oars, speared by more arrows than were needed to kill a man, drifted towards reed-beds, bumping past men face down in the water with arrows in their backs. "Why didn't King Aelle tell us the Celts now use archers and horse-warriors?" he growled to his son. Pointing a fat, wagging finger at Wuffa, he seethed through gritted teeth, "If

King Aelle knew there might be cavalry waiting for us, I'll kill the South Saxon son-of-a-drunkard's-fart!"

Having snatched the many souls of the dead, the unseen used the fear of the new to corral then herd their captives into the forest, where they would be held until the night fell and, the cave of Gwyn ap Nudd opened to welcome the slaughtered.

14.

Those who have the sight understand its burdens as well as its insights, and those who must regularly call upon the Goddess to show them images of what is to come, often feel the oppressive weight of knowing too much. That exposure-weight can sink a mind into a sucking mire of shocked madness, and sometimes the sufferer never returns to the land of the sane. In any walk of life respect is everything, and it should be total because if one slips into prejudice and judgement, two souls, not one, will feel strangled. The Merlin knows this, and will live by its meaning right up until the moment when his life is cruelly cut away from him.

Walking the earth rampart of the hurriedly built and, just as quickly abandoned Saxon fort, the Merlin turned to face the Sun setting beyond the charcoal walls of Glevum City. Since sunset the previous day he'd barely spoken a civil word to anyone, and the burden of what he knew was beginning to overwhelm him.

Keeping himself to himself, he'd spent the night sitting beneath a tree in contemplation, refusing both food and company. The images the sight had shocked into his brain had swamped him; he'd felt the first painful cut when Viroconium had succumbed to Saxon blades, and every time he closed his eyes the burning city flamed in his vision, as did the faces of the dead. The jarring thrust of the sword into King Einion's body had pierced his heart, the fleeing of the dead King's soul had had him gasping for breath. But no one saw or felt the Merlin's pain, it was his burden to carry, and though he wasn't sure on which day the slaughter had happened, he was certain that the images and feelings relayed the truth of the recent past. Shortly before dawn, Prince Cadwallon had asked him what was wrong but, all the Druid would say was: "The Wolves have feasted, soon enough the Bear will devour the Wolves."

For the four hundred spearmen of the Viroconium infantry, the march south had been fast and uneventful. Prince Cadwallon had allowed his warriors only the minimum of rest, to eat, drink and occasionally sleep because he believed the siege of Glevum was a diversion. As soon as Saxon scouts had seen the approaching Celts, shortly after dawn, Prince Cissa's army had abandoned the fort and marched for their own lands, so there was no reason for the Viroconium infantry to linger longer than necessary. Seeing the Merlin staring at the silhouetted walls of Glevum, Cadwallon climbed the earth rampart and asked him, "Are you ready to talk, we have a decision to make?"

"No, you have a decision to make," the Merlin replied, grumpily, without looking at the Prince.

"You won't advise me?"

"You are capable of making simple decisions!" the Merlin snapped. "And the choice is obvious."

"Tell me what's wrong."

"No."

"I need to know if we must march and........."

"I know what you need," cut in the Merlin, callously, "and so do you."

"You won't help?" Frustrated, Prince Cadwallon gazed across the river at the dark city walls. He felt tired and hungry, but could he order his warriors to camp here for the night, or should he begin the return march to Viroconium?

Masking the truth and the weight of what he knew, the Merlin said to the Prince, "There's nothing you can do to alter Viroconium's fate."

Cadwallon looked accusingly at the Druid. "If there's something I should know, tell me."

"What I meant was, marching tonight or tomorrow will make no difference." Having the sight meant carrying many burdens, and this was proving to be one of the heaviest. "The choice is yours to make, so get on with making your decision, procrastination is a thief."

"My warriors must rest," said the Prince, thinking aloud. "I don't know why, but when I think about Viroconium I get the most uncomfortable feeling in the pit of my stomach. My instincts tell me we must leave immediately because we are needed, common sense tells me to let my warriors rest."

"I want to return as much as you do. I know your wife and child are in the city and you are worried about them, yet the leader's job is to make the correct decisions, irrespective of family ties. Put your emotions aside and think like a prince."

"Let's walk while we talk," Cadwallon suggested.

"If it will help."

The tired infantrymen had prepared a camp for the night inside the fort. Fires for cooking had been lit, guards were patrolling the earth banks, dozens of tents made from cloaks and branches had been erected. The men were telling their Prince they needed to eat and sleep. Considering his limited options, Cadwallon made the sensible choice. “We’ll march north when the new Sun rises.” He then asked, “Tell me honestly, do you know what we’ll find when we return?”

The Merlin looked north and, he said irritably, “Yes, we’ll find Viroconium. I’ll tell you this much, Meddyf and Maelgwn are alive and well, don’t worry about them.”

“Thank you, but what about my father, is he alive?”

“Can you imagine him any other way?”

Owain and his Red Cloaks saw plumes of smoke trailing high into the blue sky long before they reached Viroconium’s meadows. Assuming the city was burning, the Pendragon ordered the Legion to charge, fearing the Saxons were about their business. But galloping into the east meadow, he couldn’t quite believe the grim scene spread over the fields. The city wasn’t burning, the smoke plumes were rising from the many funeral pyres scattered across the east meadow.

Below the arch where the fired east gates hung limp form their hinges, an ox-drawn cart carrying three white bodies, turned towards the pyres. Limping behind the cart, a wounded mourner held the hand of a child. Slowing their mounts to a respectful walk, the red-cloaked warriors pressed the corners of their cloaks to their faces, protecting their senses from the stench of burning flesh.

Owain had feared the worst when first seeing the smoke, and now, riding past the pyres and through the smoke-blackened archway, his worst fears were realised when the wreck of the city opened before him. "There's almost nothing left," he said to Bedwyr, raising his hand to halt his horse-warriors.

"Where is everyone?" Bedwyr asked, seeing the few dozen exhausted, soot-blackened people working to clear up the destruction.

"I'm guessing we saw most of them burning in the meadow," the Pendragon said. He then pointed to the courtyard at the side of the temple. "The rest are piled over there."

Bedwyr winced when he saw the bodies, and the spearmen guarding them against hungry animals and birds. "Our warriors will want to find their families."

"Order the Legion to return their mounts to the stables, if they are still standing."

"They won't like that."

"I don't care!" Owain snapped. "When they've done that they are to muster here in the courtyard, where they'll be divided into working parties." Dismounting, he handed his reins to Bedwyr as Cai walked down the bloodstained temple steps to meet him. Cai saluted then looked away, fearing telling Owain that his father was dead, so the Pendragon broke the guilty silence by asking, "Where is my father?"

"They took us by surprise," Cai burst out with, "they were inside the city before we knew we were under attack. There wasn't time to organise an affective defence, most of our men were cut down before they could join my shield-wall."

His red-rimmed, tired eyes told Owain enough of the story. He couldn't guess when his friend must have last slept and, judging by the distant look in the man's eyes there were many horrors swimming in the pool of his mind. "Where is my father?" he asked again as a girl ran down the temple steps and took hold of Cai's hand.

The City Dragon looked at Kareen, and, although his voice tightened, choking on the memory of Einion's lifeless body, out came the words that would break his friend's heart, "King Einion died killing Saxons. I found his body near the guardroom, surrounded by the blood of his victims."

"Where is his body?"

"In the temple."

"And Meddyf, is she alive?"

"Yes, as is Prince Maelgwn." Cai told Kareen to go and find Branwen, he then led Owain to the temple.

Coming to the steps, Owain stopped and pointed at the piles of bodies. "Why haven't they been burned?"

"They are unclaimed," replied Cai.

"There are women and children amongst the dead."

"The Saxons showed no mercy."

"I can see that!" He put a hand on his friend's shoulder. "I'm sorry, it's just too much to take in. How many of our warriors and militiamen survived?"

"Thirty-eight, including myself and Phelan." He watched Owain turn to look at him, guessing what the next question might be.

"How did you survive the slaughter?"

With the last shade of colour draining from his already pallid skin, Cai felt himself sway slightly, afraid of what was to come. He'd been preparing for this moment since leaving the barricaded temple, but that didn't make the telling any easier. "When the Saxons attacked, I formed a short shield-wall in the courtyard, but we were quickly overwhelmed. After we'd done all that we could to hold King Aelle's spearmen back, I ordered the surviving warriors to run for the safety of the temple. Once inside, we barricaded the doors. There, along with a few civilians, we waited until I was certain the Saxons had left, before opening the temple doors. At the time I honestly believed I had to save those that I could, but I now regret my actions, I wish I'd died killing Saxons."

Owain was lost for words. The City Dragon had proved himself to be one of the fiercest and bravest warriors in Briton, he'd fought many battles and always in the front line. How could he have run, why did he abandon women and children to the horrors of such a bloody slaughter? If King Einion was standing in judgement, he'd put Cai to death. But he wasn't his father and, there'd been enough killing. "I think, Cai," Owain began, "only you should send the dead to their next life. You'll build the pyres and carry the bodies outside the city walls. No one will be permitted to help you, and whilst you perform this duty, sections of the Legion will take it in turn to form a guard of honour for the dead. You'll carry each body through the honour guard, and only when all the dead have been placed on pyres will you burn them, then, the entire legion and those who survived the killing will watch you light the pyres. If you have the courage to do this, and it will take extraordinary courage to fulfil this task, I'll forget that when our people were being cut to pieces, you ran to save your skin."

"Thank you." Cai understood his punishment. By making him carry and burn the bodies in front of everyone, Owain wasn't just exposing him to his shame, he was giving him the chance to accept and exorcise his demons. As the people watched his struggle, to begin with they'd despise or hate him for his cowardice, but, watching him battle through the gruesome task they'd come to respect him for seeing the gruesome job through.

Standing in the sunlight at the temple doorway, Owain dismissed Cai to his grim task and, he stepped into the temple's candlelight, apprehensively looking at the dais where his father's body lay. "Clear the building," he said to the red-cloaked warrior who'd followed him in, "then leave. Close the doors behind you and stand guard, I want to be alone." Hearing scuttling feet running for the door, he waited until the heavy doors banged shut, and he marched to the dais.

King Einion's richly dressed body had been laid out by some of Viroconium's surviving women: his chainmail, which covered his body from neck to thighs, had been polished to a silver shine so it shimmered in the flickering candlelight; beneath the chainmail byrnie he'd been dressed in a pure white tunic that ran down to his thighs; his royal blue leggings with a thin seam of gold, had been slipped neatly into deer-hide boots; around his waist a belt of gold held a jet-black scabbard decorated with silver spirals; his arms lay across his chest, his fingers wrapped around the hilt of his polished broadsword, which pointed to his feet; a thin gold circlet ringed Einion's combed, dark hair; this man had been a king. Four silver candlesticks cornered the dais, their sentinel glow giving warmth and shadow to the King's death.

Gently touching the wound on Einion's cold face, Owain leaned forward, kissed his father's forehead and whispered words only the dead would hear. Feeling tears wetting the corners of his eyes, he swallowed hard as a lump came into his throat, his lack of emotional control surprising him. Hearing the door below the flickering image of Mithras open, he expected to hear the Merlin's voice. Remembering the druid had travelled south with Cadwallon, he saw a hooded woman walking towards him. Not wanting anyone to see his grief, he backed out of the candlelight.

"Everybody who met him loved him, Owain, he was a great king and he'll be remembered for many ages to come." Meddyf pulled back her hood, put her comforting arm around his waist and pulled him close, her whispering voice tender and loving. "Einion ap Cunedda, High King of the Britons, King of Gwynedd and Powys, Father of the Votadini and once Uther Pendragon, how many men have owned so many titles, how many people have lived such a life?"

Owain couldn't see the tears running down her cheeks, but he knew they were there so he raised her hand and gently kissed it. "He was the best of men," he said. "I'm not sure how I'll cope without him. He was my rock and my inspiration, I made myself into the warrior I am because of who he was. When he was alive, I could hope, not just for myself but for our people. He was so bullishly strong, the only man who could have held together the fragile union of Celtic kings."

"For the time being, Owain, forget the politics of the living, remember, feel and mourn."

"I can feel but I cannot mourn." He looked through the shimmering candlelight at his father's sword. "My first duty is to our people; I must look to their safety. The Saxons might not grant us time to burn our dead, they'll come at us again while we are weak, at least that's what I'd do if I was King Aelle."

"You do have time," Meddyf reassured him. "It is right that you should reflect upon the loss you are feeling. Be wise, feel."

"I want to, but I can't."

"You can, trust yourself."

"Why is trust relevant?"

"If you don't believe in yourself, who will? Your father knew what he was doing when he made you Pendragon, he also knew Cadwallon would rule with wisdom and guile. Together, the Warrior-Prince and the Wise-King can build something even greater than your father's achievements. You must believe that together you can bring a new age, a time when all our peoples will live in peace and prosperity. If you choose it, you and my husband can create a time the bards will sing of long after our grandchildren's grandchildren are dead. First, we must mourn our loved ones, so send your thoughts, feelings and love to your father."

Owain closed his eyes and bowed his head in silent reflection, hoping that whatever came to mind would reach his father's soul.

When mischievous and murderous woodland Dryads meld with trees and hide from the night, they do so with good reason, because the dark-time is theirs, and the forests are their playgrounds. Human noise doesn't worry them, an army can march through their woodlands without them seeking their sanctuary. But when elf-like hunters, with blackened faces and camouflaged bodies stalk their prey, the watching Dryads will scatter like windblown leaves, and leave the forest trails to the stalking hunters.

After the burning of Viroconium, the Saxons retreated south through the Middleland Forest. Fearing a Celtic reprisal, King Aelle had barely let his warriors rest until he was sure he'd put enough distance between his spearmen and the ruined city.

Three days had passed since the Celts had been slaughtered, and deciding his small army was now safe, he relented in his race to reach Andredes Caester and, he allowed his warriors the rest they needed. Having sat against a tree for most of the night, thinking about very little while most of his warriors slept peacefully beside their campfires, Aelle was about to get up and empty his bladder when he saw Algar leading another warrior towards him. "What is it?" he growled. "I need a piss so make it quick."

"This is Eric, one of the scouts we left behind to watch Viroconium."

"Yes, and?"

"The Legion have returned to their city........."

“What city!” Aelle laughed.

Eric, then said, “I counted the returning horsemen, there were two hundred and two.”

Urinating into a bush, King Aelle looked over his shoulder to ask, “They haven’t lost a single warrior? King Wihstan must have fled before battle was joined. What’s happening in Viroconium?”

“Pyres burn in the fields to the east of the city,” Eric replied.

Aelle laughed again, then became more serious. “What did the Legion do when they returned?”

“They joined the clear up, My Lord.”

“They aren’t coming after us?” the King asked as he finished relieving himself.

“No, but I did see something which puzzled me. After the Legion returned, the people stopped bringing out their dead, and one man carried out the bodies, one at a time.”

“Punishment,” the King mumbled. “Is there anything else?”

“No, My Lord.”

“They’ll never catch up with us now,” the King said to Algar.

“With your permission,” Algar requested, “I’ll go and oversee the changing of the night sentries. I don’t feel comfortable in the forest, there could be a Celtic bowman hiding behind every tree.”

“I doubt it, but yes, go.” Aelle sat against his tree again as Algar and Eric walked away.

Hearing leaves rustling in the light breeze, the King looked up, scowled at the night, wrapped himself in his cloak and began chewing a piece of dried meat. With no Celtic warriors on his trail, he relaxed into the quiet peace of the forest night.

It was so very quiet here, he thought, his heavy eyelids tempting him to sleep, quiet enough for impish spirits to work their cruel magic in the dark. Foxes no longer barked and not for some time had he heard an owl summoning forth the dead. Dark and dead silence, except for rustling leaves and cracking and spitting campfires. Realising it was unnaturally quiet, his senses pricked into life and he listened. Where were the natural sounds of the forest beasts, had they fled somewhere safer, were they hiding from their most feared predator, humans?

Getting to his feet, he drew his sword and looked deep into the dark woodland. Seeing nothing unusual, he walked to the camp perimeter. Goose bumps rippled his skin, lifting the hairs on his cold arms as instinct stopped him in his tracks. He sensed danger, but why hadn't his sentries alerted him to it, and where were the sentries? Still facing the dark woodlands with his sword drawn, his searching eyes alert to unknown dangers, he edged back to his sleeping warriors.

His instincts never betrayed him and, feeling the first pump of adrenalin sour his stomach he turned and ran to the nearest campfire. Kicking his warriors out of their dreams, he yelled, "Alarm, arm yourselves!" Running quickly to the next fire, he kicked a sleeping man in the back and slapped another across the face with the flat of his sword. "Get up, get up all of you!" Before he'd reached the next of the dozens of smouldering fires, the whole camp was coming alive with men rubbing their eyes and reaching for weapons, giving their battle-lord questioning looks as they unwrapped themselves from their cloaks. "Form circles!" Aelle shouted, running from one group to another, kicking the sleepy-eyed warriors into action. "Wake up you sons of whores! Douse the fires, raise your shields and keep your drunken eyes open!"

As far as his bleary-eyed warriors could tell, they were preparing to defend themselves against nothing. But within a few tired heartbeats they'd obeyed their king, forming four circular shield-walls around the extinguished campfires. Was the night playing tricks on their king, had his imagination run wild in the unfamiliar surroundings? "Quiet!" he shouted from within one of the circles. Nothing moved, even the wind hand dropped, adding to the clammy atmosphere only the King could feel.

His warriors watched, confused but becoming wary of unknown forces watching them from deep within the silent dark. Time passed but nothing happened. The alert warriors waited, their arms tiring from the weight of spears and shields held at the ready. Becoming impatient for the expected attack, Aelle pushed his way out from his circle and began walking around the camp, alert, expecting yelling warriors to come shrieking out from the imp-black night.

An owl hooted through the dark, a fox barked and barked again. The owl answered the fox, reassuring the King that the birds and beasts hadn't abandoned the woodlands. Accepting his nerves had got the better of him, he ordered his men to stand down. To the east he saw a faint white glow seeping through branches. Still on edge, he ordered his men to prepare for the day's march.

The owl hooted again, he heard a faint twang and a fizzing sound, followed by a blood-chillingly dull thud and a groan. Turning to see one of his men fall with an arrow in his back, he heard another twang, then another and another and before he could react arrows were flying thick and fast into Saxon flesh. "Shield-wall!" he bellowed, lifting his shield.

Circles of shields quickly formed around him, protecting him from the arrow-storm. Cursing himself, he realised he should have trusted his instincts and waited a little longer, and since when did an owl answer the bark of a fox! Warriors were falling all around the camp, pierced by the hiss of arrows loosed by unseen hands. A ripple of superstitious fear ran cold up Aelle's spine; were forest spirits attacking his warriors, were Celtic gods taking revenge for the sacking of Viroconium?

Showers of arrows fizzed through the dark, thudding into men crouching lower and lower behind their shields. More elf-arrows punched through iron-mail-rings, and men tumbled, some dying before they hit the ground, others writhing in the rotting forest mulch as pain stung deep into their flesh.

He must think, or his army would be cut to pieces before the Sun cleared the horizon. From behind his shield he could see, from the way his men were falling, that the arrows were being loosed from the north. With no option but to advance, he ordered his shield-walls forward, directly into the path of the flying arrowheads.

Squatting behind a tree, Gwen released another arrow, then she whispered into Gal's ear, "Here they come."

After hearing about the burning of Viroconium, she'd summoned all the hunters living within a day's walk of her roundhouse. Dozens of them, men and women had answered her call for revenge, and having demonstrated to King Aelle that the Celtic fightback would begin sooner than he expected, it was time for her hunters to run.

Putting his fingers to his lips, Gal let out a loud, shrill whistle, signalling to the Forest People. Unstringing her bow, Gwen heard scampering feet dash by and away, the camouflaged wraiths dissolving into the dark as if they'd never been there.

To Gwen, they were like a Faery army from the tales her father had recited when she was a child. They were there and gone, like a leafy green whisper or a forgotten sigh, real and yet surreal, images from the minds of those who believe in wistful, Dryadic fantasies. With the last of the almost silent footsteps fading into the distance, Gwen kissed Gal's cheek and whispered to him, "We've done what we came to do, now run."

Leaving a myth in their wake, they raced away from the growing light of the rising sun. Skimming around trees, leaping fallen branches and streams, swerving rocks as they put as much distance between themselves and the Saxons as they could, they chased after the hunters. Gal, running protectively behind Gwen, was amazed by her speed, not only was she beautiful but warrior spirit poured from her athletic grace as she ran for the safety of the meeting place. Risking a glance over his shoulder, he saw no Saxons following so he released a laugh of relief as he leapt a rock then splashed through a stream.

Gwen's camouflaged hunters ran until they came to a clearing where they knew they'd be safe, a tree and bush enclosed green sward, surrounding a forest pool. With rays of dawn sunlight welcoming them to their sanctuary, breathlessly they collapsed in laughing heaps beside the water, satisfied with their work.

Gal and Gwen were the last to arrive, and after splashing the heat of the chase from her sweat covered face, the Forest Queen began counting those who'd made it to safety. Forty-nine men and women had joined her hunt, forty-nine lived to tell the tale. "Just wait until Owain hears about this," she giggled to Gal.

"I'm not sure he'll believe you," he replied, splashing cold water on his face. "How many would believe that a swarm of tree spirits stalked an army of Saxons, stung death into them then vanished, leaving behind only a myth for the Saxons to fear?"

"Myth? The Saxons can wrap their defeat in a blanket of ghosts if they wish, but who'd believe such a foolish story?"

15.

If any day was meant to be cloudy, grey and wet it was this one; appropriate for the burial of a king. The windblown, swirling clouds emptied a misty rain into the grieving hearts of every man and woman who knew that today, High King Einion ap Cunedda of the Votidini, the people's Uther Pendragon, would be laid to rest on the island where some of his ancestors were buried.

This wasn't simply a day to mourn and remember a king, who for decades had kept his people safe, there was the future of the Celtic nation to reflect upon. Einion had been a strong king, so his death brought a silent, thought-provoking uncertainty to those sheltering from the weather in their homes. The defence of the nation now teetered precariously upon the young shoulders of a man who'd only two minor battles to his credit, and many feared his shoulders weren't broad or strong enough. As for Prince Cadwallon, could he rule with the iron fist his father had raised to friend and enemy, was he strong enough to bind the kings beneath the limp banner of the Votidini?

Owain, trudging with head bowed through the persistent drizzle, wiped the rain from his face. He may be walking with the funeral procession, but his thoughts were elsewhere. So many thousands now looked to him for protection, a burden he wished he'd been better prepared for. Wiping more cold rain from his face, he promised his dead father's soul that he'd meet the challenge head on, and if he failed, so be it.

Those who'd come to witness the burial, moved slowly along the raised-bank walkway that led to 'Inis Bassa' the burial place of the Votidini kings and princes. The site in the winter became a lake surrounding one large and one small island, both ringed with ditches and banks supporting wooden palisades. The two islands were linked by a raised walkway, which was met by another reaching out from the shore, joining it to create a raised, 'T' shaped path. During the summer months the lake receded to become marshland, leaving only a small pool to the east of the largest island.

Covered by a black cloth, the King's body lay on a cart pulled by two oxen. Behind the cart walked Prince Cadwallon, still tired from his return march with the Viroconium infantry, and Owain, closely followed by Meddyf and her Christian Priest, who was flanked by the Merlin. Some of the Celtic kings who'd completed the journey in time to attend the funeral, walked ahead of Bedwyr and Cai, who led a select number of the red-cloaked Legion. Along the shoreline of the rain spattered lake stood the wailing hundreds, who'd put down their ploughs and looms to come and express their grief.

There wasn't enough room for all to attend the burial on the main island, so when the procession reached the junction of the raised banks, only Einion's family, the Merlin, the Christian priest, Bedwyr and Cai and the few Celtic kings attending, turned left to walk through the palisade's open gates and on to the burial place. Two black hooded warriors, holding shovels, waited beside the grave, ready to fill it in after Einion had been laid to rest.

The oxen were halted near the grave-cut, dug near the base of the island's small hill. The Merlin drew back the black cloth, picked up King Einion's sword and walked to the head of the grave. Cadwallon, Owain, Bedwyr and Cai lifted the body off the cart, then gently lowered it into the shallow pit. The Christian Priest, assuming Princess Meddyf had brought him along to perform the funeral rites, walked over and stood beside the Merlin, made the sign of the cross and offered up a prayer of forgiveness for the dead King's soul.

The Merlin began his oration. The Druid spoke in an ancient language that Owain didn't understand, but something in the unknown words moved the young Prince. The language had a musical rhythm and feeling, releasing a shapeless image that touched the light within Owain's soul. The light flickered and pricked a supressed emotion, stinging his eyes and filling his heart with an ache that threatened to overwhelm him. When he looked around, he saw the words had touched everyone, including the Christian Priest.

When the magical words had faded into the grey clouds, the Druid nodded to the two hooded warriors, who led the oxen to the grave. Raising King Einion's broadsword, the Merlin swung it at one of the oxen. The beast slumped forward, headless, squirting a fountain of dark red blood into the grave. The second beast met with the same fate. The Christian Priest turned away, made the sign of the cross against evil and vomited into the pile of earth that would soon cover the body. Amused by the Priest's green pallor, Owain opened his hand and looked at the jewelled dagger he'd been holding throughout the ceremony. The knife was less than a thumb's length long, but was pure gold, with one small ruby worked into the pommel. He threw it into the grave and stepped back. Prince Cadwallon did the same, though Owain couldn't see what he'd thrown in.

After the Merlin, Meddyf, Bedwyr and Cai had given their offerings, the group stood in reverential silence and the hooded warriors began shovelling the earth over King Einion's body. As the earth tumbled from the wooden shovels, a horn sounded a mournful note from the shoreline, where the hundreds gathered increased their wailing and the clouds thickened with their woe-filled cries. Watching the grave being filled, Owain's thoughts turned to Gwen. He wanted to see her but he knew that until Viroconium arose from its ashes he must help with the rebuilding. For now, she must wait, he hoped she'd understand.

He'd heard how she'd led the Forest People in the attack against King Aelle's Saxons, and the success of her archers. He'd never imagined her as a warrior, though thinking about it there was an obvious logic to it, considering how proficient she was with the bow and the spear. The more he thought about it the more he realised she'd be a match for any man, as were her hunters so their skills might prove useful to him in the future.

The days following King Einion's burial hung grey, wet and cold over a nation mourning the death of its protector. While the winds howled and rains lashed the valleys, hearth-fires glowed, cracking and spitting as damp wood smoked beneath wet thatch. In Viroconium, masons and carpenters worked through the rain, slowly rebuilding a city with the help of those who'd survived the Saxon blades.

Throughout the stormy days Gwen fed her hearth, plucked her harp and stewed her fish, frustrated by the indoor life forced upon her. She became crabby, snapping at Gal for everything and nothing then regretting her quick temper. Each morning she'd lift the door-flap to check the sky's mood, but bright dawns never came, only rain.

The wheel of life never slows its turn, rarely do consecutive moons pass without change. With Gwen beginning to despair for the warmth of the sun, the grey clouds slowly turned to white, parted and the Sun broke through. Running outside to embrace the bright rays and throw herself into the lake, she stopped at the lakeside because Gal was waist deep in the water, holding a hunting spear. He raised his hand to her so she smiled back. "How long have you been fishing?" she asked, walking along the pebbly bank.

"Not long enough to feed us," he called back. He then rammed his spear into the water and cursed, "Damn it!" because again he'd missed his target.

Feeling the relief of warm Sun on her face, Gwen decided to spend some time doing nothing, so she walked around the lake until she came to where the pebbled bank blended into a grass slope that nosed into the water. Removing her soft leather shoes, she sat and slid her feet into the lake.

Tying two blades of grass into a knot, she remembered that at least a month had passed since Owain's last visit. The way he drifted into her seclusion when she least expected him held a life enhancing charm. But the waiting could be painful, and sometimes she thought she might be happier with a different man, one who'd always be there, sharing her world. Stretching her arms, she lay back on the warm grass, sighed deeply and looked up at the feathery white clouds ambling across the pale blue sky. They were a bit like her relationship with Owain, she supposed, drifting, never quite there.

Deciding the summer season was a love-making bed, she sensed an aching warmth within her that needed satisfying, and she dearly wished her lover was here. Following the thoughts, which pulled her back to the last time she'd made love with Owain, they brought a smile to her face and she felt a surge of lust warming the ache between her thighs. Sliding her dress up, she let the Sun warm her legs, her hands smoothing the soft skin at the top of her thighs. She wanted to touch herself, feel her pleasure ripple and pulsate in waves throughout her body but she was disturbed by the sound of running feet, so she quickly adjusted her dress. Looking up, she saw Gal standing over her. Lost in her private moment she'd quite forgotten he was nearby.

"Food," he said, holding up a dripping wet fish.

She returned his smile, relieved to see nothing but innocence in his eyes. It was easy for her to love the cheeky and playful nature of the boy, he had courage and an infectious zest for life that always brought something special to her day. "You are quite the hunter, Gal."

"Fishing isn't hunting, what we did to the Saxons, that was hunting."

“I’m hungry, you can cook the fish now if you want!” she joked, lying back and closing her eyes so that she could enjoy more of the sun’s warmth.

“You want me to cook?” he asked, taking his fill of her lithe young body. His gaze lingered on her legs, before slowly travelling to where he’d seen her dress hitched up. Sitting beside her, he dipped his feet in the cool lake and asked, “Don’t you ever want to live in the outside world?”

“We all have different dreams and ambitions,” she said thoughtfully. “I’ve been to Viroconium to watch how it turns, it’s not the place for me. While I was there, I constantly felt like leaving as quickly as possible. I can see why others might enjoy city life, with all its colour, gossip and news from different parts of the world. My world may be slower, but it feels natural and for me that’s a good thing.”

Gal understood, but he wanted to join the Legion and kill Saxons so he must go to Viroconium. To him, the risks and glories of a warrior’s life meant everything, however precarious that life might be. “One day I’ll join Owain in the city.”

“That’s if we ever see him again!” she half joked.

“He’ll come soon, he must because he promised I’d ride alongside him into battle, and would he say that if he didn’t mean it?”

“If that’s what he said, Gal, that’s what.......”

Their lazy-chat was disturbed by the unexpected sound of hoof-beats clattering through the forest. Riders, lots of them were thundering along the path that led to Gwen’s lake. “Get into the forest and hide," she ordered, jumping to her feet. "And remember what Owain told you, watch and listen. Go, before the horsemen see you."

"It could be Owain!" he protested.

"No, it couldn't, now go on, run!"

Reluctantly, he darted into the forest and found himself a place to hide near her roundhouse. Gwen ran to her home, emerging moments later with her fishing spear. Her worst fears came true when Huail ap Caw, with thirty warriors, charged into the clearing to encircle her.

"Hello, Gwen, we have unfinished business." Sneering lustfully at her from his mount, he swept his arm towards his warriors. "I've brought some friends with me, there's no escape for you this time. Come with me in a civilized manner or become a plaything for my excitable but still restrained warriors, it's your choice."

Gal heard every word, but the only weapon he had was his eating knife, and what could he do against so many? Seeing Huail lift Gwen onto his horse and ride away, he began his run through the forest, knowing her life depended on how quickly he reached Viroconium.

Riding across the meadow that led to the border between his kingdom and King Aelle's, King Ceredig didn't know why the Saxon had requested a meeting. He'd kept his part of the deal, Viroconium had been raised to the ground, King Einion was dead so what did the fat Saxon want from him now? King Aelle's message suggested he need only bring a small armed escort to the meeting place. Should that worry him, after all, other Celtic kings were at war with the Saxons? But Aelle had proved true to his word, so far, and he'd already been richly rewarded by him once, so why worry?

Relaxing as his horse lazily skirted a river, he breathed in the fresh sea air while enjoying the views. The river-valley led him across grassy slopes that fell away towards pebbled beaches, and the sun-shimmering sea beyond. This was gentle country, green and rolling, crossed by the occasional hawthorn hedge and backed to the north by a huge expanse of forest. The river he was following wasn't wide, and its clean water flowed sparkling and bright over a rocky bed, trickling down the slope to the sands where it emptied into the salty-sea.

King Aelle had suggested the meeting place. There was a fording-place just a little inland, crossed by flagstones. Ceredig and his four-man escort, following the final bend in the river where it passed through a copse of willow trees, saw the Saxon King and his mounted guard waiting near the fording-place. He was surprised to see beautiful, blue-eyed Gorpe with the group, but he put that to the back of his mind as he rode ahead of his escort and came to a halt on his side of the crossing-place. The Saxon King dismounted and called across the ford, "King Ceredig of the Durotriges, will you meet me in the middle of the bridge?"

The Celt dismounted and walked onto the flagstones. "It's good to see you, Aelle. I understand your attack on Viroconium was a brilliant success, I congratulate you."

"I'd like to thank you for keeping your word," Aelle replied, noticing Ceredig admiring his daughter. "I hope the gold I sent was sufficient payment?"

"It was." Ceredig decided to be direct. "What do you want?"

"I'm planning a war to split the Celtic kingdoms that form the largest part of the High King's alliance."

"There is no high king, you killed him."

"That's true!" Aelle laughed. "But I'm sure Prince Cadwallon will be crowned as soon as a gathering can be organized."

Ceredig considered this. He had spies in many camps and he wasn't so certain that Cadwallon would be accepted. "From what I've heard, some of the kings have had enough of being dictated to by Viroconium. Prince Cadwallon will have a fight on his hands if he wants to hold the alliance together."

"What you say may be true, and if it is, it serves my purpose."

"What is your purpose?"

"I intend fighting my way to Aqua Sulis. If I succeed, I'll have split the Celtic union in half, and I want you to benefit from the war."

"You need my warriors again?"

"No, I'll have more than enough spearmen by then to break the Celts."

"Then what do you want, and what's my help worth to you?"

King Aelle took a step closer to the Celt and, lowering his voice he whispered to his ally, "Your lands border mine to the east, to the west your neighbour is King Erbin of the Dumnonians. When I've split the Celtic alliance, I'll give you all the warriors you need to march across Erbin's kingdom, you'll double your lands and your wealth."

Ceredig wasn't sure it would be so straight forward, the Saxon's plan could backfire, uniting the Celtic kingdoms against him. If the stories of the new legion of 'Red Cloaks' were true, they wouldn't be easy to brush aside. As for conquering King Erbin's lands, it would be difficult no matter how many warriors the Saxon gave him, because Cadwallon and Owain were Erbin's cousins so would ride to support him if an army invaded Dumnonia. Although uncomfortable with Aelle's plan, he decided he'd no choice but to go along with it, until he knew who was more likely to win the war. "If you haven't come here to ask for my warriors, what do you want from me?" he asked.

"Allow me to march a great Saxon army through your kingdom."

"That's it?"

"Yes."

"Nothing is ever that simple, you'll need a lot more than a few hundred spearmen to take Aqua Sulis."

"Your spies aren't as competent as you think, Ceredig." Aelle confidently puffed out his fat chest. "I'll be leading thousands, not hundreds of men to war."

The Celtic king felt the political landscape shift, if the Saxon was mustering a large army, he'd be powerless to interfere. He guessed that Aelle was aware of this, so there must be more to the plan than he'd been told, and why was he asking for permission to do what he could do anyway? "How can I trust you not to turn this great army against my people?"

"Good question," replied the Saxon. He then blew a kiss to his daughter and made an offer he hoped would seal the deal. "I know you have no wife, and that's sad, every king needs a queen to birth him strong sons. I'm going to offer you a permanent alliance of mutual assistance and friendship, and to tie the bargain, I'll give you my beautiful daughter in marriage. Wouldn't she make a fine queen?"

Ceredig's blood warmed his loins when he thought about making love to Gorpe, but could he betray his own people for the hand of a Saxon princess? Lust often clouds a man's judgement, but the benefits of the alliance far outweighed his need to make love. The truth of it was that he was already considering expanding his kingdom, Gorpe would be a beautiful bonus but he'd rather have the lands, the wealth and the many beautiful women his increased power would bring to him. If he refused Aelle's offer, he was a dead man. "I accept, taking your daughter as my wife and queen will be an honour. Shall we meet in your feasting hall five days from today, to seal the deal with the marriage?"

A satisfied smile spread across the Saxon's face. "It shall be as you ask, Ceredig. From this day forward we are kin-folk, Saxons and Celts sharing a permanent union."

16.

"The high kingship isn't hereditary, Owain," Cadwallon said as he sat down on the riverbank and looked at his brother, who was leaning against a willow tree.

"Without a high king, the alliance will fall apart," Owain replied, scratching a 'G' into the willow's bark with his knife.

"The alliance might split anyway," Cadwallon suggested. "Sit down, we need to discuss this."

Owain slipped his knife into his belt, sat cross-legged beside his brother and said, "Some of our kings will remain loyal to you."

"Perhaps, but apart from King Erbin I can't think of any."

"King Ban?" Owain wasn't sure what the West-Brigantian King would do, but he had to say something, he couldn't let his father's life's work come to nothing.

"His support isn't guaranteed. I am the rightful king of the Votidini by birth, maybe I should be content with that?"

"You're giving up without a fight?"

"That's not what I'm saying. What would you prefer, the alliance to hold together with no one at its head, or war between rival kings?"

"Without a unifying figurehead?" Owain questioned. "The strongest should rule, that's the way it has always been."

"If new alliances are formed," Cadwallon said, watching a swooping kingfisher draw in its wings and dive into the river, "those unions would be strong enough to challenge us." The kingfisher burst from the water with a small fish in its beak. “I don’t want civil war; it would mean the end of our nation. You are the Pendragon, Owain, that’s already been agreed in council, so if you’re wanting a unifying force, look to yourself. The high kingship may be a thing of the past, which is no bad thing.” Brushing leaves and grass from his leggings, Cadwallon got up and looked at the city, which was rising from its ashes. “I’m not prepared to throw away the unified strength our father gave us, and like you, I believe we can only defeat the Saxons if we stand together. I also believe in the council of kings, but one man need not hold all of the power, it could be shared, rotated on a yearly basis. Times change, Owain, maybe it’s time for something new.”

“Change for change’s sake, or because there’s wisdom in it?” As Owain saw it, if the Celts were to survive, they must become one nation or Briton would be lost to the Saxons. Getting to his feet, he put his hand on Cadwallon’s arm and said, “There’s no one I respect more than you, I’ll lay down my life to ensure that you become high king. You are the only man who can lead us forward, so think about it, Cadwallon, before you throw away our nation’s survival. I’d better get back to the practice-fields, I’m supposed to be overseeing the battle-charges. Let’s talk as we walk.”

“Don’t get me wrong,” Cadwallon said as they strolled towards the city, “I believe in the high kingship, to a point, but I don’t like the idea of taking the crown by force. I don’t want to be the tyrant our father was.”

“Tyrant?”

“Yes, he ruled by fear.”

As they walked, Owain watched two swallows swooping and turning above Viroconium's west gateway. "We need a strong union," he said. "Our nobles will recognise the need for continuity, because many of them share borders with the Angles and Saxons. I'm not saying they'll fall into line without puffing out their chest's a little, but they will see sense in the end. Have faith in yourself, you'll be a great high king. If I'm the arm and heart of our people, you are the head and the soul."

"That's easy to say." Cadwallon smiled, his brother could drive a nail in straighter than anyone he knew. "I'll call a gathering of the kings to see which way the winds blow," he said with more conviction than he felt. "I'll give the kings the opportunity to puff out their feathers, see which of them needs a few of their delicate feathers plucked."

Walking alongside the city's north wall, Owain heard angry brawling, and, from what he could see a small group of the Legion were trying to wrestle each other to the ground. Then a young voice shouted the Pendragon's name from within the scrum, and he saw Gal, looking like he'd been dragged through a hedge of brambles, force himself clear of the wrestling pile. Seeing the Pendragon, he sprang to his feet and ran to reach him before he was caught again. Bedwyr grabbed the boy and pulled him to ground.

"Let him up, I know him!" Owain shouted, running to help the boy.

"It's Gwen!" Gal yelled from beneath Bedwyr, who was sitting on him. "Huail ap Caw has taken Gwen!"

“Get off him!” Owain took hold of Bedwyr’s shoulders and pulled him away.

“You must ride,” the breathless boy ordered, scrambling to his feet, “you must save her.”

“Saddle my horse, fast!” the Pendragon ordered one of the Red Cloaks. He then turned to Bedwyr. “The Legion will ride north, to King Caw’s lands. It’s the only place.........”

“No!” Gal shouted. “He hasn’t taken her to his father’s kingdom, he’s gone to your lands, to Rhuthun in Rhos, and he has about two hundred warriors with him. I passed their camp at the edge of the forest when I was on my way to find you, so I hid and listened, that’s how I know where they are going.”

“You’ve done well, Gal.” Mounting his horse, Owain gave his orders, “As soon as the Legion are mounted, Bedwyr, ride for Rhuthun, the Viroconium infantry can follow as they will. This time I’ll feed Huail ap Caw’s head to the crows.”

Temptation might feed a man of good sense and lead him astray, if only for a short time. Some men need no tempting; they know their will and they follow their needs even unto the destruction of another person’s mind or body. One person’s sin often destroys the lives of many, human history is littered with such cases.

The few people of Rhuthun who hadn’t left their homes to help rebuild Viroconium, ran up the slight rise to the fort when Huail’s horsemen rode out from the surrounding woodlands. “Why are they running?” the Pictish Prince asked Gwen, who was sitting behind him.

"They know a murdering Pict when they see one," she replied, sarcastically.

"I'm not going to kill them. I chose this fort because it's the last place your lover will think to look for you."

"He could already be on his way here."

"Impossible, he doesn't know I've taken you."

Trotting up the slope and through the open gateway, the Pict was surprised by the dilapidated state of the palisade; a good number of the stakes had rotted and collapsed into the fort's surrounding ditch, there were many gaps in the wall. "Has Owain ever been here?" he asked Gwen as he walked his horse towards the only stone building inside the fort.

"How would I know?"

Halting his mount, Huail turned in the saddle and said to her, "Do you know anything about him?"

"What I do know I'm keeping to myself."

"This neglected dung-heap is meant to be his royal seat."

"What of it?"

"He should have kept the place in better repair."

The door of the long, rectangular stone building opened and a white-hard man wearing a bull-hide cloak walked out, followed by two leather-clad warriors. "I am Cadwy," he said, walking through the small crowd towards the Prince, "and these few people are under my protection."

"By whose authority?" Huail asked as he leapt down from his horse.

"My master is Owain ap Einion, Prince of Rhos and Pendragon of the Britons."

Huail drew his sword and walked towards the man. "Not any more he isn't." He pointed the blade at the man's chest. "I am Prince Huail ap Caw of the Picts. This rancid pit of foetid poverty is now mine, and you," he jabbed the man in the chest, "will kneel in my presence. On your knees, now!" Turning to one of his warriors, Huail said, "Aillig, set your men to repairing the palisade, and post sentries along the rampart. While you're doing that, find me a girlchild." A murmur of protest rippled through the small crowd, but no one challenged their new lord.

"What do you want from us?" Cadwy asked.

"Do you have a priest?" Huail ignored the kneeling headman's question.

"Yes, he's making his rounds of the surrounding villages. He'll be back before the Sun sets."

Huail looked around his shabby conquest. Inside the palisade was a double circuit of thatched roundhouses, few of which had smoke seeping through their thatched roofing. In the centre of the fort, just to the side of the stone building, a large stone protruded from the ground. "What's that for?" he asked.

"No one knows," the kneeling man replied, "though our old stories claim it was where Bran the Blessed was crowned. Can I get up now?"

"No, stay where you are." The Prince sheathed his sword, walked back to his horse, untied the thongs binding Gwen's wrist and helped her down. "What do you think of your new home, pathetic isn't it?" She didn't reply. "Let me show you where we'll spend our first night of marriage."

"First night of rape you mean!"

Leading her past the kneeling man, he drew his dagger and pressed the point against the small of her back. "No tricks, or you die."

Inside the stone house, a central heath illuminated the sweating grey stone walls. The floor was covered in dried reeds, which hadn't been swept out and replaced for quite some time, so the smell of rotting vegetation was a bit thick. In the corner stood a small square table, and one chair. "What squalor," Huail said. "I'll have the reeds cleaned out; I'm not kneeling in this filth when we rut." Close to the hearth lay a bundle of furs. "I suppose that's Cadwy's bed." Noticing Gwen looking hopefully at the open door, he tapped her on the shoulder with his knife. "You won't escape, and if you try to, I will kill you. When I return, you'll find out how it feels to have a real man inside you. I shan't be long." Pushing her onto the pile of furs, he walked away. Stopping before reaching the door, he strolled back and aggressively squeezed one of her breasts. "Don't expect any pity from me." Smirking, he grabbed her raven-dark hair and pulled her head back. Seeing no fear in her eyes, he let go, slapped her face, felt her breast again and said, "If you need something to do, get undressed!"

"You can get up now," Huail said to Cadwy. "Have your people volunteered to help my warriors repair the palisade?"

"They weren't given a choice, My Lord."

"Good, I like efficiency." Glancing at Bran the Blessed's stone, he shivered as if someone had stolen his soul. "That must be dug up."

"You mustn't, it is sacred," Cadwy insisted.

"Do I care? When your men have finished helping repair the palisade, tell them to get rid of it."

"May I go now?"

Huail looked scornfully at him. "No, stand there until I tell you to move." He walked away, heading for the ladder leaning against the walkway above the gates. Placing his foot on the first rung, he looked back at the white-haired man and called to him, "Do you have a length of rope?"

"Yes, My Lord."

"Fetch it." Huail climbed the ladder and stepped on to the walkway. "You," he said to a sentry. "If you see warriors ride or march out from those woods, it doesn't matter how few they are, raise the alarm with three blasts from your horn." Turning, he scanned the many working parties cutting away the rotten sections of the palisade. Calculating he'd need at least three days to be ready for Owain's arrival, though it could be ten times that long before the Pendragon discovered Gwen's whereabouts, he climbed down the ladder as Cadwy returned, carrying a rope, which he held out to him. "Tie one end to a stake above the gate, then wait for me there." With his men organised into working parties, and confident his two hundred warriors were enough to defend the fort, he turned his mind back to what he was most looking forward to, Gwen's body.

Returning to the stone house, he found her sitting on the furs beside the hearth. "I hope you are ready for me," he said, leaning on the doorpost. "Stand up, woman." Unnerved by his dark silhouette, she looked into a shadowed corner. "I said stand up!"

She saw him straighten and his hand felt for the pommel of his sword. "I won't make this easy for you," she warned him, her stomach turning like a butter churn.

"So be it." He strolled casually over. "We both know what's going to happen, so why........."

"Rape?"

"Call it what you will," he sneered, grabbed her hair and yanked her to her feet. Pulling her head back so he could kiss her dry lips, he hissed at her, "I'm sure you've worked out the other reason you are here. How does it feel to be the bait in the trap?" He pressed his lips hard against hers, then winced when her teeth nipped his lip.

"How does it feel to know you'll soon be dead?" she spat back.

"You are the one whose life hangs by a thread."

"I don't think so; you've already lost this fight."

"I suggest you look at the facts, Gwen. It could be days before anyone knows you are missing, and when Owain eventually hears that I've taken you; he'll ride north to my father's kingdom." Releasing her hair, he stepped back and drew his sword. "Do you believe in miracles?"

"No."

"If your lover-boy arrives here before the next Moon wanes, it will be a miracle. I'm going to use you until you bleed, I suggest you accept your situation and make the best of it."

"You are very sure of yourself," she said, wiping the taste of him from her lips. "You think you are safe behind a rotting palisade, but you know nothing. You've given the Pendragon a reason to kill you, and that's what he'll do."

"I think not."

She looked him cold in the eyes. "You don't know as much as you think you do."

"I know that men can't walk on water and fish can't fly. By the time Owain gets here, you'll have been so well used he won't want you anymore."

"If that's what you believe, it must be true."

Something wasn't right about this, she should be begging him not to hurt her by now, yet she seemed unconcerned, why? "You don't fear me?"

"Why would I?"

"Because I was going to keep you as my plaything, but I've changed my mind." Pressing the point of his sword into the thick leather belt around her waist, he jabbed her back towards the wall. "When I've used you, I'm going to hang you from the rampart by your pretty neck. Cadwy is waiting for you on the walkway above the gate, with a rope."

"You may well rape and kill me, but you are also going to die."

"You are not fooling anyone, Gwen." His sword prodded her further back.

"Owain will kill you before the Sun falls, today."

"I want him to come; you are my bait, the fort is my net, my warriors are my shield and my sword. I only kidnapped you to lure the Pendragon into my trap. The high kingship is up for grabs and, with your lover skewered on the points of my men's spears my father will be free to challenge Prince Cadwallon. Taking you is just a beautiful bonus."

She'd guessed her role was to lure Owain towards Huail's warriors but, she hadn't realised this was part of a plan to make Caw the high king. Whatever the politics were, she wouldn't make this easy for him. "You're a week man, Huail, the only way you can get what you want from women is by force. I'm not afraid of you, and whatever happens I'll find a way to kill you. When you do come at me, you inadequate, slimy smear of dog-vomit, take care to protect your excuse for your manhood, that's where I'll strike first!"

"You may think you are being brave, but I like a woman who fights." He tried forcing a smile, but only managed an uncomfortable sneer. He believed her; she would try to kill him but he was prepared for that. "Let's get on with this." His sword prodded her back until she was pressed against the wall. "Take off your clothes." He pointed his sword at her throat.

"No, kill me."

"As you wish, your body will still be warm when I'm rutting you."

"You're an animal!"

He threw his sword across the room, punched her to the ground and drew his knife. Kneeling, he pressed the knifepoint against her breast. "I don't want to cause you any more pain than is necessary, but if you force me to, I will cut you. I know you'll never want me and, that's half the fun. For me, pain and lust go together, and making you suffer will cost me nothing. Take off your clothes."

"Kill me."

"I told you to take off your clothes!" He slapped her across the face, cutting her lip.

"Never!" she hissed, wiping the blood from her mouth. "What are you waiting for, go on, kill me!"

"I didn't want to do this, Gwen, but you've forced my hand." He called to Aillig, who entered dragging a small, screaming girl by her long red hair.

"She's the only girl of the right age I could find," the guard said, pushing the terrified child to the ground at Huail's feet.

"She's perfect." Huail was pleased with the pretty girl. "You can go," he ordered the warrior, "but remain outside the door, I might need you again."

It was hard for Gwen to believe what she imagined the Pict might do to the child, who could have no more than eight or nine summers behind her.

Grabbing the weeping child by the throat, Huail pulled her to her feet, and said to Gwen, "I've asked you to take off your clothes, don't make me ask you again because you know what I'll do to the girl if you refuse." Raising his knife to the child's throat, he smiled when the girl screamed. "I won't kill her, just cut her a little, and make you watch while I break her in. How much pain she suffers depends on you, do you like children?"

What choice did she have, the widening of the terrified child's eyes was enough to convince her that coping with her own pain would be easier than watching the girl suffer. She began slowly taking off her clothes, her every movement scrutinised by Huail's greedy eyes.

Standing naked, she tried hiding her embarrassment with her hands and arms, her long, almost ebony hair hanging loosely over her breasts. Staring at the ground, she tried turning off her senses by building an emotionless wall within her mind. But she couldn't banish the fear and feel of his clammy hands searching the most intimate parts of her body, nor could she block the thought of his slobbering mouth sliming her skin.

If the opportunity came, she'd have no reservations about plunging a knife into his rotten guts, then giving it a twist to ensure he suffered before he died. But she didn't have a knife, so decided that if she must she'd squeeze her thumbs into his eye sockets or, force her nails through the flesh of his throat and rip out his windpipe. It was vital for her to keep her thoughts clear, so when the moment to strike came, she'd be ready to kill. Until then, she'd think of her body as being a statue of cold marble, her mind disconnected from the muscle shivering touch of his fingers.

Huail lowered the knife and let the girl go. The child ran for the sunlit glow of the open doorway, screaming for her mother. Taking Gwen's hand in his, he lay the point of his knife-blade on her left nipple. "Stand completely still until I've taken off my leggings, if you don't, I'll have the girl brought back," he warned whilst struggling out of his leggings without moving his knife hand. "To begin with, I'd like to lick your skin, I've often wondered what you'd taste like." Undressed as much as he need be, he moved the dagger point to the very top of the inside of her thigh. "Before I begin, you should know that if you resist, I'll cut you where Owain has already been. I'll give you a choice, just to show that I'm a generous man who cares about his women: should I tie you up, or will you be good and play the game?"

Hoping to buy herself a more time, she said, "Tie me up, you might find it is more fun that way."

Pleased with her choice, he smoothed his left hand over her breast. His wet tongue slimed her neck, slid to her lip and into her mouth. She forced herself not to retch when his tongue flicked hers, her body shivering as his hand moved to her belly then down and between her legs. She was about to force her knee into his ball-sack when she heard a horn blast three shrill notes. Startled by the sound, Huail took a step back, shock, confusion and cold fear contorting his face.

"Is something wrong?" she asked sarcastically. "Has someone stuck a dagger up your arse?"

"It can't be!" he almost shrieked the words. "It isn't possible!" Calming himself, he smiled kindly at her. "It seems our shared pleasure must wait." Punching her hard on the temple, he knocked her out. After putting his leggings back on, he picked up his sword and ran out into the sunlight.

Walking alone towards Rhuthun's gateway, Owain heard three warning notes blast from a horn, while the gates were being closed against him. Hoping he'd arrived in time to save Gwen, he drew his sword as another horn-note melted into the pleasantly warm afternoon, and more warriors appeared on the palisade. A question slipped into his mind: why would they defend the palisade when only one warrior stood against them? It then occurred to him that Huail was occupied, so the sentries had taken the safest option. This worried him, guessing Gwen was the most likely object of the Pict's attention.

If his plan was to succeed, he must work on the minds of the watching spearmen, so he walked closer to the ramparts and called to the Picts, "I am Owain ap Einion, the Pendragon of the Britons! If you want to live, hand Huail over to me!" A gentle ripple of laughter ran along the battlements as a dark-haired man looked down from the palisade above the gates. Taking a spear from one of the warriors, the dark-haired man hurled it at the Red Cloak. Owain shifted his head and the spear narrowly missed his ear, then he called to the thrower, "You'll have to do better than that, Huail! Come down and fight me!"

"You are in no position to be making demands!" the Pict shouted. "Give yourself up for execution and I promise that only I shall rape Gwen. While you are considering that," he grabbed the rope tied to the wooden stakes, "this is for Gwen! When I've eventually had her, I'm going to stretch her neck unless you do as I ask."

Relief relaxed Owain's tight emotions as the meaning of the words registered, the Pict hadn't raped her yet, so he calmly called back, "I'll give your offer the consideration it deserves!"

"You are one-man, Pendragon," Huail replied, scanning the surrounding forest for signs of the Legion. "Did you come alone, is that how you covered the distance in such a short time?"

"There was more than one person by the lake when you abducted Gwen, so I knew what you'd done not long after you'd taken her."

"Be that as it may. If you want your woman, come and get her, though how you'll break in and kill two hundred warriors I can't imagine."

"One man with a just cause can become an army, and, a foolish man with a strong army can find himself standing alone."

"Clever words, Pendragon, but you're the one standing alone. I'll order my guards to open the gates, you are more than welcome to come in."

Owain raised his sword and circled it above his head. The edge of the forest came to life, bustling with jingling iron and snorting horses as the entire Legion of Red Cloaks led their mounts into the clearing. Halting a few paces behind their Pendragon, they mounted at Bedwyr's command. "I've nothing more to say to you, Huail, you have chosen your fate." Turning his attention to the warriors manning the palisade, Owain addressed them, "Warriors of Alt Clud, turn the son of Caw over to me and you can ride away without a single sword drawn against you. My quarrel isn't with you, but if you want to die protecting a coward who abducts women, so be it! I've no wish to make war against my brother-warriors, in fact I'd rather you joined me, I can use warriors who know how to fight from horseback. You can see only two hundred Red Cloaks, but within three days Prince Cadwallon will arrive with his infantrymen. The implications are obvious, unless you open the gates and hand Huail over to me!"

He saw heads turn as men talked, then groups of warriors moved along the rampart towards the walkway above the gates. Bedwyr rode up to the Pendragon and asked, "Shouldn't we dismount and deploy for battle? The palisade is falling apart, we could walk in."

Hearing a scuffle coming from the walkway, followed by muffled grunts, a couple of yelled expletives then silence, Owain pointed at the fort and said, "I don't think we'll need to, look."

Rhuthun's gates creaked open, and Huail, bound at the wrists, with a cut lip and a bruised and swelling eye, was pushed out. Falling onto his face, he cursed his faithless warriors while struggling to get to his knees. "My father will hear of this!" he yelled at the warriors who'd betrayed him. "Your women and children will pay the price for your cowardice!"

Owain strode towards the Pict, twirling his sword in wide arcs to loosen his arm muscles and tendons. Huail pushed himself up from his knees. Not expecting the Pendragon to show mercy, he hoped the killing would be quick, a knife across his throat or a sword thrust through his heart.

"Hold out your arms, I'll cut your bonds," Owain said, circling his prisoner.

Huail hesitated, unsure of the Pendragon's intentions. "Why would you do that?"

"We are going to fight."

"Generous, but foolish." The Pict held out his arms. A quick flick of the sword cut the leather thongs. "I've already had her," he lied. "It was enjoyable but not the best I've had. She's dirty now, a well-used whore."

Untouched by the lies, Owain called to one of the warriors above the gate, "You man, throw down your sword!" There was a dull thump near Huail's feet. "You have your weapon, pick it up."

Huail tossed the sword from hand to hand to test its weight. He may only get one chance to kill the red-cloaked Prince, so he backed away a few paces and began circling Owain, watching for any slight movement. The Pendragon turned with him, following his opponent's eyes, calmly waiting for the twitch before the strike.

Feeling the Sun warming the back of his neck, as Owain squinted, the Pict rushed at the Pendragon, swinging his sword at the younger man's head. The Pendragon tilted the top half of his body to avoid the obvious cut, then Huail's sword swung back wildly. Again, Owain calmly swayed out of the way, then flicked his blade up, nicking his opponents forearm. Huail winced, glanced at the small cut and attacked again, his sword slicing at Owain's chest. The Pendragon parried the blade, stepped in and punched his sword pommel hard into Huail's cheek. Grunting as the blow bruised him, Huail swung his sword at Owain's neck. The Pendragon ducked, rolled out of the way as the Pict's blade flashed down, then he winced when iron cut a small flesh-wound in his thigh.

"Killing me won't be so easy," Huail boasted.

"I've received worse cuts when picking fruit," Owain replied.

Growing in confidence, the Pict swung his sword in figures of eight and stepped forward, wasting his energy as the Pendragon moved back and back to avoid the wild swings. Halting to catch his breath, Huail glanced up at his watching spearmen on the ramparts, promising himself he'd have every one of them hanged when he returned to his father's kingdom.

"Tired already?" Owain asked.

"Let's find out."

Huail's blade cut viciously at Owain's knees. The Pendragon jumped and slashed his sword down, its steel biting into the astonished Pict's wrist, cutting his tendons and he dropped his sword. The Pict screamed with shock and pain as his blood dripped onto the grass. "Can you fight with your other hand?" Owain asked.

"I can."

"Then pick up your sword and fight."

Knowing he was beaten, and the next clash of swords would probably bring his death, the Pict kicked away his weapon and held out his arms. "Would you kill an unarmed man?"

"If that man was you, yes. Fight me and the killing blow will be swift, refuse and I'll cut you apart piece by piece."

Keeping his eyes firmly fixed on the other man, the wounded Pict walked to his sword, knelt and picked it up with his left hand. Still kneeling, he swung the blade. The Pendragon knocked aside the laboured stroke, and flashed his sword down hard, severing Huail's left arm below his elbow.

Huail screamed bloody-pain to the bright sun, and feeling faint he swayed to his right and he almost fell over. Blood gushed, colouring the grass where the lower part of the arm lay. Clutching his bleeding stump, everything around screaming Huail turned and spiralled into blurry-red-mists and bright sunlight. Owain grabbed him by his lank, greasy black hair and pulled his head back. Lifting his sword to strike, he was about to bring the blade slicing down when the Pict fainted, so he let him drop. Pointing his sword at Huail's neck, Owain heard a familiar voice shout, "No, not like this!" He turned to see Gwen standing in the fort's gateway, her face bruised and her lip cut. "Take him to Viroconium to face the judgement of the kings," she pleaded.

"No, he dies today."

"His crime is against me," she protested. "Don't I get a say in his fate?"

"No." Owain grabbed Huail's arm and he dragged his unconscious victim towards the gates.

"Owain!" she shouted, following him into the fort. "You will listen to me!"

"As I've said, he dies today." Seeing Bran's stone, he dragged the bleeding man over, positioned Huail's head on it and placed his booted foot on the man's chest. As the Pict regained consciousness, Owain raised his sword to strike.

Gwen took hold of his sword arm. "Doesn't everyone have the right to be judged by law?"

"Here, I am the law. Stand back, unless you want to taste his blood."

"No, I will not. Think about what you are doing, you are about to kill a defenceless man."

"He lost a fair fight; I have the right to end his sorry life."

"That right was lost when you cut off his arm. Bind his wounds and take him to Viroconium. If you kill him, it will be murder!"

"Let go of my arm, Gwen, he's a rapist and a murderer." With his sword held high, Owain looked first at the Red Cloaks, who were forming a wide circle around him, then to the far palisade where the Pictish warriors had gathered near their horses.

"Please, make it quick," Huail begged through his pain.

The sword swung down, slicing through flesh before crunching into bone. Blood sprayed in all directions, splattering Gwen who screamed and turned away. Huail made a soft gurgling noise as his body quivered. The second blow cracked through neck bones. Hacking into the neck a third time, Owain heard his sword clang as it sparked against the rock, and the headless torso flopped into the dirt. Seeing Gwen with her back to him, a pang of guilt warned him not to reach out to her. Reminding himself that by killing one man he'd prevented a battle, he began walking to the Picts, followed by his warriors.

The men of Alt-Clud had watched the killing in silence, troubled by the consequences of their betrayal. Surely their Prince had been right, King Caw would take revenge upon their families when he learned how his son had been handed over to the Pendragon. If they died fighting, their families might be spared King Caw's reprisals, so they quickly formed four shield-walls.

Owain walked only as close as was sensible, then raised his hand to halt his following Red Cloaks. "Men of Alt-Clud!" he called to the Picts, "sending your Prince out to me was a wise move, you've saved many lives today. If you ride fast, you'll save your families from King Caw's executioners, and there's plenty of room for them in Viroconium. Please, lower your weapons, there's no need for bloodshed." They remained at the ready, unsure of where the Pendragon was leading them. He walked almost up to their raised spearpoints. "I promised you'd be free to leave if you handed Huail over, a promise I'll keep. But if any of you want to join the Legion, I'll accept your allegiance." No one replied. The Pendragon recognised and appreciated their reticence, so he spoke again, "You all have horses; you can fight so you are the kind of men I'll need if I am to successfully defend Briton. Join the Legion, you'll be well fed and paid, and when the Saxons have been driven out, you'll be given their land to use as you wish. Will you join my horse-warriors?"

For a short while there was silence, then a questioning face called from the middle of the shield-wall, "Will we get to wear red cloaks?"

Owain couldn't help but smile. "You'll all receive the red cloak of the Legion when you've completed the training all my warriors go through. But as you're already horse-warriors, it won't take you long to learn our new battle-tactics."

"What about the byrnies, helmets and oval shields, will we be given them?" A Pict asked, stepping out from the front rank. "Will we be treated as equals; Picts have rarely been welcomed south of the Roman Wall?"

"That's because you raid our farms and steal our cattle!" Owain joked. "But yes, you'll be treated as equals because you'll be our sword-brothers, and you'll carry the same weapons and wear the same armour as the Legion, because you'll be a part of it. Join me, all of you."

Bedwyr, surprised by Owain's generosity, asked him, "Do you trust them?"

"Not yet, but I shall."

The Picts turned inwards to talk. Owain watched, hoping a battle could be avoided.

"We can return home to fetch our families?" one of the Picts asked.

"Yes, I'll expect you in Viroconium before the rising of the next moon."

"You are very trusting, Pendragon," the Pict replied. "If you let us go, how can you be sure we'll return?"

"If you don't, King Caw will hunt you down and kill you, only by joining my Red Cloaks can you save yourselves and your families."

Again, the Picts turned inwards to talk, then one by one they dropped their shields and spears. "We'll be with you before the rising of the next moon," the spokesman said, offering his hand to seal the deal.

17.

In the days following the Legion's return from Rhuthun Fort, Gal spent most of his time sitting beneath the wide spread of a sycamore tree in Viroconium's north meadow, watching the Red Cloaks charge and wheel and roar when their spears flew at target stakes. He hadn't seen much of Owain because Gwen needed him, which he understood, but the city was a lonely place for a boy who knew no one. He had met Kareen, and although he enjoyed her company and she was pretty, he much preferred being in the meadow, watching the Red Cloaks practising their battle-charges.

At the far end of the meadow a battle-horn punched a short note into the low clouds, signalling the rear ranks of Red Cloaks to string their bows. Recognising the call, Gal realised he should move because when the bows were strung the Legion would charge towards his part of the meadow and, loose their arrows at the lines of target posts positioned not too far in front of him.

Lazily picking himself up, he ambled to the fence that ran partway along the south fringe of the meadow. Sitting on the top rail, he watched with his usual mix of excitement and longing as the Red Cloaks galloped across the meadow. Closing on their targets, the first two ranks charged with their spears slowly lowering, while the following ranks, at the gallop, nocked arrows to bowstrings.

The battle-horn blasted and the warriors roared their battle-cry, "Britannia!" and Gal cheered when loosed arrows punched into the posts, moments before spearpoints split the stakes. The spearmen wheeled left, the archers guiding their mounts to the right, and both sections galloped back to the top of the meadow. "If I left you alone until the Solstice Sun arrived, would you spend every day here?" asked someone behind him.

Startled, Gal turned on the fence-rail and beamed at the Pendragon. "You walk like a ghost."

Leaning on the fence, Owain said, "You only have ears for horns blasting battle-commands."

"I wish I was a Red Cloak." Sullenly, the boy scratched his fingernail along the fence-rail, looking up again when the battle-horn sounded and the Legion prepared to charge. "When will you teach me to ride and fight?"

"There are good reasons for you not........"

"How's Gwen?" Gal asked, not wanting to be told for the hundredth time that he wasn't old enough to be a warrior.

"She's well, she'll return to her lake tomorrow."

"I won't be going with her, will I?"

"Do you want to?"

"I'm not sure. I'm too young to join the Legion so what am I supposed to do here?"

"I'm sorry for neglecting you, Gal." He'd promised the boy a reward for his part in Gwen's rescue, and he knew what he wanted most. Having chosen realistic rewards, he wished they didn't have such a powerful sting in their tail. "Leaving you alone was wrong of me, but Gwen needed me after what Huail put her through."

"I know, and you were right to spend your time with her." Jumping down from the fence, he said, "I feel caught between two worlds; my past in the forest and my present which is nowhere. I can't return to my cave now, that part of my life is over. Gwen doesn't need me anymore and how do you create a future when you are as young as I am?" The battle-horn blasted and the Red Cloaks charged, so Gal forgot his worries as the ground rumbled and clods of dusty earth clouded the galloping warriors.

Tapping him on the shoulder, Owain said to the boy, "Come with me, I promised you a reward and it's ready."

"A reward, what is it, are you going to make me a Red Cloak?"

"No, you're not old enough."

Swallowing his disappointment, Gal chatted with nervous energy faster than he could breathe as he walked beside Owain. The only thing he'd ever owned was his eating knife, and that wasn't worth much. He felt he would burst with excitement when imagining what the reward might be.

Entering the city, they walked past the dusty bustle of people working to rebuild what the Saxons had destroyed, not that Gal noticed, he was much too excited to care. Making their way through the streets, the boy's guesses became more practical: would he be given a new knife or a hunting bow; was he about to receive his first horse? Passing the rebuilt barracks, he wondered why they weren't heading towards Owain's villa, surely that's where his reward would be?

Coming to a part of the city almost untouched by the fires, Gal found himself standing in front of a small house built against the city wall. The building was made of stone and had been newly washed white with lime, the roof was a mix of thatch and wood, with hearth-smoke seeping lazily through the tightly packed thatching-reeds. "Who lives here?" he asked. "Is this a centurion's house, have you ordered someone to teach me how to fight?"

"No one has lived here since the Saxons ruined the city."

"Oh." The boy's head dropped, along with his expectations.

"Is there something wrong, Gal?"

"No, I'm sorry, I just thought I was..........."

"A wise man never assumes anything, the Merlin told me that," the Prince said, putting his arm around Gal's shoulders. "Come, I've something to show you." He lifted the latch and opened the door.

Inside, the house was just one room, with a central hearth for warmth and cooking. In the far corner there was a straw sleeping pallet, part of it covered by a hemp sack. Near the hearth a shelf held clay cooking pots, beakers and a couple of knives and spoons and, under the shelf stood a bucket and an iron tripod holding a small cauldron.

"I don't understand?" the boy said.

"You need a place to live when you are in the city, so I'm giving you this house. Everything in here is yours."

Unable to believe his good fortune, he looked at Owain half smiling, whilst worrying what he was supposed to do with a home of his own. Pleased with the gift but confused, he felt guilty because what he really wanted was to join the Legion. Looking around his new house, he tried to show Owain just how grateful he was, but his smile was forced. The Pendragon saw the truth in the boy's eyes, so he said, "There's more, look under the sacking."

Curious, Gal lifted the rough cloth off his sleeping pallet. His mouth opened but no words came out. Unable to believe what he was seeing, he stared at the bundle on the bed and found his voice, "Are these for me?" he asked.

"As I said, everything in this house is yours."

"I don't know what to say." Picking up the sword, he felt the pommel, almost in awe of the weapon. It wasn't the same quality as Owain's steel blade, nor was it as long and heavy but it was a well-made cavalry sword. "It is beautiful," he said, pointing it into the light coming in through the unshuttered window. Smoothing his hand along the cold metal, he imagined it slicing through a Saxon's neck. "How can I ever thank you, what does this gift mean?"

"It means you are becoming a man."

"I must give it a name, something like 'Saxon Killer' but I won't decide yet, I'll wait until I'm old and strong enough to use it in battle." Laying the sword down, his heart pumping wild in his chest, he picked up the red woollen cloak neatly folded on the straw. Uncertainty made him look at Owain, who, smiling the broadest of smiles, nodded to him. Gal knew he was too young to join the Legion, so why had he been given a red cloak and a sword?

"The gifts are from myself and Gwen, given in gratitude for your part in saving her from Huail. We are both proud to call you our friend."

Gal couldn't hold back the huge smile spreading across his face, nor the gentle tears he wasn't ashamed to shed. "They are really mine, the house, the sword and the red cloak?" he said with so much wonder that Owain had to laugh. Taking his cloak in both hands, he held its softness against his face. “What would my parents have said if they’d lived to see this?”

“They’d have told you how proud of you they were.”

Sifting through all the changes in his life since he’d met the Prince of Rhos, the boy thought about how strange the fates can be. Not many moons ago he was an orphan, alone in the forest, living off his wits and whatever nature provided. Now he had a red cloak, a sword and a new home. His journey towards avenging the killing of his family could begin. There was one question he was desperate to have answered. “When do I begin my warrior training?”

“When you return.”

Confusion replaced the joy on the boy’s face. “Am I going somewhere?”

Owain walked over and put his hands on the boy’s shoulders. “There’s something which must be done, it is vital to the security of our people.”

“It’s something dangerous, isn’t it?”

“Yes. I need someone who can run, hide, listen and watch, someone with courage who knows the hidden paths of the forest and, speaks Saxon.”

“What must I do?” His heart dropped into his stomach.

“Go to Andredes Caester. King Aelle is planning something, and I need to know what. None of the four spies I sent have returned, so they are probably dead. I’m sure you’re aware of what the Saxons will do if they catch you.”

“I know the risks.”

"I'm hoping the Saxons won't be suspicious of a boy. I know it's a dangerous gamble, but you speak their language better than any of us. I wouldn't say you are my last hope, but that wouldn't be far from the truth."

If ever a summer breeze felt like a whirlwind, this was it. He knew he couldn't refuse, nor did he want to because it would be an adventure, one he was already sensing the feel of. Owain was right to think he could go where others could not; he was small enough to use the shadows, young enough to be ignored and he had the guile and courage the mission required. "I'll do it, when do I leave?"

"Tomorrow, I want you to escort Gwen back to the lake, it's on your way so you won't lose any time." Looking proudly at the boy, he picked up the new sword and held it up to the light. "When you return," he said, "I promise that myself, Cai and Bedwyr will begin your battle-training. Within a couple of years or so, you should be strong and skilled enough to ride with us to war."

Cadwallon's hastily arranged gathering of kings in the Temple of Mithras, fell silent when King Meirchion Gul of Rheged, stood to speak. "I'm sorry, Cadwallon," he began as the oak doors opened and a latecomer walked in. After waiting for King Erbin of Dumnonia to take his seat, Meirchion continued, "Some of us don't want to be subject to a high king."

"Your father is dead!" someone called from the back of the room, causing cheering, applause and laughter.

"With respect, Cadwallon," said Meirchion, "I feel I must add that many of us aren't convinced there's a need to continue the alliance, it has long been resented." Once more the kings yelled their approval, some of them standing to shake their fists at the dais, where the Merlin, Prince Cadwallon and Prince Owain were seated. "The time has come for a vote, what do you say brothers?" the King of Rheged asked his fellow royals, sending the room into rapturous applause and cheering.

Tapping his fingers irritably on the arm of his chair, the Pendragon listened with increasing contempt for the rebellious kings. He was sick of the whole business, for three long and frustrating days he'd listened to their obstructive arguments; if they didn't want the alliance to continue, why didn't they walk out and leave him to get on with training his Pictish recruits? Closing his ears to the political manoeuvrings, he thought about Gwen. Since his father's death, all opposition to their marriage had gone, so as soon as possible he'd ride to the lake and marry her, then return to Viroconium to prepare the Legion for war.

The noise in the temple increased, two kings were locked in an argument, a border dispute, which amused Owain because they'd already forgotten about voting to dissolve the alliance. This council was going nowhere and, looking at his brother, who was listening to every word, he seriously considered leaving him to it. He was about to get up and leave when his brother stood to address the kings. A respectful hush silenced the gathering.

"I'd like to thank you all for coming," Cadwallon began. "Many of you have travelled far to attend these meetings, and I appreciate the sacrifices you've made to be here. However, it worries me that we've been at this for three days and we are getting nowhere, so maybe we should forget about the alliance and go our separate ways." He listened to the grumbled murmurs and mumbled whisperings, then he hit them hard. "You obviously believe you can survive as individual kingdoms, so go home and prepare your defences because King Aelle is mustering a massive army."

"What are you saying?" one of the kings called over the heads of the seated royals.

"I'm telling you the meeting is over, as is the alliance." He sat down to complete silence, the room suspicious, heavy with uncertainty and doubt. Turning to Owain, he spoke loud enough for everyone to hear. "Summon the Legion, I want this room cleared."

Meirchion Gul stood again. "You are prepared to abandon the alliance?"

"Yes," Cadwallon replied casually. "You can remain in the alliance or, fight the Saxons alone, it's your choice."

"I've said what I came to say," the King of Rheged grumpily said, and he sat down.

As no one wanted to speak, Cadwallon eased himself out of his chair again. Walking to the front of the dais, he set himself to make the prepared speech he hoped would begin the creation of a new kind of unified Briton. "You all fought beneath my father's Pendragon banner, accepting his rule because he conquered most of your kingdoms. In doing so, he united the peoples of Briton for the first time since the Roman legions departed our shores. Have you forgotten how easily the Angles, Saxons, Frisians and Jutes conquered the divided kingdoms in the early days of the wars? Where are the tribes of the Cantii, the Trinovantes, Atribates,

Catuvellauni and Icenii? They were once proud peoples who foolishly chose to stand alone against the invaders. They are gone now, swept away like autumn leaves in a storm." He let his words sink in, watching their faces react to their realities. "I want to offer you something new, a free vote, an open election that I hope will benefit all the people, even the lowest born because it's our obligation to protect every life within the boundaries of our kingdoms."

"Give us the meat of your idea!" King Meirchion demanded, having assumed the role of spokesperson.

"Yes, get on with it!" another voice shouted.

"What I'm suggesting is that every king attends regular councils, here, at my expense, to debate and plan, elect and dismiss with each man having one vote. There are many subjects dear to us all, such as the wars against the Saxons, the high kingship, the sharing of a common wealth and harvest, the building of roads and cities, the list is endless. Should these concerns be the responsibility of one man?"

"Are you suggesting that power should be shared?" King Erbin of Dumnonia asked.

"Yes, I believe it should be divided," Cadwallon replied.

"With Viroconium being the home of the democracy?" Meirchion asked suspiciously.

"It is the centre of our combined kingdoms," Erbin pointed out.

"We will of course require a leader for these councils," Cadwallon took up his thread again, "someone to maintain control, oversee debates and organise the voting. Whether the elected man is given a title, or not, will be your choice. Whichever title might be considered appropriate for the new office, you must vote for the man you think best qualified to serve the needs of all the Britons. I'd also like to suggest that the elected man serves for a given term, after which another election is called to replace him. I understand this idea is new to you, so you should return to your kingdoms to consider it. We could meet again the day before the summer solstice, to discuss the vote and how we might make a democracy, with an elected senate, work for us all."

King Erbin was the first to reply, "What you're suggesting has some merit. The Romans used democracy to build a republic, with two elected men leading their senate. I like the idea; I'll return for the solstice gathering." Others agreed with him.

Owain, absorbing the idea of a democratic alliance, wasn't impressed. While men argue, armies conquer, there is a time to debate and a time to fight, so if his brother asked for his opinion, he'd be disappointed. This wasn't his concern though, he was the Pendragon, elected to defend the people with sword, spear and bow. Words are fine in the game of politics, but the Saxons would come at them with swords, spears and axes.

Waking from another night as Princess Gorpe's husband, King Ceredig eased himself up the pillows so that he could enjoy looking at his beautiful, sleeping wife. Her well-formed curves made her easy to lust after, so he'd enjoyed the sex she'd been more than willing to share.

With the first rays of dawn hazily slipping through the open shutters, memories of their coupling warmed his loins. He felt a little guilty about having taken someone so young to his bed, but political marriages often throw together two people of different ages. She had come to him willingly, displaying a rare appetite for sexual learning, not that she needed any guidance, her lusts being a more than adequate teacher.

Wondering how she felt about being used as a bargaining tool, he felt a little sorry for her. Someone as beautiful and intelligent as she was should be free to choose a husband, not have one forced upon her. She did look lovely though, lying naked beside him, sleeping, her golden hair splayed loosely over her feather pillow.

Thinking about the possible consequences of his alliance with King Aelle, and the promises he'd made to satisfy his ambitions, he congratulated himself on his good fortune. He'd be safe from Saxon attacks and would receive their aid if he chose to expand his kingdom west. With his eastern border safe from Saxon raids, his people would prosper from the trade which would inevitably come. His kingdom would become rich and powerful because he'd married the daughter of the greatest threat to Celtic Briton, and that thought amused him.

Then a seed of doubt crept into his mind because the alliance may not hold if Gorpe died and, women as young as her often died during childbirth. His lands and people would be safe for a year or two, beyond that there were no guarantees. Smoothing the tip of his finger over Gorpe's cheek, he hoped she'd live a long life and give him many sons, because if she didn't, his days as a king could be short-lived.

He stared at the wood-planked ceiling, turning in his mind King Aelle's plans for conquest. The Saxon was raising a massive army, some spies claimed that six to seven thousand warriors had already massed in Andredes Caester's meadows. If the rumours were true, no one, including the Pendragon, would survive the swords of such a vast army. If the Saxon King did kill the Pendragon and cut the Celtic union in two, his own kingdom could be the next to fall.

Had he been too hasty when accepting the deal, a king's daughter and her dowry of gold in exchange for the Saxon army's safe passage through his lands? There was nothing he could do about it now; he'd made his bed and was enjoying its comforts. He then realised there was something he could do, without breaking his word to King Aelle. If he sent word of the Saxon's plans to Viroconium, that would give the Britons time to prepare. If Aelle discovered he'd warned the Pendragon, he'd kill him, so nobody except his messenger could know about his deceit, should he decide to ease his guilt with betrayal. Gareth was the most trustworthy man he knew, so if he chose to send someone north to warn the Pendragon, it must be him.

Mulling the idea, he felt Gorpe's body move. Waking, she snuggled closer to him, slipped her warm hand up his thigh and smiled when she felt his renewed excitement stiffen in her hand. Closing his eyes, he relaxed into the stimulating massage she'd already proved to be expert at.

Reluctantly and unsteadily walking through the woodlands at the edge of the Saxon meadow, Gal wiped his sweaty forehead with his sleeve, his right hand clenched into a tense fist. It would take a great deal of courage for him to walk out of the forest and cross the meadow to Andredes Caester, and he wasn't sure he had it. For two days he'd been watching the fort, so he knew what to expect and he couldn't put it off any longer, if he was to do what four grown men had failed to survive.

Climbing a tree to see what was happening in the meadow, he found a comfortable perch to watch the comings and goings. As before, he was shocked by the size of the shantytown the newly arrived warriors had built. Thousands had answered King Aelle's request for warriors, so he understood why Owain was so desperate to know what the Saxons were planning, because when this titan-swarm began its march it would be difficult, if not impossible, to stop it. Swinging down from the tree, he swallowed his fear and walked nervously into the scrublands edging the forest.

Seeing a thick patch of bracken, not ten paces beyond the scrubland, he crouched and ran for the cover, where he dropped to his knees, questioning his courage and his chances of survival. One accidental slip into the Celtic language and he'd be dead before the Sun went down, one too many questions asked to the wrong person and he'd be dangling from a Saxon rope. Between the forest and the shantytown rolled a meadow he must cross without arousing suspicion, but his courage failed so he lay back in the bracken, hating himself for being a coward.

Watching a drifting white cloud, he recalled the slaughter of his childhood village, and the burnt body of his father hanging upside-down from a tree. Cursing his cowardice, he knelt and peered over the bracken. Those thousands of spearmen could not be allowed to roam at will, hacking a swathe of destruction across Celtic lands. Others wouldn't suffer the heartache he'd lived with for two painfilled years so, forcing himself to his feet, he began his unsteady walk towards the fort.

His legs felt as heavy as stones, his mouth was as dry as newly baked bread and sweat trickled down his back, but he forced his heavy legs through the knee-high meadow grass, all the time wishing he was somewhere else. Wanting to make himself look like an escaped slave, he'd torn his clothes a little, and dirtied his skin, but would his disguise work?

He felt sick to the core, his energy sapping with every nervous step he took. There was no denying he wanted to run back into the forest, but he felt proud that Owain believed in him enough to trust him, and if the Pendragon had confidence in him, so should he. Walking unsteadily on, he realised his nerves had him veering to the left. Straightening his course, he noticed a great hulk of a man carrying an armful of spears, walk out of the fort and through the shantytown. The great hairy hulk dropped the spears on the grass, picked one up and took aim at what looked like a man, with his head lolling to one side, tied to a post.

Curious, Gal forgot his fears and wheeled left to find out if the target was one of the Pendragon's dead spies. Closing on the huge warrior, he saw that the man tied to the post was made from rags stuffed full of straw. An idea shot into his head, so he sat down to watch, less than ten paces from the spearman.

Having missed the target with his first throw, the giant Saxon raised another spear, set himself and hurled it at the straw-man. The spear flew high and wide, landing about twenty paces further on. The boy laughed to himself, it had been a massive throw but flew nowhere near the target.

Patiently watching every movement of the big-muscled man, he could see from the way the warrior stood that he'd be lucky to hit a cloud in a thunderstorm! The warrior must be a bit simple, he decided, because everyone knows you can't accurately hurl a spear with your chest square-on to the target. If this Saxon was an example of what the Celts would soon face in battle, Owain shouldn't be so worried. On the other hand, he wouldn't want to face this bull-muscled giant in a shield-wall, he could split someone clean in two with one axe blow!

After watching the Saxon cast spear after spear, each one missing the target, Gal walked over to the bearded, blonde-haired man, who turned to welcome him. "Have you come to learn how to throw a spear?" the giant growled in a deep, gravelly voice.

"I'm not sure it's my place," Gal replied, smiling at the ruddy-faced man, amused the Saxon thought he could teach him anything. "I only know how to fetch and carry."

"All Saxons are warriors." The hairy bulk looked the boy over, assuming from his ragged clothes and dirty face he must be a runaway, a servant or a slave. He'd never noticed him in the fort, and if he was a slave, he might prove useful. "If your trade is to fetch and carry, go and retrieve my spears, then we'll see what kind of warrior you might make."

The boy did as he was told, pleased the stupid Saxon hadn't the brains to suspect him. Returning with the spears, he stood beside the warrior and turned to face the straw target. "It's too far away," he said, apologetically.

"Too far?" The man grunted, and pulled the boy by the scruff of his dirty neck, ten paces further forward. "This should be close enough for a scrawny lad like you."

Aiming to miss the target, Gal threw a spear. The deliberately weak throw flew off to the left, landing in a wide patch of white clover, sending a huge bumble-bee buzzing off to find somewhere safer to fill its pollen sacks.

"You can't even kill a bee!" the warrior joked. "When casting a spear in battle, you don't worry about your aim because the target is so big, it's more about stopping a mass of advancing men before they get too close." Feeling the boy's arm muscles, he laughed again. "You need to grow a little before throwing a spear. I've done my practice for today, let's return to my hut and have some food. My woman, and she's a fine-looker, will be happy to see a young face at the table because she's given me no sons or daughters. She does have the finest teats you're ever likely to see though, and maybe I prefer them to dirty-faced young brats like yourself!" His thunderous laughter filled the meadow. Calming himself, he looked seriously at the boy. "My name is Osgar, what's yours?" he asked as they made their way through the stinking shantytown.

"Aesc," Gal lied. "I'm the son of Godric, son of Cenric, son of Aelfgar, son of Aelfred, son of Oisc, son of Horsa, son of Woden."

Looking the scruffy boy up and down, Osgar asked, "Your forefathers had good names, how come you look like you've spent many days foraging in the forest?"

Almost tripping over a muddy duckboard, Gal moved close to Osgar for protection, because the looks he was getting from the people in the shantytown were enough to worry the bravest of warriors. "My family were border people," he began his planned story. "Our village was attacked by Celts. My father was the head-man and he did try to organise our few warriors into a shield-wall, but we'd been taken by surprise so most of our men died defending their homes. I was taken to one of the Celtic towns, with the rest of the children and women, and sold into slavery. That's how I know how to fetch and carry, that being my main job in the home I was bought into. They couldn't hold me for long though, it only took me the passing of three moons to escape. When I ran, I made straight for the forest, it seemed like the safest place to be and, I've been there ever since. Not knowing where I was or where to go, I decided my best option was to follow the Sun and walk east, which would hopefully take me back to my people's homeland. Where am I, Osgar?" he innocently asked, "are we close to the borders?"

"No. Next time you run you should take someone with you who has a better sense of direction! You've come to King Aelle's capital of the South Saxons, Andredes Caester, you're a long way from your homeland. You'll be safe enough with me though, I'm a respected warrior."

Gal couldn't believe his good fortune, or how stupid this huge man was, concluding that if Osgar was so well respected, it could only be because of his size. Having thought that, he liked the Saxon, he may not be very bright but he seemed to have a good heart. He couldn't have found a more likely man to get him into the fort.

Walking through the gateway without a question being asked, Gal's eyes widened as Osgar led him through the busy hive of war preparations. "I've never seen so many blacksmiths working," he said. The Saxon didn't hear him, he was thinking about how happy his woman would be to meet the boy. "Osgar!" Gal tugged at the man's sleeve. "Why are there so many people working on weapons?"

"Isn't it obvious? You're not very clever, Aesc."

"My father used to say that," Gal lied again. "Why are there so many warriors here?"

"War."

"Are we going to kill Celts, can I come too?"

"Aesc!" the Saxon exclaimed, waving to a hammering blacksmith, "you're nothing but skin and bone! You need to grow tall and strong before joining a shield-wall. We'll feed you up and teach you to use a shield and spear, then you can think about killing Celts. You'll stay behind when the army marches, to help my woman, she'll soon fatten you up."

"I'd rather go with you."

"Next summer, when you've grown a little, then we can think about turning you into a warrior."

Walking past flaring forges and lines of seated men carving coppiced branches into spear-shafts, they came to a rectangular hut near the fort's east wall. The hut was made entirely from rough planked wood, except for the straw thatching covering the roof. Above the open doorway hung two sets of cow horns. "There's something you should know," Osgar said before going in. "My woman is not of our blood, she's a Celt. She was a slave once but she's a good woman who cooks delicious food and, when I have the horn-ups she rides the stallion like the best, so show her respect."

"If she's your woman, I'll treat her as I did my own mother."

"Just be kind to her, she had a hard life before I took her in." He walked into the smoky darkness of the one-roomed home. "Woman, I've brought us a boy."

Gal followed him into the dark hut, his eyes drawn to the glowing hearth at the far end. Walking to the table in the centre of the room, he froze, his heart almost bursting from his chest as the woman kneeling beside the fire, stirring a meat stew, turned and forced a confused smile as she looked from the boy to the man. Osgar slapped his find on the back and joked, "Didn't I tell you she has great teats?"

Gal stared at the woman in stony silence, his heart crying out to the mother he thought was dead.

18.

After spending the rest of the day following Osgar around the fort, and the vast collection of wooden huts in the meadows, Gal was emotionally exhausted by the time the warrior led him back to his hut. Although very hungry, the boy was reluctant to step back into Osgar's home because he wasn't sure he could hide his feelings for his mother, and what would he say to her without giving away his identity to the giant Saxon? He must get her alone to plan their escape, but would she come with him, just how deep were the roots of her new life?

Stepping into the limited light within the hut, he saw she had the evening meal ready. Taking his place at the table, his eyes followed her, begging her for a smile while she served the steaming food into wooden bowls. Not once during the meal did Carys make eye contact with him, which created an uneasy atmosphere they both hoped wouldn't be picked up by Osgar. The Saxon, shovelling huge amounts of stewed chicken into his mouth, noticed his woman avoiding the boy, which concerned him enough for him to think about asking her why but, reasoning her cold response was normal, with the lad not being her own, he decided that time would bring them closer.

The meal passed in uneasy silence, Carys rarely looking up from her bowl while her man, often looking from boy to woman, grunted and belched as he ate. Having filled his belly, Osgar shoved his bowl to one side, looked disapprovingly at them both then took his place on a bench beside the hearth. "I'll not be going to the main hall tonight," he growled, "I'm sleeping here."

"What about the boy?" she asked.

"He can sleep beneath the table, fetch him a blanket."

"He'll be cold under there."

"Then give him two blankets. The hearth is ours; Saxon children sleep where they are put. Anyway, aren't all young.........."

"Having spent so many nights in the forest, I'll sleep anywhere," Gal butted in to prevent an argument.

"Get some sleep, Aesc," Osgar demanded. "Tomorrow you'll work for your keep."

His mother handed him two woollen blankets and he crawled under the table.

Stretching himself along a high-backed, wooden bench, full of ale and warmed by the smoky hearth, the warrior slipped into contented dreaming. Unable to sleep, Carys waited throughout the night, listening to the big man snoring. Reckoning the Sun would soon rise, she tiptoed over to the table. Kneeling, she stroked a finger through her son's hair and whispered, "Are you awake?" She looked nervously back at Osgar, who was snoring like a blowing battle-horn.

"Mother," Gal whispered as she crawled under the table.

Taking him in her arms, she gave him a loving hug. He was about to speak when she gently pressed her finger to his lips, shook her head and pointed at Osgar. Crawling back out, she picked up a large wicker basket and, without looking back at her man she led her son out of the hut and into the remains of the night. "Don't say anything yet, other women may be heading for the wood-barn."

Stepping carefully around drunken warriors who'd slept where they'd fallen in the courtyard, the two of them skirted the warm forges, heading for the woodstore near the north wall. Patrolling the battlements, sentries stood lifeless-black, staring blankly at the woodlands surrounding the meadows. Lifting the latch of the wood-barn door, Carys opened it and pulled Gal inside. His eyes quickly adjusted to the dark, and he saw piles of cut logs stacked in neat rows, with pathways between the stacks. "Come with me," she whispered, and they walked to the dark at the back of the shed. "Fill the basket slowly, Gal, give us time to talk." Just saying his name brought tears to her eyes. Never had she imagined seeing any of the family she'd loved and lost, believing them all to be dead. "Why are you here?" she asked.

He was about to tell her he was a spy, when an emotion caught in his throat. Looking down at the logs in his basket, he wiped away a tear. "I thought you were dead, I thought I was alone."

The significance of what he'd said hit her hard, she wanted to cry but knew that she mustn't. The door-latch clicked and lifted, and a basket-carrying woman walked in. Carys and Gal crouched and hid behind a log pile, the boy watching from the dark while the newcomer collected logs. It didn't take her long, with her basket filled she left without looking their way.

"Why are you here?" Carys asked, placing a couple of logs in their basket.

"I'm here at the request of the Pendragon, I'm his spy."

"Don't be ridiculous, you are much too young!" She looked at him in disbelief. "How can a boy from a forest village know the Pendragon?"

"That's a long story, but he is my friend."

"He can't be much of a friend if he sent you here."

"He chose me because I speak fluent Saxon."

"It's madness, you must leave as soon as the Sun rises."

"I can't, I'm here to find out why King Aelle's gathering such a large army. The Pendragon wants to know where and when the Saxons will strike?"

"If I tell you, will you promise to leave and never return to Andredes Caester?"

"Yes, but how do you know about Aelle's plans? Escaping isn't going to be easy."

"I know a way," she reassured him. "As for King Aelle's war plans, Osgar told me everything when he returned from the attack on Viroconium. King Aelle will march to Aqua Sulis. By the summer solstice he wants his army inside the city, then he'll strike north, leaving Prince Cissa and part of his army behind to carve out a second kingdom."

"It's that simple?"

"There's more. Princess Gorpe has been given in marriage to King Ceredig, so Aelle's army now has free access through the lands of the Durotriges. Tell the Pendragon not to trust Ceredig."

Gal couldn't believe it, why would a British king help the Saxons? "The traitor won't live long if the Pendragon gets his hands on him."

“We’ve more important things to worry about,” she reminded him, “like getting you away without Osgar catching you.”

“I can’t just leave,” he replied, taking her hand in his. “You must come with me; you can be free again.”

“It isn’t that simple, Gal.” So much had changed in her life, so many uncertainties had grown more substantial roots. “I’ve come to love and trust Osgar, he’s a good man. I want to go with you but I have a life here, and where would I go, how would I live?”

Not understanding, his voice cracked when he tried to make her see reason. “You are a Celt, these aren’t your people, you should come with me, I’m your son.”

She could feel his pain. “I love you, Gal, but I won’t leave Osgar for the uncertainty beyond the fort’s walls. I was born a Celt; I’ll die a Saxon.”

“Why?” Hot rejection and anger flooded through him as he took a few steps back. How could she love a Saxon and choose to live amongst these savages? They were her blood enemies, had she forgotten how they murdered her family? What really cut through his bones though, was how she could reject him so easily. “You’ll never be a Saxon,” he seethed. “They are animals, worse than pigs, how can you live with such filth?”

“Try to see reason,” she pleaded. “I’m a woman, life is different for us. We can’t forge kingdoms or take up trades, our lives are given to us by the men we marry, that’s how things are. Women are never truly free, even queens are used as political offerings so that men can gain land and power. How many women do you know who chose their own paths? I’ve certainly never met any.”

He thought of Gwen and how she lived free from the world and the influence of men. He wanted to tell his mother about her, but there was no other woman like Gwen. Instead, he offered her what he could, hoping to change her mind. "Before I left Viroconium, the Pendragon gave me a house. It's big enough for us both, we could make a new life there. I also have a red cloak and a sword, so when I return, I'll learn to ride and fight with the Legion. Wouldn't you like to see that, your son charging across the meadow with the finest warriors in Briton?" He then attempted one last desperate appeal to the woman who'd fed him at her breast. "I can't lose you again, don't ask me to leave you behind."

"Don't say that, Gal." She'd suffered so much pain in her life, and as much as she wanted to be with him, she couldn't face uprooting her life again. Her heart pulled her in two directions, she could barely speak but knew what she must say. "My life is here now. I'm sorry, I'm so very sorry."

His heart hardened, feeding a defensive rage and, unable to restrain himself he told her about his sister. "Do you know how your daughter died? There was blood around her throat and between her legs. Did Osgar play a part, was it his knife that slit her throat, was he slobbering with lust when he ruined her bleeding innocence?"

"Oh, Gal." She turned away from him, hiding her tears.

"I'm sorry," he whispered into the dark. "I shouldn't have said that."

Owain needed to think. Inside the dark, unlit Temple of Mithras he spread himself lazily along a wooden bench, remembering the wise words of the Merlin: 'feel the spirit but touch the earth' which he took to mean that although thoughts, feelings and dreams might seem true, they were the images of our desires and mustn't be confused with reality.

He hadn't come to the temple to contemplate the wisdom of the Merlin; he'd sought its solitude to reflect upon a life changing decision. Although the change was something he wanted, he had his doubts: could he make the sacrifice; did he want to completely give himself to someone? Closing his eyes to think, he heard the metal doorlatch beneath the image of Mithras, click and lift and the door squeaked slowly open. Sitting up, he saw a dark figure walking towards him and, judging by the presence of the intruder, it could only be one person. "You've come here to think about Gwen," the Merlin said. "Do you mind if I sit with you?"

"No," Owain replied, and the Druid made himself comfortable on the bench. How the Merlin always knew what was in his mind was a mystery he'd never get used to. "I need her," he said without thinking.

"She needs you also," the Merlin whispered, his pleasure at the union softening his voice. "There's something I want you to remember; you'll have each other but you can never have each other."

"How can you have someone and not have them?" Owain asked, certain he'd seen the twitch of a smile on the Druid's face.

"That's something you must work out for yourself."

"You came here to confuse me?"

"Not everything is meant to be clear in the present. All moments lead to others, nothing is fixed, reality is untangled by individual perspective."

"I've known you all my life, Merlin, and you are still an enigma. I understand your wisdom often takes the form of a planted seed, and that seed must grow before the harvest can be reaped, but sometimes I wish you'd say what you mean."

"I'm not a dictator, you must think for yourself, but if you want me to speak plainly, I shall. I know you've been trying to decide if you should leave the city and marry my daughter, so I planted the seed to warn you that you'll never own her, one soul cannot own another. Think about it, you can be together but also free, you take all and give everything, it's the essence of love and it is not a mystery. You have a question, ask it?"

Owain didn't hesitate because there was no point, the Merlin already knew the question. "Is this the appropriate time to be taking a wife, when there's so much uncertainty?"

"I'd say everything is certain," the Merlin replied without having to think, "quite typical in fact. The Saxons are always making trouble, as are the British kings, so what is new?"

Owain sighed into the dark and lowered his head. His biggest concern was his brother, who was vulnerable to ambitious men and, if the Saxons attacked in strength while he was away, would Cadwallon know how to respond?

"Don't worry about your brother," the Merlin's voice silenced the Prince's thoughts. "An attack may come, but not yet, other diversions will happen before the Saxons march. Owain ap Einion is not the centre of the universe, Briton won't collapse for the want of its Pendragon for a few days. Two burdens of equal weight balance each other, two different forms of love complement existence. You can be husband and brother at the same time, one will not push the other aside."

The young Prince got up and walked over to the dais. "The scales don't feel balanced," he said, "and there are three weights, not two. My sword belongs to the people, I swore when raised on the shield that I'd serve the people before myself."

"Two weights," the Merlin corrected him as he walked over to the Prince. "Cadwallon and Gwen are as much a part of our nation as the lowest born fieldworker. Do you want to marry Gwen, it's a simple question?"

"Yes, but is it the right thing to do?"

"You alone know if it is your destiny to go to her. You should feel the power of the union drawing you in, if you cannot, the union will be short lived, perhaps destructive. Some of your life-branches bend away from my daughter, others embrace her, some will break and others can rot but as I've said to you many times, none of your branches can be avoided."

Thinking, Owain leapt onto the dais and sat in his council seat. Looking thoughtfully at the Merlin, he said, "You live by the will of the Mother Goddess Enaid, you understand why she entangles branches. What is my fate?"

"It is not my place to offer such a gift." Sitting on the bench nearest the dais, the Merlin considered how much of the future he could safely pass on. "Do you remember the story I told you when you were a boy, the one about the gathering of the druids on Mona, and the prophecy?"

"Yes, clearly, it was one of my favourite stories, though I've never understood its meaning."

"The meaning will become clear to you when you are ready to accept it. When you are riding to the forest to marry Gwen, remember how the story made you feel. If the meaning does come to you, don't be afraid of it. We mortals don't govern the world or the fates, we only play our small parts, like actors in an amphitheatre. Your part is to go to the Forest Island, Gwen will be waiting for you there, but you won't see her until the Goddess decides the time is right, so be patient."

The Merlin slipped into thoughtful silence. Satisfied he understood his feelings, he spoke again, "When the ceremony is over, I'll be proud to call you my son. I've always loved you and, watching you grow has been one of my greatest pleasures. If you need me, come to me; I'll never deny you." Again, he paused for reflection, unsure if he should plant another seed. Opening his mind to the wisdom and wastefulness of feelings, he spoke to Owain with the authority of the Merlin, "As we struggle through our many changes in life, some things are added, others are taken away. During those changes some of us take on new names, names that reflect the broken and burning homes we abandon, as well as the marbled mountains we fear to climb. Soon, and I'll not tell you when, you'll receive a new name, one you won't like but must find a way of accepting, not for yourself, but for your people. Carry that name with you, hate and fear it but wear it for those who are living now, and the souls yet to find flesh. The name you'll receive will give future generations hope and courage, meaning, pride and direction, the name becoming a symbol for a nation who'll consider themselves to be your children."

The weight of the words hit Owain like a winter storm, and he feared their cold burden. "Do I have a choice?" he asked, feeling the stirrings of rebellion. "Will this name be forced upon me?"

"Yes, and yes. Three days hence, saddle your horse and leave, and don't return to Viroconium until you and Gwen have become one in the eyes of the Goddess."

Throughout his second day in Andredes Caester, Gal had been worked so hard by Osgar, hunting in the forest and chopping logs for the communal store, that after devouring his evening meal he'd immediately crawled beneath the table to sleep. His dreams were irregular and broken, and while struggling through images of an axe wielding Osgar yelling at him to stand and fight, he felt a hand nudging his shoulder. Opening his eyes, he saw his mother kneeling beside him. "Get yourself up," she said. "If you are going to escape, it must be now."

"Where's Osgar?" Rubbing the sleep from his eyes, he looked around the hut for the big man.

"He slept in the main hall, drunk with the rest of King Aelle's personal guard."

Seeing her pick up a small, cloth covered basket he climbed out from under the table. "Where are we going?"

"To the forest with the mushroom pickers."

In the misty haze of a new dawn, they joined a large group of women and children near the fort's gate. This happened most mornings during the mushroom seasons, so Carys wasn't worried about the guards seeing them leave. Stepping out of the fort, neither herself nor the boy received a second glance from the sentries.

Walking through the shantytown and into the meadows, the women followed the path that led to the forest. Carys could barely breathe she was so nervous, her anxieties not helped by women wanting to know who the boy was and, where he'd come from. Trying to remain calm, she answered them by recalling Osgar's story of his arrival, which soon had the women clucking around him, giving him hugs and kisses whilst ruffling his shaggy blonde hair.

Embarrassed by the fussy attention, Gal kept his mouth shut, sticking close to his mother for protection until he noticed a pretty, red-haired girl who wasn't too shy to smile at him. Seeing him veer towards the girl, Carys pinched his ear and pulled him back, and whispered something to him no one else heard. Suitably chastised, he walked alongside her, occasionally glancing at the redhead, who'd also been pulled into line by her mother.

Entering the damp darkness of the forest, the group split to search for their harvests. Carys took Gal's hand and led him north, deeper into the woodlands. Walking along paths she knew well, she didn't utter a word, not until they were far enough away not to be overheard. Deciding they were well out of sight, she stopped to catch her breath. Sitting herself on the soft, mulchy forest floor she handed Gal the basket. "This is for you."

Removing the covering cloth, he saw a knife, a large piece of cheese, two small loaves of grainy bread, a hunk of salted ham and a stoppered clay water-bottle. Sitting beside her, he saw tears rolling down her cheeks, so he asked her why she was crying?

"I'm coming with you," she replied regretfully.

For the briefest moment he felt so happy that he couldn't speak, his mother would be his again. Concerned for her, he asked, "What about Osgar?"

"He'll come after us." She dried her eyes. "When he catches us, he'll kill us."

"He won't find us," Gal said confidently, putting his arm around her. "I know the forest better than him, I lived in it for two years."

"Don't underestimate him, Osgar might look and act like a lumbering fool but he's quick and cunning, he knows the ways of the forest so he'll have no problem tracking us. Hopefully, King Aelle will keep him occupied until well after the midday meal, and if we are lucky, longer. If we can get a day ahead of him, we might reach Celtic lands before he finds us, although knowing him as I do, being in British territory won't deter his hunt."

"Are you saying that at some point I'm going to have to kill him, that's the only way we'll ever be free?" It was a sobering thought.

"Yes. We'll keep running until either he is dead, or we are."

Absorbing their reality, for a while they both considered their mortality. This wasn't how Gal thought it would be. "I expected to be running on my own," he broke the silence. "Can you keep up with me?"

"I can move as quickly as you, don't forget I grew up in a forest village."

"So, we run for a while, walk and eat then run again, and if we don't stop to sleep, we might make it as far as my old cave in about four days. I'm used to forest life, and going without food for more than a day, are you sure you want to come?"

"I've survived the hardships of giving birth, regular rape and slavery, don't think that because I'm a woman I can't survive a forest run."

"I was sure you wouldn't leave him," he said while snuggling into her chest.

"I couldn't lose you again, Gal. Some of what you said in the wood-barn made sense. As you get older life becomes more complicated, you lose the courage and energy of youth because you know more about life and its pains." It hadn't been an easy decision for her, and, throughout the night she'd tossed and turned until accepting she couldn't be parted from her son again.

"How will Osgar know we've left?" he asked. "Even if we don't return from the mushroom gathering with the others, wouldn't he think we're about some other daily chores?"

Looking through the trees into the eerie darkness below the thick ceiling of leaves and branches, where here and there thin beams of almost parallel dawn light slid through the trees, she made her confession, "He'll know because before he left to join the drinking in the feasting hall, I told him you are my son and had come to the fort to find me. I owed him that much. I promised him we wouldn't leave, that we'd be a family and he took my word for what he wanted it to be, saying he'd accept you as his son, even though you are a Celt. He's a good man, and I wish with all my heart I could have stayed with him."

Gal understood, and a part of him regretted tearing his mother from her life. He supposed she'd made the sacrifice because her love for him was greater than her love for her man, as most mothers would. "What made you change your mind?"

Her mind slipped back to the day the Saxons attacked her village, and she turned away, remembering the horrors she'd witnessed and the family she'd lost. "The other night I told you I saw your father being killed; I didn't tell you everything. I saw it all, including the rape of little Elli, my own daughter, though I was led away into the forest before they cut her throat. In the forest I was raped, repeatedly, then led south to a small Saxon fort where I was used by some of their men before being taken to Andredes Caester. I suppose that meeting you again brought back the images I'd kept buried for so long, your return made me hate Saxons again."

A cold, tense silence choked the space between them while she considered how much her son should know. She decided to let her words come out as they would, "To begin with, I was kept alive only to be used as a rutting slave, and with my family gone I accepted my fate with a dead heart. My initial fear, despair and hatred quickly hardened into an emotionless, empty void of slavery. My yearning for you and Elli eventually became an acceptance that you were both dead, and slowly, to my everlasting shame, I blanked you out so that

I might survive. The months passed and I stopped hating the Saxons. I saw their joys, pains, loves, fears, laughter and hate and I began to accept them not as the savages we assume them to be, but as people not unlike ourselves. Yes, they'd destroyed my life, but war makes savages of us all. Reality changes perspective and time buries hate. Slowly, my life changed for the better. Osgar gave me a new path to follow, I was loved and respected then you returned and, the Sun broke through the clouds, I remembered how to feel a mother's love."

Gal didn't want to hurt her, but there was something he had to know. "Was Osgar there, was he part of the attack on our forest village?"

She replied with calm honesty, "No, he was not. He joined King Aelle's warriors the summer after they'd destroyed our village. I noticed him watching me, it was obvious what he wanted. Eventually, after we'd shared a few stolen moments he paid my slave-geld, set me free and asked me to share his hut. He was a good man, so I agreed. I don't like what I've done to him, he'll be like a snarling, wounded animal when he knows we've gone. His pride won't allow him to remain with King Aelle's army, he'll make hunting us down his life's work."

Opening the door of his hut, Osgar saw that Carys and the boy still hadn't returned. The other mushroom gatherers had walked back into the fort well before the Sun had cleared the horizon, and since then he'd searched every part of the fort and shantytown. Cold reasoning and instinct told him he'd been betrayed, made to look a fool by a woman and a boy. Striding over to the hearth, he kicked over a stool, picked up an empty clay bowl from the table and threw it, shattering it against the thick doorpost.

Clipping his sword-belt around his waist, he slid the blade into the scabbard and cursed his own stupidity as he slipped two knives into his belt. After putting some food into a leather bag, he felt the edge of his war-axe and slipped his hand through the looped leather thong at the end of its handle. Picking up a spear, he swore again before gathering his unstrung bow and quiver of arrows. Turning to face the light of the open door, he made a promise to his god, Woden, swearing that he'd kill the two Celts, even if that meant chasing them across the Western Sea. Nobody made a fool of him, especially a slave woman and her whelp.

Stepping out of his hut and into the bright light of the afternoon sun, he tore down the horns above the hut's door. Taking one last, regretful look at King Aelle's feasting hall, he strode out of the fort, determined there'd be no sanctuary for the fugitives, nor a day when the whore and her brat would be free to stop looking over their shoulders.

19.

Gwen had told Owain very little about the ancient people's wedding ritual, though what she had said was enough to encourage a cold sweat to worry him as he walked alone through the woods on the Forest Island. He'd no idea where the ritual would take place, all the Merlin had said was 'go to the island in the forest, Gwen is waiting for you there'. Logic suggested she'd be in the village, so that's where he'd go, assuming he could find the place again.

Lazily, or perhaps reluctantly ambling along a path bathed in sunshine, many thoughts drifted into his mind, none of them easing the tension he'd felt since first stepping onto the island. Deciding it might be wise to rest a while and try to relax, clear his head of some of the more exposing images he associated with the ancient marriage ritual, he sat beneath the wide spread of an oak tree.

Closing his eyes and taking a deep, relaxing breath, the Sun warmed him into drowsy calm. Knowing he couldn't linger too long because he was expected, he opened his eyes and listened to the many songbirds perched in the island's trees. Loosening his red cloak, he was about to remove it when the birdsong dropped into silence. His body shivered, he saw a black cloud slide in front of the Sun as a raven, hopping along a branch above him, cawed, looked down at the Pendragon, leapt from the oak and spread its wings, screeching wild as it flew low across the metal-flat lake.

The wind strengthened and rattling branches swayed as if a storm was coming. Seeing more dirty clouds darkening the sky, enveloping the Sun in a blanket of shifting greys, he squinted to where the Sun had been, and a cold and clammy hand felt his throat. Jumping to his feet, he stepped quickly around the tree, expecting to see a village child running into the bushes, but he saw no one. Feeling his neck, he questioned the experience, dismissing it as his over-stimulated imagination.

The wind gusted and clashing treetops blew one way then the other, so Owain pulled his cloak tight and crouched against the solid oak as the wind swirled around him. Before he could whisper a prayer to unknown gods, a howling gale consumed the darkening woods, ripping through thrashing branches, tearing showers of green leaves from defenceless stalks and twigs.

The rumbling heavens exploded and bolts of lightning speared silver arrows through the swirling greys. Thunder boomed, the wind howled and stingingly cold rain cut and stabbed the scattering leaves. Thinking to run for the shelter of the village, Owain got to his feet as a deafening crack of white pierced the thrashing boughs and split a nearby trunk into a smoke-blackened 'V'. Pressed against the resolute oak, he felt a feathery whisper brush his ear, warming it with a name, "Rohanna." Turning to the lake, he saw that the forest beyond the island was untouched by the storm; how could that be?

The clammy hand clutched his throat again, choking his refusal to accept reality. "Rohanna," a woman's voice breathed, and a violent thundercrack had him turning then falling to his knees. The hand tightened around his throat and, gasping for air he begged the gods to release him from this insanity. "Rohanna!" the woman's voice shrieked, his bulging eyes searching for the sun, pleading with the whirlwind to release its grip.

An ear-splitting boom shot another bolt, which sliced through one of the thicker branches above his head. It plunged like a sack of wet wheat, landing no more than a hand's width from him. "Rohanna!" the voice screamed as the choking hand released its grip, allowing him to gulp in icy air. Thunder shocked his ears and his heart leapt into his mouth as exploding light flashed across the island, throwing down hail that hammered into his shivering body.

"Rohanna!" the screeching voice revolved in his head, turning him as lightning flamed a bush into an explosion of heat. "Rohanna!" the voice shrieked, and fear curled the brave Pendragon into a foetal ball. The heavens exploded, pounding thunderous flashes across the sky, deafening him to his own screams as everything black-strobed and split then crashed into blue. Screaming for release, his exhausted mind lay him in the tree's roots, limp and wasted as hail pummelled his disbelief.

Then silence. As suddenly as the storm had erupted, it was gone and the day brightened. Still curled within the roots, he listened, waiting for another thunder-filled onslaught. Above him a thrush chirped into song and he uncurled like a blossoming flower in the morning sun. A warm breeze touched him, lifting the veil of fear from his shivering skin. Getting to his feet, he was about to go looking for the village when he saw a wet and bedraggled figure step out from behind a nearby tree. His relief made him call to the wet-feathered man, "Merlin, was the storm real?"

"Yes, of course it was real," the druid replied, stepping over a lightning cut branch. "We'll talk while we walk, come with me."

The two of them set off through the woods, walking side by side along a path the Pendragon hadn't seen until the Merlin stepped onto it. "I must warn you, Owain, there's only so much I can tell you. The storm relates to the future so must remain within the gift of the Goddess. I'm sure you heard who the creator was."

"Rohanna?"

"Yes. Having met her only once, when she was a babe, my knowledge of her is limited. You know I can't tell you her part in your future, and you don't yet need to know her past." Stopping, he took hold of Owain's arm and said, "I'm about to take you into a place that many people don't know exists. The people of the island are keen for this ignorance to continue, so I must ask you to honour their wishes. Cai once strayed into the valley by accident, when looking for one of the island men he was in love with. I'd tell you more, but secrets must remain secret."

Walking through the woods, neither man spoke for a while. The Merlin was thinking about Rohanna, weighing up how much of a threat she might be, gauging the strength of her powers and the darkness of her soul. Owain, glancing nervously at every slight rustle of leaves, was more concerned about the woods, which seemed to be closing in with every step he took. Apart from the loss of the leaf-hidden sunlight, the Pendragon realised something else wasn't right. "Are we still on the island?" he asked.

"Is that important?"

Ignoring the question, he noticed the Druid was walking with his eyes closed, deep in thought or meditating, blindly following the path as if he'd walked it a thousand times. "Are you going to tell me about Rohanna?"

"No." The Merlin stopped and opened his eyes. "Rohanna can wait until after your marriage to Gwen. If I tell you about her now, your knowledge of her may colour your thoughts during your meditations."

"Is she that powerful, or so beautiful that men can't resist her?" Owain asked as they continued their walk.

A cold shiver slicked the Merlin's skin and, within his mind he saw a beautiful, golden-haired woman and her future night of passion with Owain. Her face seemed familiar, though he didn't know her, but whoever she was she certainly knew how to manipulate the Pendragon's lusts. "Men are fickle, easily tempted," he grumbled. "Beware of your lusts, Pendragon, never turn away from my daughter."

On they walked, the path thinning as it led them deeper into the dark woodlands. With the encroaching forest cutting out almost all of the daylight, Owain realised they should have reached the edge of the lake by now. Had the Druid deliberately led him in circles to confuse him? That wasn't possible because most of the path had been arrow-straight. It had to be a druidic trick, he concluded, so he asked, "Are we going the right way?"

"Are you worried?"

"Yes, shouldn't we have reached the lakeside?"

"I've told you countless times, Owain, life isn't physical. Your reluctance to learn such a simple lesson troubles me."

“Your life may not be physical, but I’m a warrior, not a druid. This is an island and we’ve been walking long enough to reach Viroconium.”

“There’s no need to exaggerate, and are you are certain this is an island?”

“I’ve walked the shoreline, it’s an island.”

“If you say it is, it must be.”

As the trees closed in, Owain felt a cold breeze brush his cheek when he pushed aside a hanging branch. Pushing through more overhanging branches, he looked for the Sun he knew must be at its height, but he could see no daylight. “Where are we, Merlin?”

“Following the path to where Gwen is waiting.”

“Where has the day gone?”

“Nowhere, have faith.”

On they walked through battling branches and twigs. “We can’t still be on the island,” Owain said as a branch swept towards his face, forcing him to duck. “There’s something you are not telling me.”

“Have faith.”

Before he could ask the Merlin to explain himself, thin shafts of light broke through the dense canopy, making him squint through the thinning woodlands. Daylight spread above him, and to his great relief they stepped into a river-valley sheltered on either side by forested hills. “The sky is so blue, is this place real?” Owain asked, looking at the far hills, where the river cut through distant grey rocks. The river was neither wide nor deep as it flowed through grassy greens and swathes of purple clover. Not far into the meadow stood a pair of newly thatched, identical roundhouses, one on each side of the river, which was spanned by an ancient, wooden bridge. "I'll not believe you if you tell me we are still on the island."

"I wouldn't expect you to," the Merlin replied. "Do you need to know where you are?"

"What's this place called, where are we, did you bring me here by magic?"

"Where we are is where we are supposed to be!" the Merlin replied irritably.

"I only want to understand."

"Stop questioning and start feeling," the Druid ordered grumpily, unable to erase from his memory Owain's yet to be met, golden-haired lover. Believing her to be a part of the future, he realised she had the look of Graine about her, but she was much younger. If the woman was a relative, he'd never met her, which had him thinking she must be from the Summer Isle, the island of Graine's birth. "Before you begin the journey into the union, are you certain you want to commit your life to my daughter?"

"There's nothing I want more."

"Betray Gwenwyfar at your peril."

Hearing a bustling noise close by, Owain glanced to his right and he saw Gwen and her mother walk out from the woodlands, not twenty paces from him. Separated by the river, he wanted to call across but decided it might not be wise as they may have begun the first part of the wedding ritual. She didn't look at him, which had him wondering if she felt as nervous as he did?

The Merlin and Graine acknowledged each other without speaking, and the two parties walked towards the roundhouses on their respective riverbanks. Unable to look away from his beautiful, future wife, Owain saw that she was walking with her head bowed, her hands pressed together in thoughtful prayer. Arriving at the thatched houses that would be their homes for the next seven days, they turned to face each other and, the Merlin called across the river, "Are you Gwenwyfar, the only known daughter of myself and Graine?"

"I am," she replied calmly.

"Are you ready to join with Owain ap Einion ap Cunedda?"

"I have always been ready." She smiled lovingly at Owain.

Graine then called across the river, "Are you Owain ap Einion ap Cunedda, the Prince of Rhos who is also known as the Pendragon?"

"I am," he answered without any of the confidence Gwen had shown.

"Have you come here to begin your union with Gwenwyfar, daughter of myself and the Merlin?"

"Yes."

"The union will begin with thoughts," Graine announced. "Go, Pendragon. Come with me, daughter."

The Merlin held out his arm, indicating to Owain that he must enter the roundhouse, he then followed him into the hearth-lit darkness. "Before we begin, do you have any questions?" he inquired as Owain looked around the empty roundhouse. "Think carefully, because the questions you ask now will be the only ones I'll answer until you leave your meditations."

"I have two. Are we still on the island, and what do I do if the Saxons attack? Do they know about this place, am I in the real world?"

"That's four questions!" the Merlin pointed out. "But no, we are not on the island because the island as you know it does not exist, it is connected to this valley by a thin strip of land, though sometimes the lake water does rise above the join, in certain seasons. The Saxons won't come here, they have no knowledge of this place and yes, we are in the real world." Expecting Owain to ask more questions, he offered him a place to sit by the smouldering fire in the centre of the hut, and he sat beside him. "You'll be here for three days and nights, during which time no food will be brought to you, all you'll receive each day is one beaker of water, which will be placed just inside the entrance. Don't speak to whoever delivers your water because you'll break the circle of thought, and they won't reply anyway."

The Druid hummed a single note that filled the space within the roundhouse. The note died and, the Merlin opened his eyes. "Hear my words well, Owain ap Einion ap Cunedda. While you are here you will not sleep, you will want to but if you do the cycle of the ritual will be broken and the marriage rites lost to your dreams. The fire will die before the Sun goes down, leaving only your image of Gwenwyfar to comfort you in the dark. Your task is to think about your future life together, and nothing more. It's an important meditation which you should think deeply upon, using insight and wisdom. The thoughts and feelings you experience here will travel with you throughout the rest of your life, they are your awakening and your being. Allowing your mind to drift to other concerns will weaken the love you take into your marriage, so be wary of such thoughts, cast them aside as soon as they enter you. During your meditations, be concerned with how honest you are with yourself, if you can be truly honest, you'll see and feel all you need to know. When three days and nights have passed, I'll return to prepare you for the next stage of the journey. If you understand all that I've said, remain silent."

Owain said nothing as the Druid stood and walked out of the roundhouse. Closing his eyes, the Pendragon obediently thought about Gwen.

Sitting cross-legged beside the smoking hearth, Gwen closed her eyes and listened to her breathing. Before leaving her to meditate, Graine had said, "Be honest with yourself, Gwen, know your own heart."

Her first thought was to wonder how Owain might cope: would he be tempted to sleep; would he handle the hunger and could he cast aside the tightly coiled chains of the Pendragon's duties? She guessed the Saxon threat would concern him until he became used to his solitude, then, she hoped, he'd focus on the love they shared and the sacrifices they'd make. Her thoughts were clear and held no fears because if you choose to give yourself to someone, fully understanding the needs of that person, your hearts and minds will blend.

If hearts and minds can bond, is the same true of souls, or is the soul a combination of the heart and mind? Feeling that connecting with her soul might offer her a greater understanding, she looked inward, searching for the answer to her unasked question. A warm tranquillity opened her inner-being, attaching her to a searching feeling she didn't question. The sensation felt hopeful, innocently strong and vibrantly addictive as it led her deeper within herself. Through the walls of emotional restriction her search passed, moving to a place she didn't know existed. A question broke into her journey: are all souls part of a greater soul? The question touched something within her, giving her sight, insight and a channel through which she might move towards the essence of existence.

Unknowingly releasing her inner-eye, she followed its warmth through a myriad of flashing and shining lights, though when she looked closer, she felt they were more like sparks than lights, or impulses which led her through dull-browns and reds into a maze of illuminated fibres. On she travelled towards the most comforting, radiant glow, its colours shifting through various shades of yellow to white, then all the colours she knew of, before thinning to a soft gleam that pulled her into white, obscure warmth. Within the glow there were no questions, only feelings, and without thinking she understood and believed. The knowledge that every soul was part of a greater force made up of all souls, was almost beyond her understanding, but she held on to it through her desire for the truth.

Forgetting she was a physical part of nature, she willed herself to see further into the heart of all souls, wanting to communicate with it but she could find no conscious question to ask. Failing in this part of her desire, she decided it may never have been possible. The unknown question she'd longed to ask, forced its way into her mind: how can two people be together and apart?

Her soul told her that Owain could never be totally hers because he was the Pendragon: he belonged to the people, to his warriors, to Viroconium and the future of Briton. Perhaps she'd only share parts of him: she'd have the lover, the mother-seeking child, the vulnerable but gentle youth and the quietly thoughtful man who believed he'd been born to serve his people. Was she feeling the secret of their union, must she accept only parts of his life?

Could she give herself completely to a man who would never offer his full-self? She doubted it. She'd never remain in Viroconium for more than a few days, whether 'Arthur' was there or not. 'Arthur' where had the name come from? He was Owain but there must be a reason for her giving him that name, if it existed. The thought faded and she returned to her previous thread.

Would she give herself totally to a man constantly locked in a world she could never fully be a part of? Perhaps her role was to be his relief and refuge, his escape into a peace more real to him than the royal courts were. Was she to be his refuge and freedom? She liked the thought. They'd share each other when either of them had the need, moving between two opposing worlds, walking through natural doorways and closing mind-doors to keep their private world secure. She'd continue her life beside the lake knowing that when he visited, he'd need her as well as want her. What more could anyone ask for? Their souls must become one, not their physical lives and if their hearts were open to each other they'd share their love completely, even when apart. They'd be together and not together. Content with her first meditation, she wept.

20.

Run wild and run with fear, carry the burden of the hunted and run until your breath flames in your lungs, run until you drop. Use the forest shadows and embrace the night, risk the day and don't stop running because if you do you might be caught by a flying spear or a well-aimed arrow. Run, and do not sleep, not if you want to see another rising Sun because the hunter will catch you, and when he does his revenge will be bitterly-sweet.

Although Carys and her son were close to Celtic lands and relative safety, the boy would not forget the danger. His mother's fears were well-founded, Osgar would continue the chase through the forest and beyond, until he caught up with them, so they must remain alert because fighting the Saxon was terrifyingly inevitable, and could happen at any moment.

Instinct told the boy that Osgar wasn't far behind, he could feel the presence of the hunter stalking his prey. As he and his mother ran north, deeper into the darkest parts of the forest, his fear had him glancing at trees and jumping at every sound he didn't immediately recognise as being part of forest life. When the moment came to fight it could arrive without warning, an arrow flying from the dark, or an axe swung from behind a tree. He could be dead before he hit the ground, then what would Osgar do to his mother? But this journey wasn't about her, it was a mission and the fate of a nation hung on the information he carried.

The day was new and the Sun should have cleared the horizon, but only faint light seeped through the dark, tender mesh of leaves. He guessed from his mother's silence she was feeling the oppressive darkness of the place, and if he added to that her thoughts of the vicious death Osgar might have in mind for her, her tense silence was understandable.

Whenever they came to a rocky outcrop or spring-fed pool, the forest broke open to pour in showers of silver-white, misty Sun beams that angled like hazy marbled pillars. Sometimes, if there were enough breaks in the canopy, dozens of rays touched the forest floor, creating a woodland of dreamy, pillared light. It was something to see, and he always marvelled at the beauty and mystery of it, as well as the mythical imagery this natural phenomenon inspired. Not too far ahead he saw such a place, dozens of beams scything through the tangled web of charcoal branches and interlacing greens.

"It's so beautiful," Carys said at the sight of so many shafts of hazy light. Dropping her basket, she ran like an excited child, her heart racing at the thought of embracing this most beautiful of nature's sculptures. Stopping before the misty white and green columns, she marvelled at their soft beauty. Removing her shoes, in she stepped, a shifting silhouette in nature's Sun-temple, the beams catching and illuminating her swaying and turning form as she sang and danced.

Watching her flow through the soft beams like a wind-blown leaf, Gal recalled Gwen telling him that all women have the Goddess within them. He thought his mother looked more like a faery or a tree-nymph, ethereal and physical, lithe and beautiful, a released Dryad image from a midsummer dream that was only part goddess. In and out of the light she danced, her fingers stroking the misty shafts while singing a tune from her childhood. Twirling through the rays like a child caught in a faery-dance, her song leapt from her soul and into the haze that flashed from light to dark, her image skipping from one beam to another. Her tired heart was renewing itself, feeding from natures beauty after her years of loss and slavery.

The boy watched every delicate movement, he'd never seen her like this, her golden hair flowing with every sweep of her arms as they cut through the pillars. Thinking there must be an ocean of characters within her he'd never experienced, he wanted to join her, be a part of the embrace that was the soul of her dance. Caught in the beauty of her movement, he felt sure he was seeing the Goddess.

A twig snapped, and instinct turned him. He felt the touch of a feather brush past his cheek, then a dull thud and a scream cut all hope from his heart. Still silhouetted in the temple of light, Carys' fingertips touched the arrow shaft and slid over the warm, sticky liquid leaking from her chest. Holding out her bloodied hand to her son, she slowly collapsed and dropped to her knees, grasping and clawing at the rotting foliage on the forest floor, before falling sideways. The blood on her dress broke the boy's heart, yet he ran to her and took her in his arms, hoping he could do something to save her life.

"That arrow was meant for you," a familiar voice growled from behind a tree. Osgar stepped out not more than twenty paces from him. Sneering, he pulled another arrow from his quiver. "Now, stand and die like a man, or grovel in the dirt like the Celtic coward you are."

Wanting to hold his mother, Gal's eyes pleaded with Osgar to leave him be, let him have these final few moments with his mother. The Saxon would have none of it, he pulled back the bowstring and took aim. Gently, Gal lay his mother down and raised his hands in submission. "You told me Saxon warriors always fight toe to toe, so why the bow?" he asked, choking back his tears.

Osgar shrugged, threw away the bow and took two knives from his belt. "Use it," he said to the kneeling boy, tossing him a knife.

Keeping his eyes fixed on the giant-of-a-man, Gal picked up the knife and forced himself to stand. Raising the blade, he heard his mother groan, giving him a reason to kill and survive. Stepping forward, Osgar arrogantly boasted, "I'm a warrior, I fight with courage and strength, respecting my battle-foes before killing them because they too are warriors. But you are a Celtic runt who stole my woman, so you will die a slow death."

Backing away, Gal searched his cunning for a way to kill the man.

Pointing his knife at Carys, Osgar growled to the boy, "I want to give your mother what she deserves before she dies, so let's get this over with." Running his thumb along the edge of his blade, he grinned from the expected pleasure of slicing the young pup open from his groin to his chin. "I'm going to cut you, stab you, slash you until your body is lacerated flesh. But I won't let you die, not until you've seen me rut your mother's corpse."

Gal's heartbeat raced as the warrior strode towards him. He panicked, turned and ran to the nearest tree, dashing behind it as Osgar lumbered after him. "Stand and fight!" the frustrated Saxon yelled. "Are you a coward?"

The Giant's knife slashed at air and bark as the boy shimmied around the tree, using it as a shield. Osgar dodged left and right, trying to fool the young Celt but Gal was quick, always shifting to counter the threat. Frustrated, the Saxon backed away. Hearing Carys groan, Osgar said, "Come out and fight or I'll slit your mother's throat now!"

Thinking fast, the boy remembered how the Saxon rarely hit what he aimed at, which gave him an idea. During battle the man was probably a bludgeoner, a crusher of skulls and limbs, aiming his blows randomly at a wall of metal and flesh. Single combat was different, you must be cunning and accurate, every strike had to be precise which wasn't Osgar's strength. If he was quick, moved faster than the giant and only struck when certain of drawing blood, he might have a chance. Cautiously, he stepped away from his sycamore shield.

The Saxon strode at him without subtlety, swinging his knife from side to side in powerfully vicious cuts, just as Gal thought he would. The boy stepped back and back, keeping his eyes firmly fixed on the blade, following the swinging, arcing rhythm. Concentrating on the regular but slow movements, his own knife gripped tightly in his white-knuckled hand, he watched the Saxon's blade, crouching ever lower as he stepped backwards. When Osgar's knife-swing reached its widest and highest point, Gal rolled forward, came up on one knee and plunged his knife deep into the Saxon's groin.

The woodlands burst into life with squawking birds and barking foxes when the warrior let out a huge, bellowing roar. Burning pain shot through him, his knife dropped and he grabbed for Gal's dagger as he saw the boy's free hand smack onto the other, forcing the blade further into the wound.

Pushing the knife deeper into bleeding flesh, Gal turned it, twisting the blade while yanking it from side to side, every iron-jerk releasing gut-wrenching screams from Osgar. The twisting knife sliced through muscles and veins, cutting the groin to shreds. The blade scraped against the pelvic bone, sending excruciating waves of pain pulsing through the warrior, who roared to the scattering forest-beasts. As his knees began to buckle, the big man looked down at the blood-soaked boy, his eyesight dimming as his life-blood spurted free. "You can't kill me."

"It looks like I have." Although blood was pouring down his arms, Gal knew he couldn't let go yet. While his blade was savaging the Saxon's innards, the big warrior could do nothing, the pain was too great. He had him at his mercy, sooner or later the Saxon's strength would fail, and he'd drop to the ground like a felled tree. Time stood still, even though barely a moment had passed since the knife had plunged into its target. Gripping the handle with both hands, Gal yanked it down and the blade cut upwards, slicing through more flesh. He felt more blood surge warm and slick over his arms, having severed a major artery.

His arms ached but the Saxon wouldn't go down, even though the hole in his groin was wide and deep enough for the boy's hands to fill it. With his strength fading, Gal took a chance and pushed forward, let go of the knife and rolled out of harm's way. The warrior staggered backwards, the shock of death whitening his face and, he fell into the mulch with a soft-thud. Getting to his feet, Gal watched the Saxon's chest rise and fall for a few heartbeats, before it settled into death. Turning away from his first human kill, Gal vomited, then ran to his mother.

Gently lifting Carys' arm to see where the arrow had pierced, he didn't like what he saw. The arrow had punched into the left side of her chest, and she was losing blood. He guessed the arrow had narrowly missed her heart or she'd already be dead, but any jerking movement risked shifting the arrowhead closer to her heart. It must be removed, and the bleeding stopped but he'd no knowledge of how to treat wounds. Sinking into panic, he foolishly looked around for someone to help him.

"Remove it, and do it quickly," Carys gasped.

After taking the knife and cloth from the basket she'd dropped on her run to dance within the sunbeams, he ran back to his mother. Carefully, he cut the material around the arrow-shaft, giving himself just enough room to see where it had entered her flesh. She'd been lucky, the arrow had pierced her about a hand's width below her shoulder.

Taking hold of the shaft, it occurred to him that if the arrowhead was barbed, he'd never pull it free and, cutting it out might kill her. There was only one way to find out, so he closed his eyes and gently pulled, praying to the Goddess that barbs weren't holding the arrow in place. It moved, so he pulled a little harder. His mother screamed so he let go. "Don't be afraid," she gasped through wincing breaths.

"I've never done this."

"It's the same as pulling an arrow from a deer carcass."

"But........."

"Don't give me 'buts' just do it!" Her back arched and a stab of pain seared her chest.

Without thinking, he grabbed the shaft and yanked it free, and his mother's scream pierced the forest. Throwing the arrow to one side, he saw blood pulsing from the hole so he pressed the cloth firmly onto the wound, while looking around for something to hold it in place. There wasn't anything, what was he supposed to do now? If he let go his mother would bleed to death, and he could hardly carry her through the forest while holding a cloth to her chest. Her eyes opened, she moved his hand and held the cloth herself. "You see the moss on the bark of the tree behind you?" she asked.

"Yes."

"Pack it onto the wound. The moss will slow the bleeding, cleanse the wound and keep it clean until we reach a friendly village, then it can be seared or stitched closed."

"You've done this before?" he asked.

"Yes, Saxon wounds need tending just like Celtic wounds do. Now do as you've been told and fetch some moss."

After collecting a handful, he removed the cloth and padded as much of the healing plant onto the hole as he felt necessary, then he looked at her for guidance.

"Tear the hem of my dress. You might need two or three strips, and don't be afraid to tie it tight."

Doing as he'd been told, he cut enough strips to bind the wound, tied them around her chest and asked, "Is that it?"

"Get me to my feet and support me. We must find a forest village before I lose too much blood."

21.

A roundhouse, circled by the silent tread of people wearing animal skins; the men of the Forest Island tasked to be sentries and channels. For three days and nights they will tread the dust, their obedient walk a ritual to thin the wafting, feather-curtain between the physical and the ethereal worlds. Darkness, a void of nothing filling the shrinking roundhouse space and seeping up into and out through the thatching. Silence, bearable yet confusing, the need to feel a part of nature distracting the meditation-search in favour of the comfort of the understandable and predictable. The chill of the night feeding anxiety-sweats and startling reactions to nothing; the warmth of the day slowing the mind into lazy, pointless distraction. Unhooked images flash and splinter into shards, memories bloat the void and choke its open-span; no lessons grasped or learned, no windows open to guide and inspire.

Tired, hungry and frustrated, Owain looked blankly into the pile of cold ashes. He'd sat beside the spent fire for a day and a night, or so he thought, searching for the meaning of his union, without success. Having to go through this ritual irritated him, all he wanted was to marry Gwen, go home and deal with the threat of King Aelle's Saxons.

Without knowing why, he recalled the memory of a summer night spent with Gwen. While loving each other beside her lake, watching the moon's bright reflection shimmering on the dark ripples, she'd told him that all pools of water are gateways to the

Otherworld, and, if you stepped into the pool where the moonlight touched it, you might find yourself caught within Annwn, never to return.

Being the daughter of Graine and the Merlin, he wasn't surprised she was a child of nature, but perhaps she was more a child of the Goddess than she realised. Who could own such a woman? For the first time since meeting her, he realised he didn't want to own her; who can own another person's soul? Waking in the morning to look upon the sleeping peace of her face, or holding her while they watched the Sun go down, was reason enough for any man to live. Love can never be owned, only experienced, a soul cannot be caged.

Considering the possibility of free love, and its implications, he felt a wisp of cold air waft in when someone lifted the door-flap to deliver his water. Another thought took hold of him: can freedom be physical? If freedom had a physical form, it would be Gwen: when he looked at her his worries slipped from his shoulders; when he held her his place within the kingdom shrank to nothing. Realising that so long as she was free, she'd be happy, he understood that her freedom was the part of her he loved the most.

Understanding he mustn't interfere with her freedom, and never force her to fit into his world, he smiled as a touch of sadness opened him to the truth. Without her he was half a man, but maybe that was the point; together they were one, in body, mind and soul because love is a union, the meeting of souls as well as the sharing of flesh. The freedom a true union brings is the absolute value of that shared love and, should never be controlled or owned by either soul.

You can have someone and not have someone. A cloud lifted, his restrictions dissipated and he understood why this ritual was so necessary.

Leaning heavily on her son, dawn mists softening their escape from the forest, Carys stumbled out of the woodlands and collapsed on a grass ridge. Exhausted, she let Gal pick her up and sit her against a tree. After giving her a few sips of water from Osgar's bloodstained leather flask, he crawled to the edge of the ridge and looked down into the valley. "Gal," his mother called, extending her arm to him.

"I won't be long. I need to know what's in the valley."

Nestled between the forested-ridge and a gently rising slope, a mist-shrouded village of roundhouses felt the first touch of a brightening, cloudless dawn. The place was inhabited because smoke seeped through thatched roofs, but by whom? Although the village looked Celtic, this close to the borderlands it could have been taken by Saxons, so he wouldn't show himself until he was certain.

Guessing the villagers had stirred from their sleep, he must be cautious, but if he didn't find help soon, his mother might die. Crawling back to her, he took a swig from the flask and wiped his mouth on his sleeve. "There's a village in the valley," he said. "Will you be alright if I leave you here while I take a closer look?"

"Yes, unless a wolf catches the scent of my wound and decides to eat me!" She smiled at her joke, not having the strength to laugh.

"I'll return as soon as I can."

"Hurry, Gal." Taking his hand, she pressed it to her lips. "Be careful."

Watching the village from the ridge, he was about to step into a tall swathe of purple-flowered willow herbs that covered part of the slope, when he heard the sweet voice of a girl or a woman, singing to his left, and the song was being sung in his own language. The sweet voice seemed to be coming from a clump of hawthorns growing about halfway down the valley slope. Thinking that asking for help from a woman might be wise, he crouched and stalked through the long grass to investigate.

Closing on the hawthorns, he realised the voice was unlikely to belong to a mature woman because of its light, childish tone. The closer he came to the bushes, the sweeter the voice seemed, and it enchanted him. When he was little, he'd heard stories about how the Faery-folk would tempt a passer-by with the beauty of their singing, lulling them into a trance before leading them into slavery in the Faery kingdom. He didn't believe such stories but, hearing the delicate sweetness he was tempted to change his mind.

Quietly, he crawled beneath branches and pricking thorns. The Hawthorn patch was more extensive than he'd thought, so it took him a while to reach its outer limits and crawl into a spread of bracken. Carefully parting the coarse leaves, he hoped to catch his first glimpse of a Faery-woman.

Sitting with her back to him, naked in a stream that trickled out from the forest and down the slope, a girl bathed while she sang. His first thought was to wonder why she was sitting in the stream before the Sun had fully risen? His second thought brought a desire so strong that he thought he'd be sick if he didn't touch her. Trapped by overpowering lust, he couldn't take his eyes from the golden-haired Faery as her hands moved over her wet skin.

Seeing her stand and turn to face the rising sun, holding out her arms to welcome the new light, her song drifted over the valley-mists and he held his breath. Wishing he could smooth his hands over her delicate form before the rising Sun melted her back into the stream, he willed her to turn his way so that he could see her entire naked beauty. Much to his frustration, she sat down again and looked up at a hovering hawk, her sweet voice singing to the bird as it swooped and stole away a field mouse.

What was he doing? His mother could be dying while his eyes feasted on an innocent Faery-woman. Snapping out of the trance, he crawled back to the hawthorn bushes and made his way down the slope. Walking through a lower patch of bracken, he saw someone step out from a roundhouse at the edge of the village. Carrying a bucket, the dark-haired woman walked to the well near the wicker sheep-pens behind her home. Whistling so as not to startle her, he headed for the well. Hearing the tune as she was about to lower the bucket, she shouted a man's name. A man with long, grey hair walked out from the roundhouse, saw the boy and waved to him.

With his hands held wide to show he came in friendship, Gal called to him, "Good day to you. I am Gal, a friend who has come to ask for your help."

"A good day to you also," the man replied. "I am Rhodri, a village elder. Come in peace, Gal, you are welcome at my hearth."

Whilst being carried down the valley slope, Carys had passed out. Returning to consciousness on a roundhouse floor, she opened her eyes to see two unfamiliar faces looking down at her. A man with long, grey hair smiled kindly at her, and she thought he looked like a druid. The other face, a woman's, also smiled, and the dark-haired woman said softly, "Don't worry, Carys, you are with friends."

"Gal?" Carys' whispered word was barely audible.

"I'm here," he replied, kneeling beside her.

"Where are we?"

"Inside our roundhouse," said the man. "There's someone coming who'll tend to your wound."

A stab of searing pain pulsed through her chest and she winced. Gritting her teeth and sucking in air, she closed her eyes to the smoke-blackened thatched roof hanging dark above her. Hearing someone blessing the home as he entered, she tried sitting up but another jab of pain jerked her body stiff. The new voice sounded well advanced in years, and a white-haired head appeared above her and, the man spoke with a winsome joy, "I am Bryn, the village healer, I'll see what I can do to save your life. You," he said to Gal, "take a firebrand from the hearth and hold it above your mother's head without setting fire to her lovely hair. What is your name?" he asked the wounded woman while removing the blood encrusted bandages.

"Carys," she replied, and flinched when some of the dried blood around her wound peeled away with the bandage. Without protest, she allowed Bryn to remove part of her dress and, warm fingers gently pressed the bruised and bloody skin around the wound.

"Rhodri, would you pass me my bag?" After wiping away some of the encrusted blood with a wet cloth, Bryn took two thin metal rods from the woollen bag. "This will hurt, Carys, but you look like a brave woman."

Inserting the two rods into the wound, he moved them slightly apart to stretch the flesh. Carys groaned and her neck stiffened. Looking into the fleshy hole in concentrated silence, the healer nodded twice, and withdrew the metal rods. After dropping the rods into a clay bowl of water, he said to Gal, "A little lower and the arrow would have killed her. There is no chipped bone and the wound looks clean. You did well to use the moss, the flesh is neither swollen nor suppurating. Time to sear the wound I think." Taking a small leather flask from his bag, he removed the stopper. "You and your daughter hold her down," he said to Rhodri, "and make sure she doesn't move as I pour, I don't want to blister that lovely breast of hers. Carys, the liquid will sting until I ignite it, and the pain will make your eyes pop out as you scream, so keep them closed!" Chuckling to himself, he waited for Rhodri and is daughter to take a firm hold.

Carefully, he poured light brown liquid into the wound. Though it stung Carys, she didn't move, and before she could ask what the liquid was, he'd set it alight. Pain ripped through her chest and her eyes bulged as she screamed into the rafters, the smell of her roasted flesh making her want to vomit. Bryn nodded to Rhodri and his daughter, who let go of her and she shot bolt upright, screaming while the blue flame flickered and died.

"Some might say that was a waste of good 'uisge beatha'!" said Bryn. "We must find somewhere comfortable for her to rest for a few days."

"How many days?" Gal asked.

"Don't worry, your mother will live."

"It's not that; I must get to Viroconium, I've important information for the Pendragon and I can't afford to waste time here."

"Be at peace," Bryn said. "Your mother can't be moved for six or seven days at least. She's lost a lot of blood so she needs rest and food."

"If I don't get to Viroconium soon, it might be too late!"

"What do you mean?" Rhodri asked.

"The Saxons are about to march west; I must inform the Pendragon of King Aelle's war plans."

"But you are just a boy, how could you know about such things?" Rhodri asked, and he looked at Bryn, who dismissively shrugged his shoulders.

Gal told them about his mission to the Saxon fort, and what it meant for the Britons. The old man listened patiently, whispered something to Rhodri's daughter, who left the roundhouse, then he said to the boy, "We have just the one horse, not a very special horse by any standards, but it will get you to Viroconium."

"But I've never ridden a horse."

"You spy for the Pendragon but you can't ride a horse?"

“How difficult can it be?” Whilst thinking about the prospect of learning to ride, Gal saw a young, golden-haired beauty enter the roundhouse.

“Seren,” Bryn said, “this is my new friend Gal. He’s from Viroconium and has an important part to play in all our futures. Would you lend him your horse?”

Seren’s lovely, emerald green eyes smiled at Gal. “I saw you earlier, near the hawthorns. Did you enjoy my song?”

Feeling hotter than the hearth-fire, Gal blushed, not because he’d been seen watching her bathe, but because of the beautifully dreamy tone of her voice, her crystal-clear emerald green eyes and her full red lips. Realising he was staring, he blushed again. “I can only apologise. Your singing was so sweet that it entranced me, I thought you were a Faery-woman. I didn’t look for long, and I only saw you from behind.”

She knew it wasn’t her voice he was interested in, the look on his face told her as much. Since her body had developed, she’d noticed that same look on the village boys faces. “Come with me,” she said kindly, “I’ll take you to my horse. We call him ‘Shaggy Bones’ which is a very appropriate name.”

Seren spent the rest of the day teaching Gal how to ride. He fell off at least a dozen times, but always climbed back on with unflinching determination. As the day wore on, he didn’t care how many times he fell off because every time his backside hit the ground, Seren laughed, and the beauty of her smile made his heart burn wild with love. Gradually mastering the horse, he realised his heart was no longer his own and, by the time he’d successfully trotted the animal around the village, he didn't want to leave, he was in love.

Accompanied by five of his personal guard, King Aelle marched into the filthy shantytown that had almost swallowed Andredes Caester's meadows. Everyday more warriors answered his call for the Teutonic brotherhood to march against the Britons. They'd crossed the sea from Juteland, Frisia, Frankia and the old lands of the Saxons. They'd also marched from kingdoms within Briton, amongst his new army were the men of the East Angles and East Saxons, the Jutes of Cantwara had recently arrived en masse, the people of the North-folk and South-folk lands had answered his call to war, and because of this King Aelle had declared himself the first 'Bretwalda', Briton ruler, deciding he was also the uncrowned king of the Celts because he'd killed their high king.

The vast, ramshackle town now stretched north across the meadows almost to the forest's edge, and east to west as far as the King cared to see. Warriors had come in their hundreds, and he'd no doubt more would arrive before he ordered his battle-drums to beat the rhythm of the march.

Picking his way unsteadily along the walkways of slippery duck-boards, everywhere he looked community trades carried on as if this was a real town: fish and meat hung on wooden frames to dry; cauldrons boiled food in the middle of groups of huts; women sat stitching clothes or feeding their young ones; sweat covered smiths beat at heated iron in newly built forges and in almost every doorway, men ran whetstones along blades. This foetid, stinking dung heap was a town preparing for war.

These men had come because King Aelle was a strong leader, and if they survived the fight there'd be rich rewards for everyone. Even the lowest spearman could expect a small farm, whilst the high-ranking sons of nobles would be given towns, cities and even kingdoms to rule. When his warriors marched, he'd put every Briton to the sword, man, woman and child, his intention being genocide.

Walking back to the fort, he took a cloth from one of his warriors and used it to cover his nose as the small party avoided a stinking, communal cesspit. Passing through the fort's gateway, he dismissed his guards and climbed the steps to the battlements. Leaning on the west wall, he looked down at the shantytown, his chest swelling with pride at the sheer number of warriors who'd answered his call for spearmen. There had to be five or six thousand warriors in the meadow, every one of them a brutal killer. Some were the second, third and fourth sons of kings and chieftains, who wouldn't inherit their father's lands and wealth. There were hundreds of mercenaries, who'd fight for profit before moving on to the next war. Others were the scum of society, cut-throats, thieves, rapists and murderers but he didn't care, all who could kill were welcome to fight beneath his banner.

When he was ready to march, he'd have an army that could not just fight its way to the Western Sea, but also turn north to conquer as far as the Roman Wall. The Celts had no idea a storm of spears was coming, and once they realised the storm was a tidal-wave it would be too late for them to successfully defend their lands.

Since the death of King Einion, the Celtic kings had gone their separate ways, or that's what King Aelle's spies had told him. Cadwallon had about four hundred infantrymen, and the Pendragon had no more than three or four hundred horse-warriors, which would be useless against his massive shield-wall. There was no one in Briton powerful enough to stop or slow his march west, and once he'd defeated the hostile kingdoms, he'd kill King Ceredig and take Princess Gorpe back. He'd missed her and couldn't wait to have her youthful joy and beauty illuminating his hall again. Soon, Briton would be his and he'd rule it with an iron grip.

22.

Throughout his life, King Ceredig had murdered, raped, stolen, betrayed, manipulated, conned and tortured to get what he wanted. But after receiving King Aelle's message, his underworked conscience troubled him, and he knew why. Having broken his fast in a foul temper, he decided to walk the city battlements, taking King Aelle's parchment with him. The grey clouds and increasing winds did nothing to lighten his mood and, walking the east wall he cursed his own stupidity, unrolled the parchment and read it again.

The Saxons were coming and there wasn't a Celtic army large enough to prevent the conquest of Briton. Angrily tearing the parchment, he tossed the pieces over the battlements. Destroying the message didn't help his mood, he'd betrayed his people and the ever-darkening storm clouds warned him that the next storm might be one of fire, metal and murder.

Facing the sloping meadow that climbed north to the forest, he wondered how the Pendragon would react if he discovered the back door to conquest had been opened by lust for a beautiful woman. Considering his options, he dismissed the idea of sending his small army to fight the thousands mentioned in King Aelle's parchment. He could warn the Pendragon, but would his message reach Owain in time? Seeing Gareth walking the ramparts towards him, he made a quick decision. "I've a task for you that must be accomplish quickly, and in total secrecy."

"I'm your servant, My Lord."

"You know about the deal I made with King Aelle."

"Have you changed your mind?"

"Yes." Ceredig looked east to where the wolfpack would soon begin its hunt. "When Prince Cissa returns from the continent, the Saxons will advance. I've given King Aelle permission to march his army through my lands, but I can't allow it."

"We haven't the numbers to stop them."

"Unless we build a wall. I want you to ride to Viroconium and inform the Pendragon of King Aelle's plans. Do you know the valley that forks west and north below Caradoc's Hill?"

"Vaguely."

"That's where the Saxons plan to enter my kingdom. Tell the Pendragon that I'll blockade their march where the fork divides, which should force the Saxons to follow the valley north to the abandoned fort overlooking Badon. If the Pendragon prepares his defences there, it might give the other kings time to muster their warriors and join him. When the Saxon army has passed my blockade, I'll wait a day or two then follow, cutting off their retreat. Leave now, and remember, only Cadwallon and the Pendragon must know of the plan."

As the warrior saluted and walked away, Ceredig turned and saw Gorpe standing no more than ten paces from him. She looked beautiful, wrapped in a blue woollen cloak trimmed with foxtails. Her golden, unbound hair was blowing in the wind, which surprised him because she was no longer a maiden, and only maidens wore their hair loose. She was looking east at the grey hills on the horizon, no doubt thinking about her homeland. Had she overheard his conversation with Gareth? There was one way to find out, so he strolled over and kissed her cheek.

"It's a cold day, Husband." Slipping an arm around his waist, she smiled warily at him. "I wonder if the coming days will be colder?"

"Why would they be?" he asked, not liking her double meaning.

"Because the gods have sent a wind to chill my bones."

"Weather constantly changes."

"My father says that warm winds come from the east, they are like an old friend, strong and reliable."

"Who can trust the weather?" asked Ceredig, making a mental note to have her watched until the war was over.

The leather door-flap lifted, flooding Gwen's meditation roundhouse with shafts of bright sunlight. Sitting naked, cross-legged beside the cold ashes as she'd been instructed to do by Graine, she had such a feeling of exhilarating understanding that she wanted to continue her meditation and not be separated from her bliss-experience.

Feeling a warm breeze feather her skin, her reborn senses picked up the sound of drums beating a slow and steady rhythm. Opening her eyes, she saw the shades of three women, dressed in animal skins, standing in the shafts of daylight. Recognising her mother, who was holding a small clay jar, she felt less certain about the other two, both of whom were carrying garlands of ivy and chains of buttercups. “Has it been three days?” she asked, her dry throat reducing her voice to a cracked whisper.

“Yes,” her mother answered. “Your time of meditation has passed. I hope it bore fruit?”

“I saw, felt and I understood.”

“I’m pleased. It is time to prepare you for the next part of the ritual.”

“I am willing.” Knowing what to expect, this was the part of the union Gwen feared the most. The problem wasn’t so much being naked in front of her mother and the hand-maidens, or that she’d be oiled from head to toe and tested for moon-blood, what worried her was standing naked before the entire Forest Island tribe, a trial Owain would share with her.

“Stand up,” Graine ordered. “Your mind, heart and soul have touched Owain’s, now comes the joining of the flesh.” The two hand-maidens approached and, the three of them dipped their fingers in the clay jar. “Love-making can be rough, crude, hurried and selfish which is not acceptable to the Goddess,” said the Priestess, placing the oil jar on the floor. “For your souls to become one during your coupling, your loving-making must be smooth, relaxed, caring and born from love. Oiling you from head to toe will aid the meeting of your flesh and souls.” Gwen gasped as the women began massaging the cold oil into her skin. “I sense fear in your heart, Gwenwyfar, restrictions must not cloud your mind. The next part of the ritual is solemn, and is understood to be so by those witnessing your journey. We are not like the childish outsiders who mock the human form, we understand that cluttering the mind with winks, lust and jests at the expense of others, is a betrayal of our natural humanity."

"I understand," Gwen replied, slipping easily into the movement of the rotating, oiled hands smoothing her skin. She noticed the oil was perfumed with something familiar, though not sweet like crushed petals or herbs. The scent was earthier and hypnotic, reminding her of the forest.

"Open your mouth and taste the Goddess," Graine ordered. She touched her daughter's tongue with an oiled finger. Psilocybin.

The bitter, earthy taste made Gwen think of the forest as she smoothed her tongue against the roof of her mouth. The tang wet her tongue, its metallic shiver tingling a shift within her that she'd never experienced. Happy to relax into the movement of the women's hands, she swayed to the rhythmic drumbeats, her open eyes glassy, their lids heavy, the room softening into changing shades of light that rolled like a swelling sea. Caught within the cresting waves and the beating drums, her senses moved inward and she hummed a mellow tune. Could the women hear her, were they also humming?

The humming increased, weighting her eyelids so she closed them. Feeling the tone vibrate between her closed lips, she slipped into a bright light, a warmth that might overwhelm her if she was wise enough to leave it be. Her light, airless breathing slowed to almost nothing, fading into her consuming hum. With the tune circling inward, she felt the space around her fill with perfectly beautiful harmonies. If she opened her eyes, she'd know how many had joined her song, but she couldn't, her senses being channelled by the scented oil, the beating of the drums, the taste of the forest and the gentle movement of hands slicking her skin. Why not drift, she thought as the light within her swayed her one way then the other.

Her mother's voice broke into her trance, "The Goddess demands that I test your moon-cycle." Gwen felt her mother's hand move between her thighs, and a finger slipped inside her. "If there is moon-blood, the ritual must be delayed. You must understand that this is not a mystery but, it is essential nonetheless." Removing her finger, the Priestess said, "You are clear, Gwenwyfar, your womb is ready to accept the seed of your chosen man."

With this small test over and, Gwen's body fully oiled, the two serving women picked up the ivy-garlands and buttercups.

"Daughter," Graine said, taking a blood-red poppy-head from her pocket, "nature's flowers and twines shall be all you'll wear when you join with your man. These gifts are an offering to the Mother Goddess Enaid, in the same way that your womb is hers to breathe life into."

The women began twining the ivy and buttercups around Gwen's body. Tying a strand of ivy around her head, they slipped buttercups between the leaves; a crown representing the woman as the Goddess. The second garland they tied around her chest, making sure her nipples were exposed; a symbol of the nurturing mother. The third garland of ivy circled her hips, to show that she was fertile and capable of bringing new life into the world. Graine then tied the poppy-head to the garland around her waist, so that it rested on her womb. This, Gwen was told, symbolised her virginity, which amused her because she wasn't a virgin.

"You are ready, your journey towards the union of life can continue," Graine said, stepping back to look at her daughter. "Is there anything you want to say or ask before we lead you outside?"

The beating drums stopped abruptly; Gwen turned to the sunlight flooding into the roundhouse. "I have no regrets; I am ready to give myself to the seed-giver."

"That is as it should be." Graine laid a gentle, comforting hand on her daughter's arm. "Come, now you must feel the breath of the Goddess."

Her mother led her by the hand into the bright, sun-filled day. Gwen stepped into the warmth and heard welcoming birdsong, which lifted her heart. After three days inside the dark roundhouse, it took her eyes a few moments to adjust, but when they did, she saw the entire Forest Island tribe standing naked in front of her, reverentially solemn. They were her kin, her soul family and she felt no naked shame at their presence, so she turned to face the wooden bridge her man would soon cross.

Naked and oiled, Owain followed the Merlin and a Forest Island man carrying a red deer-hide, unsteadily across the bridge. Seeing Gwen waiting for him, dressed only in ivy twines and buttercups, a lust-filled smile spread across his face, the earthy, metallic tang in his mouth tricking his eyes into seeing two Gwen's. Psilocybin.

After crossing the bridge, the Merlin raised his hand, turned to the Pendragon and nodded to the hide-holding man, who tied the forelegs of the deerskin around Owain's neck. "You were the

Pendragon," the Merlin began, his voice echoing inside Owain's head, "now you are the seed-giver, for three days and nights only. Do you have any questions?"

Looking over the Druid's shoulder, Owain couldn't take his eyes off Gwen's naked beauty. "If I am the hunter, is Gwen the Goddess?" he asked, wondering if the glow surrounding her was real?

"In a way, all women are a part of the Goddess. When you enter the hut, she will become your prey, but only inside the roundhouse. When the three days have passed, I doubt my daughter will remain subservient to your sexual desires, because you will never own her soul or her body."

Gwen's eyes widened when the Sun caught the young warrior's oiled, muscular body. A warm sensation between her legs stiffened her nipples, goose-bumps spread over her skin and her lips parted, hungry for the feast of sexual union. He looked so handsomely wild, every bit the seed-giving hunter. "Must I be his prey?" she asked Graine. "Can I not hunt the one who wears the antlers?"

Supressing a laugh, the Priestess replied with, "The worm is eaten by the mouse, the mouse is devoured by the hawk, the eagle swoops to feed on the hawk but when the eagle dies the worm enjoys feasting on the bird, so which is the hunter?"

Walking towards his bride, Owain saw her not as the woman he knew, but as a shining goddess of nature, oiled, naked and pure. His eyes followed the flow of garlands passed her breasts to the red poppy-head, and he couldn't control the stimulated reaction her body had upon him. Although aware of the people gathered to witness the ceremony, he made no effort to suppress his erection, and why would he, why would he deny the most basic of nature's demands?

Instructed by the Merlin, Owain circled his prey three times, his eyes taking their fill of her womanhood. Turning within his circle, she saw his burning lust and ached for him to take her there and then, uninhibited and free. Completing the third circle, Owain took her hand. Tickling her palm with his forefinger, he looked at the Merlin, unsure of what to do next.

The Merlin said to Gwen, "Being your father, I am not permitted to lead you through the ceremony." Turning to the only fully-clothed man standing with the Island People, he beckoned to the stranger.

The man walked forward, his flowing, long brown hair catching the Sun which gave it a reddish hue. Wearing black tanned-leather from neck to toe, and a black, bull-hide cloak the man bowed slightly to the Merlin and turned to face the young couple. Gwen thought she saw a wicked glint of playfulness in his eyes, though when she looked again it was gone. "This is Marcus ap Trefor," the Merlin said, "he's a druid from Llanrwst. He will bind you together." He then waved forward a naked, red-haired man who was holding a small harp.

By the woad-coloured patterns etched onto his skin, Gwen guessed he must be from the north. Having heard about the Brigantian Celts, who were said to be an aggressively warlike race, she was surprised to see him carrying a harp. "May I introduce you to Cieren ap Callum," the Merlin said to the lovers. "He is a

Brigantian bard from a place he calls Merryfield, in the region of Elmet. He's the finest of bards and will sit near your roundhouse for the next three days and nights. His harp will give rhythm, feeling and soul to your union of flesh, the notes weaving a spell of love and lust until you emerge on the final day. How he can do this is a mystery, but he'll not let a single note drop from the seed-music, nor will he eat, drink or sleep."

Gwen was more interested in Marcus ap Trefor, wondering at his years because he could have no more than twenty summers behind him, which was young for a druid. Concluding there must be something special about him, not only because he was a young druid, but because her father had chosen him to conduct the ceremony.

Graine passed an ivy twine to Marcus, who held out his hand and spoke to the lovers, "Owain the hunter, give me your right hand. Gwenwyfar the hunted, give me your left hand." Laying the ivy loosely over their wrists, he closed his eyes and turned to face the sun. Raising his arms, he hummed a long, resonant note. Time seemed to slow and spiral as the note grew in intensity, silencing the birds and for a few heartbeats stilling the light summer-breeze. The resonant hum travelled, first through the flesh of the Island People, then up and over the green forest, soaring to the Sun as the note grew in strength. For a while the hum held all heartbeats within its tone, all thoughts forgotten until the note faded. Lowering his arms, Marcus turned back and said, "Owain the hunter, you will speak your chosen words to your lover."

Owain looked at Gwen, searching for the prepared words his heightened senses had swallowed into the metallic tang in his mouth. Shaking his head to clear it, he succumbed to the earthy taste of the forest, and spoke from his heart, "Gwenwyfar, from the first moment I saw you I knew I could never love another woman. I choose to share my soul with you because without you I'd have no soul, you are my life. I know you are a woman of nature and I'll always respect that: you'll be free to choose, to live and to give only by the wishes of your own heart. I promise to demand nothing from you, only ever requesting what is yours to freely give or withhold. I'll listen to you when you are not speaking, love you well beyond our existence in this world and never will I share the bed of another woman. My seed, my life and my eternal soul are yours."

Marcus spoke again, "Gwenwyfar the hunted, reply to the seed-giver."

She looked down at Owain's still erect manhood, then deep into the eyes of his soul. "My love and my lover, I can think of nothing I desire more than to give myself to you. I know you are high-born and a part of you must always be given to your people, that is as it should be. I am your consort, not your ruler so I choose to share your soul, not dominate it. You were not born free like myself, so I'll always try to understand the burdens you carry. My love has always been yours, and however many lives we live in the future, I shall be at your side. I give you my heart with its love, my womb with its fruit and my soul with its eternity."

Marcus tied the ivy-twine around their wrists, and the Island People respectfully applauded. He then warned the lovers, "Nature's twine is the bond between the Mother Goddess Enaid, your union and the earth. We are spirit, but we are flesh, we live then return to the earth. This cycle cannot be broken, nor must the ivy twine break, be cut or fall from your wrists during your lovemaking. Only I can remove the twine, which I'll do when you return to the world bound into one soul. Understand this, if you break the twine your souls will not become one, the marriage will be void and the Goddess will demand a sacrifice. No one born of flesh knows what that sacrifice might be, nor the pain it could bring not just to you, but also our nation." He led them to the hut Gwen had spent the last three days and nights meditating in, and he cupped their ivy-twined hands in his. "You go into this first home as young lovers, when you return to the world, you'll be one life and one soul, just as everyone who walks the earth are one life and one soul."

Marcus nodded to Cieren the bard, who walked over to a stool placed a discreet distance from the roundhouse. Sitting, he set his harp on his lap and began plucking the strings. The music had a strange rhythm, neither a dance nor a lament. Some might say the plucking mirrored the beating of two separate hearts, which was a skill few bards ever mastered. The Merlin knew it's meaning and why, as the three days of love-making progressed, the beat would alter its pattern to become a single heartbeat.

Marcus pulled back the leather door-flap. "Go, become one within the soul of the Goddess."

Once more, everyone applauded, and the lovers disappeared into the darkness of the roundhouse.

"Remember when we were young?" the Merlin whispered to Graine.

"We never were," she replied softly, "we knew too much. Will you come to me tonight, Gwion?"

"I will. Shall we meet on the island, or would you prefer the forest?"

"Do you remember the cave where we first made love, the night Gwenwyfar was conceived?"

"I'll never forget it. I'll go there before the stars guide secret lovers to their trysts, to light a fire and prepare a place for our love-making."

Marcus lowered the roundhouse door-flap and walked away. Cieren, softly plucking his harp, looked up from the strings and saw a jet-black raven glide over the roundhouse. A name slipped into his mind, 'Rohanna'. Hearing Cieren's thoughts, the Merlin looked up as the raven cawed a warning, then the name 'Morrigan' touched something warm within his soul and, he smiled, though he didn't know why. A heartbeat later the warmth turned ice-cold, and the Druid watched the bird fly south.

23.

Cadwallon couldn't trust Ceredig, yet the King's idea was workable, assuming he adhered to his part in the plan. Sitting with Gareth in Viroconium's guardroom, Cadwallon looked suspiciously at Ceredig's messenger, while toying with the pros and cons of relying on Ceredig to divert King Aelle's army north. Sipping a cup of wine, he mulled over what might happen if the plan failed and, the Saxons reached Aqua Sulis. Viroconium's only reliable ally was King Erbin of Dumnonia, so if Aqua Sulis was captured and a wedge was driven between the lands of the Votidini and the Dumnonians, Cadwallon and Owain's influence and power would be greatly reduced.

Ceredig's diversion was a sound tactic, so he'd pass it on to Owain if he returned from his marriage ritual in time to lead the Britons to war. Cadwallon knew Sulis Hillfort well, having used it many times as a base when hunting with his father and brother, and the fort's defences were basic but in good repair, as it had been necessary to refortify many of the old hillforts because of the Teutonic invasions and Irish raids. More could be done to strengthen the walls, and provisions would be needed if King Aelle laid siege, so either Cai or Bedwyr should be sent south, which is why he'd summoned them to the guardroom.

Bedwyr and Cai arrived and took their places at Einion's old table, both looking warily at Gareth. Before either had a chance to speak, Cadwallon said, “The Saxons intend to march west and take Aqua Sulis, and King Ceredig has given them permission to cross his kingdom.”

“If that’s true, what’s he doing here?” Bedwyr asked, pointing at Gareth.

“He has brought a strategy from Ceredig, and in my opinion it is sound.”

“Can we trust Ceredig?” Cai asked.

“We might not have a choice,” Cadwallon replied. He then ordered Gareth to tell them the plan.

Gareth shuffled uncomfortably on his chair, took a sip of wine and thought for a moment before saying, “Ceredig regrets his alliance with King Aelle, so this.........”

“That’s of no interest to us,” Bedwyr cut in. “Just tell us the plan.”

“King Aelle intends crossing into Ceredig’s lands before the summer solstice, on his way to Aqua Sulis. Ceredig’s wall will divert the Saxons towards Sulis Hillfort, where they can be held up long enough for other Celtic kings to muster their armies.”

“Is that it?” Bedwyr asked. “What if the diversion doesn’t work, what if King Aelle smashes through Ceredig’s defences, what if the Saxons follow a different route? There are so many floors in the strategy.”

Not knowing what else could be done, Cadwallon asked, “Do you have a better idea?”

“What we should do,” Bedwyr began, pouring himself some wine, “is ride around the Saxon army and attack Andredes Caester, which will force King Aelle to march back. By the time he arrives we'll have destroyed his fort and run."

"That's madness," said Cai, scathingly. "We should message the kings, muster a great army and attack the Saxons while they are laying siege to Aqua Sulis. Don't forget that.........."

"Mustering so many warriors would take forever," Bedwyr cut in, "and you know how fickle the kings are, they'll hold back and wait for Owain and Cadwallon to be killed in battle, then fight each other for the throne."

"Ceredig's plan will be followed," Cadwallon insisted. "What I need you to tell me, is when we should march?"

"Today," Bedwyr said without hesitation. "If Owain was here, our warriors would already have left."

"Bedwyr is right," Cai added. "We must strengthen the hillfort's defences as soon as possible."

Cadwallon wished Owain was here: why had he chosen this time to marry, why couldn't he have waited until after the invasion? Being a proud Christian, he'd refused to attend the wedding, not wanting to be seen taking part in a pagan ritual. He'd told Owain that the Legion wouldn't be permitted to attend the rites, because they must be ready to ride if the Saxons attacked. This had caused an argument between the two brothers, the first harsh words they'd exchanged since they were boys.

"What are your orders?" Bedwyr asked.

"I'm not sure," Cadwallon spoke honestly. "If I knew Ceredig's diversion would definitely work, I'd feel more comfortable with giving orders."

“The earth wall will be built high, and it will run right across the valley,” Gareth said. “The chances of Aelle attacking it are slim at best, because he’ll lose too many warriors in the fight; he’s certain to follow the north fork.”

“Nothing’s that simple,” Bedwyr insisted.

“Bedwyr, you and a dozen Red Cloaks will ride to Badon,” Cadwallon ordered. “Use the local tribes to strengthen Sulis Fort’s walls and gather food.”

“And the rest of our warriors?” Cai asked.

“They’ll follow when Owain orders them to march.”

A shimmering heat-haze arose from the sparkling Forest Lake as the midday Sun warmed the Merlin and Marcus, who were sitting on rocks at the lakeside, dangling their feet in the cool water. It was the sixth day of the wedding rites and, they were both looking forward to dusk, when Marcus would cut Owain and Gwen’s ivy twine, and the celebrations would begin. “Do you ever wonder how Cieren plays for so long without dropping a note?” Marcus casually asked as tiny fish nibbled at his feet.

The Merlin lifted a foot from the water and looked at his toes. “He has a gift from the gods,” he replied, plopping his foot back into the lake. “Why do you ask, are you thinking of returning to Mona to learn the higher bardic skills?”

“No, I was just being curious.”

“The druids on Mona speak very highly of you, Marcus, some have suggested you might be the next Merlin.”

"Not while you are alive," Marcus enthused. "There hasn't been a Merlin so well regarded as yourself since the great Gwydion passed over to the Otherworld."

"I can't agree, there have been many Merlins held in higher esteem than myself. My predecessor Emrys was one, his wisdom was legendary, as were his seeing skills. When did you first realise you had a calling to the priesthood?"

"It wasn't a calling," Marcus said, "it was more like a need. A feeling I can't explain grew within me, pulling me where it would."

The Merlin understood because it had been much the same for him. He wouldn't describe the beginning of his journey as being a search, it was more like reaching out to embrace what you knew you were. "Has your ability to see into the present and the future ever been a burden?"

"Definitely, though not for me. I think my parents sent me to Mona because they were fed up of me always telling them what was about to happen!"

They both laughed. Few outside the druidic-brotherhood understood the ways of the sight. It was an essential part of the life of a priest or priestess, giving them an unquestionable power over the people, though never were they allowed to use it for personal gain; the sight was only to be used in the service of the people and the Mother Goddess Enaid. Prophetic in nature but never fixed, the sight was more of a possibility than a direct path, which could be altered by man's actions if the Goddess willed it.

"Do you ever wonder what being of the world must be like, instead of being of the Otherworld?" the Merlin asked.

Marcus considered this whilst watching a heron swoop low over the water, scoop up a fish in its long beak then soar high over the forest to find its perch. "I think we are in both worlds, a foot in either camp you might say. We have wives and lovers, take up the sword and go to war, we make children, we eat and drink, we love and suffer just like other mortals. I'd say we are more a part of this world than the Otherworld, even if the two do run parallel. Fortunately, because of our learning we can go to a place where the untrained never go, which I think is the greatest of our many gifts. I suppose the question must be asked as to whether there are more than the two worlds we know about? I've often considered this question, what if there are countless worlds that move through time and space parallel with each other, side by side so to speak? The possibilities are infinite, and I'd give anything to travel through those worlds and times. I know that during our meditations we can go anywhere and be anything, but wouldn't it be marvellous to physically cross the barriers of time and space?"

Though the Merlin was surprised by the reply, he was also impressed. "Have you taken a wife?" he asked, wiggling his toes in the water to scatter the nibbling fish.

"Oh yes, and what a wild beauty she is. Her name is Tanwen, which means 'white fire'. She has the most beautiful long, strawberry blonde hair, and let me tell you she is pretty, oh yes. But she's no precious little daisy, she's as strong as an ox and has the shapeliest form of the healthiest of child-bearers. She's not big mind, just healthy. If she were royal, she wouldn't be a princess she'd be an empress, such is her stature."

"Don't you worry about leaving her alone so often, we druids spend very little time in our chosen places?"

"I'm proud to say I never have to worry about her. I go on my travels and when I return, she welcomes me with a lusty warmth you wouldn't believe. She's a giver, see, and is as lust-filled as a Beltane gathering!" Laughing, he nudged the Merlin in his ribs. "I'd say she'd break the back of a man not as strong as myself, maybe that's why she chose me for a husband! Oh, while I remember, she's the finest swordswoman you'll ever come across, she's skewered a few Saxons in her time and, enjoyed it too! She's also outthrown, with the spear, all the men of our valley, and people say she can bring down an eagle with her bow, which is useful because every day she's out hunting in the forest. When the forest beasts are wise enough to keep out of her way, she truffles in the undergrowth until she has enough wild mushrooms to fill a pot. She's a rare woman my Tanwen, though sometimes I wish she'd sleep inside our roundhouse. I built it for her, but she prefers being outdoors, which can be a bit embarrassing when she has the urge to make love."

The Merlin had never known any man speak with such enthusiasm about a woman. "I'd like to meet her."

"Maybe you would, but would she want to meet you? She makes her own decisions, see, she's quite free."

"Have you ever been tempted by another woman? Do you still join the ritual ruts?"

"I used to, it being my druidic duty. But since I met Tanwen I've never strayed, it would be more than my life is worth! There was someone before her, a travelling girl who was not quite a restless soul, more like an adventuress I'd say, seeking out the joys of life in every place she visited. Rhosyn was her name, I met her at the festival of the new-sun, and naked she was, laid out on the warm grass without a care for those who might see her. Thousands came to experience that solstice, so thousands saw her naked splendour." The memory of his time with Rhosyn made him chuckle. "That night it was me she chose to bed with, even though a handsome young man had travelled all the way from Gaul to be with her."

"What happened to her?"

"She continued her travels. Sometimes, when I'm walking the pathways from village to village, or sleeping alone beneath the wide spread of our mother-oaks, I remember her easy-beauty."

"She must have been quite something."

"Oh yes, and she had the most fantastic nipples, like ripe raspberries they were! You're asking a lot of questions, Gwion, why?"

"Do you need me to tell you?"

Covered in dust and sweat from his journey, Gal slid from Seren's horse, tied the shaggy animal to a branch near Gwen's Forest Lake roundhouse, looked across the glistening water and was surprised to see what looked like the Merlin and another man, cooling their feet in the lake. Gwen's boat was in its usual place, so he pushed it into the water, jumped in and pulled the oars through the glassy surface.

"That looks like trouble," Marcus said, pointing at the boat.

The Merlin stood to get a better look. “Is that you, Gal!” he called across the water.

Without missing a stroke, the boy called back, “I must find Owain!” The boat ran up the pebbles at the lake’s edge, he leapt out and ran to the druids. “I’ve been to Andredes Caester, the Saxons are ready to march, thousands of them!”

“Calm yourself,” the Merlin demanded, “take a few moments to breathe. Anyway, you can’t speak to Owain yet, he’s into the sixth day of the marriage ritual and the spell cannot be broken.”

“Spell?” The boy looked suspiciously at him.

“Not quite a spell, more a journey, but it mustn’t be interfered with under any circumstances.” Looking at the ragged and panting, sweaty boy, he could see that he’d been through quite a journey. The lad looked older; something was different about him. “Take a moment to gather yourself, then I’ll take you to where the marriage rites are taking place. I must warn you though, Owain won’t leave the roundhouse until after the Sun has set.”

Gal matched the Merlin’s quick pace, following the two druids across the wooded island and into a valley he never knew existed, which was strange because he knew every blade of grass and sheltering leaf within three days walk of the lake. Seeing the valley for the first time, he found it difficult to believe he could have missed the place, with its climbing hills, soft grassy meadow and wooden bridge spanning the river.

Following the Merlin towards the gathering of naked Island People, he saw a bard sitting near one of the two roundhouses, playing music with the strangest of rhythms, a melody gently ringing over the top of what sounded like a heartbeat.

It was obvious to Gal which of the two roundhouses Owain and Gwen were in, and his first instinct was to ignore the Merlin's warning and make a dash for the door-flap. But while walking through the woods, Marcus had warned him about the dangers of breaking the union, so he hesitated. But every passing moment was vital, the nation's security depended on him delivering his message. Choosing to follow his instincts and risk severe punishment, he shimmied past the Merlin and ran. The Druid made a grab for him but he was too slow. "Come back!" he shouted. "Stop that boy!"

Others raced after him but he was too quick and agile. Closing on the roundhouse, he shouted, "Owain! Owain! the Saxons are ready to march, thousands of them!" Reaching the roundhouse door-flap, he slipped and fell and a naked man grabbed him and pinned him to the hard earth. "Owain!" he shouted while struggling to free himself. "Come out, Briton needs you!"

The door-flap lifted and dropped again. Cieren the bard stopped plucking his harp and looked angrily at Gal. "Do you know what you've done?" he asked, then he told the naked man to release the boy.

"I'd no choice," Gal pleaded.

The Merlin caught up and turned the boy to face him. "I don't know what the consequences of your actions will be, but a wise man would assume they'll be severe. What Owain will do to you I cannot guess at, and however he reacts I may not be able to protect you."

The boy saw concern in the Druid's eyes as the door-flap lifted again, and the two lovers stepped out like naked gods into the bright sunshine, their ivy-twine unbroken. Gal turned and saw Gwen in all her naked glory, her angry eyes cutting hard into his soul, so he quickly looked at Owain.

As his head lowered, all that had happened to him flashed through his mind: he'd risked his life in a Saxon fort; found his mother; fought and killed a giant; carried his wounded mother through a forest; fallen in love with an angel-star all to get a message to the one person who could save Briton. He couldn't fail at the final hurdle, whatever Owain's reaction might be he had to deliver his message. "I'm sorry about breaking the union," he began, "but King Aelle plans to reach Aqua Sulis in time for the summer solstice. King Ceredig, and I am ashamed to say this, has given the Saxons permission to march across his land. He has formed an alliance with our natural enemy, having married the Saxon King's daughter. I've also found my mother and discovered what love is." Shaking his head and cursing himself for telling the Pendragon the last part, he composed himself and continued, "I really am truly sorry for interrupting your marriage, but what choice did I have? Our people need you more than Gwen does."

The Pendragon held out his hand. "Give me your knife, Gal."

The boy hesitated, then nervously he placed his knife in his friend's hand. Owain cut the ivy-twine and said to his young spy, "You've done well. If we act fast enough to intercept King Aelle's army, you might just have saved a nation." Aware of his nakedness, he called for clothes, then he said to Gwen, "I'm sorry to do this, but there's so little time if I'm to stop the Saxons from reaching the west coast. We've spoken our words and made the union, so our marriage is good. When I return, we can have the final day's celebration, if that's what you want but now, I need you to do something for me."

"What?" she asked, hiding her sorrow.

"I need you and Gal to gather all the Forest People who can throw a spear or aim an arrow, and you must do it quickly. There's a small army of hunters in your forest, I'm going to need them all, men and women. I'll tell you more after we've dressed." Turning at the sound of galloping hoofbeats, he saw a red-cloaked rider charge into the valley. Cai reined in his mount in a cloud of dry, dusty earth. Leaping from the saddle, he made straight for the Pendragon. "Owain, please forgive my intrusion but Cadwallon insisted I stop the wedding because the Saxons are ready to march."

"I know, Gal just told me."

The Merlin looked at Marcus, who returned his worried look. They both knew that cutting the ivy-twine meant trouble, but when the punishment would be delivered, no mortal knew.

Striding purposefully through Andredes Caester's gateway, Prince Cissa was grabbed in a massive bear-hug by his father. The Prince had been across the sea far longer than intended, and although the fruits of his labours had made it a worthwhile trip, he was glad to be back.

"You've done well," Aelle beamed, "thousands of warriors have joined us."

"Word spreads fast amongst idle spearmen," Cissa replied when his father let go of him.

"Come, there's plenty to organise before we march." The King led his son through the bustle of warriors and smiths preparing for war, to the feasting-hall.

"When do we leave?"

"I've sent foraging parties out to steal livestock and grain from Celtic border villages," Aelle said, kicking open the feasting-hall doors. "They should return today or tomorrow, so we'll march the day after tomorrow."

Walking past one of the three hearths, Cissa asked, "How long will it take us to reach the Western Sea?"

"It depends on the weather, seven or eight days, maybe more. As Ceredig has given us safe passage through his lands, it will be at least five days before the Celts know we are marching. By then it will be too late for them to prepare strong defences, so we'll roll right over them, assuming they are foolish enough to fight. Do you know what I'm hoping for?"

Cissa laughed and suggested, "A ready supply of Celtic women to pleasure you during the long march!"

"No, but it's a good idea. I'm hoping the Pendragon rides south to fight us; I can't tell you how much I want to kill him."

24.

King Ceredig wiped the sweat from his brow, took a big gulp of watery-ale from his leather flask, thrust his wooden shovel into the piled-up earth and looked along the lines of the hundreds of men and women working hard in the dry heat of the midday sun. Many days they'd laboured below Caradoc's Hill, and he hoped the impressive defences, which had risen to the height of two men, would be enough to divert King Aelle's army towards the hillfort overlooking Badon Village.

The rampart was wide enough for half a dozen men to march along, shoulder to shoulder, so all it needed now was a wooden palisade along its entire length, with a raised walkway for his spearmen to stand on. In the valley behind the wall, the first oxcarts piled high with sharpened stakes for the palisade, were creaking towards the rampart, where a chain of workers were ready to unload and pass the stakes along the wall's length.

Ceredig had somewhere near six hundred men ready to man the defences, but almost half were not trained warriors, they were hunters, townsfolk and villagers who knew how to throw a spear or loose an arrow. As soon as the Saxon army was sighted, a horn would sound and his people would man the ramparts, presenting a formidable obstacle to King Aelle's ambitions.

Hills protected the ends of the wall, and just to make certain King Aelle wasn't tempted to send his warriors up the hills to outflank his defences, he'd ordered women to collect rocks and pile them on the hillside, then throw them at the Saxons if they attempted to climb the hills. He could do no more to divert King Aelle's army towards Badon, his precarious fate now depended on the Saxons dislike of siege warfare.

Running down the rear slope of the rampart, as the first oxcart was being emptied of its load, the King saw a rider galloping fast towards him. Gorpe, sitting astride her white pony, with a look of grey thunder on her beautiful face, reined in her mount and looked down at him. "Do you want my father to kill you?" she hissed at him.

"It won't come to that; he won't waste his warriors on us."

"You are a fool. I've seen how he deals with traitors, as soon as he defeats the Pendragon, he'll march against you: your people will be butchered or enslaved; your towns and cities torched; the land laid waste from your northern forests to your coastline. When he gets hold of you, he'll peg you out, slit you open from your cock to your neck and leave you alive for crows to peck at."

"I must protect what is mine," he said, unable to look her in the eye. "Men have fought and died so I might rule this land, not that it's any concern of yours."

"My father trusted you!" If she had a weapon, she'd slice open his guts.

"I don't answer to you, Gorpe. I told you to stay in Durnovaria, go back and remain there until the danger has passed."

"All traitors are cowards!" she spat. "Your betrayal has dissolved our marriage; I am no longer your wife so I'll return to my own people." Raising her hazel crop to whip her pony forward, she kicked out at Ceredig when he grabbed the reins. "Let go!" she screamed, "I'm no longer your property!" Her crop slashed a bloody smear across his cheek. Down it came again so he grabbed it and pulled it from her grip.

"You'll return to Durnovaria and remain there, under guard." Holding tight to her pony's reins, he waved over two mounted warriors. "Escort my wife back to the city," he ordered, "and make sure she remains there. If she escapes, I'll have your heads."

"You wouldn't dare imprison me!"

"You think so?"

"We are finished, Ceredig the Betrayer," she seethed with every drop of hatred in her young soul. "Watch your back and sleep with your eyes open, fear poison in your food and ale, trust none of your friends because I'll need another lover, and the price for my body will be your death!"

"No man will be allowed near you. I know you'll never look upon me as your husband again, so when I return from the wars, I'll cut off your pretty Saxon head." He turned to her escort and said, "take her away, lock her up and make sure no one goes anywhere near her. When I return to the city tonight, I'll organise a food and water rota for her."

Sitting at the table in his candlelit, private room, Cadwallon listened without complaint to the stern words of his wife's priest, Gildas ap Caw. The brother of Huail had prayed his way to the conclusion that the present 'Woes of the Britons' were entirely down to the evil, sinful indulgences of the ruling classes, especially the Pendragon. Meddyf, standing reverentially beside the seated monk, spoke her halleluiahs every time Gildas raised his hands to ask God to forgive the sins of the Celtic kings, even though she didn't believe they were worthy of Christ's mercy.

Being the youngest of King Caw's many sons, Gildas wouldn't inherit any of his father's wealth, so he'd reluctantly joined the priesthood at his mother's request, unable to refuse her dying wish when he'd knelt in prayer beside her deathbed. He was a dark-haired, brown-eyed Pict, and his face may have been handsome if it hadn't been for his long, thin nose, which gave him the look of a weasel. Ashamed of his ridiculous nose, he walked everywhere with a stoop, hunching his head into his shoulders while picking his way through crowds. To say that he was an unswerving, fanatical fundamentalist would understate his character. Having taken religious vows, the more he'd learned about the Christ, the more fundamental he'd become. To him, there was only one word, and that word was Jesus. Relating everything in life to the teachings in the bible, he took every commandment at face value, and to its extreme. His mission was to evangelise the Celtic nation, and anyone who wouldn't bend the knee, first to God and then himself, was the spawn of the Devil.

"It's your own fault, all of it," the Priest raved. Leaning across the table, he pointed a bony finger at Cadwallon. "You allowed your brother to take a pagan wife, so there'll be a reckoning. You claim the Devil's ways are not yours, yet you don't have the conviction to control one sinful brother. What kind of a Christian are you?" Scraping the legs of his chair on the stone-flagged floor, he got up and began pacing the room, Meddyf's worshiping eyes following him. "You had the power to stop your brother," he continued his rant, "but you cowered before the evil-one, permitting open sin to blight your kingdom. Nor did you punish the Devil's own Pendragon for the murder of my innocent brother Huail! Do not doubt that the Pendragon will answer to God when Gabriel's trumpet sounds, as will you, unless you kneel before the Christ." With the proud veins in his neck tightening, his face purpling and spittle gathering in the corners of his mouth, he shrieked, "Mend your ways, cast out your sins and repent before it is too late!"

Cadwallon had nothing to say, but his wife did. "Can't you see the truth, Husband, has Gildas not made clear to you the path you must follow? As for your brother, is he not the most wicked of men, has he not taken a pagan whore for a wife?"

"Owain isn't evil," Cadwallon insisted, "and Gwen is a good woman,"

"You say so," she replied instantly, "but I do not."

"You'll treat her with respect," he ordered. "She's my brother's wife, their marriage cannot be evil because it was born out of love." He turned to Gildas. "You are wrong, evil is not what you say it is."

"You dare to question me!" Gildas shrieked at him.

"Apologise!" Meddyf demanded.

Cadwallon got up from his chair, walked over to the window and looked out at the royal gardens. He'd had enough of the monk and his ravings; he only tolerated the man because he was his wife's confessor. "I've nothing to apologise for," he said to Meddyf. "Gwen will be treated with respect when Owain returns. She is family now, and a more caring, loving, gentle and wise woman you'll never meet."

"If she's so wonderful, perhaps you should have married her!" Meddyf screamed at him.

"The Pendragon is due to return, when?" Gildas asked. "He'll have his Devil woman with him? that cannot be allowed."

"I was powerless to stop their marriage, although I ...."

"Don't you realise your actions reflect upon us all?" Meddyf cut him short. "You may not have been able to prevent the marriage, but you should have condemned it, publicly."

"I'd never condemn my brother's choice of wife."

"You are the next king of the Votidini, your word is law!" the Priest raved. "Do you not fear for your soul? The fires of Hell have welcomed better men than you. Beware the wrath of God!"

"Owain's conscience is his own!" Cadwallon replied, angrily. "I cannot and will not dictate how a man feeds his soul!"

"How dare you raise your voice to the Lord's servant on earth?" the monk yelled, pointing a dirty fingernail at Cadwallon. "Kneel and repent, now!"

By God's law the Priest was right, but who has the right to dictate another man's conscience? If someone isn't free to think and feel, what kind of freedom does that person have? He fully understood what Gildas was saying but, questioned the truth of his words because Jesus preached peace, love, acceptance, forgiveness, tolerance and understanding for all people, there was no hate or prejudice in any of the Christ's teachings. Yet hatred was all this bitter Priest spat into the world, and Cadwallon wondered just how holy the weasel-faced man really was? For the sake of his wife, he'd toe the line, but it galled him. "I'll seek forgiveness through repentance, but I'll never order anyone else to do the same." Kneeling in front of the monk, he pressed his palms together. Gildas was about to begin a prayer, when there was a knock at the door. "Enter!" Cadwallon shouted with a little too much relief, and he got to his feet. The door opened, in walked the Pendragon and Cai. "Owain, you've returned not a day too soon. I take it you've heard the news Gareth brought from King Ceredig?"

"Yes. What have you done to prepare for war?"

"I've sent messengers to the kings to ask for their help, organised foragers for food and sent Bedwyr south to oversee preparations for the defence of Sulis Hillfort."

Owain nodded, glanced at Gildas then asked his brother, "Have you ordered the Viroconium infantry to march?"

"Not yet, I was uncertain of the required strategy."

"The infantrymen should have been despatched immediately; it will take them days to march to Badon." Owain turned to Cai. "You'll order the immediate departure of all the infantry and, you'll be leading them. Take everything we have in the armoury, don't leave behind a single spear or arrowhead. Tell the Legion to be ready to ride before the Sun reaches the middle of the day." Thinking, he glared at Gildas and spoke again to Cai, "Order the Legion not to take their red cloaks with them."

Puzzled by the last part, Cai saluted and left the room.

"Is it wise to leave Viroconium undefended?" Cadwallon asked.

"There's little point in more than a small city-guard remaining, King Aelle will need all his warriors for the battle he knows must come, and no one else is likely to attack the city."

Gildas stepped forward and threw a not so confident question at Owain, "Is it not Cadwallon's place to decide who goes to war and who stays, he is the next king?"

"Who are you?" Owain asked, trying to place the man's features.

Cadwallon replied for the Priest, "He is Gildas, a priest of the Christ God. I summoned him from the north at my wife's request."

"He is a good man," Meddyf added, "you should listen to him."

Owain glanced contemptuously at his brother's wife, then he walked slowly over to the Priest. "Gildas, from the north?"

"That is my name, what of it?" The Priest backed into the corner when Owain stepped towards him.

"Didn't Huail the murderer, abductor and rapist have a brother called Gildas?" Owain felt his blood warming.

"I am the youngest brother of Huail." Drawing on the power of his god, the monk foolishly spoke what he thought, "My brother had every right to do with Gwen what he wished, because she's a pagan. Surely you know that the laws of the civilised don't apply to those who follow the Satanic ways of the Goddess?"

"Watch your mouth, Priest." The Pendragon stepped closer, amazed the man would insult his wife in front of him. But if he wanted to die, that was his choice.

Gildas dug his hole a little deeper by saying, "You should remember, Satan's Pendragon, you are also a pagan."

"Speak your filth again, Gildas the whelp, and I'll rip out your throat."

"You and your whore are pagan scum! I don't fear you because I'm protected by Jesus. Touch me and you'll burn in the fires of Hell!"

"Owain!" Meddyf yelled when the Prince grabbed the Priest's neck. "Step away from him at once!"

Ignoring her, the Pendragon seethed at the Priest, "You are a snivelling drop of rat-shit, the slime from the bowels of an eviscerated dog, and you've said too much. No one calls my wife a whore!" With one hand he lifted Gildas to eye level, and pressed him hard up against the wall. "If I survive the battle with the Saxons and return to this city to find you still here, I'll kill you. Now take your weasel-faced carcass out of this city." Relaxing his grip, he dropped the Priest.

War-drums boomed, and battle-horns blasted defiant notes to the thickening grey clouds as King Aelle, followed by his personal guard of twenty mounted warriors, trotted his horse along the ranks of his cheering warriors. The vast army was ready to march and, no Celt would be spared as they progressed to the Western Sea.

With rainclouds obscuring the rising sun, King Aelle took one last look at Andredes Caester and, signalled his spearmen forward with a wave of his arm. Beating a steady marching rhythm, the war-drums smothered the farewells shouted by women and children from the fort's high walls, and the massive army rumbled west.

For most of the late spring and early summer the Sun had been bold, so why today of all days, Aelle asked himself, must it hide behind clouds? The light drizzle was the last thing his heavy baggage carts needed, and he feared that if the rain persisted his army might become bogged down in clinging mud.

Leading his army out of the valley, he sat astride his horse with a grim expression on his face, not because of the strengthening rain, but because he was remembering how young he'd been the last time he'd fought in a full-scale war. In those days he'd lived for the smell of Celtic blood, the rich spoils of war and the taste of Celtic women. Today, the aches and pains of age told him his rattling bones would be happier beside the hearth-fire.

This would be his last campaign, kill the Pendragon and his Red Cloaks, then give his warriors to Prince Cissa. War was for young men, and if he'd had the choice Cissa would have led the army. But his warriors wouldn't follow him yet, not until he'd proved his worth in full-scale war. Looking at the young warrior riding beside him, he felt proud of the tall, strong and handsome man he'd fathered, and he dearly hoped his son would show his metal when battle was joined.

As the vanguard marched out of the valley, the self-proclaimed 'Bretwalda' of Briton turned in his saddle to laugh along with the army, who'd begun a bawdy marching song about a hairy woman and a well-endowed stallion. The raucous chant reminded him of his youth, when he'd marched to war singing about gods and heroic warriors; how times change! He pulled his cloak tighter as the rain poured, flowing cold down men's helmets, necks and chainmail as they marched, chilling their bones as the strengthening wind cut cold. "Damn this rain," Prince Cissa cursed.

"Today, rain waters the land," Aelle said, "soon it will be Celtic blood."

"The warriors might take the rain for a bad omen," his son suggested.

"Tell me, Cissa, from which direction is the wind blowing?"

"The east."

"Yes, they are Woden's winds, so they are a good omen." Looking to his left he saw dark clouds hanging over the rolling swell of the grey, Southern Sea, which made him thankful he'd chosen to move the army by land. He didn't believe in omens, so as the wind strengthened and the rain poured, he looked ahead to the distant Celtic horizon, to a land that would be his before the next Moon waned.

Climbing onto the east-facing stone wall of the old fort on Sulis Hill, Owain scanned the surrounding countryside, his focus the east valley along which the Saxons would certainly swarm towards the village of Badon. They were coming in their thousands, and he didn't doubt that when they did swarm up the hill's slope, they would pour over his few hundred warriors and slaughter them all. If a small miracle did happen, and the besieged held out beyond the first attack, there was a small possibility that the fort's defenders could hold out for two to three days, if King Aelle mismanaged his attacks. Two to three days, that wouldn't give the other Celtic kings time to muster their armies and march to Badon, assuming they had the inclination to join the fight.

Below him, four valleys met at the village, which straddled the banks of the Afon. Rising above the east and south valleys loomed the treeless Badon Hill, which levelled to a plateau that could easily house a similar fort to the one on Sulis Hill. The north and east valleys were overlooked by the densely wooded Forest Hill, its grassy ridge falling into the meadow cut through by the Afon.

He could see why this place had been chosen to make a stand. The fort overlooked all four valleys and the view into the distance was long and wide, so it would be impossible for King Aelle's army to take the fort's defenders by surprise. Leaping off the wall, he ran down the rampart's slope and stood in the outer ditch to view the defences, reckoning that together with the stone wall topping the earth-banks, the ramparts rose about the height of two men, three in parts. The walls were wide enough for the defenders to stand on three lines deep in places, and, running along the ditch towards the main gate, he laughed up at the grey sky because he couldn't imagine a better fighting platform.

The ramparts were cut from slopes which ran at least two spear-throws down into the valleys, so if the Saxons chose to fight their way in, their attack would be exhausted before it reached the walls. The surrounding ditch was a death-trap for the warriors who survived the downpour of spears and arrows, and those who reached the ditch must then find a way of scaling the defended walls. Reassessing the situation, Owain reckoned that an army could be hacked to shreds trying to take this fort, King Ceredig's choice was the perfect place to stop the Saxons.

Climbing back onto the wall, he looked east to the distant hills partially obscured by clouds. Somewhere beyond those hills, King Aelle's army was marching west. Flicking a loose stone from the top of the wall with his boot, he closed his eyes, raised his nose to the grey clouds and drew in some of the humid air. Rain was coming, he could smell it, not that a few showers bothered him because the hill's slopes would become slippery underfoot. On the other hand, Bedwyr was hoping the extended dry spell in the west would continue, at least for a few more days because he'd planned a few dirty-tricks, and dry weather was essential for his underhand tactics.

Having led the advance party, Owain's foremost Dragon had spent his days productively. He'd gathered from the nearby villages a strong workforce, and formed them into working parties. Walking along the walls, Owain was more than impressed by what had been achieved in such a short time: all the walls had been repaired; at both the southern and northern points of the triangle, where the fort's walls met, the two entrances had been strengthened with solid oak gates, and while they wouldn't withstand a fire-attack, they would hold back an assaulting force long enough for the defenders to gather, and repel it.

Inside the fort, Bedwyr had ordered posts and railings erected so that the Red Cloaks would have somewhere to tether their mounts. Also, a collection of over twenty roundhouses had been thrown up in the centre of the fort, not enough to house the entire Celtic army, but a good part of it. In the centre of the cluster of roundhouses, a larger one had been built for the use of Owain and his Dragons. Close to the central roundhouse, huge water barrels were stacked, and they'd be needed because defending walls at the height of summer was thirsty work. Dozens of barrels filled with birch-bark-tar had been brought to the fort, as well as a large cauldron, though Owain wasn't sure what Bedwyr planned to do with them. Hundreds of cows, goats, sheep and pigs had been driven into the fort and were now bellowing, bleating and snorting their disapproval of being corralled into pens near the northern point of the triangle, where the west and east walls met. Slaughtered poultry, gutted hares and fish-fillets were drying on prepared frames, hemp sacks of wheat and barley had been acquired and piled high behind the rows of drying meats.

Sitting on the wall, Owain looked east again, trying to imagine how fierce the coming battles would be. Feeling a slight tension and sickness in his stomach, he blew out a deep sigh that proved to be more discomforting than his tension was. Questioning his courage, he hoped some of the other British kings would rally to his cause and bring hundreds, perhaps thousands of warriors to add to the few hundred he'd have under his command. If the kings didn't come, he'd be forced to fight an army of thousands, with only four hundred Red Cloaks and the few hundred spearmen of the Viroconium infantry, who he hoped would arrive before the Saxons marched into the valley.

He'd never experienced battle-fear, but this fight would be very different from the few skirmishes he'd fought in, and with the odds so heavily stacked against his small army, his chances of surviving were slim at best. His palms were sweaty, his stomach ached, his mouth was dry and for the first time since arriving earlier in the day, he wished he wasn't here.

His mind turned to his wife as he looked up at the Forest Hill, with its woodlands falling north into a plain where the smear of trees met the Middleland Forest. Somewhere within those woodlands, he hoped Gwen and Gal were gathering an army of hunters; he could certainly use their killing skills. He'd never tell her, but he wished she was far away from the wars, and he with her. They'd spent so little time together, even their marriage had been cut short and if he was to fall in battle there'd be little for his wife and people to remember him by. But this wasn't the time for regrets, he and Bedwyr had prepared enough surprises to ensure that the Saxons limped away with Celtic victory songs loud in their ears, but only if other Celtic kings brought their armies to the fort.

Eased out of his reflections by the smell of roasting pigs on spits, he licked his lips at the thought of the feast. Tonight, brave songs and boasts would be drunkenly offered around many campfires, his warriors forgetting they'd soon be fighting bloody battles. Walking amongst his warriors as he moved from fire to fire, he'd encourage them with his own exaggerated boasts of how easily they'd defeat the Saxons; how many would believe him, who amongst them knew the vast numbers they must fight?

He was about to walk to where the pigs were dripping their delicious fats into the spitting fires, when he saw a red-haired horseman galloping along the east valley, kicking up parched earth as he charged towards the fort. Driving his mount hard up the dusty cart track that led to the south gateway, the rider could only be bringing the news Owain didn't want to hear. The messenger galloped through the gateway, dismounted, tethered his horse and looked around for the Pendragon. Seeing him sitting on the wall, he ran over. Bedwyr had also seen the rider, so putting aside the arrow he was fletching, he ran to hear the news. "You've come from the east?" the Pendragon's question was obvious but necessary.

The warrior saluted, and breathlessly he said, "They are on their way, hordes of them, about seven thousand I'd say, possibly more, and they should........."

"How soon will they get here, Cieren?" Bedwyr asked eagerly.

"You have about three days to prepare for battle, perhaps less. The size of their army is slowing their march, and they are moving west though not yet in this direction. I've seen King Ceredig's wall and only a fool would waste his warriors attacking it, so King Aelle must take the north fork if he wants to reach Aqua Sulis with his army intact."

"Can you get a message to King Ceredig before the Saxons reach his wall?" Owain asked.

The Brigantian bard, whom the Merlin had recently enlisted into his circle of spies, hesitated before replying. There were risks involved in making the return journey, and he wasn't sure he wanted to be there when King Aelle's army reached Caradoc's Hill. "The Saxons are only a day's march from the earthwork, so I must leave immediately, and I'll need a fresh horse."

"Tell Ceredig this," the Pendragon began, jumping down from the wall. "When the Saxons march away from his wall, he must remain where he is for at least three days, I want King Aelle to think he doesn't have to watch his back." Cieren saluted, and was walking away to find a fresh mount when Owain called to him, "When you were in the forest, did you see or hear any signs of Gwen and the hunters?"

"No, but the forest is vast, they could be anywhere."

A horn blasted from the distant, Middleland Forest. "Look, emerging from the woodlands." Bedwyr pointed to the vanguard of an infantry force. "It looks like Cadwallon is with them."

Just about able to make out Cadwallon's banner, the red dragon on a green background, Owain angrily shouted, "It's madness! If we are both killed, who will wear the Votidini crown?"

25.

Below thin wisps of white cloud, a horn sounded three long, sharp notes and hundreds of King Ceredig's men ran to man the wall, while their women, hundreds of them, climbed the slopes of the flanking hills. Cieren the bard, standing next to the King in the centre of the battlements, rested his bunch of spears against the wooden palisade and waited for the Saxon horde to turn into the valley. "Shouldn't you be riding back to Badon?" Ceredig asked him.

"I want to see what happens. If the Saxons don't head north, Owain will need to know."

"There could be fighting."

"I doubt it, but if I'm wrong, I'll die killing Saxons." Cieren took hold of one of his spears and, he ran his sweaty palm along its shaft.

"Spears ready!" Ceredig called to his warriors, he then nervously said to the bard, "Do you think King Aelle knows we are here?"

"If he doesn't, he should abdicate and give his crown to Prince Cissa." Before Cieren could add to his opinion, Saxon battle-drums began pounding a warning in the approach to the valley.

A heartbeat later a small group of riders, followed by ranks of warriors beating battle-drums, turned the corner marked by the slope of a hill, and progressed towards the earth-wall and wood-palisade. The sound was deafening, shaking the dust from the dry earth as thousands of battle-ready infantrymen marched in ordered lines behind the riders and drummers. Halting his horse, King Aelle raised his arm to silence the drums. "I'll slice off his balls and stuff them in his mouth," he seethed to Cissa, "then stitch up his betraying mouth so that he swallows them. If he hasn't died from the shock, I'll have his eyes slashed with knives and his skin flayed. The man will regret betraying me!"

"Are we going to attack?" Cissa asked, his stomach churning after his father's overly vivid description.

"I'd like to," Aelle growled through clenched teeth.

"It could take days to breech that wall, and their flanks are well protected, I wouldn't like to guess how many men we might lose if we attack. Do you think he discovered your plan to turn against him?"

"Perhaps, though I can't think how. I won't waste my warriors here, but I do want to hear what he has to say." Drawing his sword, he said to his son, "Come with me."

Ceredig watched Aelle and Cissa ride towards him. Nervously licking his lips, he questioned his decision to betray the Saxons, but word had come from one of his spies, and Aelle would turn his army against him, when the Pendragon had been defeated, so he'd little choice but to defy the Saxons.

The two royal Saxons trotted to a halt about a spear's throw from the wall and, Aelle called to his Celtic son-by-marriage, "We had a deal, Ceredig! Does your word mean nothing?"

"You plan to attack my kingdom!" Ceredig called back.

"That's nonsense, didn't I promise not to march against you? You are family, I gave you my daughter in exchange for free passage through your land!" Raising his sword, he pointed it at Ceredig. "I'll give you one chance only; honour our agreement and I'll forget this insult!"

"You speak false, Saxon! But I promised I wouldn't raise my sword against you, and that promise still stands! If you march away, my warriors won't attack you!"

Aelle's anger broke. "Your days are numbered, Celt, my army could roll right over your pitiful defences!"

"If that's what you believe, do it!" Ceredig shouted back, then he said to Cieren, "Give him a warning."

The Brigantian threw his spear. It's silver point, watched by everyone in the valley, caught the Sun when it reached its height, glinted then dropped, punching into the dry earth just in front of King Aelle's horse. The animal reared, almost throwing the Saxon off its back. Regaining control of his mount, Aelle spoke quietly to his son, "You know these valleys; will the north fork take us to Aqua Sulis?"

"Eventually, yes, but there's a fort on the hill where four valleys meet."

Looking at Ceredig and the hundreds of spearmen manning the rampart, Aelle spoke his concerns to his son, "He wouldn't dare stand against us alone. But would he form an alliance with the Pendragon when he hates the man?"

"If he has, our spies haven't heard about it. The Dumnonians might have joined him, their lands adjoin his."

"No," Aelle replied, "they've no army to speak of, only Viroconium has the warriors needed to help Ceredig. The Red Cloaks could have refortified the hillfort you mentioned, which would explain why we are being forced north and west."

"The Pendragon couldn't have discovered our plans and ridden south so quickly. We don't have to march blind; we can send riders ahead to scout the fort."

King Aelle patted his snorting horse whilst mulling his options. "We go north and west," he decided. Pointing his sword at Ceredig again, he shouted a warning, "I'll be back, Celt, and I'll kill you and lay waste your pathetic kingdom! Not a single blade of grass will survive the burning, and your valleys will be piled high with bleaching, crow-picked corpses, not one Celt will survive the slaughter!"

"You won't harm any of my people!" Ceredig confidently yelled. "Gorpe is under close guard, and if any of your warriors set foot in my kingdom, I'll give her to my warriors to rape, then I'll hang her naked from Durnovaria's battlements until she shits out her final, sobbing breath!"

Taking a last look at the formidable defences, Aelle spat on the land of the Durotrigues and, he rode away.

Three days after Cadwallon's arrival with the Viroconium infantry, the Celtic Dragons were seated around the table in the large roundhouse, when a low rumble disturbed their midday meal. "Did you hear that?" Owain asked, looking at the roundhouse door-flap.

"Be quiet and listen," he said, raising his hand. "There it goes again, rumbling thunder."

"It can't be," Cai suggested, "the sky has been cloudless all day."

"Thunder doesn't have a marching rhythm," Cadwallon added.

"Thunder is a fair description," the Merlin said, "but inaccurate."

"You know the sound?" Bedwyr asked.

"Yes, though it's been many years since I last felt the fear instilled by Saxon war-drums." All eyes turned to the Merlin. "Why look so surprised when you all know about their pre-battle tactics?"

"They know we are here," Owain suggested.

"Not necessarily." Searching his memory, the Merlin took a sip of his wine. "They could be warning the people in the valleys that they must run or die."

"They've lost their element of surprise," Cai pointed out.

"The drums are a weapon, Cai," the Pendragon felt the meaning of his own words.

"Owain is right, they are a weapon," the Merlin agreed. "Before King Aelle brought his warriors to Briton, an equally ambitious Saxon marched thousands of warriors to war. Einion chose a defensive position on a ridged-hill overlooking the Tamesis River. For an entire day our warriors listened to the same sound you are now hearing, the cracking and booming, roaring thunder of dozens of war-drums. You are all proven warriors who've faced Saxons in small battles and skirmishes, but none of you have faced a massed Saxon army, nor have you endured the constant pounding of war-drums and the fear they drive into every man. By the time Einion's warriors finally caught a glimpse of the Saxons, their imaginations had run wild with fear, and if it hadn't been for the timely intervention of the late arriving Brigantian King and his warriors, that fight might have been lost, all because the courage of our warriors had been undermined by their imaginations."

"I'm going to have a look," Owain said, walking to the door-flap.

Outside, the Pendragon saw others heading for the ramparts. Pushing through the gathering warriors, he climbed onto the wall and looked to the far end of the east valley, expecting to see the Saxon vanguard. All he could see in the distance was plumes of smoke rising from burning villages and farmsteads, dozens of them climbing into the blue sky. In the valley below the fort, hundreds of villagers and farmers, the refugees from the burnings, were driving their cattle towards Sulis Hill. The drums had begun their work, Owain felt it in his guts and saw it in the eyes of his silent warriors. The Merlin was right, fear is the first weapon of battle.

Walking along the wall to estimate the number of refugees, the first of whom were climbing the slope towards the main gate, his attention was grabbed by a blasting horn behind him. He turned to see many of his warriors moving to the centre of the fort, crowding around a newly erected flagpole. Villagers mingled with the warriors, though few could see Cadwallon and the Merlin standing beside the pole. But they could all see the Votidini banner of Gwynedd and Powys being raised as horns blasted a salute to Cadwallon. Owain pushed through the cheering crowds, belatedly taking his place alongside his brother. “A useful diversion, but your banner looks lonely!” he joked.

“You could raise yours,” Cadwallon suggested. “It would lift everyone’s spirits.”

“I didn’t bring it; I don’t want King Aelle knowing I’m here. He’ll be expecting my Red Cloaks to block his route at some point. I want him to worry about where my warriors are, and when they will strike.”

“That’s why you ordered the Legion to leave their red cloaks in Viroconium?”

“It is.”

Their conversation was cut short by the arrival of an armed rider, galloping his horse through the open south gateway. After dismounting, he pushed through the crowd and saluted the Merlin of all people. “I am Gwyn ap Marc of the Cornovii. I have a message for Cadwallon, from King Erbin of Dumnonia.”

“I am Cadwallon.” He took a step forward. “If you’ll follow me into the roundhouse, you can deliver your message there.”

Inside the roundhouse, Gwyn began his message as the Dragons took their places around the table. “Lord Cadwallon, since King Erbin received your request for help, he’s gathered as many of our countrymen as he could. Having marched them as far as Aqua Sulis, he’s camped outside the city for the night, he’ll complete the journey here tomorrow morning. He wants me to reassure you that all his six hundred warriors are battle-hardened spearmen, so they won’t run from a fight.” Flinching at the sudden increase in the volume of the Saxon war-drums, he completed his message, "King Erbin would like to know if you have any orders for him?"

Cadwallon turned to Owain, amused to see a small spark of hope in his eyes. He knew what this news meant, one king had answered the call to war, so others might also be coming.

"How many horse-warriors do you have?" Owain asked.

"None," Gwyn replied, "we are infantrymen."

Owain nodded. "It would give everyone in the fort a much-needed lift if they were to see your King's flag flying beside Cadwallon's, do you think you could ride to King Erbin and return here before dusk, with his banner?"

"Yes."

"Tell King Erbin this: if he follows the Afon up the valley, he'll see the fort on his left. I'd like him to deploy his warriors along the valley bottom, on our side of the river. This will protect our right flank, I don't want the Saxons attacking two walls simultaneously, that would overstretch our resources. Dig a ditch and bank, because once King Aelle sees you, he'll send part of his army against you. Thank Erbin for his help, it is timely and welcome. Some of my warriors will begin digging your ditch and rampart as soon as the Sun rises, unless the Saxons attack the fort before then."

A warrior entered the roundhouse, saluted Cadwallon and spoke to Bedwyr, "The dry brush and brambles you ordered cut have been piled in bushels near the south gate, it's more of a forest than a stack. What would you like us to do with it?"

"When I give you the order, light the cauldron, heat the birch-bark-tar until it becomes fluid, then soak the dry brush and brambles with it," the Dragon replied. "You'll find barrels of the tar behind the roundhouse."

"Birch-bark-tar?" Owain asked in the hope that Bedwyr would tell him what he was planning to do with it. The tar was usually used to fix arrowheads to shafts, and could also be used as a resin to seal boats.

"Yes, tar. I had barrels of it brought form the Muddy Valley, where they use the stuff for sealing their fishing boats. Have the villagers gathered all the rocks and stones I asked for?" Bedwyr inquired of the warrior.

"They have, and you could build another wall with them."

"How are the men reacting to the war-drums?" Owain asked.

"What do you mean, My Lord?"

"I want to know if the constant throb of thunder is getting to them?"

"No, I don't believe so."

Owain saw right through him. "When you are sitting at your campfire tonight, tell your friends that the men beating the war-drums bleed like all men do. Tomorrow, we will fight the Saxons and win the battle."

With the shimmering red Sun sinking into burning scarlets and purples, King Aelle raised his hand to halt the march and silence the drums. As he did so, an out-rider descended the gentle slope of the sparsely-wooded hill to his right. Pulling up in front of the King, the rider saluted and said, "Celts, My Lord, hundreds of them."

Prince Cissa galloped over, eager to hear the news.

"Where?" Aelle demanded impatiently.

"In the fort on the hill where four valleys meet."

"How many of the flee-riddled cowards are inside the fort? I take it you remained hidden long enough to estimate their numbers?"

"Yes, My Lord. They have seven to eight hundred spearmen."

"Did you see any horses?" Cissa asked.

"They have about four hundred mounts." The rider reached for the ale-flask in his saddlebag.

"Who are they?" Aelle couldn't see how anyone but the Dumnonians could have reached the fort so quickly. "Was King Erbin's flag flying from the ramparts?"

Taking a quick gulp from his flask to wash away dust, the scout gargled and spat. "I saw only the red and green Votidini flag of Gwynedd and Powys."

"That's not possible," Cissa said, absorbing the implications.

"It is if Ceredig warned Cadwallon." King Aelle realised the extent of the betrayal. "I'll kill the bastard, breathe life back into him and murder him again!" Thinking, he looked at the messenger, held out his hand and grunted. The rider passed him his ale-flask. After taking a deep drink of the warm brew, Aelle asked, "What about the Pendragon's banner?"

"It wasn't there."

"Were any of the warriors wearing red cloaks?" Cissa asked "Think, it is vital."

"There were enough horses to mount the Pendragon's Legion, but no one was wearing a red cloak. From what I could see from the Forest Hill, Cadwallon has only spearmen with him."

"If Cadwallon is in the fort, the Pendragon must be close by, shadowing our advance perhaps, waiting for his moment to strike," Aelle said, scanning the surrounding hills.

Cadwallon was no great war general, the Saxon King knew that. Owain was the true successor to King Einion but, where was he? Looking at the hills again, he asked himself what he'd do if he was the Pendragon. He understood that mobility and speed were the strengths of the Legion, and inside the fort they'd be spearmen with no more advantage than any other warrior, so the Red Cloaks must be riding the valleys and hills, waiting for an opportunity to attack and kill then run. He decided to immediately send scouts out in every direction, the last thing he wanted was well-drilled cavalry taking his marching warriors by surprise.

THE BATTLES AT BADON

DAY 1

It was such a warm night, where an army had gathered within the ancient walls of a Pretanic hillfort; warriors sweaty with fear; cold with nervous jesting; thoughts of battle deliberately stifled, the smell of oatcakes cooking on campfires being a much more pleasurable and tolerable sensation. Few would choose the peace of sleeping during this night, most would avoid the solitude of dreams because there was comfort in the jests and laughs, as well as the insults the boasts and the wineskins so the camaraderie of warriors would defend what might prove to be, for so many, their final night of life.

Inside the large roundhouse, the hearth-fire released the faint, sickly smell of burning chestnut wood, and Owain, uncomfortable in his chair while watching the glowing wood shimmer with heat and spit embers into the ashes, closed his eyes and sent a silent prayer to any god that was listening, asking to be sent more kings and their armies, because if no other royals brought warriors to help his cause, he would certainly be killed before the solstice Sun died.

He couldn't sleep, his worries about Gwen and the idea of battling thousands of Saxon killers, was keeping him from his bed. Bedwyr had sat with him beside the hearth, long after the others had gone to their beds, and the more they'd talked, the less likely it seemed that they'd survive the first Saxon attack. But at least King Erbin's army would fight with them, though that was small comfort.

The Pendragon's small army of Red Cloaks and infantrymen may hold back King Aelle's swarm of spearmen for a while, but with only eight hundred trained warriors defending the fort, he'd need more than a miracle to inflict a bloody defeat on the Saxons. King Erbin's warriors would help, but the east wall and south gateway would be very exposed, and he guessed that was where the hardest fighting would take place. There was still the possibility that other Celtic kings were mustering their warriors, but he doubted they'd risk their lives to save his.

Irritated by Bedwyr's snoring, he went outside to get some air. Pulling the hood of his black cloak over his head, he walked around the campfires, unsurprised to see that like himself few of his warriors were sleeping. Standing between Cadwallon and Erbin's limp banners, he watched his spearmen: some were praying while their friends griddled oatcakes and thin slices of pork; others checked their weapons and chainmail-byrnies; most, sensing the coming battle, looked thoughtfully into their campfires, silently wishing they were at home with their loved ones.

Having made his way to the east rampart, Owain climbed onto the stone wall. Looking beyond the hills and valleys to the east, where the first touch of the Sun had softened the black night, he sat on the cold stones to watch the opaque rays creep over the dark and distant hills.

Understanding he might never see Gwen again, the thought saddened him and he realised he wanted to run, and live. Feeling overwhelmed by his emotions, he drew his sword and kissed it. Thinking he should fling it away and slip over the wall, find Gwen and search for a place to live where nobody knew them, he wrapped his fingers around the sword-hilt and pulled back his arm. Swinging the blade, he almost released it but he couldn't cast aside his responsibilities, his conscience wouldn't allow it. He was the Pendragon, his warriors looked to him to inspire their courage during the fight, so for their sakes he wouldn't run.

He was about to climb down from the wall when he heard a pulsating, dull rhythm. Holding his breath, he listened and his heart sank into his bowels as battle-drums boomed and echoed, the Saxons were coming. A battle-horn blared from between the two flagpoles, and in the fort the scramble to arms began. Fires were doused and warriors strapped on helmets; friends kicked their sleeping sword-brothers awake; lines of propped up spears were grabbed and warriors ran to man the walls. The momentary panic confused the villagers and refugees, who picked up their wailing children and ran for the north gate, pleading with the sentries to let them out. Feeling like his feet were sinking into the hard earth, Owain watched the panic, his fear preventing him from switching on his mind and taking control.

Realising he'd nothing to do because his warriors were manning the ramparts, he breathed out a cold sigh and calmly untied his hooded cloak, lay it on the wall and forced himself to walk to the flagpoles, where Cadwallon, the Merlin, Bedwyr and Cai were waiting for him. After seeing his spearmen run to the walls without a backward glance, he felt ashamed for wanting to abandon them.

They were prepared to fight, not one of them hesitated when the battle-horn sounded; could he do less? With his sword still drawn, he said to his brother and friends, “Take your places and fight.”

Ready to face the expected onslaught, Owain turned and strode purposefully back to the wall. Steady in his heart, willing to fight and kill and die for freedom, he felt the expectant glares of his warriors watching him. With the beating drums growing ever louder, pounding and cracking from rock to rock in the valley, he leapt onto the wall. Silhouetted against the brightening dawn, he called to his warriors, “You all know what you must do, kill Saxons, or die!” Thrusting his sword high, he yelled to his ancestors, “Britannia!”

“Britannia!” the defenders of Sulis Hillfort repeated, chanting the Legion’s battle-cry as Saxon drumbeats clattered against and echoed from the fort’s walls.

With their battle-drums pounding an earth-shaking death-beat, thousands of Saxons marched in a foot-stomping cloud of dust, into the valley below the Forest Hill. The sea of spearmen came to a juddering halt before the abandoned village of Badon, and their drums fell eerily silent, the dust settling as the Sun rose above the distant hills. King Aelle looked scornfully up at the fort, sneering his contempt for the few hundred spearmen manning the walls.

“Should we send our entire army against them?” Prince Cissa asked, coyly.

“No, half will be enough.”

“I’m not so sure, those walls look high and strong.”

"We'll soon know." The King placed a hand on his son's shoulder. "I want you to lead the first charge."

"It will be an honour, but shouldn't we offer the defenders the chance to leave peacefully; they'd be much easier to kill out in the open?"

"They'd guess that game so would refuse, and I want to get this over with." Assessing the fort's well-prepared defences, he considered how many warriors he might lose in the fight. "I've changed my mind. Lead the entire army against one wall, and kill every Celt except for Cadwallon, I want him to beg me for mercy before I put him to death."

"It will be a pleasure."

Looking over his left shoulder, the King took the measure of the plateaued hill. "Up there," he said, pointing to the sloping plateau, "that's where you'll find me; bring me Cadwallon in chains." He was still worried about where the Pendragon's Legion might be, so by making camp on the highest point of the hill, he'd see an attack from the Red Cloaks long before they could do any damage. He then looked at the Forest Hill. "If we don't take the fort in the first attack, remind me to send a few hundred warriors up that hill, I don't want the Celts using its height against us."

"Our first attack won't fail," Cissa promised.

King Aelle waved to his drummers, an order was barked and the crashing drumbeats began again, a swirling cacophony of chaos beneath a brightening sky, and the Saxon army advanced. Deafening and terrifying, each thumped beat brought the Saxon dust-cloud closer to the fort's dry and crumbly slope, the warriors clanging their weapons against shields while chanting, "Woden! Woden!" to every pounding beat.

Expecting the Saxons to attack two walls simultaneously, Owain had divided his warriors equally between the east and west walls. Standing on the rampart, he could see the army wasn't going to split, so he yelled across the fort, "To me, every warrior to me!"

"You heard him!" Bedwyr, commanding the west wall, stepped back from the rampart and shouted over the din of the drums, "every man to the east wall!"

Bedwyr's warriors changed positions in time to see the Saxon drummers peel away. As they marched to the rear still banging their drums, a horn sounded, the beating ceased and the army of thousands came to a dusty halt.

Jumping down from the wall to stand with his spearmen, Owain admired the neat lines of helmeted warriors. "I'd be proud to lead such an army," he said to Bedwyr.

"You admire them, I'll kill them," the Dragon replied, grinning a smile some might describe as being lust-filled.

"Why haven't they divided to attack two walls?" Owain asked, surprised they were making such an obvious mistake.

"Maybe they are expecting to swarm over us?" Bedwyr suggested, "and why wouldn't they when they are so many?"

"I'll make them pay for their stupidity. Are the gates sealed and protected?"

"Yes," Bedwyr replied, "front and rear. Both sets open outwards, so when they were closed in the night, I had rocks piled high in front of and behind them. It will be a death-trap for anyone trying to shift the rocks."

The Pendragon was about to thank his friend when the Saxon war-drums boomed again, and their warriors began beating their weapons against shields to the shouts of, "Woden! Woden! Woden!"

"Archers to the front!" Owain bellowed.

There was a general shuffle as warriors changed places along the wall, the Red Cloaks stringing their bows as they stepped forward. Behind them, the Viroconium infantry formed lines of spearmen, while the refugees from the villages nocked arrows to bowstrings. A Saxon horn blared and King Aelle's roaring warriors began a steady walk up the parched and brown, dusty slope.

The Pendragon waited, judging the distance for the ideal killing ground, hoping the Saxons would keep on coming just as they were. Pointing his sword high, he shouted his order loud enough for it to be heard in Viroconium, "Raise bows!" He swept his sword down and shouted, "Loose!"

Hundreds of arrows flew high, a dark arc of killing-rain, and the Saxons stopped to gaze at the unexpected death-storm. At the summit of their flight the arrowheads dipped, pulling the feathered-shafts into a heavy fall. Aelle's men instinctively raised their shields.

"Loose!" Owain repeated his order, and a lower aimed flight twanged from hundreds of bowstrings.

As the first flight fell towards upheld shields, the second, low-aimed flight ripped into the exposed torsos of hundreds of warriors. In the front ranks the dull thud, thud, thud of piercing arrows mingled with warriors screams as scores of them fell, blood spurting from punctured chests, arms, legs, necks and faces. Some of them, gut-shot, dropped to their knees while those with lesser wounds sat on the parched earth, clutching their wounds and cursing the Celts who weren't standing toe to toe to fight as they believed all warriors should.

"Loose!" Owain cried out. "Loose!" he called again. "Loose! Loose! Loose!" repeating the order time after time, only pausing long enough for men to nock arrows and pull back bowstrings.

The stinging death-rain kept coming, flight after flight thudding into the massed ranks of confused Saxons. The front three ranks dissolved into chaos, not knowing whether to raise their shields or hold them forward. Those behind them, caught between the lines of dead and wounded and the on-coming ranks of marching men, had nowhere to go so they instinctively turned to force the rear-ranks back down the hill. Because of the pounding drums, few in the rear-ranks heard the calls for the army to turn, so they kept on coming.

"Loose!" Owain almost sang the order, delighted by the unfolding chaos. "Loose!" More arrows flew, easily finding exposed flesh and, the chaos spread. "Loose!" The killing rhythm continued. "Loose!" The dry and dusty, corn-gold hillside became blotched with pools of red.

Throughout the Saxon ranks, desperate scrums developed and wounded men pushed to get through the thousands still wanting to get at the Celts. And the arrows flew high and low, killing and wounding while desperate warriors kicked and punched to escape the thudding points of iron. Panic spread, and hundreds of Saxons tried to run back down the hill but the rear ranks still hadn't reacted to the chaos.

"Loose!" Owain bellowed. "Loose!" he yelled again. "Loose!" he laughed as he shouted, almost drunk on the slaughter his warriors were causing. "Spears!" he shouted and raised his sword. "Loose!" his blade fell and the heavy spears of the Viroconium infantry were released.

Warriors fell like autumn leaves in a rain-lashed gale, there was no escaping the showers of death. The Saxons at the rear finally got the message and they turned and ran. Seeing the confused ranks breaking to retreat, Owain called out, "Spears and arrows, arc them high, loose!" Spears and arrows darkened the summer sky, dropped and hit with their sickening death-thuds, adding to the bloody chaos. "Hold!" the Pendragon shouted as the panicking Saxons ran for the bridge spanning the river.

The Celts cheered with a mix of relief and battle-lust as the Saxons fled. Most of the defenders had expected to be slaughtered by the huge army, not do the slaughtering themselves. They'd killed and survived and shown King Aelle they could not be so easily marched over.

Owain looked along the wall at his cheering warriors, and down the slope at the hundreds of dead and dying men. Pitying them, he sent two hundred Red Cloaks over the wall to slit the throats of the wounded, recover as many arrows and spears as they could and, take weapons and shields from the many dead, to better arm the villagers and refugees. Putting the wounded to death was savage but merciful, and who wants to listen to the screams and moans of slowly dying men?

Estimating that perhaps as many as five hundred Saxons, maybe more, lay dead on the hillside, the Pendragon was pleased by how easily the first attack had been repelled. His archers had given King Aelle a warning, and a bloody nose, so Owain knew the next attack would be more measured, and deadly. Watching the Saxon stragglers cross the bridge, he heard a horn blast so he turned to the west. Cadwallon, unstringing his bow, shouted to his brother, "King Erbin has arrived!"

From his vantage point on the plateaued hill, King Aelle took an honest measure of his arrogance, while watching the Celts on the slope of Sulis Hill, put his wounded warriors to death. He felt very foolish, hundreds of lives had been wasted on a rash attack because he hadn't thought the situation through; he'd allowed his contempt for Celts to blind him, he wouldn't make the same mistake again. He had plenty of spearmen to waste though, so he wasn't too concerned about their loss, and, once he'd reassessed the situation, he guessed that his damaged pride would swell into the conviction of certain victory.

Watching the survivors making their way up the slope towards his banner, a pole with three wolf-heads hanging from a wooden crosspiece, he saw more Celts marching into the west valley, which had him wondering how many other Celtic kings might come to help the defenders? The sooner he took the fort the better, but his warriors looked a sorry sight, and well they might after being put to flight so easily.

His defeated spearmen slumped down on the hillside to check their weapons, armour and minor wounds. Many had lost friends in the chaos and, seeing his warriors looking across the valley to the killing-field, Aelle sensed their desire for revenge, so perhaps he shouldn't wait too long before ordering them to muster. For the next assault he'd divide the army and attack the east and west walls simultaneously, forcing the Celts to fight on two fronts, which is what he should have done in the first place.

His scouts were still searching the surrounding hills and valleys for the Pendragon and his Legion, but they should return soon, so he'd wait to find out where the Red Cloaks were before sending his army back up the slopes of Sulis Hill. A messenger approached and saluted. "My Lord, I bring news from Prince Cissa."

"Well, get on with it." Aelle couldn't hide his frustration because the new Celtic arrivals were making camp below the fort, which meant he'd have to fight through them before attacking the west wall.

"King Erbin has joined the Celts," the messenger began, "with about six hundred spearmen. Prince Cissa would also........."

"I know, I do have eyes!" the King yelled. "What else did my son say?"

"Only that the Dumnonians are digging a ditch and rampart extending from the river, almost to the west wall of the fort."

"Bastards!" Aelle shook his head and breathed out a frustrated sigh. "Bastards!" he repeated, kicking the pole holding aloft his banner, knocking it to the ground. “Pick that up, then go and fetch my son!”

Attacking the new rampart meant wasting the lives of many warriors, but he’d no choice, two walls must be attacked simultaneously if he was to capture the fort. “Damn those archers!” he swore through gritted teeth. “I’ll chop their hands off and release the butchers to starve in the forest, or bleed to death, whichever.”

King Erbin, forgetting his royal dignity, climbed over the west wall to the amused cheers of the defenders, and was met by Bedwyr, who immediately hugged his friend and stepped back to look at him. “You are looking tired around the eyes, too much wine and too many women I’d say!”

“You would because that’s how you live!” the King replied. “I’ve heard you’ve put aside women and returned to the pig-runs you enjoyed in your younger days, before the two summers you spent with me, civilised you!” There was a short pause before the two friends burst out laughing.

“You are late, as usual!” Bedwyr joked.

“Such gratitude, consider yourself fortunate we came at all, and as for having to climb over the wall, what kind of a welcome is that for a king?”

“Needs must, you do know we are fighting a war!”

The two of them joked about old times as Bedwyr led the King to the roundhouse. Entering the smoky, hearth-lit round they saw Owain, Cadwallon and the Merlin sitting at the table. Cadwallon stood to formally greet the Dumnonian. “You are welcome, King Erbin of the Dumnonians, as are your warriors.”

“Being faithful to the alliance agreed between our fathers, I wouldn’t have refused your request.”

The formalities over, Cadwallon walked around the table and clasped the Dumnonian’s hand in both of his. “It’s good to see you, Cousin. Please, take a seat, we’ve much to discuss.” After ordering refreshments, Cadwallon sent a message for Cai to join them.

Breathless after his run from the north gate, Cai entered. Sitting next to Erbin, he shook the King’s hand. “I’m sorry I’m late,” he said to Cadwallon, “I was handing out weapons to the refugees.”

Servants entered and placed on the table dishes of cold meats, cheeses and bread, as well as jugs of wine. Filling a cup and handing it to Erbin, Cadwallon said to him, “We repulsed their first attack without them reaching the wall.” He then turned to Owain. “What will they’ll do next?”

“They’ll attack your rampart,” Owain said to Erbin, “they’ve no other choice.” Accepting a cup of wine from Cai, he guzzled the contents down. “Before the arrival of the Dumnonians, Aelle would have assaulted the west and east walls simultaneously, to stretch us beyond our limits.”

“That won’t be so easy now,” Cadwallon suggested.

“You are right, they must take the new rampart and send everything they have against at least two of our walls, perhaps all three. If I was Aelle, that’s what I’d do, it is………”

“Should we help dig Erbin’s defences?” the Merlin asked the Pendragon.

"I don't think we've much choice," Owain replied, "his ditch and bank must be high and wide."

"We haven't much time," Erbin said, certain the Saxons would attack before his rampart was finished. "Will your spearmen help us?"

"Yes," the Pendragon said, and he looked at Cadwallon.

"You are the battle-leader," his brother pointed out.

"Would a ditch and rampart protect Erbin's men long enough to make a real difference?" The Merlin didn't often join in tactical discussions but, he felt sure there was a flaw in the plan. "Wouldn't it take at least three days to build a rampart high and strong enough to withstand an attack?"

"Probably longer." Owain saw the worried expression on Erbin's face. "Building the rampart isn't about stopping Aelle, it's a delaying tactic, the longer we keep the Saxons from reaching the west wall, the more time we'll have for reinforcements to arrive."

"Assuming help is coming," Cai said negatively.

"Couldn't we send a rider to ask King Ceredig for help?" Cadwallon asked.

"I've already sent him a message," Owain replied, "though it wasn't to request his help. If we can hold out for two or three days, I've a surprise in store for King Aelle, and Ceredig has a part to play in that."

"So, we continue digging the rampart and hope we can hold out for two or three days?" Erbin cautiously asked, understanding his warriors were sacrificial lambs.

"The Saxons can't cross the river so they must attack you from the front," Bedwyr pointed out. "There is no fording place between here and Aqua Sulis, it would take them days to march over the hills and come at you from behind."

Owain's eyes shot a question at his Dragon, but he said nothing.

"My warriors are strong and willing," Erbin offered. "We don't fear battle, if any spearmen can buy you time, it's the Dumnonians."

Owain nodded to Cadwallon, who spoke to the door-guard, "Take this message to the centurions: every man of the Viroconium infantry will help King Erbin's warriors dig their ditch and bank, and the villagers are to join them. If the Saxons attack, the villagers must return without delay."

The guard saluted and left the roundhouse.

"The river flanking your camp is too deep to be easily forded," Owain said to Erbin, "and Bedwyr was right to suggest the Saxons won't try crossing it, unless they can find enough boats to ferry an army." Again, he looked questioningly at Bedwyr, then asked him, "Why are you so certain King Aelle's men won't cross the river?"

"They won't find any boats within a two-day march," the Dragon replied with a smile. "I anticipated that possibility, so before your Red Cloaks arrived, I sent the villagers out to burn every boat and coracle they could find."

"In conclusion, Cousin," Owain said, wondering how many more surprises Bedwyr had in store, "the Saxons will attempt a frontal attack. My Red Cloaks on the west wall will support you with spears and arrows, hopefully, that will be enough."

For much of the warm and dry morning, the Dumnonian spearmen, the Viroconium infantrymen and the refugees worked hard to dig King Erbin's rampart, and, it didn't take long for so many people to raise the defensive bank from the earth. The workers sweated, heaved with wooden shovels and hacked with picks, all the while glancing over their shoulders to see if King Aelle's hordes were massing to attack them.

By the time the midday Sun hung bright over Badon village, close to half of King Aelle's army had mustered and were filing over Badon's wooden bridge. Seeing sunlight reflecting from chainmail, helmets and hundreds of spearheads, King Erbin dropped his wooden shovel and bellowed to his warriors, "Grab your weapons, villagers get back to the fort!" His warriors didn't need telling to arm themselves, most were already running for the piles of spears, shields and helmets stacked behind the dirt-wall. As for the villagers and refugees, they weren't slow to scramble up the parched grass slope of Sulis Hill.

Bedwyr, having ordered some of the village women to warm the large cauldron, left his post on the wall to supervise the melting of the birch-bark-tar. Barrels were opened and the contents emptied into the hot cauldron; instructions were given to the women, who used pitchforks the bundle over the dry brambles and brushwood, and Bedwyr returned to stand beside Owain at the wall.

Having crossed the bridge, the Saxons formed a rectangle, almost sixty men across and fifty ranks deep, their shields and spears pointing towards Erbin's assembling shield-wall. Behind the earth rampart, the Viroconium infantry waited, hoping the Pendragon would signal their return. Having promised Erbin he'd leave the Viroconium infantry in the valley, Owain, watching from the fort's west wall, said to his brother, "I didn't think they'd send so many against so few, I should signal the return of our spearmen."

"We can't abandon Erbin," Cadwallon pleaded. "If our infantrymen return the Dumnonians will be slaughtered!"

"You must recall them; the defence of the fort is our priority!" Bedwyr insisted.

Owain wanted to help Erbin, but how many warriors could he afford to lose? "I'm sorry," he said to Cadwallon, "but I have no choice."

"You promised Erbin infantry support."

"I know!" Owain shot back at him, "but I didn't think King Aelle would send so many warriors. The Dumnonians are lost, we need our infantrymen here."

"It will be murder."

"That's the reality of war," Owain coldly replied. Ordering two horn-notes blown to signal the return of the infantrymen, the Pendragon looked guiltily at his brother. "All warriors know their possible fates when strapping on helmets and swords."

"The Viroconium infantry would have balanced out the fight." Cadwallon wasn't giving up.

"Not by much, and we need them here." Guilt was a burden every commander carried, someone had to make the difficult decisions.

"I could order you to send our warriors back," Cadwallon said, grabbing his brother's arm to turn him around and face him.

"No, you couldn't. Our people are yours; the warriors are mine."

King Erbin's defensive rampart and ditch began well up Sulis Hill's slope, almost reaching the fort's west wall, and ran down close enough to the river for water to permeate into the lower section of the ditch. The Dumnonians first three shield-walls, sixty men in length, stood ready on top of the rampart, the seven reserve ranks waiting on the lower ground behind the earthwork, were ready to fill the gaps as their sword-brothers were cut down.

A distant voice shouted an order in Saxon, a high-pitched cow-horn shrilled a command and King Aelle's warriors marched. At the rear, the now familiar booming battle-drums pounded into the bright sunshine, shocking into flight the jet-black carrion crows feasting on the corpses on the east-slope of Sulis Hill.

Owain clenched his fists as three thousand Saxons marched towards Erbin's six hundred. Marching to the pounding drums and the clashing of spears on shields, they came on through the heat of the day, a calculated, terrifying rhythm of sound. Above the marching spearmen, the high Sun caught their metal, sending shafts of reflected light flashing through the dust cloud as the warriors stomped across the valley.

Those who'd never experienced the stomping march of the shield-wall, could be forgiven for wanting to run, but none of the Dumnonians fled. Shoulder to shoulder they waited, watching the mass of metal, dust and flashing light closing with every thumping heartbeat. As the sun-glinting dust-cloud neared, and his breakfast slipped into his lower bowels, Erbin called to his warriors, "Hold your ground and kill! Ready spears!" Standing in the centre of his front rank, he squeezed the sweat-soaked leather straps of his shield. His clammy fingers had already slicked the wooden shaft of his spear, which had him wondering if he'd have the grip to throw it.

Standing sideways with legs apart and shields raised, the Dumnonians pulled back their spear-arms. The Saxons were close now, near enough for the Celts to make out individual faces and pick their targets. Just a few more strides and the first few sweat-stinking ranks would be in range. Erbin pulled back his throwing arm, focused on a shining Saxon helmet, and he yelled his order, and six hundred spears flew towards the marching swarm.

For this attack, the Saxons were better prepared. The moment the spears were released a horn sounded and their drumbeats ceased, bringing them to a juddering halt. All but the front rank raised their shields to fend off the falling iron, and it worked, most of the spears clattered off wood and metal. Some spears did get through, here and there painfilled screams and groans matched the shrieks of the circling carrion crows. A horn sounded, the drums beat again and the Saxons marched on, the few wounded or killed stepped over as the grim rhythm closed on the rampart.

Reluctantly acknowledging the Saxons had learned their lesson, Owain watched with horror as the flight of spears failed to have much impact. From his vantage point he could see a flaw in the Saxons attempt to form the 'Roman Tortoise' they'd covered themselves from above and to the front, but their flanks were exposed. With the formation closing on Erbin's warriors, the Pendragon knew what he must do.

Giving Bedwyr and Cai orders to pass along the line, he joined his warriors as they climbed onto the wall. Rocks from Bedwyr's pile were quickly passed along, and at his command warriors climbed over the wall, followed by villagers carrying bows and spears. With the Pendragon, Bedwyr, Cai and Cadwallon at their head, the hundreds ran down the slope, yelling and screaming their battle-cries while hurling rocks into the swarm. Stones crunched raised shields, breaking bones and knocking men off their feet. At the Pendragon's command, the villagers shot arrows and threw spears into the exposed Saxon-flank, but Aelle's warrior turned and lowered their shields as soon as they recognised the danger.

Erbin saw Owain's charge, the damage caused and the Saxon flank lowering their shields, so he ordered another flight of spears, "Aim to their right!" he bellowed as more villagers' arrows flew.

A curving arc of spears dropped out of the sun, clattered onto shields and punched into flesh, halting the flank as the rest marched on, their drums pounding through the dusty summer heat. The unwounded on the damaged flank stepped over their fallen sword-brothers, marching forward to make the formation whole again.

As there was nothing more he could do, Owain ordered his men back to the fort, where the village women were dipping balls of brushwood and brambles into the melted resin. Nearing the top of the hill, Owain looked back and he saw Erbin raise his sword and shout an order he couldn't hear above the din of the battle-drums.

"Lock shields!" Erbin yelled to his terrified warriors.

The Saxons reached the part-flooded ditch and came to a halt with shields still raised, waiting for Prince Cissa, who was somewhere in the middle of the tortoise, to shout his command. The drums fell silent, their job done they peeled away and marched back to the bridge. A battle-horn sounded, the Saxon's raised shields came down and thousands of spears flew towards the Celts, whose three ranks collapsed in a writhing mess of blood and spears.

The rear ranks ran forward, hurriedly cleared the dead and wounded and took their places on the earthwork. Three ragged battle-lines reformed amongst the screams of the dying as they were dragged away, three shield-walls to hold back a tidal wave. The Saxon horn blasted again and, yelling their battle-cries the first rank of Saxons ran forward and leapt the ditch, clambered up the earth bank and cut into the Dumnonian spearmen, none caring how they died so long as it was with the blood of Celts on their swords and battle-axes.

"Push and stab!" Erbin shouted as a two-handed battle-axe cleaved his shield in two. Thrusting his sword, he felt the blade punch through chainmail and slide into the axeman's sticky guts. Grabbing a shield from a dead comrade, he shouted again, "Push and stab! Hold your ground!"

More Saxons leapt the ditch as Erbin's men hacked down at the battle-crazed axemen throwing themselves against Celtic shields. It was a desperate struggle, Saxons thrusting up while Celts hacked down. The Saxon attack seemed unstoppable, pushed from behind by the increasing numbers of warriors splashing into the ditch and making their way up the blood-slicked, muddy slope, their weight of numbers forcing the Celts back from the lip of the rampart.

Blades from both sides hacked into flesh, cutting through muscle and cracking bones, slicing open veins to send clouds of fine red mist and fountains of blood splattering and spraying in every direction. Sword-hands swung then span away, sliced off by the chop of a battle-axe. Spears rammed through splintered, blood-soaked chainmail, sword-blades punctured throats and cut through gaping jaws. Hands, fingers, ears and guts were trampled underfoot as the warriors struggled back and forth in the push to hold or take the rampart.

Erbin's Dumnonians were being cut to pieces, so Owain called for archers. The Saxons not yet fighting raised their shields as soon as the archers climbed onto the fort's wall, so the falling arrows had little effect. There was nothing more he could do, and he certainly wasn't going to waste more arrows, so Owain impotently watched the death-struggle.

In a hot and sweaty, blood-soaked fight for their lives, Erbin and Cissa's warriors fought toe to toe. There was no careful sword play and no well-aimed spear thrusts, this was the killing ground so desperately vicious hacks, slices and thrusts were necessary. If you couldn't stab or chop you kept your head low and pushed for your life, using all your strength and weight behind the shield to force a gap wide enough for you to cut and thrust into.

With more Saxons crossing the ditch, the press against the Celts became overwhelming. Slowly the Saxons forced the Celts back, with every heartbeat more axemen made it to the top of the earthwork, adding their weight to the shove. Bit by bloody bit the exhausted defenders gave ground, backing into their rear ranks whose locked shields pushed them back into the wall of Saxon blades.

Jammed within the crush of pushing warriors, Erbin's feet lost contact with the rampart but he didn't fall. Held upright by the press of surrounding men, his crushed lungs fought to suck in air as a Saxon blade knocked his helmet spinning backwards. Carried one way then the other, he realised the Saxons were pressing in from the flanks, shrinking his fighting line. Desperately trying to free his sword arm, his suffocating anxiety had him screaming for release as bloodied blades hacked at those around him. Barely able to breathe, and unable to swing his sword, he shouted an order above the din of battle, "Break and run! Break and run!" Thinking no one had heard him because his ranks hadn't thinned enough for him to turn, he yelled again, "Break and run!" The head of the man next to him toppled in a spray of red, squirted blood soaking the side of his face. "Break and run!" he yelled again when his feet found the rampart. The terrified rear ranks turned and ran, releasing those in front. Erbin's words may have been lost in the din, but warriors know when a battle is lost.

Sucking in air, Erbin raised his shield to deflect a chopping sword, lost his footing and tumbled backwards down the rampart. Rolling to his feet, he fled with his retreating warriors towards a reforming line of spearmen some way back from the earthwork. Running for the gap in the centre of the forming shield-wall, he wondered who'd had the wisdom and courage to reorganise and prevent a rout.

Owain's attention was caught by movement on the plateaued hill the locals called Badon Hill, where the other half of the Saxon army was forming two battle-groups, no doubt to attack the fort's east and west walls when the Celts in the valley had been slaughtered. Now he felt vindicated for recalling the Viroconium infantry, soon his warriors would be fighting for their lives.

Seeing the Dumnonian's forming a new shield wall, the Saxons on top of the earth rampart hesitated. They were just as exhausted as the Celts so they breathed in warm air, took sips from their ale pouches then began locking shields before launching the final attack.

King Erbin glanced up at Owain as Saxon weapons once again beat out the killing rhythm, clanging blades against shields as they streamed over the rampart. The Dumnonian King's eyes were pleading with the Pendragon to help him, but what could Owain do, the Saxons on Badon Hill would soon march into the valley and the fort must be held? Bedwyr nudged the Pendragon in the ribs. "Leave this to me," he said, "I've had the balls of brushwood and brambles soaked with the tar."

A large group of the villagers, holding firebrands, moved towards the west wall while a larger group with pitchforks and spears pulled balls of tar-soaked brushwood from the stacks. At Bedwyr's command they climbed over the wall, lit the brushwood and bramble balls and ran down the slope as far as they dare. Bedwyr shouted his order and they hurled the dozens and dozens of fiery-balls at the massed ranks of Saxons.

Weeks had passed since the last decent rainfall had soaked the thirsty hills overlooking Badon village, so the grass was bone-dry, and as brittle as the dusty earth. The fireballs rolled, tumbled and bounced into the lower valley, igniting the parched valley grass with frightening speed. The bouncing balls of flame crashed into the Saxon flank towards the middle of their advancing army, and once it has been ignited, birch-bark-tar is difficult to extinguish. Shocked warriors pushed inwards, screaming their pain and warnings as their clothes caught fire.

More of the fireballs tumbled, sparking and bouncing down the slope before exploding into the tightly packed mass of men. Some of the Saxons to the rear broke and ran from the spreading field of flames as more fireballs burst against the flank. The wind, blowing from the west, whipped up the flames and drove them eastward, the scorching licks of flame running through the panicking massed ranks. Men became human torches, others pushed against their sword-brothers, kicking and punching each other, anything to avoid the growing firestorm. More fireballs tumbled and the dry fire licked across the valley bottom, lapping fiery tongues at Saxon flesh.

The smell of burning flesh drove men to madness and, panicking warriors scrambled over each other to escape the surge of flames. Some were crushed in the press, others stabbed at their sword-brothers in their desperate bid to escape. Living men became running torches, twisting and turning, their screams driving them in every direction, it was an horrific chaos.

King Erbin saw the opportunity. The Dumnonians charged and smashed into the Saxon front ranks, hacking and stabbing, pushing with renewed ferocity. As the fire swept along the valley bottom, consuming those who couldn't force a pathway to safety, the Saxons broke and ran to escape the flames.

Owain ordered his archers to shoot their arrows into the mass of running, unprotected Saxons. This time there was no organisation, no raised shields because the Saxons feared the firestorm, so the arrows found their marks. King Aelle's arrow-pierced men dropped like stones, the badly wounded consumed by a gale of flames. Owain looked away as acrid columns of smoke hung over charred and screaming, burning and dying men.

The lower meadow, right up to Erbin's rampart, was now a smear of scorched and burning earth and bodies, the black smudge trailing flames almost as far as Badon village. The black smear stank of greasy, well-cooked meat where fire-consumed men lay writhing on the smoking earth, shivering and shaking in hot pain. The battle was over, so Erbin's men followed the retreating flames, putting to death those still writhing in pain.

From the summit of Badon Hill, King Aelle watched the unfolding hell, unable to comprehend it. His mind unhinged by the sight of hundreds of burning men, he turned away and blanked the slaughter. Three thousand of his warriors looked on helplessly, not one of them turning away.

Those who'd outrun the flames, about half the warriors who'd attacked Erbin's rampart, crossed the bridge and joined Aelle's warriors on the hillside. Slumping down in small groups, their smoke and soot-blackened faces streaming with tear and sweat tracks, they couldn't look back at the meadow where some had killed their sword brothers in a desperate bid to escape the flames.

There were no cheers of victory from Owain's warriors; within the safety of the fort, they endured with sickened hearts the hellish screams of charcoaled men. Most turned their backs, not wanting to see the blackened bodies crawling out from the dying furnace. It was a pitiful sight, and as Erbin's warriors continued putting to death the horribly scorched Saxons, many of the Red Cloaks wondered if the victory justified the horror.

Owain realised it was unrealistic to expect Erbin's warriors to hold their earthwork again, more than half of them had been killed or badly wounded, so he sent a messenger down, inviting the Dumnonians to join him in the fort. Another attack was unlikely today, the Saxons would need time to recover from the horror. They'd been bloodied and burned, but Owain knew they'd come again, probably when the new Sun rose. Inviting the Merlin to walk with him, he strolled away from the west wall, not wanting to look upon the scorched field of shame.

The Forest People, led by Gal and Gwen, had run for many days, the small army growing in numbers as hunters joined the race to reach Sulis Hillfort in time to help the defenders repel the Saxons. Throughout the run, breaks for water and food were regular but short, as was their sleeping time during the humid forest nights. No one resented the hardships; they knew what must be done if they were to save Owain's warriors from being slaughtered.

There wasn't time to look up while they ran, so neither Gal nor Gwen could judge the time by the height of the sun, nor did they know how many had answered the call to war. Even when they occasionally glanced left or right as they ran, trees hid their numbers, so they could only guess at how many were with them. What they did know was that the hunters weren't all men, if women and older children were strong enough to draw a bowstring or throw a spear, they'd joined the forest army as it raced through the dark shades of green.

When he took the time to listen, Gal heard hundreds of feet pounding the paths as he leapt bushes and fallen branches, swerved trees and splashed through cooling streams. He wanted to rest but the relentless pace couldn't be slackened, Owain needed them and their arrival might mean the difference between victory and defeat. Sweat must pour and lungs must burst, feet must bleed and hearts must pound against ribs, if they were to get there in time.

The battle could already be lost, but as long as there was breath in his lungs and strength in his muscles Gal would run, hoping the Pendragon and his warriors still held out against the Teutonic swarm. Glancing left, he saw lines of equally tired runners, bags of food slung across their backs, bows and bunches of arrows held tight in their sweating hands. Looking to his right he saw equally determined groups of runners, one of whom was a woman with a baby strapped to her chest. He guessed she didn't have anyone to look after the child but had joined the army anyway and, seeing her made him feel proud to be a Celt.

The Merlin, standing with Owain on a pile of stones next to the closed south gateway, watched the Saxons collecting their dead from the still smoking, charred battlefield. King Aelle's warriors might have lost the battles, but the south, east and west valleys were now theirs to control, only the northern approach remained open to the Celts.

King Erbin's exhausted survivors were now inside the fort, sitting with their backs to the west wall, letting the afternoon Sun soothe their aching bodies. Cai had organised water-carriers to bring them cool drinks, but all the Dumnonians wanted was to wipe from their minds the images of human savagery. Killing a man in battle was one thing, the agonized screams of burning men, sickened the soul. No human deserved to die like that, so the Merlin said to Owain, "Are you proud of that?"

The Pendragon didn't reply immediately. Turning away from the savage scene, he sat on the stones, rubbed his sweaty palms on his leggings and said, "I'll never forget it."

"It was murder."

"Necessary murder," Owain replied curtly. "Did you know about Bedwyr's plan?"

"He hinted at it."

"You might have warned me."

"I didn't think he'd do it. Will they'll attack again today?" the Merlin asked, changing the subject as he sat next to his friend.

Owain didn't really want to talk, so for a moment or two he ignored the question. Leaning back against the oak gates, he watched circling carrion birds, drew in a warm breath and sullenly replied, "They'll cremate their dead before launching another attack."

"Don't they usually burn their dead at night?"

"Yes, that's why they are building pyres on Badon Hill."

"And after that?" the Merlin asked.

"They'll attack two walls."

"Why just two when they could send a force up the Forest Hill and around the back to attack the north wall?"

Owain looked across the fort to the north wall, trying to work out how many warriors he'd need to defend it. "If the Saxons did attack the west and east walls," he said, thinking, "they could still send at least a thousand spearmen against the north gate." Jumping to his feet, he looked up at the Forest Hill. "Archers might do the job. If I send fifty of my best, under cover of the night, they could be in place before the Saxons light their pyres."

"Will the hill be easy to defend?"

"Yes, there's no cover below the ridge, anyone climbing the hill could be easily picked off."

"Wouldn't King Aelle simply send more warriors up the slope?"

"I doubt it, sting them once and they'll avoid the nest." Climbing onto the east wall, he looked north. There was an easy enough route for his archers to take, so he waved Cai over. "Choose the best fifty archers from the Legion and give them as many arrows as they can carry," he ordered his Dragon. "When night falls, cross the valley where the hawthorns run down to the brook, and make your way to the top of the Forest Hill. The forest runs almost to the edge of the ridge so, if you can, remain hidden in the trees, I don't want the Saxons knowing how few you are. If Aelle sends warriors up the slope, kill them without being seen."

On Badon Hill, dozens of Saxon funeral pyres burned long into the night. Gathered around the pyres, warriors dressed in full battle-armour, their swords pointing skyward, sang the souls of the dead on to the next life. Standing beside his banner, King Aelle felt the guttural hymns of death, his heart touched by the gentle tones of his singing spearmen. Reflecting on the slaughter and how dishonourably the Celts had killed, he could only describe the day as being a disaster. If he hadn't so many warriors, he'd accept defeat and go home but, returning to Andredes Caester a defeated king wasn't an option.

In Sulis Fort, Owain watched the Saxon rites from the east wall, drawn to its sadness by the mournful shades of the funeral dirges. Although the plateau of burning pyres was a reminder to him of the earlier horrors, the scene was impressive, and he wasn't surprised to see his warriors manning the walls to witness the rites. All dressed for battle with swords pointing to the pyres, they paid tribute to the dead Saxons, so Owain drew his sword and followed their lead.

"I'll not salute them," Bedwyr said.

"We all live according to our consciences."

"What's that supposed to mean?"

"It means there'll be no more fire-battles."

"But my tactics saved King Erbin and his warriors," Bedwyr rightfully claimed, "and if I hadn't done it, we could be dead now!"

"The end justifies the means?" Owain asked, looking into the eyes of his Dragon. "Does it not matter how a warrior dies, so long as he dies?"

"Kill or be killed, that is war!"

"There's a difference between war and murder."

"There's also a difference between being dead or alive."

Owain took the point for what it was, the realistic truth. "Your tactics won the battle, but if the Saxons hated us before, that hatred will have cooled into vengeful loathing, tomorrow they'll kill without mercy."

"Do they ever kill any other way?"

Owain turned back to the pyres on Badon Hill. "I'm not going to argue the point, there'll be no more fire-battles.'"

"There can't be, we used all of the tar."

DAY 2

Beneath the fading stars of the dying night, the Saxon pyres on Badon Hill collapsed into smouldering heaps of white ash, while a thick mist settled over the four valleys and their hills. Having crossed the bridge spanning Badon's river, a thousand grey figures mingled with the mist, awaiting the order to climb the Forest Hill.

In the scrublands fringing the hilltop, where the long grass met the top of a ridge, wisps of mist hid Cai's archers, who were crawling through the long grass. Lying flat at the top of the ridge, Cai peered down into the valley, eager for the hundreds of dark figures to climb the slope and be killed. Since hiding from the Saxon destruction of Viroconium, he'd waited for an opportunity like this one, an opportunity to banish his guilty demons by proving to his warriors that he wasn't a coward.

In the days following the Viroconium slaughter, many had called him a coward, mostly behind his back, occasionally to his face. While carrying Viroconium's dead to the pyres, some onlookers had spat at him then turned away, including some of the Red Cloaks and every look of disdain he'd met with since had been a hot knife burning into his heart. At times the disgrace had been unbearable, and in the privacy of his home at night, while Kareen slept, he'd occasionally shed a few tears, regretting the choice he'd made. Now he had the chance to reclaim his worth, Owain had asked him to do a job and he'd do it, even if it led to his own death.

Whistles akin to the night song of a blackbird, told him his fifty prone archers were ready, so he peered over the ridge again, to see the valley mist bristling with Saxon spearmen. The hilltop and valley may be shrouded, but most of the slope, the killing ground, was clear of the thicker mists and believing the hill to be theirs for the taking, King Aelle's warriors casually emerged from the grey fog as they climbed the lower slope, laughing and joking with each other as if they were walking to an alehouse. Up the slope they climbed, hundreds of spear and shield carrying warriors, a black cloud of killers leaving behind them the grey, pre-dawn mists, killers who were strolling towards their deaths.

Using the ghostly hoot of a tawny owl, Cai ordered his warriors to ready themselves. Turning onto his back, he suppressed a laugh while fitting an arrow to his bowstring, this was going to be so easy. Rolling onto his stomach, he picked his target. More Saxons emerged from the mists to tempt his aim, their chainmail byrnies and scabbards jingling as they climbed the hillside. Having waited for his target to climb halfway to the ridge, Cai relaxed his fingers and he heard the bowstring twang. His fifty bowmen did the same and arrows punched cold iron into dozens of shocked warriors. Before their screams had pierced the night, another flight of silent death-bolts hit their marks, and the Red Cloaks nocked more arrows. The hundreds of Saxons not pierced by the first two flights threw themselves to the ground, scanning the edge of the mist covered ridge for bowmen.

Every double heartbeat each archer loosed more stinging death at the dark patches of prostrate men, most of the iron-tips finding flesh. This was too easy, Cai thought, hitting targets who couldn't move because of the fear of being hit; the irony amused him. More arrows flew from his bow and, hearing the thuds and groans that told him another soul was either dead or dying, he felt release and relief.

With their Saxon sword-brothers being easily picked off, someone had to make the decision to either stand and fight or, run. But Alfric, the warrior who'd led them up the hill, had been killed by the first arrow, so for a while the spearmen lay prone and leaderless, waiting for someone to take command.

With storms of arrows fizzing down the slope, a Saxon voice shouted, "Raise shields!" and reluctantly, hundreds of the wary-black figures lifted their shields whilst rising to their knees. They couldn't see their deaths coming, but they heard the whoosh and thud as arrows flew and struck. "Stand!" the Saxon voice yelled as two iron-darts punched into his shield, and the kneeling men forced themselves up. "Charge!" the Saxon shouted, but too many of his comrades had already fallen, and those still unharmed weren't willing to risk being hit. All but one spearman turned and fled down the hill, sliding, rolling and tumbling to reach the mists, anything to escape the arrows. Seeing them run, the lone warrior turned and ran then fell as half a dozen arrows pierced his back.

Running targets make for easy pickings, and more flights stabbed into the backs of fleeing Saxons before the bulk of them dissolved into the valley mists. Satisfied with the wasp-sting he'd delivered, Cai's tawny owl hoot signalled his bowmen to return to the forest. Crawling back into the woodlands, he laughed, because so far King Aelle had received a bloody nose, had had his beard singed and now his arse had been stung by wasps!

Dawn broke slowly over Sulis Hillfort, the thinning mists dissolved from the four valleys and light, feathery rain brought a fresh glow to the surrounding hills. After weeks of almost continuous sunshine, the rain was welcome but as the clouds lifted on the gentle breeze, it didn't look like the light shower would last.

Stepping out from the roundhouse, carrying a campstool, Owain saw the fort coming to life: food and drink were being passed around campfires; weapons and byrnies were being checked and he noticed some villagers mingling with the warriors. Sitting with his back against the wicker wall of the roundhouse, he watched the bustle of life while considering the next Saxon attack. Today, to protect the west and east walls he'd split his warriors into two groups, because King Aelle would surely throw his full battle strength at the fort.

Worrying about the unprotected north wall, he got up to stroll amongst the warriors gathered around the many campfires. None of them seemed concerned about their prospects, which was unusual, but who can see into a man's soul? On he walked towards the north gate, returning peoples greetings but refusing their food when offered. Coming to where the animals were penned, he noticed their numbers were greatly reduced. Although he took comfort from the smell of roasting animal flesh continually drifting around the fort, the stocks wouldn't last, at some point his small army would have to go out and fight because warriors cannot do battle on empty stomachs.

Cheers broke out near the east wall when Cai and the archers climbed back over the rampart. Walking through the cheering crowds, the Pendragon was pleased to see a smile on the Dragon's face; redemption is good for the soul he thought, as Cai happily accepted the congratulations. "You did well," Owain said. "Because you and the archers were prepared to risk your lives, you've made it more difficult for the Saxons to defeat us."

"It was easy," Cai replied modestly. "Aelle's men ran before they got near us. They don't like archers, which makes me wonder why they don't bring their own to battle?"

"They believe that killing from a distance carries no honour," Bedwyr said, having joined them.

"That's true," Owain agreed, "though I find their lack of bowmen contradictory because they throw spears, which is killing from a distance."

"We should be grateful they only use bows for hunting," Cai added, yawning.

"You should get some sleep." Owain waved him in the direction of the roundhouse.

The Dragon saluted and headed for the roundhouse. Ignoring Bedwyr, Owain walked to the south gate, where his brother was waiting for him.

"The food won't last much longer," Cadwallon said, looking at Badon Hill, where thousands of Saxons were walking down the hillside.

"We must limit the rations," Owain replied, "and hope to wear down the Saxons before the food runs out." Across the river, King Aelle's army formed two equal battle-groups, so Owain said to Cadwallon, "They'll attack two walls simultaneously. They might also attack the north wall, if they do, I don't know how we'll stop them getting into the fort, we don't have enough warriors to protect three walls."

"I could defend the north wall with the villagers and refugees," Cadwallon suggested. "There's enough of them to hold back an attack until we are reinforced, even if they are untrained for battle."

"The villagers might have weapons, but they don't know how to fight." Owain didn't like the idea. "They'd be slaughtered, and how would we reinforce them? No, I don't like it." But what other choice was there? He couldn't man all three walls with his trained warriors. Reluctantly, he said to his brother, "Take them to the north wall, along with a horn-blower. If you can't hold out, three horn-blasts will summon help, if we've any warriors to spare."

The west and east valleys shimmered with metal as thousands of Saxons marched towards Sulis Hill. This time no war drums thundered as the two armies progressed across the valley, instead, the drummers carried shields and spears. It was quite a sight, thousands of helmeted heads bobbing like silver-waves on the rolling swell of tanned leather and polished chainmail. Impressive yet terrifyingly deadly, an ocean of killing spears that King Aelle hoped would flood right over Sulis Hillfort.

Below the west and east slopes, the tidal waves came to a shimmering halt, creating an eerie, deathly silence occasionally punctured by the ghostly cawing of hovering crows. A high-pitched note blasted from a Saxon horn and, the two armies raised their shields above their heads, except for the front ranks, who locked shields to make a defensive wall. A second note shrilled and the thousands marched up the two slopes. Rank after rank of glittering warriors trudged slowly towards the walls, their raised shields a warning to every Celt that the previous day's slaughter would not be repeated.

Standing on the east wall next to the south gate, Owain didn't know what to make of the silent march. Unaware he was nervously licking his dry lips, he realised his archers would be of little use, so he called to his nervous warriors, "Bows down!" Along both walls, bows and arrows were passed back and collected by women and children, and swords were nervously drawn, shields pulled close and spears raised.

King Aelle's warriors continued up the slopes in silence, eager to avenge the previous day's butchery and burning. It was a nerve shredding, blood-chilling sight and Owain felt waves of cold fear shivering his skin. About a spear's throw from the walls, a horn blared and the two Saxon armies came to a metal-clanging halt. Why had they stopped, Owain wondered as a buzzing fly pestered him, the only sound beneath the pale blue sky? Swotting it away, he licked his lips again and nervously ran his thumb over the pommel of his sword. A horn blew, and the Saxons shields came down.

A warrior, richly armoured and wearing a recently polished, shining iron helmet, the nose and cheek pieces decorated with intricate gold patterns, walked forward, followed by three of his sword brothers. "Celts!" he called to the fort. "I am Prince Cissa, the son of King Aelle and I've come to make an offer to your leader!"

Tying the chin-straps of his helmet, Owain walked along the wall so that he directly faced the Saxon, and he called back, “You don’t need to know my name, Saxon, just like you didn’t know the names of those whose lands you stole, and the many innocents your warriors raped and murdered! There’s nothing you can offer us; this is our land so your words mean nothing. You may call yourselves kings and princes, but I say you are thieves, rapists and murderers!” His warriors raised their spears and swords and cheered him. “You might take this fort today!” he shouted, “but it will cost you the lives of thousands of your spearmen!” Again, his warriors raised their voices in support. “And the war won’t end here!” he yelled with a joy shared by every Celt, “even if you kill everyone in the fort, other armies will march against you, our nation will never surrender! Now, I’ll give you a choice, Cissa the arse-born Prince of nothing, lead your armies back to your hovels, get into your boats and sail back to the sows that whelped you, or order the attack and send your warriors to their certain deaths!” The fort irrupted with a mix of cheers, jeers and laughter, the Celts banging their weapons against shields, inviting the invaders to come and taste Celtic iron.

Prince Cissa looked along the wall at the battle-charged warriors, and realised there was no point offering them the chance to peacefully retreat. Striding closer to the warrior on the wall he believed to be Cadwallon, he drew his sword and pointed it at him. “You’ve made your choice, Celt, and when this battle is over, I’ll not only rape your dead women, I’ll abuse your slaughtered children! All your naked dead will then be impaled through the arse and planted in the valley as a warning to all those who defy Saxons!

When this war has been won, I'll hunt down your wife and have my way with her, before slicing off her breasts to make into moneybags! Before I return to my warriors, Celt, won't you tell me the name of the man I am about to slice open from his chin to his cock, because if you are Cadwallon, I'd like to know so that I can boast about the day I spilled your guts."

The Saxon's words drove hard into Owain's soul. He couldn't help but picture the grinning Saxon raping Gwen, the image igniting waves of hot, angry fire in his belly. Unable to control his anger, he grabbed a spear from the warrior behind him and threw it. The spearpoint smashed through chainmail, splitting links as the heavy blade drove deep into Prince Cissa's belly. Gripping the bloody-spear with both hands and, falling to his knees, the Saxon looked at Owain through shocked, questioning eyes. "Take that back to your father!" Owain yelled at the bleeding man, more from the shock of what he'd done than anything else. Although he'd just broken one of the unwritten rules of war, he nevertheless felt exhilarated.

Those standing in front of and behind the east wall, Saxon and Celt, looked on in stunned silence. Killing in cold blood a man who'd come to parley was unheard of, and as warriors hurriedly grabbed Prince Cissa's limp body and began dragging him back through the Saxon ranks, one of them shouted, "Murderer!"

Word of the atrocity spread like a forest-fire and, seeing their dying battle-lord being carried down the slope, thousands of angry warriors began banging their weapons wildly against their shields, not in the rhythm of the march but a faster, more frenzied thrashing, whipping the warriors into a violent killing rage. The front ranks broke and charged, hurling themselves into the ditch and up the earth rampart to climb the fort's wall.

"Onto the wall!" the Pendragon shouted, and hundreds of warriors clambered into place.

Owain thought about calling for archers but it was too late, ladders were already planted against the walls and the roaring Saxons were climbing. The Celts began chopping and slashing down, throwing themselves into the battle with the same frenzied, blood-boiling violence as the Saxons. Blood spurted and body-parts flew, metal sliced and chopped, the blood-splattered walls became slick underfoot, making warriors slip when they swung their blades. Both sides stabbed and slashed with equal ferocity, killing in the frenzied savagery of hate-war.

The overwhelming press of so many spearmen was too much for the Celts, and although they fought with courage, they couldn't prevent Saxons from clambering onto the walls. Celt and Saxon fought toe to toe, trying desperately to hold their ground, each man driven by their fear of the killing blow. Minds quickly closed to the appalling slaughter, every warrior fighting for the few stones they either stood on or faced.

And the Saxons kept coming, climbing, pushing, hacking and slashing at legs and feet, sending limbless Celts tumbling from the walls to where ravenous Saxons rammed their spears into them. It didn't take long for King Aelle's axemen to gain footholds on sections of wall, then they turned inwards to fight along the ramparts, leaving space for more Saxons to climb onto the blood-smeared stones.

Not far from where the Pendragon was hacking at weapons and flesh, death was coming at the Celts from all directions, except the rear, the significance unrealised by the defenders because they were too busy protecting themselves from the storm of blades. The Saxons on the wall had a killing rhythm going, slash and move, thrust and step, hack and kill. Both sides were fighting for every stone but there was a definite, if unplanned agenda to the Saxon attack, that was yet to be noticed by the Celts. All the Saxons on the east wall were fighting towards the man who'd murdered Prince Cissa.

The Merlin, organising flying-squads of archers behind the fighting, saw the Saxons take sections of the wall but not follow up their advantage by jumping down into the fort, and he knew why. Handing out bows and arrows to the women, and any child strong enough to draw a bowstring, he realised the Pendragon had been targeted, and if something wasn't done Owain wouldn't survive. After ordering his squads of archers to shoot at the sections of wall held by Saxons, he ran forward to join the fight.

Killing towards the nameless warrior, the Saxons fought with murderous hatred, their determined lust for revenge driving them on, cutting away the Celts on either side of the murderer. With every swing of their blades they killed, and stepped closer, slicing a bloody path to the Pendragon.

Finding himself holding his small section of wall alone, Owain cut and slashed in huge killing arcs, desperate to live as snarling warriors came at him. Feeling the slick blood of the dead sliding his feet in directions he didn't want them to go, he battled to keep his footing while severing heads and limbs. Saxons were coming at him from both sides as well as from the front, so he swung his sword in every direction, killing, wounding and maiming whilst calling for help. But none came. Thinking faster than his swinging blade killed, he ducked and cut, jumped and slashed, driven by his fear of death and the one thought swimming inside his brain: kill Saxons.

More warriors came at him, wild, angry men who wanted nothing more than to kill the nameless murderer. He held them off as best as he could, his steel sword a tool of death, its razor-sharp blade slicing into more victims than he could count: chainmail burst in showers of metallic blood; split helmets oozed brains, blood and bone onto the blood-covered stones; blades were sliced clean through, nothing could withstand Owain's lightning steel weapon.

He kept telling himself he must survive but his lungs were burning and ready to burst, his legs felt so heavy that he thought he'd been buried to his knees in sand, his arms ached so much that he feared he'd soon be unable to hold his weapon. But his desperately exhausted senses drove him on, until a rising spear cut a thin trickle of red across his forearm. Screaming, his mind went blank and his eyes misted, though he was sure his sword was still scything through Saxon flesh. Without him realising it, the battle-frenzy had come upon him. Seeing nothing but his hacking blade as it sang, it's metallic-light flashing in every direction, he fought like a man possessed: limbs dropped; guts spilled; heads rolled and severed hands spun high. It felt like a frenzied dance to him, uncontrollable and savage yet beautiful in the patterns of the blood-sprayed light that trailed in the wake of his cutting blade. Almost blinded by a mix of sweat and blood, he knew that at any moment the killing blow would come, and his head would topple into the flesh-filled ditch.

Then a song hummed in his ears as the sound of clashing blades mingled with the slow melody. The 'Battle Awen' was consuming him, his sword swinging with lightning speed as a voice, not unlike the Merlin's, sang to him about the Bear of the Britons, each word joyfully touching his soul, driving his screaming heartbeats faster as they throbbed in his aching head.

His sword cut and swung and the voice sang a new song about the blade the Island People had forged for him, the sword of steel that could slice through chainmail and blade, the unbreakable sword that would save a kingdom. He felt the trance and embraced it, loving the song of his soul. Was he also singing, he wondered as his blade hacked through another Saxon's neck? He couldn't be sure about anything, not even knowing if he was in control while he twisted and turned, killing and maiming, his savage blows bright in his eyes, his body moving without the need for his guiding will. Swords and axes flashed around his head, spears thrust and fell as the song inspired every fibre of his nerveless body, giving renewed life and energy to his exhausted strength. Blades clipped and cut his flesh, spears punctured his skin, he could feel his blood trickling warm and pungent from many minor wounds but his killing dance continued. Although Saxons were coming at him from three directions, none could deal him a death-blow because they weren't fast enough, so they died where they stood, and every time his sword sliced through iron or flesh, he felt and saw their deaths as he joyously cut all who came too close to his swinging sword.

The battle-song drove him on, pulling him into a dreamlike trance of killing lust. Was he making love, he questioned himself as a severed head fell dripping from his blade? Rational battle-thought slipped away, and he found himself thinking about Gwen while he fought. Just as his sword bit through flesh and bone he heard himself call to her, feeling the warmth of her love kissing him softly on the cheek. As Gwen's love touched his lips another Saxon's head rotated in a bloody-loop from the edge of his sword. While Severing the leg of an axe-wielding warrior, he heard the gentle whisper of Gwen's voice telling him to kill and kill and keep on killing because she needed him, he must not die.

Then the song and her whisper faded to nothing, and he felt alone as a sword cut across his knuckles. From the corner of his eye, he saw an axe-blade swing towards his neck. He wanted to raise his sword to deflect the blow but his arm was thrusting his blade into a Saxon's guts. Turning his head, his movements slowing to accept his death, he saw sunlight glint from the virgin axe as it swung towards his throat. Speaking Gwen's name for the last time in this life, he braced himself for the jarring hack that would severe his head.

The axe-holding hand flopped onto the wall when a blade sliced through it. A hand reached up, grabbed Owain from behind and pulled him backwards, dragging him hard onto the earth which knocked the trance out of his head. Shields locked above and around him, preventing the death that had been a heartbeat away. Forcing himself to his feet, he pushed through the protective shields and looked around, relieved to see that his warriors still held the walls, but only just. Children's voices caught his attention and he turned to see joy on their faces as their mothers, dozens of them, shot arrow after arrow into the hordes of Saxons on the walls.

Then through the clashing of iron and the screams of wounded men he heard three blasts from a horn. Panic turned him to the north wall, where Saxons were pouring into the fort, brushing aside the helpless villagers who were fighting in vain to stem the battle-tide. He must think fast; his brother was there and if he couldn't get reinforcements to him, Cadwallon must surely die. Calling to the warriors closest to him, he pointed his sword at the north gate and charged.

Running, he saw his brother surrounded by Saxons, their blades hacking at the small group of villagers bravely protecting him. Seeing bloodied axes and swords rising and falling, Owain roared with rage and, lifting his sword to kill he threw himself into the savage scrum, desperate to force his way through to his fighting brother. He heard a crack, felt dull pain and he collapsed into unconsciousness.

Swimming-red, spinning images of hacked-flesh and slicing blades, chopping and stabbing; blood-mists and flashing metal colouring sun-nightmares; the cries of the wounded tolling death-bells, throbbing and snarling the bloodied faces of the dead, forcing the sleeper to reckon he was just about to awaken into the next life, wherever that was though he didn't care so long as he shifted free of the horrors being heaped upon horrors within the uncontrollable, bloody nightmares of his dreams.

Opening his eyes, Owain was surprised to find himself sitting in a chair beside the hearth in the big roundhouse. His head ached as if a dozen hammers had pummelled it, and he could feel pricking, itchy pains criss-crossing his arms and legs; his battle-badges sore. His chainmail byrnie was blotched with red and there was a small amount of blood encrusted on the side of his mouth, so he picked at it while looking through the smoky half-light within the roundhouse. He wasn't being guarded, which puzzled him.

Assuming the Saxons had taken the fort, he must be a prisoner. But why was he alive at all, why hadn't they killed him? If they knew who he was his death would be cruel and slow, unless they planned to ransom him. He quickly dismissed that idea, King Aelle would want him dead.

Not wishing to suffer too painful a death, he decided he needed a credible name and identity. They would have looked at his byrnie, helmet and sword and realised he was a man of means, though a fighting druid would be dressed and armed much the same. That would be as good a cover as any, the Saxons would have very little knowledge of the druids, so he decided to call himself Dewi, the Druid of Rhuthun.

Getting unsteadily to his feet, he made his way to the entrance, still confused as to why there were no guards on the inside of the roundhouse. Lifting the door-flap, he expected to be challenged by Saxon guards on the outside, but again, there was no one, all he saw was bright shafts of daylight that stung his eyes and made his head spin a little, so he closed his eyes. Leaning for balance against the roundhouse, he was about to open his eyes and look around the fort when a voice he recognised called to him, it was Cai! His head began to spin again, and a spasmodic surge forced his last meal up from his stomach. Vomiting, his knees buckled and he fell face down onto the earth. Feeling Cai lifting him back to his feet, he couldn't help wondering why the Saxons hadn't overrun the fort?

"You took one hell of a blow to your head," Cai said, holding his friend steady. "Without your helmet you'd have been killed. I'll help you back inside." Sitting the Pendragon beside the hearth, he wet a cloth from a water-bucket and gave it to Owain so that he could wipe his face.

"What happened, Cai, why are we still alive?"

"They couldn't breech enough of the walls, and you have the Merlin to thank for that. He organized women and children into groups, ordering them to shoot arrows into any breeches the Saxons made. It worked because men fighting hand to hand combat can't defend themselves against archers. It was the bloodiest battle I've fought in, for a time our survival looked unlikely, the slaughter was horrendous. But our warriors never took a step back, they were true heroes, although without the Merlin's archers we'd all be dead."

"We won the day?"

"We are here aren't we. We lost more warriors than we can afford to, as did the Saxons, and most of the villagers and refugees died defending the north gate."

The north gate! An unpleasant memory flashed painfully into Owain's aching head; an image of his brother being battered by a shower of bloodstained blades. "Cadwallon! What happened to him, where is he?" He forced himself to his feet. "Is he alive, I must go to him?"

"We couldn't reach him in time," Cai's sad voice told its own story. "You might have saved him if an axe-blow hadn't knocked you unconscious. We eventually cut through to him, just before the Saxons turned and ran, but he was already dead."

"Dead?" Owain's stomach tightened. "He can't be, he's my brother!" The truth overwhelmed him and he wailed into the roundhouse rafters. Memories passed before his tear-filled eyes: two boys with wooden swords fighting a mock battle; two young fishermen laughing when their father slipped and fell into the river; the pranks the two boys had played on the Merlin and their father, and the punishments they'd received. "Take me to him," he demanded.

"Now?"

"Yes, that's an order!"

Cadwallon's hacked, cut and sliced corpse lay on a table in the adjacent roundhouse, where the Merlin and Bedwyr were cleaning and stitching the body, a job usually given to women. "He died well," the Merlin said as the Pendragon walked in, though from the look of pain in Owain's eyes, he guessed his words weren't registering. "He killed many Saxons before being overwhelmed, and if he hadn't blown the horn to warn us that the north wall had been breached, we might all be dead now. He must have known he'd be killed when lowering his sword to blow the warning, he gave his life for us."

With tears streaming down his face, Owain looked coldly at the Merlin, then he walked to the table and took his brother's cold hand in his.

"He is at peace," Bedwyr whispered softly, offering small comfort.

"He may be," Owain's reply was cold, hard and almost spat through gritted teeth. "We have a war to win, and I swear upon the body of my brother that we shall win. His banner must come down, he is no longer with us."

"Why?" Bedwyr questioned. "Our warriors will lose heart if it is lowered?"

"Take it down I said, I'll give our spearmen other reasons to kill Saxons!" The Pendragon let go of his brother's hand and he looked over the horribly hacked, almost unrecognisable body, revolted by the number of shocking facial wounds. "Our people need a king but there is no one," he whispered, trying to understand why Cadwallon had sacrificed himself. The moment he realised that he was now the leader of his people, a door opened and Owain understood many of the lessons the Merlin had taught him. Broken ends joined and loose strings tied, so he turned to the Merlin and looked him straight in the eyes, wanting him to know that he understood.

The Merlin nodded his understanding, and said, "If we take down the flag, King Aelle will know Cadwallon is dead. Are you sure you want to give him that advantage?"

"I want Aelle to know. We'll burn my brother's body tonight, maybe in death there is one last gift he can give to his people."

"You can't burn his body, Owain, he was a Christian," Cai pointed out. "His body must be taken back to Viroconium and buried. His god doesn't permit cremation, it's a........."

"As I said," Owain angrily turned to his Dragon, "we'll burn his body tonight! If his god is so forgiving, he'll understand." Cai and Bedwyr looked at each other, not realising what the Pendragon was getting at, but the Merlin understood. "Build a pyre," Owain ordered, "and build it high because tonight we are sending a noble man to his god."

The night shone star-bright black over Badon Hill, where King Aelle walked alone. The last of his three legitimate sons wouldn't live through the night, so he looked up at the stars and asked Woden to open his feasting hall doors for Prince Cissa's soul. Ahead of him lay the task of taking blood-revenge for his son's murder, and from what his warriors had told him, Cadwallon had thrown the killing-spear, so it would be his head he'd hunt for during the next battle. Only when the Celt was dead would he think again about conquering Briton.

From where he stood, he could see into Sulis Hillfort, and he was more than interested to see that the Celts had built a pyre. It had to be for someone important, perhaps one of their Dragons had been killed because every warrior had gathered around the pyre, many of them holding firebrands. He continued watching because the solemn proceedings were about to begin, and he wanted a clue as to who would be cremated.

As the not-too-distant firebrands began circling the pyre, he saw Cadwallon's banner being lowered; the filthy-royal-piece-of-stinking-cow-dung was dead, depriving him of the pleasure of killing him. Raging with anger at not being able to take personal revenge against the man he believed had murdered his son, he swore that he'd skin alive every member of Cadwallon's family, when he eventually swept north to Viroconium. He then wondered why they were lowering the flag when they should have let him believe that Cadwallon stilled lived? "Strange people these Celts," he whispered to the night. The torch-holding, circling Celts came to a halt, a single note blew from a horn and the firebrands were thrown onto the pyre, which burst into an orange glow, consuming Cadwallon's body as Cymry voices sang a song of celebration.

Aelle watched the pyre burn, hypnotised by the twists of flame and the joyful songs the Celts sang to the stars. He then realised that with Cadwallon dead and, the Pendragon's whereabouts unknown, the Celts in the fort were leaderless so there'd be little fight left in them. Tomorrow, he'd attack all three walls simultaneously, and put every Celt to the sword.

After his brother's pyre had collapsed into smoking ashes, Owain walked alone to the north gateway. Climbing onto the night darkened wall, he remembered seeing hundreds of Saxons pouring over this wall and into the fort, and he couldn't help feeling this wasn't much of a place for his brother to have died. Above him, stars disappeared in clutches as clouds began to swallow the night. The north star could still be seen, which made him think about Gwen:

was she close by; would her army of Forest Hunters reach the fort in time? Seeing the north star disappear behind the thickening clouds, he sat on the wall and tried to imagine Gwen holding him during his time of grief, which would be short because the Saxons would attack when the Sun came up.

Glancing back to where the white embers of the funeral pyre had been abandoned by everyone except the Merlin, who was staring thoughtfully into the smoking ashes, he dearly hoped Gwen's journey had been without incident, he couldn't face losing her as well. Looking across the north valley to the forested flatlands, he imagined her sleeping peacefully beside a campfire. Gal would be close by, no doubt keeping a protective eye on her while she slept.

Tomorrow, because food and water supplies were running low, he'd leave the fort and lead the Legion in a desperate charge against the Saxon shield-wall, though he knew there was little chance of success against so many warriors. They could no longer defend the fort, they hadn't enough fit warriors left to protect one wall, let alone three, and having discussed battle-tactics with Bedwyr, Cai and King Erbin they'd decided that while the remaining warriors were still strong enough to fight, they should try to breakout.

Thinking back to the Merlin's story about the 'Bear of the Britons' he closed his eyes and asked the gods to send him that hero. What a sight that would be, a heroic warrior riding out from fire-blooming clouds on a charging warhorse, swinging his light-catching sword as he galloped down from the fire-belching heavens to smash into King Aelle's shield-wall. But it was fantasy, no warrior of the gods would turn the tide of battle, only mortals would charge to death or glory when the Sun climbed.

Although he was excited about the planned battle-charge, he realised that few of his Red Cloaks would survive. But there was a small crumb of satisfaction to be taken from their sacrifices, because even if the battle was lost, so many Saxons had been killed that they'd have to forget their plans for conquest and return to Andredes Caester. His warriors would die losing the battle, but the war would have been won.

He was about to jump down from the wall when he thought he heard something moving in the long grass, not too far from where he was. The rustling sound could have been a trick of the night, or Saxons stealthily moving into position to launch a surprise night attack. Quietly and slowly drawing his sword, he held his breath and looked along the rampart towards the north gate, where he thought he saw something dark moving quickly up the defensive ditch. Looking again, his sight adjusting to the darkness below the wall, he saw someone scrambling onto the wall, not ten paces from him.

Assuming the Saxons had sent assassins to eliminate sentries before attacking, he searched the long, breeze-blown grass for other cloaked figures. Seeing no one else, he ran towards the shadowy-figure, who'd just about pulled himself onto the wall. "Move and you die," he challenged the hooded intruder, pressing the point of his sword into the assassin's back.

The dirt-blackened face of the figure turned at the prick of the sword, pulled back his hood, looked up at the Pendragon and smiled at him with a white-toothed grin. "You wouldn't kill the best friend you ever had, would you?"

"Gal!" Owain shouted, and a smile as wide as the boy's spread across his face. Taking the boy's arm, he helped his young friend to his feet. Realising that if Gal was here, Gwen must be close by, he pointed his sword to the wooded hill and asked, "Is Gwen up there?"

"No, she went there to assess your situation, now she's in the lower forest."

"Why didn't she come with you?"

"Because we've a battle to win, and she could hardly lead our army here when we don't want the Saxons knowing that hundreds of hunters are preparing a nasty surprise for them. Come on, Owain, you're the Pendragon, you should know about these things!" Laughing, he watched Owain's face crack into a deliberately restrained smile. "Seriously though, over four hundred hunters ran south with us."

"Where are they?"

"Gwen ordered them to fell and trim trees in the lower forest, and, wanting to oversee their part in her battleplan herself, she sent me here instead. Being the craftiest fellow in the Legion, and there's lots of Saxons about, if you hadn't noticed! she entrusted me with her message, which is more like a set of instructions. Do you want to know about her plan, or would you prefer to stand there looking dreamily up at the hilltop?"

Owain smiled at the pure cheek of the boy. "Come with me, we'd better find Bedwyr, Cai, Erbin and the Merlin."

"What about Cadwallon?"

“He is dead.”

DAY 3

Through the night the exhausted warriors slept, their dreams weeping for the dead, the carnage of battle and the horrors and stench of roasted flesh imprinted forever in their tormented memories. There is nothing glorious about battle, killing another human being is not a triumph it is a grotesque burden that fixes into the conscience and memory of every mortal soul who suffers battle's butchery; the distress of aftermath is beyond our understanding.

Before the night had fully given way to the new day, King Aelle had his warriors deployed for battle. Having watched the Celts remove the stones blocking the south gateway, he guessed they were coming out but why, when remaining inside the fort was to their advantage? After what had happened over the previous two days, he couldn't help thinking they had another surprise in store for him, though with the number of warriors he still commanded, what had he to fear from a few hundred battle-weary Celts, especially now that Cadwallon was dead?

Out in the open, he had the advantage of greater numbers and the strength of his shield-wall; the Celts must throw themselves against his spears and shields, where they would die. His army had mustered then split into two equal sized battles, one on either side of the river. By dividing his army, he was forcing the Celts to do the same or be outflanked, further reducing their attacking strength, so his battles would devour the miserable vestiges of Celtic strength. Because of the surprises the Celts had thrown at him, he'd taken the precaution of holding back two hundred of his most experienced warriors, to protect him should the Red Cloaks arrive. From where he stood, halfway up the gentle incline of Badon Hill, he could see the entire valley floor, so that's where he'd command his armies from. Not wanting his drummers drowning out his battle commands, he'd ordered them to join and fight in the shield-walls.

While he was considering moving his command-post higher up the hill, so that he could see into the fort, Sulis' gates opened and the few hundred Celtic infantrymen still capable of fighting, marched out in four snaking columns. "Lock shields," he said to the horn-blower standing beside him. Three horn-blasts cut across the valley, and his warriors on both sides of the river locked shields.

Tactics had been discussed with those commanding the different sections of his army: his warriors would hold their ground and let the Celtic remnant break itself on their shields and spears; and then, when the Britons were exhausted, he'd order his shield-walls forward to break what remained of the Celtic resistance. When his warriors advanced, he'd lead his two hundred reserves down the hill, he wanted the glory of the final attack and rout for himself.

Pleased the Celts were finally playing into his hands, he watched the battle-weary Britons march down the slope of Sulis Hill, then halt before the bridge over the Afon River. Estimating that about two hundred Celtic infantrymen had marched through Badon, he wondered where the rest were because he'd seen at least twice that number in the fort. Thinking he should walk up to the summit to see what the rest of the Celts were doing; he was about to begin the gentle climb when the Britons trooped over the bridge. "It's suicide," he said to the horn-blower. "Surely they know I'll march my other army over the bridge and attack their rear?" He looked at the fort's gates, wondering why the rest of the Britons weren't coming out. "Why would they play such a reckless game?"

"Are they baiting a trap?" the horn-blower asked.

"How can they be?" Aelle replied. "There's pitifully few spearmen left in the fort, and we'll see them leave long before they attack us." Were the Celts about to launch another savage surprise, was there something he'd missed? "The Pendragon!" he shouted, and he turned to his horn-blower. "Have our scouts returned?"

"Yes, there is still no sign of the Legion within a day's ride of here."

Inside the fort, Owain walked along the lines of nervous horse-warriors, and they should be nervous because they were about to ride out and fight against overwhelming odds. They'd trained hard for this but they'd never charged at an army of thousands, and although they'd become a well-trained fighting unit, their tactics remained untried in full battle. Only the Pendragon, the Merlin, King Erbin, Gal and the Dragons knew of Gwen's battleplan, so the waiting warriors assumed they'd lose the battle but win the war, a sacrifice they were prepared to make.

Coming to the end of the lines, Owain turned to give the order to mount. He was left speechless by what he saw: his warriors had reached into their saddlebags, taken out their red cloaks and were hurriedly clipping then on. Looking away, he hid a smile while they fixed their red plumes to their conical helmets. They'd defied him, but he loved them for it and why shouldn't they wear the badges of the Legion during the last battle?

Bedwyr trotted over, reached into his saddlebag, took out the Pendragon banner and the very first red cloak, the one Gwen had woven. Taking them from his Dragon, Owain felt the softness of the cloak's red wool, remembering the look of love in Gwen's eyes when she'd given it to him. "Mount!" he called to his warriors before handing the banner back to Bedwyr. "Tie it to your spear," he said, "you will carry my flag into battle." After fastening his cloak around his neck, he took hold of his reigns and mounted his horse, then raised his hand to an archer and, an arrow shot high into the thick clouds.

In the valley below Badon Hill, Cai saw the arrow fly so he called to his infantrymen, "Fight for each other! Fight for your families! Fight for Briton!" Standing next to him, the Merlin saw fear in the Dragon's eyes, so considered offering him words of comfort, but there weren't any. Although only half of King Aelle's army had massed on this side of the river, the Celts were about to engage a force at least five times larger than their own.

King Erbin, standing on the other side of Cai, nodded to the Dragon, who raised his spear, shouted an order and his four columns of infantrymen wheeled to face the Saxons in four ranks of almost fifty warriors. Raising his spear again, Cai swallowed hard, closed his eyes and asked his god to take care of his adopted daughter Kareen, should he die. Pointing the spear forward, he led his warriors slowly towards King Aelle's massed ranks. "Shields!" he shouted, and the front-rank locked shields while the three behind raised theirs to deflect the expected volleys of spears. Glancing over his shoulder to the fort, Cai hoped the Pendragon's second signal wouldn't be long in coming.

If he thought he'd known fear before, he was wrong. Marching in the centre of the front rank towards the many ranks of Saxons, he felt his bowels aching to squirt their contents onto the parched grass. With sweat pouring down his face and back, he set his mind for battle, thinking that whatever happened today, whether his infantrymen ran or held their ground, he'd fight until he was cut down, he wouldn't run from this battle.

"Raise spears," King Aelle said, and two short horn blasts sent his command. Watching the Celts closing on his ranks, he held his breath until the cloud of dust and metal was within killing rage. "Loose." Four short notes began the battle.

Thrown high by roaring Saxons, a cloud of black killing darts flew and fell, plummeting into Cai's warriors. The Celtic lines staggered, shuddering to a halt with a collective groan as the blizzard punched into shields and flesh. Shock met the recoil of the sky-born death, then blood and all the slippery gore of battle squirted and gushed onto the dusty earth. Cries of pain echoed from shield to shield as men clutched at bloodied spear-shafts. Where gaps in the ranks appeared, and there were many, unbloodied men stepped forward to strengthen the wall. With the gaps filled, the Celts moved forward again.

"Loose," Aelle casually repeated his order, and the horn notes released hundreds more pointed-blades.

As before, Cai's warriors came to a blood-splattered halt, with anguished cries spreading throughout the ranks of terrified Celts. Blood poured, bowels opened and warriors vomited from the horror of seeing their comrades speared. But they had to keep going, it was their duty to march again and hope that enough of them still lived when the opposing shield-walls met.

Appalled by the sight, smell and taste of the slaughter, Cai swallowed bile and looked again at the fort, hoping to see the Pendragon's second arrow fly. "Where's the signal?" he heard his own half-panicked words. Half of his warriors were either dead or wounded, and if Owain didn't act soon, he'd have nothing left to fight the Saxons with! Seeing their Dragon circling his spear above his head, the warriors still able to fight closed around him, moving swiftly into two ranks of fifty. Pointing his spear forward, Cai led what was left of his small army towards almost certain death.

Seeing the snarling faces of the blood-lusting Saxons above the rims of their shields, Cai marched towards overwhelming odds, surprised that in the moment before impact his fear had fled. Before he'd even thrust his spear or drawn his sword, his terror at the thought of being hacked to pieces had triggered the battle-calm, or 'frenzy' as some warriors called it, so he shouted his command, "Lock shields!" The clanging of wood and metal told him a tight line had formed on either side of him. "Halt!" he bellowed, and his two lines came to a dusty stop, a few paces short of the Saxons. Gritting his teeth before the attack, he chose a wide-eyed Saxon to be his first victim, emptied his mind of all worldly thoughts and, he yelled, "Charge!"

With a crash like echoing thunder the remnants of Cai and Erbin's small army smashed into the Saxons. The churning mass pushed and slashed the combat into life, cutting, butting, kicking and stabbing, hacking at everything that moved in the panic to survive. Celtic spears punched forward and swords stabbed. Saxon axes swung, hooked onto shield-rims and pulled them down to expose the carrier to iron-sliced death. Cai smacked his helmeted-head into the face of an over confident warrior, who'd foolishly lifted his head too high above his protective shield. Hearing teeth crunch and the man's nasal-bones crack, Cai frantically thrust his sword. Warm, stinking-blood gushed along his blade and up his forearm when he rammed his sword into the Saxon's gaping mouth. A sword narrowly missed his throat, cutting instead into his lifted shield rim, which splintered but held the sword fast. He sliced his blade across the Saxon's wrist, leaving the severed hand clinging to the wedged sword. An axe swung at his head but was deflected by King Erbin's protective blade. A shield rammed into his, and a bearded, snarling Saxon shoved hard, trying to force him off his feet. Pushing back with all his strength, Cai saw Erbin's blade slice clean through the Saxon's leather helmet, splitting the man's head which oozed brains and blood.

Stabbing his sword into another Saxon's face, Cai cursed the Pendragon for not sending the signal as an axe sliced through the top of his shield, its razor-edge cutting a thin red line across his face as it passed. Feeling sharp pain pulsating below his eye, followed by warm blood trickling down his cheek and neck, he stabbed frantically as angry tears slid from his blood-spattered eyes.

"Owain!" he stupidly yelled; aware the Pendragon couldn't hear him. His warriors couldn't hold their line much longer, the weight of the Saxon press was way too heavy and if relief didn't come soon his men would be slaughtered, and he'd die with them. What was the Pendragon waiting for?

Although King Aelle's warriors had been content to absorb the initial Celtic push, Cai knew that soon the Saxons would advance. When they did, a smothering blanket of flashing swords, chopping axes and stamping feet would march right over his sword-brothers, unless the Pendragon's arrow flew. Desperation ached his bowels as he pushed against the solid shields with his last ounce of strength. With tears streaming down his bloodied-face, his sword thrust again and again into face and flesh. He wanted to turn and run, free himself from the gore-stinking savagery of this appalling battle, but he couldn't, a battleplan had been devised and he must play his part to the full.

The Saxons on the Forest Hill side of the river-valley, numbering as many as those on the opposite bank, watched the battle unfold, cheering on their sword-brothers. From what they could see the Celtic attack was being cut to pieces. It wouldn't be a glorious victory, the Britons were too heavily outnumbered for this fight to be remembered by the bards, but it would be their first victory at Badon.

King Aelle still felt uneasy with the Celtic tactics. Instinct told him to beware of the unknown, and he wished he'd remained higher up the hill, so that he could look down into the fort. Having seen the signal arrow order the Celtic infantry forward, it confirmed his suspicion that the Celts in the valley weren't their only warriors. Finally, he ordered one of his warriors to climb to the summit and find out what was happening inside the fort. There was a reason the Celtic infantry had been sent out to fight alone, and he must know why before committing to battle the other half of his army.

He'd seen the horses tethered in the fort, automatically assuming they were the mounts some of the warriors had used to carry them south. But what if he'd been wrong, could the horses belong to the Red Cloaks? Then again, if the Pendragon's Legion had been with Cadwallon's infantry, he would have seen their banner, which would surely have been flown during the siege. It would have been impossible for him not to notice the famous red cloaks of the Legion but, could Owain and the Legion be in the fort, had the Pendragon kept his presence a secret while directing the Celtic defence? He couldn't be certain of anything, but the goose-bumps prickling his skin told him to be wary, the Pendragon must surely be inside the fort.

Shaking his head in disbelief at his own stupidity, he looked back to the top of Badon Hill, impatient to receive the report from his spearman. He'd have made the climb himself but he couldn't leave his position now that the fighting had begun.

Hearing the screaming wounded and the din of battle, the Pendragon decided he'd waited long enough. The Saxons had been sucked in so he ordered his archer to release the fire-arrow.

Watching the one-sided battle from the edge of the woods on the Forest Hill, Gal and Gwen were relieved to see the fire-arrow cut a smoky trail. Stepping out from behind a tree, Gwen waved her hunters forward. With arrows nocked to bowstrings, like stalking cats her small army moved quickly to the forest's edge.

Carrying a small cloth-bag in her left hand and, her bow in her right hand, Gwen walked through the long grass to the hill's ridge, proud and beautifully magnificent in tight, tanned black leather leggings and tunic. Standing at the edge of the ridge for all to see, she put down her bow, opened the bag and took from it a piece of shining silver, and placed the silver circlet neatly over her long, raven-black hair. The gift from her hunters told all who saw her that she was Queen Gwenwyfar of the Forest.

Picking up her bow, she looked down at the blood-stinking savagery and, raised her weapon. Pulling back her bowstring, she called to the Goddess then watched her arrow fly. A cloud of arrows followed, then another and another and three flights of iron and flint cut through the sky. Spent, the shafts plummeted into both Saxon armies.

Still watching his warriors slaughtering Celts, King Aelle hadn't seen the arrows fly and fall, but he saw the aftermath. No Saxon had seen the hunters emerge from the forest, nor heard their twanging bowstrings above the battle-din, so no Saxon shields were raised. Aelle could do nothing but look on in horror when his warriors fell, hardly an arrow missing the tightly packed targets. He looked up at the hunters as the next flights flew. "Raise shields!" he shouted too late, "raise shields!"

The Celts on the hill nocked and fired, nocked and fired faster than they could breathe, loosing thousands of arrows into the collapsing ranks of Saxons. Arms, legs, chest, stomachs, eyes, backs and necks felt the sting as iron and flint thudded into the massed ranks.

Hundreds of Saxons screamed as they clutched at arrow-shafts lodged deep in their punctured flesh. Blood flowed slick over the dry earth, streaming crimson trails into the nearby river, colouring its banks red as dying men tumbled beside its languid flow. Those who'd survived the first arrow-flights raised their shields but it was too little too late, the thousands of arrows had done their worst, cutting to shreds the Saxon armies on both sides of the river.

Cai saw Owain's fire-arrow fly and fall and, relieved but exhausted he ordered his blood and sweat soaked warriors to disengage. What was left of his infantry retreated and turned to watch the hunters' arrows fall. His small army had come close to annihilation, too close in his opinion, the Pendragon had almost released Gwen's hunters too late.

Wiping blood from his sweat-beaded face, he saw that less than half of his warriors had made it through the first stage of the fighting, though that would be enough to form one final shield-wall. To his relief, the Merlin and King Erbin were unhurt, which was a miracle considering what they'd been through.

Watching thousands of arrows drop into the chaotic carnage, dissolving the Saxon army into a mass of half-panicked, confused warriors, he set clearly in his mind the next part of the battleplan.

His charge must be timed to perfection, if he got it wrong, he could waste the lives of his remaining warriors. As the last arrow buried into Saxon flesh, he shouted his order to his weary warriors, “Shield-wall!” and the infantrymen dragged themselves into line.

Although the Saxons had been cut to pieces by the arrow-storm, the front two ranks below Badon Hill had barley been touched. Cai knew that if they could push them back upon their wounded and dead, they’d cause a chaotic, panic-driven slaughter that would finish the battle on his side of the river. “Charge!” he yelled.

The battle-weary Celts charged, smashing their shields into the Saxon wall, pushing and stabbing for all they were worth. “Push for your lives!” Cai shouted above the clash of shields and metal; the order repeated along the line. The shock of the impact forced the Saxons back and off-balance just enough to give Cai’s warriors hope that their tactic might work. Their strength returned with their growing confidence, and step by step they forced the Saxon wall back into the squirming mass of wounded and dying, arrowshot men. Stumbling backwards over fallen bodies, the two ranks of Saxon shields broke apart, making them easy pickings for Celtic-blades.

All along the line the Celts pushed forward while stabbing down, forcing their enemies to tumble blindly over their fallen comrades, and as they fell, they were mercilessly butchered. Cutting further and further into the writhing mass of arrow-punctured, bloodied flesh, stride by stride Cai’s warriors drove the thinning wall of Saxons back, the unrelenting pressure preventing Aelle’s men from reforming to counter the charge.

The Saxons fought desperately but the wall of stabbing swords and butting shields never relented and, kill by kill they were being put to the sword. Realising this part of the battle was lost, the surviving Saxons broke and fled towards Aelle's personal guard on the slope of Badon Hill.

Shocked by what he was seeing, King Aelle didn't realise that all he had to do was order his guards forward, locking shields as they marched down the slope to engage the remaining Celts. The battle could have been won but would now be lost, because in the back of his mind Aelle was worried about when the Red Cloaks would strike.

Stepping over the carpet of bloody savagery, Cai couldn't believe how fast the battle had turned, the tide of war changed by a timely downpour of iron-tipped rain. He looked up at the hill where Gwen stood alone, and raised his blood-smeared sword in salute to her, knowing exactly where her hunters had gone and, why they'd disappeared into the woodlands. Seeing the surviving Saxons join their king, he considered reforming his warriors to pursue them, but quickly dismissed the idea. His spearmen had earned their rest, he wouldn't risk their lives in a pointless charge.

Across the river, the other Saxon army, which had recovered from the storm of arrows and was reforming coherent ranks, looked on as their surviving countrymen ran from the battle. Cai, forming his men into a defensive wall just in case the Saxon King got a grip of the situation, could see there were still hundreds of fit Saxons on the opposite bank of the Afon, and they looked more than ready to fight and kill. They could yet cause a twist in the fortunes of this war, should the next part of Gwen's plan fail.

In the quiet time before dawn, Owain had considered what he'd say to his Red Cloaks before leading them out to fight. Trotting his horse along the lines of mounted, red-cloaked warriors, the words he'd chosen seemed inappropriate after the blood-bath Cai's infantry had just endured. Coming to a halt where Cadwallon's banner had recently flown, he stared blankly at the top of the flagpole, not yet able to feel the sadness of his loss.

A stiffening breeze blew through the fort, taking the edge off the solstice heat as thick, dirty grey clouds drifted over the hill. Squinting into the humid sky, he saw a hawk hovering over the valley beyond the east wall, its golden eyes fixed on its prey. He watched the bird, thinking how nature creates imbalance so that every creature might thrive. There's no contest between a hawk and a shrew, just as there's no chance for a worm once the shrew has found it.

When the hunting Saxons had first marched into the valley there'd been an overwhelming disparity, but less than three days later the Red Cloaks were about to become the hunters. The hawk pulled in its wings and swooped for the kill, diving beyond the east wall. Looking at the faces of the hunters he was about to unleash, Owain saw fear in their eyes, which pleased him because while fear kept men alive in battle, it also made them kill.

Patting the neck of his snorting horse, he took a swig from his water-bottle, replaced the stopper and slipped it back into his saddlebag. Straightening his back, he spoke to his warriors loud and clear, "We've come a long way since the first of you joined the Legion. We've grown together, learned to ride and fight, becoming one arm, one spear and one shield. We are a fighting legion of brothers, and this is our moment to show what an efficient killing machine we are. News of what we'll achieve today will spread throughout our nation; the day we charged the Badon meads will never be forgotten!" He looked at the vacant flagpole again. "We may have lost friends and brothers in the defence of this hill, but there are enough of us left to take the battle to the invader. We won't be charging to death and defeat, today we ride to victory!" The Legion cheered loud enough for the Saxons to hear them.

King Aelle looked across the valley to the fort: was he about to face the Pendragon's Legion, would their swords clash at last? The spearman he'd sent to the top of Badon Hill, returned and saluted. "What did you see?" Aelle asked, though he'd already guessed.

"Red Cloaks." He waited for the King to speak but, Aelle remained silent. "Shouldn't we call our army back from across the river?"

"No, has your backbone been so weakened by the savagery of the Celts that you can no longer fight?"

"Forgive me, My Lord, I just thought that........."

"You thought what, that we should accept defeat, retreat to the top of the hill and form the death circle because the battle is already lost? We still have double their numbers, the battle is ours to win and I shall have the final victory."

Having sent her hunters back into the forest to prepare the next phase of her battleplan, Gwen watched the defeated Saxons on the other side of the river, run up Badon Hill. Hearing her hunters returning, she saw them dragging and carrying dozens upon dozens of chopped and trimmed tree trunks to the lip of the ridge, each one about the length of a man. Now everything was in place to win the battle and the war for the Pendragon, savage and bloody murder was about to be unleashed and if the hunters had their way, not a single Saxon would survive.

Gal had been the instigator of this part of the battleplan, and with hundreds of Saxons waiting to fight, close to the bottom of the hill, Gwen could see the merits of his idea. Unfortunately, the Saxons looked like they were preparing to march away, perhaps back to defend King Aelle, so Gal's plan must be executed immediately.

Gwen raised her hand and a fiery trail of smoke flew high above the valley. She knew the signal could lead to the death of her husband, but this was war, a plan had been agreed so it must be followed. Anyone might die in battle, kings and lowborn foot-soldiers alike, the point of a spear or the edge of a blade knows neither rank nor status. Watching the fire-arrow climb into grey clouds, she whispered a short prayer to the Goddess, "Please, Enaid, keep my lover safe."

Gwen's fire-arrow fell and clattered onto the fort's east wall, bursting into showers of sparks as it chipped away a small piece of stone. "Raise the Pendragon banner," Owain ordered.

Bedwyr lifted his lance and, resting the butt-end on his saddle he looked with pride at the snarling red dragon on its black background. It had been many years since the banner had led the Britons into battle, and a sharp, hot blade cut across Owain's heart when memories surfaced of his father marching to war from Viroconium's east gate, the banner flying at the head of the column. At least ten years had passed since that fading memory had been a reality, and, tightening his grip on his reins he hoped his father's soul would see the snarling dragon lead the Celts to battle. "To victory!" he yelled. Nudging his horse forward, he signalled the advance with a swing of his spear.

The Legion trotted out of the fort, their red cloaks hanging limp from their shoulders, the red, feathery plumes in their iron helmets blown by the stiffening breeze. Down the dusty cart track and into the valley bottom they cantered, where they split into two sections. The smaller part, numbering less than fifty horsemen, galloped through Badon village and over the wooden bridge to support Cai's survivors, just in case King Aelle sent his unwounded warriors and reserves against them. The larger section galloped into the valley to attack the Saxon army below the Forest Hill, perfectly wheeling into four battle-lines before coming to a halt between the river and the hill.

Feeling a spot of rain splash on his cheek, Owain looked up and saw Gwen standing on the ridge of the hill, wearing the silver circlet her people had given her. She looked magnificent he thought, a true queen and battle-leader. She lifted her sword, pointed it to the heavens and waved it to show him that her hunters were ready.

Along the Legion's battle-lines horses snorted, champing at the bit, hoofing the hard ground, pulling against their riders steadying hands, eager to make the charge they instinctively knew was coming. Raising his spear, the Pendragon clicked his horse into the trot. His warriors rode forward with him, their concentrating minds focused on the wall of shields and spears awaiting them. Those who'd wanted to say a final prayer had done so before riding out, this wasn't the time for reflection or regret, this was the time to kill and only those who could smell the blood of the kill and ram their spears home, would survive. Raising his spear again, the Pendragon signalled the gallop. Dust swirled around thundering hooves as warriors pulled their oval cavalry-shields tight. Lowering their heads and couching spears, they picked their targets as they halved the distance to the shield-wall. "Britannia!" Owain yelled above the clattering hooves.

"Britannia!" the Red Cloaks replied through the rising dust-cloud, and the warriors charged at the hundreds of Saxons.

On the slope of Badon Hill, King Aelle couldn't help but hate and be impressed by the charging Red Cloaks. With their brightly polished chainmail, and their red plumes flowing from their shining conical helmets as they galloped towards his warriors, they were a sight to be feared and admired. Their horses muscled, sweating coats shimmered like polished jet as they galloped headlong across the valley, forcing a scowl of jealousy from him, making him wish the magnificent horse-warriors were his. Cursing the Pendragon's deception, while admiring him for his cunning and tenacity, Aelle thought what a magnificent Saxon the Pendragon would make. If he was lucky enough to meet him in the afterlife, he'd happily share Woden's hunt with the 'devil of a warrior'.

Below Gwen's hill, the Saxons locked shields and raised their spears, ready to meet the charge of the Legion. Standing side on with legs apart to take the weight of the impact, heads looking over their left shoulders at the fast approaching, thundering swirl of dust, horses and warriors, the Saxons nervously closed ranks, bracing themselves for the death-clash of metal and wood.

As the Red Cloaks charged, cheering bellowed from the top of Gwen's hill, drawing King Aelle's attention away from the charging horse-warriors. To his absolute horror he saw dozens of tree-trunks tumbling and bouncing violently at speed down the slope. His heart sank as all along the Saxons right flank, elms, beeches, sycamores and chestnuts, Briton's most ancient defenders, smashed mercilessly into his warriors, crunching great swathes of bone-crushing pain, deep into the terrified ranks.

More tree-trunks rolled and, gathering speed they tumbled and bounced and scythed into men who'd no protection against the heavy wood. Scores more felled trees smashed into the shattered army, cracking bones and crunching heads, then the hunters picked up their bows. Before they could react, the Saxons saw hundreds of arrows falling from the sky. The army quickly became a seething, writhing tangle of shattered bodies and arrow-punctured flesh.

Only the front four Saxon ranks still stood, and although their comrades behind them were screaming in pain, begging their sword-brothers to help them, the wounded and dying had to be ignored because Red Cloak spears was racing towards their shields. Those from the rear ranks who could still fight, ran forward to bolster the shield-walls, leaping over their wounded and dead in their haste to join the fight.

To the rear of the charging Celts, a horn blasted two shrill notes, and the three ranks behind Owain's pulled back their bowstrings. Again, the horn sounded and at the gallop arrows were shot into the grey sky, the Red Cloaks casting aside their bows as the arrows fell. Seeing the pointed shafts falling, the Saxons raised their shields, hoping to lower them again in time to meet the impact of the charge.

Not a heartbeat after the arrows thumped into raised shields, Red Cloak spears punched into chests, guts, faces and necks. The Saxon wall collapsed as rearing stallions' broke skulls, swinging swords severed limbs and heads, and piercing spears punctured blood-spurting holes through chainmail and flesh. Brave as the Saxon spearmen were, their courage wasn't enough and they were cut to pieces.

Unable to recover from the Legion's charge, the surviving Saxons turned to run but where could they go? Before they had time to decide, another bellowing roar erupted from the top of the hill, and four hundred hunters, led by Gal and Gwen, drew their long knives and hurtled down the slope to join the Red Cloaks for the final kill, yelling like screaming banshees as they ran and tumbled down the hillside. They fell upon the Saxon carpet of crushed and broken warriors without any thought for mercy, stabbing at moving flesh like wild animals, raising and plunging their knives, crawling on their hands and knees through the smear of bloodied flesh in a frenzied killing orgy. For so many years they'd suffered because of these savages from across the sea, now they would have their revenge, even on those already dead. They stabbed and chopped until nothing moved, and then, covered in blood and gore they searched for more victims, their lust for revenge unsated.

King Aelle watched the slaughter, disgusted by the savagery, appalled by the sight of blood-soaked, screaming and shrieking Celts moving on hands and knees through his massacred army, stabbing down at everything and anything, hacking through a writhing blanket of dead and wounded warriors, ensuring that no Saxon left this valley alive.

Finally resigned to total defeat, Aelle turned away from the merciless murder. This valley of death he'd entered just a few days ago, riding like an arrogant emperor at the head of a massive army, had become the knife with which he'd cut his own throat. He'd been beaten every time he'd sent his men to battle, his great army reduced to almost nothing. A wiser man might throw down his weapons and surrender, stop the slaughter and allow himself a humiliation he never would have thought possible. But he knew the Pendragon wouldn't let him live, or allow his few hundred remaining warriors safe passage back to their own lands. All he could do was walk with his survivors to the top of Badon Hill, set a defensive position on the plateau and, await the Red Cloaks.

Covered in Saxon blood and gasping for breath, Owain turned his horse and looked for more Saxons to kill, there weren't any.

Hundreds of butchered, blood-soaked corpses lay strewn amongst arrow-shafts and gore splattered tree-trunks, a sight that turned his stomach. Searching for more victims, Gwen's hunters picked through the corpses but all Saxon life had bled out of this battle, the sea of dead flesh had given up its harvest of souls.

Hearing his name being called, Owain saw Gwen running along the edge of the crows-feast, her clothes and face splattered with blood. Relieved to know she'd survived; he sheathed his sword and dismounted. She threw herself into his arms and pressed her lips gently against his, the kiss lingering long enough for their warriors to see and cheer their embrace. He didn't mind the taste of blood or the smell of her sweat, knowing he probably tasted and stank much worse. Feeling someone pulling his arm, he released her. "I hate to break up your fond reunion," Gal said, trying to keep a straight face, "but don't I get a kiss as well?"

Owain had to laugh, and for a moment he was tempted to embarrass the boy by kissing him. Then something caught his eye on Badon Hill, so he said to Gal, "Do you see King Aelle's wolf-banner, up there on the hill?"

"I do," he replied apprehensively. "You have another job for me?"

"No, you've already done more than most would do in a lifetime but, if you can lay King Aelle's banner at my feet, along with his head, then I'll kiss you!"

Gathering his warriors around his banner at the highest point on the plateau, which was some way back from where Badon Hill sloped down into the valley, King Aelle considered a fighting retreat with the remnant of his army. He had less than three hundred warriors, most of whom were his personal guard.

He's was about to order the retreat when a horn blasted a series of triumphant notes from the east, and his stomach turned cold when he saw King Ceredig's Durotriges in the distance, cutting off his escape. Another horn shrilled through the heavy grey clouds, and a great cheer erupted from the river valley; the Celts, he assumed, were about to climb the hill.

Because the summit was long and almost flat, the Pendragon's Red Cloaks had plenty of room to make a full charge. With no choice but to defend his position, and certain an arrow storm would come, Aelle ordered his warriors to form six short shield-walls in front of his banner. With his small army arranged for the final battle, he watched the edge of the plateau.

His warriors, no doubt thinking about their women and families, waited in silence for Celtic spears to crest the ridge. Aelle thought about his wife, Queen Aelice, wondering what she'd do when news of the slaughter reached her: would she choose the quick slash of a blade across her wrist, believing that death was preferable to suffering Celtic revenge; would she return to her ancestral home in Germania? The latter was the most likely, either that or she'd gather whatever warriors she could and hide in the forest, raise an army then march out to repulse the Celts from Andredes Caester. She'd been a good wife, giving him strong sons, and the most beautiful daughter a man could wish for. Whilst he'd never treated her as an equal, he had shown her the respect a wife of a king deserved. In his way he'd loved her, as she had him, and their union had been mostly happy, even if he had spent as many nights as he could in other women's beds.

With grey clouds dropping spots of rain onto the parched, dusty earth, the Red Cloaks crested the edge of the plateau. Behind them came the blood covered Forest People, holding bows and handfuls of arrows, many of the shafts and points smeared with blood after being plucked from the dead. When Cai and Erbin's infantrymen had made their way on to the slope, Owain raised his hand to halt the advance as a rider galloped to him. "Cieren," he said to the dusty rider, "has Ceredig secured the east valley?"

"He has, My Lord. Do you need his warriors?"

"No, the battle is almost over."

"With your permission, might I join you?" the bard asked. "I want to bloody my sword."

"I'm not sure you'll get close enough."

"You have a plan?"

"Yes," Owain replied as his Red Cloaks formed two lines for the charge. "If you ride alongside Bedwyr you might get the chance to kill, but only if my idea for ending the fighting fails."

"Thank you, My Lord." Cieren manoeuvred his horse into place beside Bedwyr.

Gwen, who'd climbed the hill with her hunters, walked with the Merlin through the lines of horsemen. "Owain, do you want my hunters fighting from the flanks?" she asked.

"No, if we are to kill without being killed, your archers will be needed elsewhere."

"What do you mean?"

"Do you remember, Gwen, back in the spring when I drew you a battleplan in the dirt outside your roundhouse?"

"Yes, vaguely."

"I explained how to defeat a shield-wall without the need for hand-to-hand combat; have you forgotten the hidden tactic?"

"Now I remember," she replied. "You called it the 'unseen rain'."

He looked up at clouds which were now releasing light, drizzly rain but threatening something heavier. "If we don't get moving the rain will ruin my plan. Go and prepare your archers, Gwen."

"I think I know what you are going to do," the Merlin said, looking sceptically at the Pendragon. "Have you considered the risks?"

"Nothing is ever certain," Owain replied, "you taught me that. Too many of our people have died in this war, so I'll finish off King Aelle from a distance. Arwyn!" he called over his shoulder to one of the Red Cloaks, who trotted his horse forward.

"Yes, My Lord?"

"Ride next to me. When I give you the order, blow four quick notes on your horn, and whatever happens you must not hesitate, timing is everything."

The success of the charge now rested on Gwen's shoulders, the speed and accuracy of her archers being vital. The Red Cloaks had tried the tactic and it did work, but that was in Viroconium's practice fields and, if the hunters failed the Legion would have to charge headlong into a well-prepared shield-wall. Looking to the left and the right then over his shoulder, to make sure everyone was ready, Owain clicked his horse forward.

Such was King Aelle's fear of the advancing Red Cloaks, he could barely move his hand when feeling for his sword. Death was closing on his pack of wolves; the hunter had become the hunted. There would be no chase, no attempt to run because his wolves were cornered and, his great army had been reduced to a wounded beast. At least the Red Cloaks weren't going to finish off his men with arrows, Aelle thought as the horse-warriors closed, so his spearmen would die killing Celts.

Having anticipated the Celtic-charge, he'd organised his wolves into a series of defensive shield-walls; his front rank down on one knee, shields locked with spears raised to rip into horseflesh; the second rank crouched with shields protecting the heads of the warriors in front; the third line stood side on with shields held at chest height but slightly forward, to protect the second rank; the fourth, fifth and sixth ranks had formed the standard shield-walls. When the Red Cloaks crashed into them there'd be few gaps for Celtic spears to penetrate.

Through the oppressively close, thickening humidity, two lines of cavalry, their spears pointing at the darkening clouds, trotted calmly over the black ash smears left by the Saxon funeral pyres, towards the wolves. Bedwyr's voice cut across the plateau, and the Legion broke into a canter. A single note from Arwyn's horn chilled the waiting wolves and, hooves pounded and a dust cloud swirled across the plateau. Releasing a battle-roar, the Red Cloaks raced to the gallop like a wave ripping across a storm-swollen ocean. Choosing their targets and lowering their spears, the Legion roared, their charging stallions kicking up clouds of dust.

Checking his lines to make sure all shields were locked and facing the Celts, Aelle felt the charge rattling his nerves. The cracked and crumbling, thundering earth rumbled beneath his feet in a quake that shook his banner lose, toppling it as the blood-red cloaks closed on him. Within the charging dustbowl, hundreds of blood-smeared spearpoints had him transfixed with fear, they all seemed to be pointing at him. "Brace yourselves!" he bellowed through the thunder.

The only Red Cloak without a spear, Owain gripped his sword tight in his white knuckled hand and felt the first twinges of battle-lust soak his stomach with adrenalin. Reason told him to control the battle-fury, this wasn't the time for it to drive him into the slaughter. Deliberately relaxing, he exhaled, searching through the hoof-kicked dust for a glimpse of the wolf-banner. His horse felt like a giant bird beneath him, gliding with the roaring cloud of Red Cloaks, their battle-cry, "Britannia! Britannia!" driving them across the plateau. But this wasn't his killing time, and just before the cloud should have hammered into Saxon shields, he nodded to Arwyn, who raised his horn and blew four quick notes. The well-drilled Red Cloaks split and galloped around the flanks of the surprised Saxons, leaving a dust-cloud in their wake.

King Aelle watched the Legion part, then he groaned as hundreds of iron-pointed shafts flew from the dustbowl. “Raise shields!” he bellowed too late. Misty fountains of blood, and guttural groans choked his hopes and, his protective wall disintegrated.

Galloping around the Saxons, Owain stood in the stirrups and looked over his shoulder to see if the hunters timing had been precise. He whooped with joy as the arrows fell, Gwen must have ordered the flight from her running warriors as soon as the first note from Arwyn’s horn had blasted through the dust cloud. He’d been right to assume that on earth as dry and crumbly as this, hooves would kick up so much dust that the hunters, charging on foot behind the cavalry, would not be seen by the Saxons.

To a man the Saxons had believed that the Red Cloaks alone were charging to finish them off, so their shields had been firmly locked forward to meet the charging spears. Arrows had flown, and arrows had killed, and after three days of bloody slaughter the fighting was just about over. Circling the rear of the bloody carpet of dying men, Owain joyfully twirled his sword above his head.

King Aelle couldn’t accept the defeat, his mind cracked as he tried rationalising what had happened. He’d lost everything: the last of his sons had been skewered on the slopes of Sulis Hill, and his army of thousands had been systematically and brutally slaughtered. The final blow to his crumbling pride would be the tip of iron that ended his life, though under the circumstances he felt that his death might be a blessing.

Most of his remaining warriors were now dead or wounded, though a few still stood with their shields raised to protect him.

Expecting another flight of arrows to fizz towards his remnant, Aelle looked up and lowered his shield, hoping to welcome a death-arrow. His glassy-eyed gaze searched the grey clouds but no more arrows fell, it was over and he hadn't shed one drop of Celtic blood. The dust-cloud thinned and settled, revealing the dusty figures of Gwen's hunters as King Aelle sheathed his sword and sank to knees, absorbing his loss of everything. With his tired mind closing out the moans of his wounded, he licked his lips and spat the dust from his mouth as two riders trotted towards him, one of them holding aloft the Pendragon banner.

The red-cloaked warriors, watching to see what their Pendragon would do, steadied their restless mounts, their spears pointing at the few souls protecting the Saxon King as Owain, with his sword still drawn, rode towards the edge of the slaughter, alongside Bedwyr. "What will you do with them?" the Dragon asked.

"Let them go."

"Why, they invaded our land and raped and killed our people?"

"Some should return to spread the word that the lands of the Celts aren't easily conquered."

"And King Aelle, will you let him go?"

"He will die, he is mine to kill."

The two of them dismounted. "You don't need to risk your life," Bedwyr said, punching the Pendragon banner into the ground. "Leave him to our archers."

"I want his people to know that I killed their king in single combat."

"I don't understand you, Owain, one lucky swing of his sword and you could be killed!"

"Think about it, Bedwyr. Our armies faced each other in battle and we destroyed them. But the Saxon nation isn't its warriors, it is their king, so if we shoot arrows into him, they'll say it took many men to kill King Aelle, which might encourage them to regroup and try again. Their defeat won't be total unless I kill him, it has to be this way." Taking a few steps towards the arrow-punctured dead, Owain saw for the first time the man wearing a thin gold crown around the rim of his helmet, so he called to him, "The war is over, Aelle, your crown is now mine and I want it, as well as your life!"

"Come and take it, Pendragon!"

"Wait." Bedwyr took hold of Owain's arm, turning him around. "Let me fight him, the result and the meaning will be the same. You can't risk your life, you are now the uncrowned king as well as the Pendragon, your people need you."

"I am not your king and I never shall be."

"But, Owain, what about the........."

"I will fight Aelle and that's an end to it!" Turning back to face the Saxon, he looked King Aelle cold in the eyes and asked, "Will you fight me, to the death?"

"I will, but what about my remaining spearmen, what happens to them if you kill me?"

"My Red Cloaks will escort them back to Andredes Caester, where they'll be released unharmed."

"And the women and children of my kingdom, will they receive your mercy?"

"You have no kingdom. Your people won't be harmed so long as they peacefully accept Celtic rule."

"And what if I kill you?" Aelle asked, walking towards the Pendragon.

"You won't," Owain replied, looking up as thunder rumbled and steady rain began to fall.

Ignoring the fine rain sweeping over Badon Hill, King Aelle and Owain faced each other with their swords drawn. The Merlin, standing aside from the human amphitheatre of cheering and jeering warriors and hunters, glanced up at the darkening clouds, wondering at their sudden arrival and the hint of yellow within the greys. Feeling a cold finger bristling the hairs on the back of his neck, he turned sharply to see who'd touched him. But no one had, the nearest person was a woman and she was well out of reach.

Ignoring the encouraging shouts from his warriors so that he could concentrate on the edge of King Aelle's sword, Owain backed away from the crowd, making room for himself to turn and move when the Saxon attacked. Taking a few steps back towards where the rope-bound Saxon spearmen were sitting, he too felt something cold touch his skin. He dismissed the feeling, assuming a trickle of rain had dripped from the rim of his helmet.

"Will you keep backing away like a coward, or will you fight?" Aelle growled. Raising the point of his sword, he jabbed it at Owain's face, teasing the Celt into making a rash move.

"I hear you've titled yourself Bretwalda," Owain mockingly replied.

"That is my right." The Saxon immediately realised his claim was ridiculous under the present circumstances.

"Bretwalda!" Owain laughed. "How many Saxons and Britons do you rule?"

Aelle took the bait and ran forward. Pulling his sword-arm back, he lifted his blade in such a clumsily laboured manner that someone across the valley could have seen the strike coming. Bending his upper-back to avoid the predictable cut, Owain laughed. "Is that the best you can do?" A rumble of thunder rolled across the sky.

Aelle came at him again, thrusting his sword in repeated jabs, each stab flicked away with ease. After diverting a slash of Saxon iron aimed at his neck, Owain cut his steel blade across his slow-opponent's chest. The iron mail-rings burst, and the steel cut a thin gash across the King's leather and wool jerkin. The watchers burst into robust applause, shouting support for their Pendragon who'd drawn first blood. Stepping back, Owain rotated the point of his blade in Aelle's face, teasing him with the words, "You are too slow, old man."

Running his left hand across the thin cut, Aelle felt warm blood. "It's a scratch, I've received worse from the many Celtic slaves I've rutted." He sounded brave but he was worried by the speed of the Pendragon's swordplay.

Aelle's blade flicked out again, narrowly missing Owain's top lip. The Pendragon, turning away from the slice, ducked as the iron-blade flashed back and clanged against the top of his helmet. The Saxon's sword jabbed forward again, slightly clipping Owain's forearm. "I've fought better men than you," Aelle boasted. "First blood means nothing, the one who delivers the final blow is always the victor."

Another rumble of thunder rolled over Badon Hill as the two blades clashed, flashing like lightning beneath the turbulent skies. Rain poured, Owain parried a thrust and slashed his steel across the Saxon's shoulder, inspiring more cheers. Aelle yelled into the grey mass of yellow tinged cloud, feeling the pain of the cut that must have slashed deep enough to scrape against his collarbone. With warm blood streaming down his chest and arm, he rashly threw himself forward, putting everything into all-out attack, swinging his sword wildly as he strode forward, hoping brute strength would force his blade through. He hoped in vain, their blades clanged hard, jarring his wrist so he stepped away as a bolt of lightning shot across the sky.

"Rohanna," a feathery voice whispered into Owain's ear, distracting him long enough for iron to slap into the ringed-mail protecting his ribcage, knocking him off balance. Aelle's blade slammed down again and again, forcing the Pendragon to his knees.

"Rohanna," the word kissed Owain's wet cheek and the heavens roared, vomiting rain that blurred his sight as he raised his steel to protect himself.

The Saxon beat his sword heavily down with both hands, convinced his time for revenge had come. The worried crowd fell silent as Owain was hammered down into the wet, cloying mud the torrential rain had daubed under foot. Holding their collective breath as the Pendragon pulled himself away from Aelle's thrashing-blade with his free hand, the crowd gasped as iron hammered down repeatedly against retreating steel.

Parrying stroke after stroke as thunder boomed and burst, Owain's feet slid in the slurry as they searched for purchase where a Saxon pyre had cremated some of the battle-dead. A bolt of lightning exploded across the sky, startling him to such an extent that he almost missed the next cut, which he caught just below the hilt of his sword. Unable to get to his feet, the desperate Pendragon kept his blade high, doing just enough to glance away another heavy blow. Aelle's sword swung back at him, shattering the mail that had already been crushed, slicing a small cut a hand's-width below the Celt's armpit. Time and time again the Saxon hammered his sword down, its iron blade sparking against steel as he tried to kill the Celt.

Out of sheer desperation the Pendragon rolled away, narrowly avoiding a pointed thrust that rammed into the mud not a fingers width from his neck. Deflecting another hack, he scrambled to his knees and threw himself bodily forward, his iron helmet butting Aelle hard in the guts. With the air punched from his lungs, the Saxon staggered backwards as he fought for breath. Exhausted, the Pendragon stepped away, giving both men the chance to catch their breath.

The erupting sky thundered and crashed, a bolt of lightning cut through the swirling grey and their swords came together again, this time in viciously equal battle, sparks flashing from blades as each sought the advantage both were unwilling to give. Back and forth they struggled, trading blow for blow in the slippery mud.

Forward the Pendragon strode, flashing cuts and thrusts so fast that Aelle could only step back and back, desperately fighting to protect the life he feared the Celt was about to slice away. Steel cracked hard against iron, shocking Aelle's fingers into loosening their grip. Steel beat against his weapon again and it slipped free, plopping into the mud. About to skewer the defenceless man, Owain heard the whispered name again, "Rohanna," and a bolt of lightning flashed across his vision, blinding him with a light so bright that his sight blurred into white.

Retreating, he closed his eyes and shook his head to clear his vision, opening them just in time to see the Saxon's reclaimed sword thrusting at his throat. He instinctively fell away to his left, rolling twice before parrying a heavy, doublehanded downward slash. "Rohanna," the voice chilled his ear as Aelle's arcing blade cut towards his neck. He rolled away again, shouting Rohanna's name to the Merlin as he jumped back to his feet, ready to meet the charging Saxon, who, believing he had the upper-hand, doubled his efforts to find the killing-blow.

The Merlin, certain of what was happening and what must be done, ran to the edge of the plateau, to where hawthorn bushes grew. He pulled a thorn from one of the branches and dropped to his knees. Slashing the palm of his hand with the thorn, he spat on the blood, closed his hand around the spittle-blood, and muttered words not of this world.

The thunderstorm continued, the downpour churning the mud slick beneath the dancing slog of the duellists' feet. Aelle, being older and fatter than the Pendragon, felt his muscles strain and his chest tighten as he threw cuts, slices and thrusts at the man he thought he'd beaten. Wheezing and gasping for air, he raged with anger, forcing himself into one last desperate attack upon the Celt. The attack came to nothing.

Stepping back to catch his breath, Aelle drew in deep lungsful of wet air, wiped his wet sleeve across his face and charged at the Celt, his sword twirling above his head as he stepped into the killing zone, aiming cut after cut at the retreating Pendragon. Owain happily gave ground, drawing more and more lung bursting strokes from the rapidly tiring, fat old Saxon.

Parrying another heavy blow, Owain thought he heard a woman scream as he circled the Saxon. With a fresh wind suddenly gusting over the hill, blowing the grey clouds away to the east, he let the Saxon waste his strength and energy when slashing wildly through the drying air. Convinced he'd succeeded in banishing the Otherworldly threat, the Merlin returned to watch the duel.

Aelle swung his sword down hard, aiming to slice through the Celt's iron-protected skull. The crowd cheered when Owain swerved deftly away from the heavy chop, but Aelle swung again, his breath rasping as the Pendragon casually flicked the blade aside. Shifting his balance onto the front foot and, throwing his weight forward, Owain drove his blade through the Saxon's chainmail, the sword skewering the fat man's guts. Blood belched up the Pendragon's blade, slicking his hand. Wincing at the feel of another man's warm, sticky-blood he yanked his sword free and the wound gushed as Aelle dropped his sword and slumped to his knees.

Standing over the kneeling Saxon, for the briefest moment Owain felt pity for the man clutching at his blood-pumping wound. Rocking back and forth, Aelle felt another ripple of pain skirt the rim of his open wound. Recovering from his initial shock, he realised he wasn't holding his sword so he rocked forward and slid his hand through the blood-slicked mud, grabbing for it before his escaping life-blood sucked away his soul.

Owain's metal-studded boot crunched down, pinning the Saxon's arm to the mud. Yelping, Aelle looked up at the Pendragon, his eyes pleading with the Celt to free his arm. His anguished scream pierced the souls of his ancestors when the point of Owain's sword punched through the Saxon's reaching hand, skewering it to the earth. Screaming from the pain, Aelle didn't want to beg but what choice did he have? A Saxon must die holding his sword, so clenching his teeth against the pain, he screamed at the Pendragon, "Please! My sword, I must die with it in my hand!"

The Pendragon shook his head. "This is for the many Celts you murdered, raped and enslaved because you're a greedy, barbaric, fat old Saxon animal." Pressing his full weight onto the sword pommel, he drove the blade deep into the earth. Aelle's hand folded upwards as the steel slid through it, its fingers locking into an air-grabbing claw. Owain felt no pity, he'd be damned if he'd allow the soul of this murdering rapist, a place at Woden's feast.

Gasping for breath through pulsating pain, Aelle raised his watering eyes to his killer, and he begged, "Please, put my sword in my hand. Are you so full of hate that you can't permit such a simple request?"

"I'm denying you your journey to Woden because it's the only reward I'll receive for defeating you."

After kicking Aelle's muddy sword away, he pulled his blade free, raised it above his head and swung it down hard. In a mist of blood King Aelle's severed head plopped into the mud. Picking up the Saxon's sword, Owain kicked over the torso and walked to the crowd. Feeling the first touch of emotional relief stinging the backs of his eyes, he called to his people, with both swords held aloft, "I have taken the sword from the Saxon; the war is over so most of you can return to your homes and your loved ones. It has been a costly victory, we've all lost friends but our freedom has been won so spread the word, this island belongs to the Britons!"

After kicking Aelle's head towards the survivors of the great Saxon army, Owain looked across the valley to the fort where his brother had died. The Merlin walked over, placed a hand on the Pendragon's shoulder and said, "I know how much you've lost; I also grieve for your brother but our people need a king. Cadwallon's son is an infant at the breast so he cannot rule, you must wear the Votidini crown until he is ready to take it from you. I know you won't do this for yourself, will you do it for the people?"

Owain smiled ruefully before replying, "Yes, I'll sit on my father's throne, though not as a king, and only until Prince Maelgwn is old enough to rule."

Cai, Bedwyr, Cieren and Erbin walked over, wanting to congratulate him and, just as the Merlin had done, ask him to take the throne. But Owain wanted to be alone to grieve for his brother and father. Walking away, he stopped and turned when someone shouted, “Arthur!” Then the entire crowd began chanting, “Arthur! Arthur! Arthur! Arthur!” Not understanding, Owain looked to the Merlin and asked, “What does this mean?”

“‘Arthur’ means ‘Bear’. They are giving you a new name.”

This wasn’t what Owain wanted to hear. “Tell them to choose another bear, I deny the name.” Listening to their raised voices acclaiming him, “Arthur! Arthur! Arthur!” a shiver of cold fear ran down his spine.

“I’m sorry, Owain,” the Merlin said, “but you are the ‘Bear of the Britons’. I’ve known this since the day you were born because the Goddess whispered that truth to me when you took your first breath. Your father understood and accepted your destiny, that’s why he had you worked harder than anyone else in the practice fields. I’ve always known you wouldn’t accept the name, but your destiny cannot be avoided. Your people have raised their voices in tribute to you, they and the Goddess have given you a name never before known or heard in our islands, it is up to you how you use it.”

TAWELWCH...

There are five books in the series.

1. The Black Book of Badon.

2. The Blue Book of Viroconium.

3. The Grey Book of Trevena.

4. The Red Book of Camlann.

5. The Green Book of Isca.

Pendragons Books Email: cieren.callum@yahoo.com

KEVIN BAYTON-WOOD AUTHOR | Facebook

Cover created by Rhian www.rhianwynharrison.com

Printed in Great Britain
by Amazon